COMING HOME TO
PENVENNAN COVE

Linn B. Halton

HEAD
ZEUS

An Aria Book

First published in the the United Kingdom in 2020 by Aria,
an imprint of Head of Zeus Ltd

This paperback edition first published in 2021 by Aria

9 7 5 3 1 2 4 6 8

A CIP catalogue record for this book is available from the
British Library.

ISBN (PB): 9781800245938
ISBN (E): 9781838938000

Typeset by Siliconchips Services Ltd UK

Printed and bound in Great Britain by
CPI Group (UK) Ltd, Croydon CR0 4YY

Aria
c/o Head of Zeus
First Floor East
5–8 Hardwick Street
London EC1R 4RG

www.ariafiction.com

To live with hope is truly a blessing because every day is a blank page just waiting to be written. The dream is to fill your blank page with happiness.

April

The Happy Hive offices
in London

1. This Country Girl is Going Home

'I can't believe you're really doing this to me, Kerra,' Sy declares.

In a fit of pique, he raises the roll of packing tape to his mouth, using his teeth to tear off yet another strip. The horrible ripping sound grates on my nerves, sending a shudder through me.

As if today isn't tough enough as it is, the last thing I need is a petulant assistant who knows my Achilles heel. And he's giving the performance of his life playing the *poor, abandoned me* role.

'For the last time, Simon, please do me a favour and stop doing that. Use these.' I thrust the scissors in his direction. 'If you break a veneer, I'll feel obliged to hang around and sort you out.'

He hates being called Simon, because it reminds him of his mother, who refuses to shorten it. It pulls him up rather sharply when he isn't playing nice; it's our little code to remind him he's overstepping the mark.

'That's the general idea. Anyway, who's the assistant here? I'm supposed to be packing up this lot, not you.' He flashes a withering look in my direction. 'The Happy Hive offices just won't be the same without you... and *my* life won't be the same without you.'

Letting out an exasperated sigh, I'm struggling to face the fact that in less than an hour my things will be all boxed up and ready to go. It signals the end of an era, one that ruled my entire life and that's why it's time to move on.

Sy has been my right-hand man for the last five years and he's acting like I'm divorcing him. Which is ridiculous, although one look at my face and Sy can pre-empt my every need. He's the only person who ever makes my coffee to perfection and he instinctively knows when I'm pushing myself too hard. The number of times he's appeared in front of me with my coat in his hands and given me that stare of his, well—he was the one who kept me sane.

But I'm leaving him in capable hands, with a shiny new job title and a rather nice pay rise. It's time for me to teeter forward and begin the next stage of my life. So, I can't find it in my heart to be angry with Sy, even though the way he's tugging on my heart strings is stretching them to breaking point. We both know there is no going back, but knowledge of a fact is one thing, accepting it—for my darling Sy—is another.

'I know and I'll miss it. And you, too—that goes without saying—and the team. But I'm not the boss anymore, Sy, and the handover is complete. My baby is all grown up and it's time for me to accept my job here is done. The Happy Hive is now a part of a much bigger concern and it's about to grow exponentially.' I try my best to brighten my voice, enthusiastically.

The Happy Hive is all about connecting people with a need, to people who have the skills to fulfil that need.

Members pay a fee to join the community and interact via geographically based groups at regional and local levels. It's a simple idea that works beautifully, because the website only puts people in touch. It's then down to the parties concerned to decide whether money will change hands, or whether there will be an exchange of services. Simple. Effective. Personal. And scalable. It's also a convenient bolt-on for social media phenomenon, Keeping in Touch.

When one of the biggest social media outfits going, comes knocking on your door because your little business excites them, it isn't just about seeing pound-signs. It's about realising what you've created is morphing into this... monster that you never envisaged. My life had become tunnel-visioned and I can now admit that the stress was almost overwhelming at times.

The frown on Sy's face tells me that my attempt to reassure him has fallen on deaf ears.

'Traitor. I never thought you were the type of woman to take the money and run.'

Staring at him, I raise a disapproving eyebrow and Sy hangs his rather handsome head in shame.

We both know he doesn't mean that, but as a creature of habit he hates change. And he hates goodbyes even more. He's like the younger brother I always longed to have when I was growing up. My best friend had one and he adored his big sister, despite the fact that having a little shadow following her every move annoyed her intensely. Sy latched on to me in much the same fashion from day one. He was a godsend and he isn't just an employee, but a dear and valued friend. I trust his opinion because he always has my back and I have his.

'Cornwall is where I grew up and it's time to go back, Sy, to reconnect with my roots. You can come and visit anytime you want, so think of it as a free holiday whenever you need a break.'

The look I get in return makes me stifle a laugh. Sy looks like a startled rabbit.

'What—you expect me to head down to the land that time forgot?'

That would have been funny if he wasn't being serious. Cue the commercial—I need to be painting a picture here. In my smoothest tones, I imagine I'm doing a voiceover.

'Cornwall is a beautiful area, with stunning scenery, Sy. It's a place made for romance, steeped in history and with wonderful walks that make the heart want to leap out of one's chest.'

He gives me a sour look. 'Sounds wonderful if you like that sort of thing, but I'm not fooled; you're just trying to appease your guilt at abandoning me. Wellies have never been fashionable in my book, or remotely of interest to me.'

'From lush green pastureland,' I continue painting the picture, 'to sandy beaches washed by fingers of foaming, salty water, to cresting waves and spray that stings your face, making you feel truly alive. Nature is a gentle reminder of the wonders all around us: the things that ground us and remind us what really matters. What's not to like?'

Sy takes one step back, crossing his arms in front of him and resting his chin on one hand.

'Hmm. Let me think. Would it be the narrow, winding lanes without a motorway in sight? And there are probably more bright lights in one square mile in London, than there are along the whole of the southwest coast. Not forgetting the fact that there's either a camper van, or a herd of cows around every bend. It's a hazardous place to live and the parking is abysmal. The Wi-Fi is rubbish, too, I hear!'

I give up. He's being purposefully antagonistic now.

'It's the countryside, Sy. It's all about community—but the real thing, not the online variety. This is life in the raw, versus...' How can I put this into context? 'As opposed to virtual reality—which doesn't always bear much resemblance. There is life outside of London, it just has a different dynamic. It's more sedate, neighbourly. People get to know each other on a more personal level.'

'I like work, and wine bars, and theatres, and crowds of people I don't know—and don't care to know up close and personal. I hate the thought of strangers being privy to my business and I have no desire whatsoever to be on more than nodding terms with either of my neighbours. They could be serial killers, for all I know.'

I, too, have loved the sense of anonymity that living in a metropolis brings with it. No one has time to notice you, unless you want to be noticed. The truth is that the day I signed on the dotted line I did waver, there's no denying it. I watched my hand shake as I focused on forming each of the letters of my name. My head was telling me that it was the right thing to do for the survival of the company and to ensure the livelihoods of my loyal staff. But my heart felt it was at breaking point—I was being pulled in two directions. Work on the one hand and family on the other.

When Mum was diagnosed with terminal cancer, I travelled home every weekend so we could all be together during those final few months. We laughed, we cried and we reminisced. But it's a mean beast and although she was ready to go when the time came, we weren't ready to let go of her. What it did for me, was put everything into perspective.

Going back is never easy; going forward was all I knew, until now.

It eased my conscience a little to see my team through the transition, giving them time to adjust to the new regime. It was meant to be a period in which we'd all feel proud of what we'd achieved and I'd leave them with a sense of excitement about their future. But the last few months have been a blur of activity and, naturally, upheaval.

And now, Sy is right—I feel like a deserter, walking away as if I can't already see the problems beginning to stack up on the horizon. Big business is fierce and while it was all smiles and handshakes at the start, it's now deadpan faces and long emails detailing the new procedures. Did they really want the business, or just the ready-made audience to add to their already huge database? Equally as soul-destroying is the fact that I'm beginning to feel I've been disloyal to our customers, too. The press release put a very positive spin on it, of course, but some of the benefits seem one-sided to me. I'm hoping I'm proved wrong.

This little website I set up, working every evening and weekend while I was at uni studying for my computer sciences degree, began as a tiny seed of an idea. The experience I gained as a database administrator after I qualified, spurred me on. It became my sole focus in life to the exclusion of everything.

I vividly remember the day I handed in my notice at the day job, much to the horror of my parents and everyone I knew. All I had was a team of one to take my ideas forward.

But every time I shut my eyes at night it took over my dreams. There wasn't room for anything else in my life because I became obsessive. As it grew, and more and more subscribers signed up to pay their monthly fee, each member of staff I recruited knew their input made a difference; they counted for something. I lovingly nurtured it for nine years as it grew into a sapling and then into a little tree. But the handover has only served to make us all feel like pawns in a game of chess, overshadowed by the mighty castles and the knights who came sweeping in with solutions to problems we didn't even know we had. So now I feel like I sold out and that's my Achilles heel—for me it was always about the people, regardless of whether they were employees or customers.

Being faced with technical wizardry far beyond even my—not inconsequential—IT abilities was a sharp and timely reminder that I was doing the right thing. Of course, a multi-million-pound company can afford to pay for the brightest of whizz kids. And some are young, very young—making me feel old at the age of twenty-nine. The saving grace for my team is that I hand-picked the best.

It was a great idea that worked at a micro-level, as well as for much bigger things—everything from exchanging babysitting duties, to finding a local tradesman and being able to choose someone with a degree of confidence. Scanning through the feedback shows that it reflects a true sense of community, not least because of the launch of Help-a-neighbour, a free service. There are a lot of lonely, isolated people out there and a call to action by a member to rescue an elderly person's overgrown garden, for example, can achieve a staggering influx of offers to help.

And more and more we began to see an increase in the number of people offering a simple exchange of skills. That alone saw one of the biggest jumps in enrolment and word spread quickly. Keeping the subscription fee low was key to making it accessible for as many people as possible.

None of my family and friends really understood what I'd built. It's my own fault, as I was too busy to realise I had distanced myself from them all. No one outside of the business wants to have a conversation about websites, bugs and download speeds, though. As soon as you mention you work in IT, people's eyes tend to glaze over and they change the subject very quickly. And there was always an emergency at work—a reason to cancel a trip home to visit the parents, or bow out of a dinner date. But now I no longer have a business to run and technically I no longer have a job, so there are no more excuses—just an obscene amount of money in the bank and a whole raft of contacts offering me consultancy work. And that holds no interest for me whatsoever, as I don't see myself as an entrepreneur in the truest sense of the word. It was all about the challenge of building and running a website that fulfilled a genuine need. I should be feeling ecstatic and I would be, if it wasn't for this monster of a guilty conscience weighing me down for jumping ship.

'I have responsibilities to take care of, Sy,' I say, my voice sounding a tad more emotional than I'd hoped. 'Since Mum died, Dad's been struggling and it's time for me to be there for him, as he was for me when I was growing up.'

Sy, being Sy, throws his hands in the air, but he knows that I'm speaking from the heart. Now is probably not the time to remind him of the bonus I gave each of my team when the electronic transfer hit my account. It was a nice little nest egg in case corporate life and the perks on offer turn out not to be quite right for them. I know it's a whole new world and it won't be the same, but nothing stands still forever and that's life, I'm afraid. If it does, in this day and age, then it signals the beginning of the end. It means people have run out of ideas and that's a red flag.

'That's what weekends and holidays are for,' Sy retorts, still needing to vent. The desperation in his eyes is hard to witness.

'After years of being a neglectful daughter, it's time to head home and get him back on track. My parents asked nothing of me and gave me their support every step of the way. Mum would expect me to do the right thing now and don't pretend you don't understand, Sy, because I know that's not the case.'

'It doesn't mean you have to move back to a little village in the depths of Cornwall and leave behind the delights of London. You'll stagnate! You're used to spending your days in meetings talking about server speeds and demographics... and...' He pauses, casting around for the right words, which are clearly eluding him as he teeters on the edge of a meltdown. '...software updates.'

I shake my head, walking over to give him a big hug.

'And that's precisely why I'm done, Sy. I'm overwhelmed and tired. I put my life on hold for the last nine years and became almost a stranger to the people I love. The regrets I have weigh heavily upon me and it's time for me to step up. Mum's passing made me realise that it's foolish to take anything for granted.'

My words have the required effect and he begins to relax.

Wrapping his arms around me in a resigned gesture, we hug, acknowledging the moment has finally arrived.

'I know, but it's so hard to let you go. I want you to be happy—we all do. But this is personal. You're the sister I never had, Kerra. Who is going to stop me getting myself into trouble when you're gone?'

I push back a little, so I can give him a purposeful look.

'Just keep your head down at work and keep doing what you're doing. Our customer services team has an enviable track record for speed of resolution and you are a good organiser and motivator, Sy. Their success is entirely down to you. Your new boss is going to see that and you will learn a lot from him. When it comes to the ladies… well…' I heave a sigh. 'I wish I had the answer to that one. You're a lost cause, Sy, and I don't quite know what to say.'

He at least has the good grace to nod, because we both know it's true.

'I'm on a mission to find your perfect match. And when I do, I'll be in touch immediately. I promise. In the meantime, you'll just have to do what you usually do, but try not to let every single one of them break your heart.'

'So you'd waft temptation under my nose, knowing it's too big an ask? That's almost as bad as leaving me in the lurch.'

Aside from his firm belief that London is the centre of the universe, Sy prefers to connect with people via social media. And that's usually how he finds his next girlfriend. He's like an F1 racing car. He goes from zero to top speed in seconds, when it comes to falling in love. The reality, once they meet—after weeks of scintillating texts—is always a bitter disappointment and that's my point.

'Sy, you need a hobby to get you off your phone and meeting people in a non-work environment, without pressure.'

'Me—a hobby?'

'Yes. I think you'd enjoy amateur dramatics.'

Immediately turning my back on him to stack another box on the table, I'm glad he can't see the huge grin I'm trying to contain. It also means that I don't have to witness his reaction.

'I'm done here, if you'd be kind enough to finish sealing up the boxes,' I call over my shoulder. 'It's time to say one final goodbye to everyone and then Cornwall, here I come!'

2. The Future Starts Here

There are tears in my eyes as I drive away from my London life, but there is also a huge sense of relief. Dad is trying his best to keep Mum's dog-sitting business—Home from Home—going, but he was only ever a weekend helper before he gave up work. While there are perfectly good kennels in the garden, on my last trip home every available seat in the house had a dog curled up on it. He told me they only howl if he tries to use the bespoke accommodation. The truth is that they, too, miss my lovely mum and are pining for her. They don't understand what's happening and, sadly, neither does Dad. Mum would be horrified at his total lack of control and expect me to sort him out, which I will. But he needs time to adjust and I can't just wade in; it would only add to his anxiety.

People came from miles around to entrust their beloved fur babies into Mum's care, because she was a professional and had a true affinity with animals. They would return home better behaved because she was a nurturing woman, able to dispense tough love when it was required. Dad, on the other hand, is a pushover. If there was something I really wanted, I'd ask him first, then break the news to Mum. She would usually look at me, narrowing her eyes admonishingly. I'd keep my head down and stay out of her bad books for a while, until she eventually forgave me.

But running a business requires a multitude of skills. The fact that Dad isn't good with paperwork or using the computer to figure out the electronic booking system, was a growing problem. However, it took a phone call about six months ago to alert me to that fact. My old school friend, Tegan Richards, rang me one day to give me an update and I realised that while Dad was telling me everything was fine, it wasn't.

'Your dad needs rescuing, Kerra. He really does. We're all worried about Eddie. I don't think the word "no" is in his vocabulary and it's getting ridiculous. It was pouring down the other day and I caught up with him on what was obviously not his first walk of the day. He had three large and extremely energetic canines straining on their leashes wanting to get on. We spoke briefly and he apologised for having to rush off. He was already soaking wet at that point and admitted to me that he had another three lots of dogs to walk.' I'd heard a real sense of concern in her voice and guilt had hit me squarely in the gut. 'It's too much for him without Meryn,' she'd added sadly.

The mention of Mum's name had instantly made my eyes prickle with tears and a trip down the following weekend turned them into tears of despair. However, slow and steady is the required approach with Dad and there was little I could do from a distance. I was heavily caught up in contract negotiations for the sale of the business at that point—something I didn't want to bother him with, as I knew he'd worry. I wasn't in a position to go anywhere until that was done and dusted. There was also the matter of getting my loft-style apartment in London ready to rent out. And serving notice to the tenant living in the little cottage I'd inherited from Grandma Rosenwyn, or Rose as we called her, in Penvennan Cove.

But that particular day I'd had to grit my teeth, in need of a quick fix.

'I'll ring my cousin, Alice, and ask her to pop over to see if there's anything she can do. Thanks for being my eyes and ears, Tegan, you are a life-saver.'

Normally, I wouldn't thrust Alice on anyone. However, I was desperate and as Mum always said, 'family is family, no matter how much they don't like each other'—and she was right.

'We're all looking out for him, Kerra, as best we can so try not to worry. But Eddie is a very private man and he's cautious about what he shares, and with whom. That means he's not always easy to help,' she'd declared, and I had to agree.

Tegan's latest update, a fortnight ago, was a little more encouraging, mainly because Dad is so excited about my return. She'd said he'd mentioned he was concerned that I'd 'quit my job and intended to work from home'. Tegan had sounded a little dubious about that herself. It made me realise what a true friend she is and always has been over the years. And that's despite the fact she knows nothing at all about my life in London, because whenever we catch up I'm desperate for news about home. A part of me has never left Penvennan, and she knows that.

'Are you getting nervous about coming back here for good, now you're on countdown?'

For some reason I'd hesitated for a second. 'Not really

nervous, just anxious to get settled in as quickly as I can. How's my tenant doing?'

'I told Mr Mills you'd booked me to clean through after the removal men have been and he was very grateful. He's a strange man, Kerra. I still can't fathom out what exactly he does for a living. Anyway, I'll have a whole day to get it sorted before you arrive. Oh, and I mentioned in passing to James, that Eddie is finding the dogs a handful. I might have mentioned to Eddie, too, that James was looking to earn a little cash.' I remember hearing a distinct chuckle in her voice. 'He's a nice young man, isn't he, and Eddie jumped at his offer, apparently.'

James and his parents, Tom and Georgia Hooper, live next door to Dad.

'Ah, thank you—that means a lot, Tegan. I should have thought of that myself.'

That particular call had left me even more desperate to wrap things up and be on my way. I've been working a six-day week to get everything tied up. On the seventh day it's been all about packing cases to store away the more personal items in the apartment. The expensive, designer furniture and furnishings I was happy to leave behind. The new tenant will only use the apartment Monday to Friday, as his family home is a large manor house in Somerset and he wanted something set up ready to go.

And it's all about home, isn't it? I kidded myself that my life was bigger and better in London, but it wasn't—not really. The closer to Cornwall I get, the more it now feels like I was castaway on an island. A place where there was an alternate reality. And my family bought into that, too, unable to fully comprehend how very different my life was to theirs. There was absolutely no crossover between the two, but they were happy for me because they felt I was living my dream.

After the funeral, Dad insisted I head back to London. He assured me he had plenty to keep him occupied because Home from Home was going to remain open for business. To Dad, though, a dog is a pet. And that's how he's treating all of his tail-wagging guests now, who are clearly missing Mum's firm, but loving hand.

The irony of the timing of the offer to sell my business wasn't lost on me. I realised fate was offering me a chance to redeem myself and I grabbed it.

I'm nervous and that's only natural given the situation. Returning to the place where people remember you growing up means their view of you is very different. And going back will probably rake up memories of the first love of my life. You never get over the first one, do you? All those fantasy 'what if?' daydreams, although in my case it was more *if only*… I was way too shy, in those days, to let my feelings be known. He also happened to be the one guy every girl I knew wanted to date and every guy wanted to be him. Intelligent, cool and charming without even having to try, he stood out from the rest. But for me it was all about those eyes and that charming smile. One glance in my direction and suddenly the sun began to shine and my heart would start to dance.

Ironically, our paths never crossed during any of my trips home and when I heard he'd married I was glad of that. I would be a sad and hopeless individual indeed, to still feel something for someone who never really noticed me when we all hung around together at school. 'Well, mister, you're the one who missed out,' I say out loud, laughing to myself. My words are tinged with a hint of contempt and a huge dollop of self-satisfaction. *You are a self-made woman, Kerra, and when you are good and ready you'll choose someone worthy of the love you have to give. The focus now is on keeping a low profile until people are used to seeing you around again. Simple. You can do this. Fading into the background is a skill you were particularly good at back then. It's a coping mechanism that will come in handy, I suspect.*

Finally, I pull up outside of Pedrevan Cottage and the enormity of this moment almost takes my breath away.

My heart weeps and all I can do to show Mum how much I regret the days we didn't have together, is to be here for Dad. And now I'm actually going to live in the cottage in which my mum was born and brought up, for the very first time. That would have warmed my grandma's heart, too.

Switching off the engine, I immediately grab my phone and press speed dial. 'I'm here, Dad.'

'I'm on me way.'

Walking up to the front gate I stand for a few moments to take it all in and I'm awash with emotion. I knew that someday I would come back here to live, but the picture in my head was a totally different scenario.

'I've got this, Mum,' I whisper, softly to myself. 'Dad's in safe hands now. Your daughter is finally home to stay.'

Unlocking the door and stepping over the threshold instantly transports me back to my childhood. I can picture Grandma stopping to welcome me with a big sloppy kiss on my cheek, as I'd breathe in the smell of biscuits fresh from the oven wafting through the cottage. Fairings, they were called. Sweet and spicy, made with fresh ginger, they were deliciously crumbly in the mouth.

Giving myself a little shake, I step forward with determination but the moment I head into the sitting room I let out a groan.

'Oh dear!'

The stack of boxes sitting neatly in the middle is a sharp reminder that I didn't bring very much with me. Sy would point to things and say, 'You'll need this, and that…' but I kept shaking my head.

Suddenly, I hear a key in the door. 'Only me and I've brought another friendly face,' Dad calls out. I turn around to see him and Tegan, standing in the doorway grinning at me.

'Group hug time, I think.'

As I stride across to join them, it feels good to be wrapped in the arms of two people who have known me forever. I'm just Kerra again now. No need to wear my work armour and fear people will see the chinks in it. Or lie in bed at 2 a.m. worrying after a stressful day. This is the start of a new life and a new me. It's time to live in the moment and enjoy each day as it comes.

'Your mum will be smiling,' Dad says, his voice breaking up and Tegan and I hug him even tighter. So many memories come flooding back and it's bittersweet, every smile raising a tear simply because she's no longer here.

Reluctantly we disentangle ourselves, smiling through the tears.

'My things arrived, then,' I say as cheerfully as I can.

'This is everything that was in the van. Where are the rest

of your things?' Tegan asks, glancing at the pile behind me with a frown on her face.

'That's it. A new bed and a couple of other items will be delivered before five this afternoon. I thought I'd paint through first and buy things as I need them. Thanks for getting your team in and cleaning through, Tegan. Everything sparkles.' It's tired, this little cottage, but soon the décor will sparkle as brightly as the windows.

Tegan and Dad exchange a worried look but say nothing. The truth is, I haven't had time to think about home comforts, or exactly how I'm going to bring this place up to date. As long as I have somewhere to sleep and the internet, I'll be fine for the time being.

'Dad, has the engineer been in to install the Wi-Fi?' My heart misses a beat or two, until he nods his head. Starting over is a shopping nightmare and I suspect I'll be doing quite a bit of it online. I also have this little software programme where I can replicate the room sizes and move items of furniture around. I'm looking forward to having a play with it.

'Yep. It's in the front bedroom as you requested. Logan, the Williams' boy, is our local engineer. He said if you have any problems at all just give him a call. Day or night. I told him you're working from home and it's IT work.' Dad's tone automatically lowers as he utters those last two words. Goodness knows what he's telling everyone.

'Logan Williams, my—he must be what, almost thirty now?'

'Thirty-one. He's a couple of years older than us,' Tegan replies. 'Wife and two kids and two very energetic dogs in tow.'

Dad laughs. 'I can vouch for that.'

'Hello?'

An unknown voice calls out from the hallway and I shout out a good-natured, 'Come on through.'

The man who appears is tall, has short, dark brown, curly hair and isn't dressed like a delivery man. He's wearing some paint-splattered jeans and a somewhat grubby T-shirt emblazoned with the words *Don't ask*. Which immediately makes me want to ask the question, 'Why?' as he produces a bunch of something green from behind his back.

'Some herbs from the garden. I'm Drew, Drew Matthews. I live next door.'

Rather surprised at his offering, I take it and return his smile.

'Kerra Shaw,' I reply. 'Thank you, Drew. These will come in handy, I'm sure.'

If I can find a jug to put them in among these boxes, I reflect. And there is the slight problem that it's been a while since I did any cooking at all.

'Oh, I know who you are. Alright Eddie, Tegan? She's home then.'

I almost feel like an interloper as the three exchange meaningful glances. So I'm the talk of the village. Again. But then I always was, branded as never being satisfied by a few less charitable folk.

Tuning back in to the three of them now chatting away quite happily as if I'm not here, I cough to clear my throat.

'If you give me a few moments to investigate, I'll find the box with the mugs and the kettle, and make a drink.'

'Oh, don't do that,' Drew insists, taking charge. 'I'll bring a tray around. Tegan won't mind giving me a hand, will you?'

Tegan looks absolutely delighted.

'There's a paint brush that needs putting in water first, so give us a few minutes. I bought a cake from the shop to celebrate your arrival.'

'Well done, Drew,' Dad says. 'Nothing beats a slice of cake and a cup of tea to celebrate a grand occasion.'

Tea? I've only been here ten minutes and I'd cheerfully attack a glass of wine. I can't even recall seeing Drew around the village on my trips back. Why have Dad and Tegan never mentioned him, when clearly he's one of the trusted circle? I'd assumed next door was a holiday cottage.

That's another thing about village life. There are circles. And some you don't want to join. Others, well, you need an invite. Me, I'm going to create my own little circle because I've suddenly remembered one of the reasons why I left in the first place. Square peg, round hole. Hopefully, life has given me the confidence to knock off a few of those sharp edges and stop putting up unnecessary barriers. This is where my future lies and if each one of us was the same, life would be plain old boring. There is nothing wrong with being different, I've learnt, only in letting other people make you feel uncomfortable about that. Nicknames like Little Miss Clever and Miss Laugh Not a Lot made me want to run and hide as a sensitive, and rather serious, six-year-old. Little did I know that as the years passed, those very qualities would stand me in good stead. Now who's laughing?

Ding-dong, ding-dong, ding-dong.

Glancing over Dad's shoulder, I see a blue delivery lorry is parked just inches from the back of my car.

'Oh, good. The bed has arrived.'

As Drew and Tegan head off, Dad and I lead the delivery men upstairs. There's a bit of scratching of heads as they look at the rather tight turn at the top of the stairs.

'Might be tough to get it round that,' one of them says to the other. 'What do you think?'

'Hmm. These cottages are always a nightmare. We'll do our best, lady.'

I look at them with a sympathetic smile on my face. 'Well, thank you, guys. I have a twenty-pound note here to make up for the inconvenience.'

They're back out to the van quicker than a cat after a mouse.

'Nothing changes then, Dad?' I muse and he laughs.

'And neither do you, lovely. You're a breath of fresh air.'

3. Friends and Neighbours

We're standing just outside the back door, gazing out over the lawn that is badly in need of a cut.

'I can't believe you're really here! I finally have my old friend home for good.' Tegan throws her arms around my shoulders enthusiastically, sounding a tad tearful.

It makes me gulp down a lump that begins to rise in my own throat. Life hasn't felt this real in a long time and yet I had no idea how distant I'd become from the people who really care about me.

'Is everything okay?' Tegan's frown reflects genuine concern as the seconds pass. 'You aren't regretting your decision?'

Taking a deep breath, I pull myself together. 'No, not at all. It's great to be back. I know it'll take a while for me to get the cottage sorted, but I'm not in a rush.'

'Eddie told Logan you had to be online as a priority. Eddie was getting stressed about it as there was a fault on the telephone line, apparently, which Mr Mills never bothered reporting.'

'It's no big deal and I keep forgetting that I'm a free agent now. I have my phone and I doubt I'll be setting up the computer until I've decorated the room I'm going to use as an office.'

Tegan looks at me, wearing a rather unflattering frown. 'I assumed... I mean, Eddie said you'd be anxious to get yourself up and working again as quickly as possible.'

'There's a lot of painting to do and furniture to buy, first.'

'Oh. Right.' Her frown deepens and I look at her, trying to fathom out the reason she's choosing her words so carefully.

'What exactly has my dad been saying?' As our eyes meet, she looks a little embarrassed.

'Not much; Eddie isn't a great talker at the best of times. But people are curious and you know what some of them are like. Poor chap can't even walk the dogs in peace without fending off questions from everyone he passes.'

'But what has he told *you*?'

She swallows hard, her discomfort growing by the second.

'It's not what he's said, so much as what he hasn't said. He's worried about you, Kerra, because he knows you love the buzz of London life. If you're back for good, then he thinks it...'

'What?'

'...was all becoming too much for you.'

I almost drop the mug I'm cradling in my hands.

'Oh, Tegan. I sold my business because it was time to come home. When you are looking thirty in the face it's a turning point. Don't you feel that, too?'

The frown has disappeared, only to be replaced by a slightly blank look.

'Well, I suppose I do in a way.' I can tell she has no idea at all what I'm talking about.

'Maybe it was losing Mum that was the catalyst for me. It made me realise I miss this life.'

She laughs, but it comes out as a bit of a sarcastic snort. 'But you couldn't wait to get away. I can't even imagine how exciting it must be to live in a big city with so much to do and see.' Her tone has a distinctly wistful edge to it.

'Oh, it is exhilarating and I felt really alive walking the streets with a purposeful stride, because I fitted in. Me, Kerra, the girl from a little village who had a big dream. But I've learnt that things change and it can also be a very lonely place at times. I've been there, done that and now I can walk away from the pressure and begin all over again. It's exciting, but in a different way.'

Tegan takes a sip of her drink and when she lowers the mug she gives me a sideways glance.

'So, everything really is okay and there's no need to worry?'

I nod. 'Everything is perfect, actually.'

'You'd better sit Eddie down and have a frank talk with him, then. He's been telling them down at The Lark and Lantern, that anyone in business should have a website these days and if they haven't, they should hire you.'

I let out a groan, as I look up to the heavens. 'Thanks for the heads-up, Tegan. If anyone asks, I'm not taking on any new clients for the foreseeable future. Hopefully that will put an end to the speculation.'

'Of course, and I'm happy for you, Kerra. If anyone deserves success, it's you, because you've always worked hard.'

'It takes one, to know one,' I reply, but she grimaces.

'Well, running a cleaning company isn't anywhere near

as glamorous,' she chuckles. 'The rubber gloves are on more than they're off right now. I'm two staff down again at the moment. Weekdays it's mainly domestic cleaning jobs and it's not so hectic, but I'm praying they will both be well enough to get back to work on Saturday. It's changeover day for the majority of the rental properties.'

As we exchange a look of commiseration, to my horror her eyes begin to fill with tears and seconds later we're hugging like we did when we were kids. Tegan lost her husband, Pete, two years ago and he was her rock. Mum's been gone six months now but there are still times it doesn't feel real. I know what it feels like, though, when suddenly a big part of your world is missing and nothing else can fill it.

'Listen. If you need help, I'm here for you. Cleaning is cathartic and we always made a good team. If you get stuck, you know where to come. I'm hoping to shed a few pounds by getting active again, but it doesn't matter whether that's from painting walls, or cleaning bathrooms.'

'It's going to be just like the old days,' she replies, her eyes sparkling. 'Remember when your mum let us take over the old shed and we turned it into a clubhouse? We were painting buddies back then and I can't wait to help you bring Pedrevan Cottage back to life.'

It's humbling to be reminded that true friends are there for you, always.

What a frenetic day it's been, with a stream of people coming and going. The kitchen looks like a bakery, with a whole array of welcome home gifts—homemade cakes, biscuits, jams and chutneys.

And finally, here I am, sitting in my garden, cradling a mug of hot chocolate and staring up rather contentedly at the twilight sky above. Even the typical nip in the air of a spring evening isn't enough to tempt me back inside.

I find myself taking in a slow, deep breath and, instantly, it conjures up thoughts of my childhood. The air is different here, not just that bitter, salty tang when the wind is blowing in from the sea, but it has notes, like a perfume. The streets of London smell of lots of things, many food-related or that pungent odour of exhaust fumes. In summer there's that dusty dryness that feels stifling as the heat builds and travel by tube becomes unbearable—it's no wonder people head to the nearest open spaces. Just taking half an hour lounging on the grass and revelling in the green vista of towering trees, makes for a revitalising lunch break.

Sitting here, my nose is curious as I begin to distinguish some very familiar smells. A whiff of woodsmoke from a garden fire. And other fragrances. Definitely jasmine, but also that slightly earthy, leafy smell. Maybe it's from the hedges nearby and the new spring growth as it begins to open out. There's a sweetness to it that connects with something inside my brain. It's rather comforting, in a déjà vu kind of way and tonight I need that. My fear is that I'll quickly tire of the novelty of being back and then what do I do? London is like a drug and people either embrace it and thrive, or end up feeling lost. But I was tired and grieving. That's a good enough reason to come home, isn't it?

A movement in the far corner of the garden makes me lean forward. Squinting, I imagine I can see two eyes peering back at me from beneath one of the bushes. It's all so overgrown that anything could be hiding in there as it extends way back. I'm wondering what on earth it can be, when suddenly the form of a cat streaks across the garden and takes a flying leap to clamber up onto the fence to the left of me. It's not being chased, so maybe I startled it as much as it startled me.

Suddenly, a lone voice breaks the silence.

'Hey, neighbour. Well, day one is almost over, and you survived.'

Unable to see Drew, who is the other side of the two-metre-high hedge, I have no idea how long he's been there. I can only hope I haven't voiced any of my tumbling thoughts out loud.

'I did. I wasn't expecting such an overwhelming response, to be honest with you.'

'That's village life for you. What are you doing?'

'I'm just listening and looking.'

'At what?'

'The silence and the stars.'

'Oh. Do you do that a lot?'

It feels funny talking to a hedge.

'No. Not usually, but then there's so much buzz going on in London at all hours of the day and night, that sitting in the communal garden contemplating wasn't a thing.'

'And now you're back here, it's a thing?'

Hmm. He obviously doesn't intend to do the gentlemanly thing and leave me in peace.

'It's disconcerting sitting here talking to a hedge. Would you like a hot chocolate?'

'I wondered when you were going to offer. I'm on my way.' The enthusiasm in his voice catches me off guard for a moment, before I head back into the kitchen.

When I return Drew is sitting in my seat, having used the side entrance, and his legs are sprawled out in front of him, head tipped back.

'There are a lot of stars visible tonight. A full moon and a clear sky make it look very different up there. Surreal.'

I ease myself into the wooden chair alongside him, mirroring his pose.

'I'd forgotten what it's like to look up, not just at buildings and billboards and glitzy lights. It's other worldly and with the lack of light pollution it's mesmerising. In London everything at ground level seems to rise up and steal your focus. Busy colours, busy people, lots of noise and bustle. I can't remember the last time I was out in the night air, feeling truly alone and staring up at the universe. Well, present company aside, that is.'

He turns to face me as I take a tentative sip from my mug.

'And I've spoilt the moment. Sorry, and thanks for the chocolate, it's been a while since anyone made me this sort of nightcap.'

'Really?'

'Really. My girlfriend is more of a Prosecco-at-any-time-of-day, person.'

I was that party girl once, then the entrepreneurial businesswoman who stuck to bottled water. But now... this is rural, coastal living and it might as well be a million miles away from London. That part of my life is firmly behind me and I have no intention, or desire, to go back.

'Each to their own, as they say,' I reply good-naturedly.

'Hmm. Indeed.' He sounds disheartened. Maybe he's missing her because, clearly, she's not around.

'The rumour mill hasn't reached you yet, then. It will.' Drew's mouth forms a playful smile.

'Give it a day or two,' I reply, only half-joking. 'Hot chocolate reminds me of my mum. She always said that a cup of hot chocolate is the equivalent of a hug, when you need it.'

Drew's body shifts position so he's looking directly at me. 'Guess that makes two of us, then. I suspect it's not easy picking up the strands of a life you left behind.'

Raising the corners of my mouth to form a grateful smile, I can see in his eyes that the sympathy is genuine.

'I have no doubt at all that some of my visitors today came to see if the rumours are true, that I'm back because I failed.'

Drew does a double-take.

'As an outsider I don't get to hear everything, but the impression I have is that you're the one who made it. Eddie is certainly very proud of you.'

Good old Dad. Tegan was right, he's careful about what he says and to whom.

'I didn't fail, I chose to walk away. There's a big difference, but I can see why people would jump to the wrong conclusion. So why are you a topic of conversation among the gossips?'

He lowers his head, peering down into the mug between his hands, before looking back up at me. This time his eyes are shining, mischievously.

'Felicity is referred to as the *girlfriend* in a hushed tone. There's a rumour going around that she doesn't actually exist. Well, only in my head.'

My eyebrows shoot up into my fringe. 'That's downright mean!'

'Quite. Admittedly, she's only been here once, when we first viewed Tigry Cottage. It was the name that attracted me, of course. I love kestrels and the Cornish translation is perfect. I have fond memories of holidays spent here when I was a child and I saw it as an omen. Felicity wasn't quite as keen, as she would have preferred something detached, but the fact it was such a short walk down to the cove swung it in my favour. It was supposed to be our weekend retreat, until I was made redundant and finances dictated the need to make this my permanent base.'

He pauses, raising his mug as I sit quietly, leaning back and turning my eyes upwards again before I begin talking.

'Sorry to hear that, Drew. It must have been tough facing two massive life changes at the same time. I'm sort of going through the same thing and I'm feeling distinctly overwhelmed.'

He settles back, half-lying in his chair now.

'Your arrival has done me a favour, actually.'

'It has?'

'Well, Felicity isn't likely to put in an appearance for a while yet. Most weekends I end up at her place in the Cotswolds, so I'm a continuing puzzle. However, if the locals are too busy figuring out the details of your return home, then I won't be the only conundrum for them to muse over.'

I start laughing. 'Oh, thanks.'

'It's easier for you. You belong here and I'm only an *emmet*, a newcomer who will probably never really fit in. I do my best work at night and often sleep during the day, which can be regarded as a little antisocial.'

'Ah, I haven't heard the term *emmet* in a long while, but my Grandma Rose used it frequently. Anyway, you're being rather hard on yourself.' It's just an observation, but thinking back I'm pretty sure I remember Dad telling me that the cottage had sold a few months before Mum died, so he hasn't even been here a year yet.

'It's been slow going, I will be honest. The only room I've managed to complete so far is my office. The rest is tidy, but I have a vision.'

'What line of work are you in?'

'I'm an architect,' he replies, watching for my reaction.

'Oh. That's interesting.'

'I've drawn up plans for an extension to the rear and before I submit the planning application, I'd like to show them to you. There's no point ploughing forward if I'm going to upset my only neighbour, is there?'

Ah. He has an agenda.

'I'd love to take a look. I'm used to having a lot of space around me and while I love this little cottage because my mum was brought up here, it's not really *me*.' I snap my mouth shut. 'Ooh, that sounds a tad pretentious, doesn't it? Sorry.'

Drew sits upright, stretching his back and repositioning himself ready to stand, but he pauses for a second.

'You're worried that if you aren't careful about what you do and how you do it, people here will think you've outgrown them?'

I stand up and reach for his mug as he eases himself up off the chair.

'Well, something like that. My cousin lives nearby, and she thinks moving away is about distancing yourself from family. It's not, although that's what often happens. But it's about being flexible enough to chase the opportunities that otherwise won't come your way. Some people simply can't see it, though, so they take it personally, like a rejection.'

We stand, a look of irony passing between us.

'It's nice to meet a fellow non-conformer. Some people weren't made to simply fit in Kerra, you do know that?'

I give him a grateful smile.

'Maybe you're right. But I owe it to my dad to give it a try.'

4. A Helping Hand

It's mid-morning before I eventually head across the road to Dad's place. He'll be back from the doggy walks and will have had his second cup of coffee by now. As I approach the garden gate, I'm amazed to see that he's in the process of giving the kennels a thorough clean.

'Morning,' I call out, not wanting to make him jump. There isn't a dog in sight, though, and I suspect they're all inside watching TV.

'Mornin' lovely. Nice bit of blue sky we have today.' He straightens, grimacing a bit and places his free hand on his back, giving it a quick rub.

'Want some help?'

'No. I'm good. Just giving it all a bit of a spruce up.'

It looks like a lot more than that to me, judging by the array of cleaning materials in the plastic crates next to the hosepipe and a jet washer.

'Now I'm back I have plenty of free time, you know,' I respond encouragingly. 'I could lend a hand, help you get the dogs back into using the kennels properly again.'

Dad's brow furrows. 'You don't approve, and you think Mum wouldn't approve, either. But I like a bit of company in the house.' He looks a tad offended.

'But it's not right, Dad. They aren't *your* pets, although I know some of them regard this as their second home. But Mum was always very particular, and everything ran smoothly. It is a business, after all and you do need to have a bit of a life outside of it.'

'I know, don't nag. This is my mess and I'm the one who needs to sort it out.' He's not cross, but he is adamant.

'You had no choice but to take charge and keep things running because you knew what it meant to Mum. But it was never your thing, was it?'

He smiles. 'She never realised that, of course, because I didn't want to upset her.'

'You know Dad, this wouldn't take long to sort out with two of us working side by side.'

'Let me think about it, Kerra. Knowing your mum, she's watching me. This is one test I want to pass with flying colours because if I can do the right thing, then I know she'll be able to rest easy.'

What can I possibly say to that? 'I'm here to talk when you're ready, because a problem shared is a problem halved.'

He smiles, leaning in to give me a brief hug.

'Ha! I've said it enough times to you over the years to know the day would come when I'd hear you throw it back at me. The dogs I look after are the ones who miss her as much as I do. When the time is right, I'll get things up and running properly again. Now that's enough about me. How was your first night in Pedrevan Cottage?'

It's obvious this is going to be a gradual process and there's no point in pushing him when I've only just arrived. The only heartening thing is that at least he's talking about getting things back onto a normal footing. And that's a huge development, given the months of total chaos.

'It was fine. I invited Drew over for a nightcap and we sat in the garden for a while, chatting.'

Dad slots the bottles of various cleaning materials into the tubs, stacking them before lifting them up and using his chin to steady the top one. He turns to walk back up towards the shed. I grab the jet washer and follow on behind.

'It's nice to know you have a good neighbour, there,' he calls over his shoulder. 'There are a few young women hereabouts keeping an eye on him, but he's always busy and often away at weekends.'

It's never easy getting information out of Dad, as he's not one for general chatter but he's rather cheerful today. Is this his way of letting me know he thinks Drew is trustworthy?

'Yes, I gather his girlfriend lives in the Cotswolds.'

'Oh, he mentioned her, did he?'

Dad cocks an eyebrow, seemingly surprised, as he turns to look at me before easing open the shed door with his boot and stepping inside.

'He did. Did you know he's drawing up plans for an extension on the back of the cottage?'

Dad steadies the crates on the work bench, then turns around to take the load from my hands.

'No. That's rather ambitious.' The tone in his voice is a little disapproving. 'It's a perfectly good little cottage as it stands. And that could be a lot of mess and noise for you.'

He gives me a worried look.

'Oh, it's fine. He said he's going to show me the drawings before he submits them to the planning office. Besides, I'm used to noise at all times of the day and night; it's the quiet that I'm finding strange. Did you know that Drew is an architect?'

Dad starts laughing. 'Rumour has it that he's a writer, because the light in his study is on until the small hours most nights during the week. That'll surprise a few people if it gets out.'

Why on earth do people do that? Make assumptions based on virtually no information at all?

'They won't hear it from me,' I reply rather caustically and Dad gives me an affirming nod.

'Me neither. But you can't worry about what's said behind your back. People are naturally curious when not a lot happens, especially in our sleepy neck of the woods. Anything new is automatically the focus of attention but the vast majority mean well. There's only one or two mean-spirited people and that's a fact of life, wherever you live. It's just more noticeable in a smaller community.'

He lifts the two crates up onto their allotted shelves and we step back outside.

'I know, but now I'm back I don't want you to feel awkward.'

'Because you don't have a job, you mean?'

'Look, Dad, I... well, at some point I'll figure out what I'm going to do next. The thing is, I'm not in a rush. I want to slip back into village life quietly, with minimal fuss. My old life is now firmly behind me, but there will be a period of adjustment.'

He takes a moment to shut the door, double-checking the latch as he continues talking with his back to me.

'So, you really are alright for money? Because you only have to say, you know. Your mum and I made sure we had a rainy-day fund there for you, just in case. And when I get this place up and running properly again—'

I step forward, throwing my arms around him, giving him the hug he so deserves. Leaning my head against his shoulder, I notice that his jumper has dog hairs on it which start to tickle my nose. I'm not the only one badly in need of a fresh start.

'There is nothing at all I want,' I reply softly, 'other than time to turn the cottage into my dream home. I'm back for good and people will soon see that. I've worked hard to earn the freedom to do exactly what I want, and it will all have been wasted if it doesn't totally change my life going forward. It's going to be fun setting everything up and then looking for a new challenge. And if *you* need anything, Dad—'

He cuts me off, his voice firm. 'Then I'll ask for your help.'

Lines have now been drawn, but how easy it's going to be to stay on the right side of our respective boundaries, who knows?

I might not have many boxes to unpack, but I've handled enough over the last couple of months to be anxious to see the last of them. Today's challenge is to be box-free by the end of the day and have them flattened, ready for the recycling. The good thing about a fresh start, especially when you are moving into a little old cottage, is that it's a great excuse to let go of *stuff*. The bulk of the boxes are clothes carriers and the rest are destined for the kitchen. Admittedly, my chef's apron rarely saw the light of day as it was always easier to eat out, rather than entertaining at home. Even having left a reasonably well-equipped kitchen behind for my tenant, as I make a start decanting the boxes I realise that I could easily fill the cupboards here several times over. What am I going to do with it all?

The sound of the doorbell makes me jump and I sit back on my heels, my shoulders sagging. I stand and head for the front door. At this rate I'll be living with boxes for the foreseeable future. I suspect I'm going to struggle to fit in enough hanging space for all of my clothes, too, even when everything is straight.

'It's just your friendly, local telecoms engineer doing a routine check, Madam.'

The smiling face in front of me takes me back almost a decade.

'Logan! It's wonderful to see you. Come in. I'll pop the kettle on.'

He's hardly changed, well, except for the work outfit and the substantial-looking, dark grey tool bag.

'Tea or coffee? I hope you're in need of a sugar fix, because half the village have popped in with baked goods and there is only me. The kitchen looks like a stall at the summer fair.'

He nods enthusiastically and I notice Logan still has the same, lop-sided grin.

'You bet. Coffee, please. The wife is cutting back on sugar and fat at the moment, so that means I am, too. I figure that I'm due a large slice of cake, as long as you don't tell on me. She says I'm like her third child and I'm more trouble than Oscar and Cadan put together.'

'Well, all credit to her for keeping you all in line. You're happy though, I can tell and that's a blessing.'

'Everything that matters to me is here and I'm grateful for that. Work is just a means of paying the bills and giving my family a reasonable standard of living. Sienna has a little part-time job at the school, working in the office, and that pays for a nice holiday abroad every year. It's only three days a week and she is looking for something a little more challenging, but it needs to fit in with the school runs. I'm a happy man as long as my wife is smiling and she smiles a lot. So, life is good.'

'It's funny to think you used to sit together in school and all these years later, you're still together and have a growing family. That's special.'

'I'm lucky and I knew I'd found a good one from the start. We both wanted the same thing and that was to settle down. At a time when a lot of our friends were heading off in different directions, we were saving like mad. It sounds boring, but life is full and there's never a dull moment in our house.'

'I'm glad you're happy, Logan. It's easy to get caught up with things that don't really matter and family is everything.'

It's funny to think how worried I've been about bumping into old friends. And yet the years in between seem to fall away, as if they are irrelevant. Maybe they are if you've always stayed true to yourself and it doesn't matter what different directions your lives have taken, because there's still that connection. The old Kerra that Logan knew still exists, she's just mellowed a little when it comes to feeling she has something to prove. It's not money that gives you confidence, I realise, but self-worth. Now I'm free of that burden.

'Is it bad timing?' Logan asks, as we walk into the sitting room and he surveys the pile of boxes.

I shake my head. 'No, it's a welcome distraction. I set myself a target, but this one is making me lose the will to live. Even travelling light, I seem to have overestimated the amount of storage space I have.'

Logan deposits his tool bag on the floor and follows me through into the kitchen.

'These old cottages are lovely, but they are small. I imagine it's a bit of a culture shock for you. Still, at least I can make sure you have the best broadband speed available in the area. Eddie told me to move the main point up into the front bedroom, as that was going to be your office. But he wasn't sure where exactly to locate it, so I'm here to switch things around if necessary. He said it's a priority to get you all set up.'

Not again; oh, Dad! 'That's so kind of you, Logan and now I feel bad. Getting my computer up and running seems pointless until I've assembled the desk. And I need to sort the mess in here, first. I know the Wi-Fi is working, as I've already ordered a few things using my phone. But as for proper work, well, it's sinking further and further down my to-do list. Here you go. I haven't unpacked the plates yet, but I do have napkins.'

Logan grabs a mug of coffee and his eyes light up as I hand him a large, Cornish saffron bun, an old favourite from our childhood.

'Mrs Moyle's?'

'Yes, bless her. She said it was nice to be welcoming someone to the area who she knew, for a change.'

'So many cottages that come up for sale are bought as

holiday rentals, these days. At least it brings visitors here all year round to keep the local shops and businesses going, but it's not quite the same, is it? Villages need new life breathed into them by an influx of permanent residents, but that doesn't seem to be happening. Still, Tegan's business is doing well out of it. That woman deserves a break, after what she's been through.'

'Losing the love of your life must put everything else into perspective,' I reflect sadly. 'It's easy to forget what really matters.'

'It's a tragedy, for sure.' Logan pauses for a few seconds to savour a mouthful of bun. 'I'd be lost without Sienna, so I can't imagine what it's like for Tegan. She and Pete worked as a great little team and it must be really hard to go it alone.'

Logan is already popping the last morsel into his mouth and I watch his eyes as they glance hungrily over at the plate on the worktop.

'Another one?'

Nothing beats a little sugar lift when mulling over the vagaries of life.

'Why not? It might be a while before I get a chance to indulge again. If you don't mind me munching as we walk, shall we take a quick look at your office?'

As we head upstairs, the emptiness of the place makes everything feel unloved. It's clean and had a paint-through eighteen months ago, but it's all rather basic. The front bedroom is south-facing and this morning the sun is streaming through the double-aspect windows.

We stand in the middle of the room gazing around, as I try to visualise where everything will go. The boxes containing the components for the desk are leaning up against the wall in the corner, a stark reminder that it's going to take a lot more furniture to kit this room out.

'Is that the desk?' Logan enquires.

'Yes. But now I'm having second thoughts. It's so bright in here, which gives it a wonderful ambience, but it's a nightmare for a computer screen and I'll need blinds for when I'm working.'

'I didn't like to say anything to Eddie, but I thought the same thing. Look, if you decide you want it somewhere else, I can move the point and get that desk assembled for you. As long as I'm out of here by noon, it's not a problem.'

There was a time when both Tegan and I used to purposely dream up ways of crossing paths with Logan. He was two classes above us and captain of the school football team. We were two giggling girls in awe of him. And now he's my friendly telecoms guy, offering to give me a hand. How life has changed.

'What's funny?'

He finishes his coffee and places the empty mug on the windowsill.

'Oh, just old memories that keep popping into my head. You always were kind-hearted, Logan, and I was delighted when I heard that you and Sienna were together. I can't wait to meet your boys.'

'They're a handful, for sure, but I wouldn't change a thing.'

He remained in the village and he made it work, so life here can't be that bad. There's hope for me yet.

5. The Old A-Team is Back in Business

'Kerra, it's Tegan. I know you've only just arrived, but I have a huge problem and I'm desperate. I hate asking, but there's a chance I could lose some of my best customers if I mess up today.'

She sounds stressed and more than a little tearful.

'Whatever it is, the answer is yes. I owe you big time, Tegan, and I'm here for you.'

'It's a big ask for anyone, I'm afraid. I'm three people down and even re-arranging everyone else's lists and calling in favours, it leaves me with less than four hours to turn around the two biggest contracts on my books. Saturday is always crazily busy anyway. But pulling this off will need a small miracle.'

'Give me ten minutes and I'll be outside, waiting. Is there anything you want me to bring?'

'Just your very capable hands. You are an absolute angel.'

Tegan isn't usually a fast driver, but as the white minibus sporting the Clean and Shine logo pulls up in front of me, it screeches to a halt. She leans across, flinging open the passenger door.

'I feel really bad. I know you still have lots of unpacking to do. Mum and Dad, bless, offered to sort out the luxury bungalows up at Rosveth, as it's closer to them. That leaves the two of us to deal with Treeve Perran, the other side of Polreweek, and Treylya up on the headland. Buckle up, because time isn't on our side.'

Hmm. Four hours, at least one of which will be spent travelling as we are heading in two opposite directions.

'Treeve Perran, that's the farm, isn't it?'

She nods, hands gripping the steering wheel so tightly her knuckles are beginning to turn white.

Tegan turns left onto the main road and the minibus bounces along as she drives at the maximum speed limit of sixty. It's a bumpy ride and I can hear a few things clattering around in the back.

'Yes. The pigsties are all gone now, and the central courtyard is a car park surrounded by holiday cottages.'

'It sounds nice.'

'It is, but there are five of them.'

As I turn to look at her, even sideways on I can see her jaw is set in a grimace.

'And the bad news is that Treylya is that big glass building up on the headland. We can't do that one first, which would be the sensible thing to do, as I've had a text that they've overslept and will be a bit late leaving. Overslept! It has six bedrooms and six and a half bathrooms.'

This is crazy. No wonder Tegan is panicking.

'Is it like this every Saturday?' I ask, thinking that's a lot of pressure to handle in a short space of time.

'Well, it's always hectic picking everyone up and dropping them off with just the two minibuses. I do the longest run, though, and ferry around emergency supplies if people run short of anything. But when staff ring in sick at the last minute, then it's a complete nightmare. The turnaround time is tight between guests leaving and the new visitors arriving.' Tegan is talking so fast that her breathing is very shallow, which can't be good for her.

The moment she stops, she finally sucks in a deep breath and expels it seconds later as a long, drawn-out sigh. It's heart-rending to hear her sounding so distraught. Pete would have been her rock, of course, jumping in to drive and helping rejig schedules to avert a crisis. Maybe even donning rubber gloves himself to clean a few bathrooms, because he was that sort of guy.

'Don't worry. We've got this, Tegan. We will whip through this lot with no problem at all.'

I stop short of crossing my fingers in front of her as I utter the words, but she's so tense I have to say something to reassure her. Tegan's profile softens a little, I note with relief, but she keeps her foot firmly pressed down on the accelerator.

We travel in silence for a while and, gradually, Tegan's shoulders become less hunched. It's a relief when she begins speaking again, her voice sounding much more composed this time. 'Are you making progress with those boxes?'

'Not really. Right now, I don't have a master plan for Pedrevan. I could list the problems with it, but until I know what the overall solution is going to be what's the point of unpacking? I think it's more about the shock of leaving behind an orderly life, where I had a routine and lists with tasks I could simply tick off as I worked through them. It's what I know. Now, all I have is a blank page and I have no idea where to start.'

I come to an abrupt halt, realising that it sounds like one big whinge and given what Tegan is going through, my problems are pathetic.

'Oh dear,' Tegan replies and at least I've made her smile. 'A little cottage isn't really you, is it?'

I shake my head, sadly. 'No. I should have bought something else and continued renting it out, but I know Dad would have been disappointed in me. If it's going to be my home I can't just paint through and pretend that's going to make me happy. Or make me want to stay for good.'

Tegan changes into a lower gear as we turn onto the gravelled track leading up to Treeve Perran.

'I remember coming here to the old farm shop with Mum, when I was a teenager,' I tell her, staring out of the window. 'For me there's a memory at every turn and it's like that at the cottage. It's a comfort on one hand and a dilemma on the other.'

'You can't live in the past, Kerra. I don't think our loved ones who pass over would want that, anyway.'

Aww. The sadness in her voice isn't just for my loss, but also for hers. Days like this she must miss Pete so much. As she parks the bus in the courtyard, I can't help thinking that maybe it's better not to find one's soul mate, rather than to experience happiness with your true love, only to lose them forever.

'Well, what a laugh today turned out to be. We were like a whirlwind,' I tell Dad, as he stares at me in awe. 'We stripped and changed beds, mopped floors and cleaned mirrors so fast it would have made your head spin.'

'I bet it was a sight to see,' he laughs. 'You and Tegan were a handful whenever you were together, you know. Your mum called you—'

'The terrible two. I know. I remember.' It's good to see him smiling and talking about old times with fondness.

'Always up to something, the pair of you and I know it means a lot to Tegan to have you around again. I'll pop over when I get a chance and mow that lawn for you.' He inclines his head and I follow his gaze. It's annoying me, too. 'It'll be one job less on that list of yours, when you aren't making much progress inside. But I'm glad you were able to be there for your old friend, today.'

Gazing out over the garden, I notice that a whole raft of healthy-looking weeds seem to have shot up overnight. As someone who likes everything just so, I'm eager to get stuck in, but it's not easy to know where to start. Anyway, more important than a bunch of weeds and a straggly lawn, now might be the time to tackle what is fast becoming the biggest obstacle threatening to hold me back.

'Dad, I need to talk to you about this place.'

'This *place*?'

I stifle a sigh. 'The cottage. It's lovely, so cute and full of memories for both of us. Which is wonderful, but...' I slow to a halt, casting around for the right words to explain how I feel. 'But it isn't *me*. I mean, my style. I like clutter-free space around me, with lots of storage and light.'

His eyes widen a little, in surprise. 'Pedrevan isn't big enough for you? Families with two, sometimes three, children live in cottages like this all over Cornwall. It was good enough for your grandma and grandad, when they were bringing up your mum.'

Now I've upset him.

'I know and I love it, I just wish... My bedroom growing up was twice as big as the master is here.'

Dad shakes his head, sadly. 'This is history, our place across the way is just a 1960s box. Big rooms, I grant you that, but no character. It suited your mum's needs when she wanted to start up the business, but she always hoped you'd settle here at some point in the future. Are you having a change of heart because you're used to fancier things? I want you to be happy, Kerra, because if you aren't then you won't stay.'

'I do love it here, Dad, but living in a cottage is a whole new experience for me. I just feel a bit... hemmed in.' My mind begins to wander and I find myself thinking out aloud. 'If only I could knock through into the cottage next door.'

Wow—that idea came out of nowhere and just popped into my head. Ironically, though, that would be the perfect solution.

'Imagine, twice the garden and a massive patio coming off the back of the cottages,' I paint the picture, my excitement growing. 'I could knock the second and third bedrooms in each property into reasonably-sized en-suite rooms and use the current masters for guests, as they are adjacent to the main bathrooms. My office would have to be located downstairs, of course, and this would need to be extended out.'

I wave my hand in the direction of the back wall of the property. My head is reeling with possibilities and then I look across at Dad, who is staring at me.

'Kerra, have you totally lost the plot? Even if it was up for sale, you'd have to win the lottery to do all that!'

I swallow hard, my cheeks no doubt beginning to colour up as I realise how silly that would have sounded to Dad. But it's a daydream I could easily make happen if I convinced my neighbour to sell up. Drew sort of admitted he'd ended up here due to circumstances beyond his control and if he's missing his girlfriend that much, he might jump at the offer. I wonder if I dare to broach the subject? It would save him the trouble of getting all that work done and he'd have cash in his pocket to start over at a convenient location of his choice. Drew said this was supposed to be a place to come to get away from it all at weekends and that means he never envisioned living here permanently.

'But if I could make it happen, Dad, do you hate the idea?'

'What do you mean, *if* you could? You aren't making any sense at all, Kerra.'

I lapse into silence for a moment, or two, while Dad scans my face intently.

'Dad, when I sold the business it... well, it... you do know that people make a lot of money when websites change hands these days, don't you?'

Dad shifts in his chair, one eyebrow raised as he stares at me sternly. 'You can't go frittering your little nest egg away when your future is so uncertain, Kerra. I know you've always had big ideas, and that has been a bit of a worry for your mum and me over the past few years, I freely admit. Oh, we were always proud of the fact that nothing seemed to hold you back, but we always thought you had your feet firmly planted on the ground. We brought you up to be level-headed, not the sort to get into debt in order to follow a dream. If life here isn't going to make you happy, digging yourself into a financial hole to make it more attractive isn't going to help. Besides, big ideas don't sit well in a small village.'

From what Tegan has already told me, it's clear that Dad's interpretation of my having told him I'd 'done well' is nowhere near the reality of the situation.

'Dad, I have the means to do this if I get the opportunity. I want to keep it just between us, but I walked away with a seven-figure deal.' His expression freezes and he stares at me with his mouth open, unable to speak. 'It's not about spending money for the sake of it,' I continue, 'as I want this to be my forever home. I don't want to look elsewhere for a house I can just move into, when it won't mean anything to me. I'm close to you here, and the location couldn't be more perfect. But I have to be honest with you, because it's not working for me unless I can drag the cottage into the present and make it special.'

He lets out a puff of air, his lips rattling together making a little trumpeting sound.

'Well, I never. Mum always said she'd love to see you living here but didn't think you ever would. She knew about all those ideas inside that head of yours and she'd understand better than me about changing this place. But this website thing, that's incredible. And the deal is really done, there's no chance it will fall through?'

I smile softly, my heart tugging in my chest at the way Dad is trying to look out for me. He thinks I'm still that little girl who was so intent on pushing forward, she sometimes forgot to savour each milestone.

'The money is in the bank. Maybe I'll keep an eye out for a small business that would benefit from an online presence. I put in a little injection of capital to give them a boost and then set up a website to kick-start the e-commerce side of things. After all, that's where my skills lie and then after that I step back and become a silent partner as they grow the business. If it works out, then I can then look for the next opportunity. But money only represents a safety net, it doesn't solve all of the other problems that life presents us with, does it? So, I'd rather people here didn't know.'

'And there I was, offering to help you out, silly old fool I am. I should have known that me daughter had her head screwed on right.'

'Well, save your judgement for the time being, Dad. Somehow, I want to ease myself back in as if I'd never left. There will be a few who won't like me pulling this place apart, for starters. And I need to at least look like I have a job of some sorts, or the gossipmongers will have a field day. Tegan needs help, that's clear, and maybe I can convince her that having something to do for a few hours here and there would be helping me out.'

Dad breaks into a beaming smile, tapping the side of his nose with his finger. 'Ha! That's my girl. Always there to help someone out when they're in need. I worry that Tegan's barely making ends meet, as Pete handled the finances and he was always worried about cash flow.'

That's the one topic that Tegan hasn't mentioned and I knew it was for a reason.

'Okay. Seems like a plan then, Dad.'

He levers himself up out of the wooden chair.

'Who would have thought, eh? You get that brain of

yours from your grandma and your mum, that's for sure. But the practical side of solving a problem comes from me.' And with that, he gives me a wicked wink.

A sudden noise makes me spin around, but it's only a bird, foraging in the hedge.

'So that means your own little housing dilemma is on the road to recovery?' My frown leaves him in no doubt at all that I'm not going to let him off the hook.

'It is, that. I know I've been remiss, but I needed a bit of company, Kerra. Now you're back, things are already beginning to feel different. When I was cleaning the kennels this afternoon, Rufus, the Thomases' red setter, went missing. I found him curled up in the run at the back. It's the first time he's ventured in there since your mum passed.'

'Aww, Dad. It's a start, isn't it? And they can feel it, too. You're doing the right thing.'

We stand and throw our arms around each other for comfort.

'Change is good; we mustn't lose sight of that. And we're here for each other, lovely. Mum's up there smiling down at us, for sure.'

6. Hiding in the Shadows

When I finally return to my little mountain of boxes, I have a change of plan. There's little point in trying to cram everything I can into the bijou kitchen, just for the sake of it. Most of this might as well go up into the loft for the time being. A few minutes later I head out into the garden and as I step out onto the patio I hear a noise, close by. Clearing my throat rather loudly, I call out:

'Drew, are you there?'

Mere seconds later a distinctly reluctant and very subdued, 'Hi neighbour,' filters back through the hedge. OMG—was he sitting there the whole time? A sense of panic rises up in my chest as I try to recall exactly what I said, and I figure I have to assume he heard every word of it.

'I um… I have a proposition for you. Are you busy?'

There's the sound of a chair scraping on concrete and his voice gets louder as he walks closer. This is ridiculous.

'We're talking through the hedge again. Maybe we need a gate,' I laugh.

'I'm just finishing off a little job online. It will take me about an hour to get myself sorted. If you aren't doing anything this evening, how about popping round, say sevenish? I have a pizza I can throw in the oven.'

'Great. I'll bring a bottle.'

'Sounds good.'

Inside I'm cringing. It's not that I don't think he's discreet, or that he would have listened on purpose. But I thought he said he saw his girlfriend most weekends, so I didn't even give it a thought he'd be around today. A cold sweat begins to trickle down my back—what must he be thinking? He was probably too embarrassed to make a noise once he heard the topic of our conversation. I'm gutted. So much for keeping my personal affairs close to my chest.

Ringing the doorbell to Tigry Cottage, I feel a tad jealous that Drew's cottage is named after the kestrel, whereas Pedrevan means newt, but that's the charm of the Celtic language in making even the ordinary sound mystical. Anyway, I tell myself, a newt is a curious little creature, different—just like me, so it's very apt.

As the door opens, a rather embarrassed-looking Drew gives me a slightly hesitant, albeit welcoming, smile. 'Hi there Kerra, come on in.'

He turns, leaving me to shut the door and I follow him inside. I'm immediately rather surprised, as I hadn't realised the layout had been changed over the years and the cottages are no longer mirror images.

'This is very nice,' I remark, walking into the open plan area. The walls between the dining room and kitchen have been taken down and it's much more practical. 'Oh, here you go. I hope you like red wine.'

I hold out the bottle I'm carrying and as Drew takes it from me, he flashes me a cagey glance.

'Look, this is rather embarrassing. I owe you an apology for this afternoon, Kerra. I should have made a noise, or something, to make you aware I was working outside. I'm terribly sorry—I hesitated for a moment and then I didn't like to interrupt your flow.'

'You're perfectly entitled to sit in your garden, Drew, so no apology needed.' I can't bring myself to look directly at him, so instead I try hard to play down a growing sense of mortification. Instead, I look around, taking in the bright, clean and tidy surroundings.

'I'll, um, just grab some glasses. Make yourself comfortable.' With that, he heads over to the kitchen area in silence.

This was obviously done quite a long time ago. Even so, the enormous difference it makes only serves to confirm the fact that I can't possibly live with the existing layout next door. Just making the ground floor into one flowing space without extending it, makes a hell of a difference.

'I love how this has been opened up,' I remark, as he walks back to hand me a rather generously sized glass of ruby red wine.

'Yes, it was one of the attractions for me. Anyway, I thought a large one might be in order. Seriously, I can't apologise enough and if it happens again, I'll make it very clear I'm within earshot. It's certainly not something I make a habit of, eavesdropping.'

I suspect he was in shock when I threw out the idea of knocking the two cottages into one. If it had been the other way around, I'd have been horrified. Instead, he's being the perfect gentleman, when he could easily be angry, or demanding I explain myself.

But the fact that he did hear it all makes my mouth go very dry. I blurted everything out, eager to reassure Dad about my financial situation, too, and inwardly I groan as I recall my words. And then I went on to... hell, I just got carried away. *Act normally*, Kerra, I tell myself. Damage limitation.

'It was a conversation I was dreading and it wasn't really planned. I was simply throwing out ideas rather randomly without engaging my brain.'

Could this get any more awkward? We're now staring at each other very uneasily and I force myself to continue.

'The truth is that I've never been a twee little cottage sort of person. Even standing here seeing what difference taking down two walls makes, is telling me I'm right. My place feels like a series of tiny little boxes and already it's driving me mad.'

The instant I say that, his eyes light up and I see, with relief, that he understands exactly where I'm coming from. 'Let's take a seat at the dining table. I think it's time I showed you my little project, because I might have found the perfect solution for you.'

After sharing a family-sized pizza and then popping back to grab the last of the saffron buns for dessert, everything certainly feels a lot less like a major balls-up on a full stomach. That large glass of wine has also helped to ease the evening along rather nicely. But the saving grace has definitely been Drew's ambitious plans for Tigry Cottage. His talent as an architect is really something and as he runs through the design in detail, his enthusiasm overcomes any sense of awkwardness between us. And now he's sitting back, looking rather pleased with himself.

'You don't have any reservations about the proposed redesign of the rear elevation, then? I wasn't sure if when I put in the application, I'd get any objections. Obviously, your views carry the most weight as we're semi-detached. You will get a little bit of shadow from the extension falling across your garden, at one point in the day as the sun moves around. Is that a concern to you?'

I'm still trying to take it all in, as Drew has the detailed drawings playing on a continuous loop. What I'm marvelling at, is the fact that he's picked up on every little thing on my own wish list. Clever storage solutions and clean lines to maximise the feeling of space. The rear of the ground floor extension is a wall of glass that, once opened, will turn the garden into a seamless transition from the main living area. A large deck stretches out, almost doubling the living space and this contemporary design will bring a very dated layout firmly into the present.

'It's a lot to take in, Drew, and I love that it's a total transformation. This is an amazing plan and I'll be honest, I'm envious.'

He settles back in his seat, a lot less nervous now he's seen my initial reaction.

'It's taken a long time for you to get it to this stage, so I bet you can't wait to get the plans approved and start work.'

Drew stares down into his wine glass, his right hand sliding up under the curve of the bowl to give it a gentle swirl.

'It's my turn to be honest with you, now. It's been ready

for several months and I've just been tinkering with it. At the moment, even if it sails through planning, I can't afford to press the go button and get things started. I'm not a risk-taker and being self-employed is very different from having a regular salary coming in to rely on.'

My pulse begins to quicken.

'Ah. Life happens and plans change?' I enquire gently. 'I was only brainstorming when I was talking to Dad this afternoon, but if your situation has moved on and you're thinking of selling up, I'm serious about being interested.'

Drew purses his lips, raising his glass and taking a quick sip.

'I wish it was that easy, Kerra. I can work from anywhere, so that's not the problem. Felicity struggles to get away and even this weekend is yet another example of... well, let's just say that working for the family business and with two siblings each vying to be the second in command, it isn't easy on anyone. However, we haven't given up hope of this being Felicity's home away from home, too, once her situation eases. So, in the meantime, I'm happy enough living here and grabbing time with her when I can; it's quiet and the walks are amazing. I mean, who wouldn't love living in such a scenic place?'

'Oh, right. I understand but I'm sorry to hear it's so complicated for you both, Drew. That can't be easy.'

He nods, making a face that indicates it's not something he can influence.

'Until her father retires, and it's all sorted, our relationship is on the back burner. The last thing she needs right now is me putting pressure on her for us to move in together permanently. And, financially, I'd be taking on debt I'm not sure I can afford. So, I might as well be here; especially as I don't get on with her brother at all and I don't want to end up saying something I'll regret. Invariably, the weekends that we do manage to spend together it's expected that we'll lunch at her parents' place. Her brother, Scott, makes it his business to make sure he and his wife are always around. I get on great with Felicity's mum and dad, which irritates him immensely. Felicity thinks he sees it as a bit of a threat.'

I feel sorry for Drew.

'That's tricky. I'm sure Felicity will want to be involved in every aspect of the renovation work on the cottage then, and it must be so frustrating for you.'

Drew jumps up, walks over to turn on the coffee machine, then ferries the empty plates across to the sink. I think I've touched a raw nerve.

'Well, what's annoying is having to wash up by hand, because I miss having a dishwasher,' he moans. 'But, joking aside, it's not so much that dilemma, as sinking everything I have into this without due regard to the future.'

Money is such a pain. Rarely does anyone have just enough for it not to be a concern. But his edginess is telling me there's more to it. The decision is all his, as far as I can tell, but what if he's been looking for her approval to reassure him about their future together?

'That's a real pity. Let's face it, though, these cottages are an investment and there'll always be a purchaser willing to snap them up. Whether it's renovated to a high spec as a luxurious weekend getaway, or as a fixer-upper. Location is key and it doesn't get any better than here.'

I can see he's impressed that I'm not coming at this solely from my own perspective but trying to be objective.

'What if...' I pause, thinking I've already gotten myself into trouble for brainstorming out loud once this afternoon. Dare I risk making the same mistake twice in one day?

Drew stops pouring out the coffee, waiting for me to continue.

'What if both cottages were extended at the same time? I presume there'd be a cost saving for us both, not just because it would be an even bigger project, but there would be other, knock-on savings, too. Would that, together with the fees you'd be charging me, allow you to commit and get the ball rolling?'

He turns away, finishes the job in hand and walks back to the table carrying the mugs.

'There would be quite a saving, so yes, if you are serious. I mean, you like my design enough as it stands to consider it as an option?'

Drew is just checking that I understand it only works if I don't start tinkering with the layout, as then the ad hoc costs would start to mount up.

'I do. The bonus is that the project manager lives on my doorstep,' I throw in and he laughs. 'If you can give me a detailed estimate in terms of cost and how long it would take, I won't hang around making a decision. I'm already sold in here,' I tap my head, 'I just need to see how it stacks up on paper.'

His expression alone tells me I have nothing to worry about, because this would solve a big problem for him, too. He's excited, heck, we both are and neither of us can hide that fact.

'There's one condition, though,' I add, looking him firmly in the eye. 'If you ever decide to sell up, I want first refusal on Tigry Cottage at market price. If I'm going to plough a considerable amount of money into this place, then if you move on, I might not get such an accommodating neighbour, next time around. I need to be sure my investment is safe.'

This is business, after all. I hold out my hand to him and he immediately offers his and we shake. The deal is as good as done.

'Oh dear,' I groan. He looks at me as I begin to frown. 'So much for coming back home and keeping a low profile while I settle in. What people will make of you and me joining forces, I have no idea.'

Drew looks distinctly amused. 'I'm sure there are endless possibilities and I look forward to hearing them all,' he replies. 'Give me forty-eight hours to rework the figures and I'll get you a detailed breakdown in terms of time and cost.'

'I'll look forward to that, Drew. And thanks.'

'For what?'

'The… pizza.'

He knows that's not what I mean. We're not simply neighbours now, he's gaining a client, too and that means anything between us is confidential. My secret is safe.

'I'm glad you're not doing the cottage up just to sell it on, Drew.'

'Why would I do that when I now have a half-decent neighbour to look after my cat, Ripley, when I go away?'

'Ah, I did wonder about my very hesitant little visitor. Ripley? That's unusual. Not Ripley, as in the film Alien?'

'The very same. She's fierce, well, no—not fierce, as in she'll scratch you, as she's more likely to run in the opposite direction until you gain her trust. But she's a character and that's why she can't go into a cattery. She thinks she's a person and it would screw with her head to put her in a cage.'

I try, unsuccessfully, to suppress a laugh and am relieved to see his own mouth twitch a little.

'So I'm officially your cat-sitter now, then?'

'You are. One who makes a half-decent hot chocolate, too. You can always tell when someone was brought up in a village,' he grins back at me. 'No Starbucks within walking distance,' he explains. I like that he's feeling comfortable enough to joke around with me. Any sense of awkwardness has now disappeared.

'I'm sure Ripley and I will get on very well indeed when she's good and ready to introduce herself properly. She was hiding in the bushes again, last night.'

'Your garden has been her hunting ground, as she's a good mouser.'

'I have mice?' Just the mention of the word makes me instinctively draw my feet up off the floor.

'She's eaten most of them. Mr Mills complained he often came back to find one lying prostrate on the doormat as a little gift. You might spot the odd one running around until she trusts you enough to visit again.'

That's a friendship I need to work on, then.

Lying in bed relaxing in the semi-darkness, I feel like a huge weight has been lifted from my shoulders. I can't believe my luck. Financially it's a no-brainer. Wearing my business hat, a modern extension tacked on to next door would leave the rear of Pedrevan looking odd, out of kilter. However, developing both properties in the same way ensures the balance and overall aesthetic will be maintained. It's a win-win situation.

When I was helping Tegan out yesterday, going from the very country-style holiday lets at the farm, to the iconic and contemporary home named Treylya, up on the headland, I knew then that I couldn't settle for a twee little extension to the kitchen and an upgraded bathroom. That's precisely why I broached the subject with Dad, so at least the news that I intend to gut the place, won't come as a total shock.

My phone pings, disturbing my chain of thought and I reach across to grab it.

Are you awake?

It's Sy. Goodness, that seems like another lifetime ago, already.

Yes. Lying here thinking and planning.

I add an emoji, a face laughing so hard it's crying.
Seconds later the phone rings.
'That wouldn't involve planning your return, would it?' Sy's voice sounds hopeful.
'No. Planning the alterations to my new home. How are things there?'
'Strange. Lots of meetings behind closed doors and new faces appearing.'
I try not to let out a sigh. 'It's how big business works, Sy.'
'And my boss isn't my boss, anymore. They're bringing in a new guy.'
That stops me in my tracks. 'Already?'

'All I know is that there's an important presentation next week when all will be revealed. Rumour has it that this is to do with big changes at the top.'

Sy sounds utterly dejected. Rumours can do that to you—shift the floor beneath your feet by sowing fear and doubt. I wish I could say, hand on heart, that it doesn't hurt to hear this, because it does. Did I make the right decision? I wonder. Should I have stepped away for a month or two, taken time to grieve properly and then thrown myself back into it?

'Try to see it as an end to the uncertainty and the beginning of the next phase.' It's time to change the subject, as it's clear he's in the mood to wallow and my conscience is weighing me down. It's a case of the least said the better, for fear of making it worse. 'So, were you out on the town tonight?'

'No. I ordered a takeaway and watched both the *Deadpool* films, back to back.'

That is not a good sign.

'What you need is a bit of company. You must make a concerted effort to get out and about Sy, especially until things settle down at work. If you don't, you'll sit around overthinking everything and becoming more and more stressed. Hopefully, the worst is over and it will all fall into place very quickly now.'

The silence is telling.

'At least things are going well at your end,' he says, trying hard to muster a little enthusiasm.

'I wouldn't say it's going well, exactly. I spent half of today cleaning holiday lets, and stripping and making beds, to help out an old friend. And then I had a bit of a heart-to-heart with Dad which might, or might not, turn out to have been a mistake. And I put my foot in it with my neighbour, but I did manage to redeem myself tonight, hopefully.'

He snorts. 'It's not so easy to blend into the background, is it? London has a lot of perks and one of them is anonymity whenever you want it.'

At least that perked him up; there's a definite element of *I told you so* in his tone.

'Point taken,' I laugh softly. 'But I know I've made the right decision. Sy, if you're miserable there now, remember that you don't owe them anything. You could just look for another job.'

His frustration is obvious, and I've never heard him sounding as low as this before.

'That would mean facing even more changes and upheaval. I feel like I don't fit in, Kerra. What's worse is that I seem to be the only one who is struggling. You might be right, but I keep thinking if I just hang on it will get better. But what if it doesn't?'

Aww. Poor Sy. He's always joking around and people think that means nothing pulls him down, but he goes to great lengths to hide his insecurities from the world. And one of them is his fear of rejection. It's a continuous circle he keeps travelling, fuelled by his fragile love life. Every time a relationship falls apart, he's back to square one. He needs his work life to be a constant he can count on, because it bolsters his confidence. Sometimes it's all he feels he has in life, because he doesn't have anything to do with his family. And now I've left his side, too.

'Why don't you arrange to take a few days off? It will do

you good. If I'm not equipped to put you up here by then, Dad has plenty of space. There are lots of things to do and a change of scenery can be cathartic.'

'You're serious?'

'I am.'

'Okay. As soon as I can break out, I'll be on my way. Are wax jackets and wellies obligatory?'

I burst out laughing.

'You can mock all you like, but a dose of reality does us all good from time to time. One of the diversions I have in mind for you is helping Dad to walk the dogs.'

'Dogs? I do hope you're joking. I'll be in touch as soon as I can.'

'I'm not joking,' I say out loud, after pressing end call. Sy needs a distraction or two—and then the craziest of ideas pops into my head. A real light bulb moment. Whenever there's a problem it's a simple case of finding the right solution. But what if you take two very different problems and put them together?

7. Some Things Never Change

'Good morning, Mrs Moyle. How are you today?'
I grab one of the wire baskets and walk over to the counter, where she's restocking a display of homemade cakes.

'I'm fine. It's good to see you in here, Kerra. It's like old times.'

'Thank you again, for the saffron buns. It was a real treat. I haven't had one since I moved away and I'd forgotten just how delicious they are.'

'You've eaten them all already?' She stops what she is doing to look directly at me and I shake my head.

'No. I shared them with a couple of my visitors.'

'I didn't think so, 'cause there's hardly anything to you. It's all food fads and diets up in London.'

It's so hard not to break out into a smile.

'My neighbour, Drew, and Logan Williams, polished off a few of them quite happily.'

'Guess you'll be getting a steady stream of visitors now word is getting out that you're back. You'll be sorting your dad, no doubt, and that's what your dear mum would have wanted.'

I like Mrs Moyle because she says exactly what she's

thinking, so you know where you stand with her. A quick nod and I head off to grab a carton of milk and a loaf of bread, but she continues talking as I shop.

'If you don't mind me saying, I do believe that if it weren't for the kennels he'd have lost his mind living there all alone. I won't forget that Sunday, when the ambulance whisked your mum into hospital with the blue lights flashing and you and your dad following behind in the car.'

We look at each other and Mrs Moyle's empathy is touching.

'I don't know if it's true what they say, but I felt Mum hung on until my plans to return home were underway. She was ready to let go and knowing that I was going to be there for Dad in the future, she felt at peace.'

A look of understanding passes between us.

'As tough as it's been for him, at least having the dogs to sort out kept him occupied. It was a reason to get up each morning and there's no better lift to the spirits than having a purpose. But there's a marked change in him since your arrival. He's more relaxed and I see he's started straightening things up. I bet that's down to you.'

'Only indirectly. He won't let me help, but I think it's a comfort knowing I'm around and it stops him worrying.'

She gives me a knowing look. 'It does, that. And he needed something to remind him that he has a lot of living still to do. Have you bumped into Nettie Pentreath, yet?'

I scrabble inside my purse for three one-pound coins, my hand shaking a little as her words send a chill through me. Dad's been struggling, that was obvious, but is she saying he's been depressed, or something?

'No, I haven't seen Nettie since Mum's funeral and we didn't get a chance to talk. Is she well?'

Mrs Moyle slides the carton and the bread back towards me, taking the coins and dipping into the cash register drawer to extract my change.

'She is and active. She only works one day a week helping out at the vet's surgery now. Semi-retired she calls it. Don't see much of her, so it's obvious she finds things to do, but busy people are never content to simply sit around, are they?'

Okay. Figure this one out, Kerra. What exactly is Mrs Moyle trying to say?

'Just a thought,' she adds breezily, giving me a parting smile.

The moment I step out onto the pavement I hear my name being called and I turn around to see my cousin, Alice, heading straight towards me.

'Uncle Eddie said you wouldn't have gone far. Welcome back, Kerra.'

My relationship with Alice over the years has been interesting. Sy has a very apt term he uses—frenemies. Given that she's a relative, it sounds a bit mean of me to put her in that category, but it fits. She's all smiles whenever we cross paths, but people who talk about you behind your back rarely get away with it. Gossip goes full circle and Alice, I've heard, can be a little mean whenever my name comes up in conversation. I always laughed it off whenever the rumours got back to me because I gave up on Alice a long time ago. A careless comment she made caused a rift between Tegan and her brother, one that has never really healed. She'll say what she wants to say about me and anyone, even if she doesn't know all the facts, so the less I say, the better.

'Thanks, Alice. How are you, and Auntie Marge and Uncle Alistair?'

Almost five years younger than me, Alice is very pretty and she knows it. She does that flick of the head thing, tossing her perfectly curled hair away from her face as if she's in a shampoo ad.

'We're all good. How about you, though? Did Uncle Eddie drag you back, or were you missing us?'

She flashes her pale blue eyes at me, unable to hide her curiosity. *Not quite as clever as you thought you were and found out you couldn't hack it?* That's the question she'd like to ask.

'A bit of both.'

'Oh dear. I do hope nothing has gone wrong. London is such an exciting place and yet here you are, home for good. It must be difficult to leave behind such a glamorous life. A bit of a shock trying to fit back in, when that's the reason you left in the first place.'

I begin walking back to the cottage and she falls in alongside me. Our conversations are always a little stilted because we're very different people with little in common. But it's more than that. I never feel comfortable around her as I know she doesn't like me.

And Alice is on form today, so I really do need to be careful what I say as it will be repeated—well, Alice's version of it, anyway.

'I promised Mum I'd come back and I'm happy to be here. It's time for me to relax a little.'

Trudging up to the front door of Pedrevan Cottage, I know I have no choice but to invite her in for a cup of tea, as it's clear she isn't done with me.

'Are you in a rush to get on?'

'No,' she replies brightly. 'I dropped in purposely to catch up with all your news.'

As she follows me inside and we step into the sitting room, her face drops. The boxes I have earmarked for the loft are still in the middle of the room, but I've brought in one of the wooden garden chairs as I was tired of sitting on the floor.

'You don't have any furniture,' she exclaims, clearly appalled and so shocked she stands rooted to the floor.

'You're right, I don't. I do have a bed and Logan Williams was kind enough to assemble a desk for me, upstairs. We can sit up at the little breakfast bar in the kitchen; there are two stools and what I do have is lots of cake.'

Leaving her to stare in absolute horror at the sad little pile in front of us, I head off to pop the kettle on. There is absolutely no point in explaining, as Alice simply wouldn't understand. The sooner I brew up, the sooner she'll drink up and be out of here to report back. It sounds horrible, but in all honesty, I don't care what she thinks, because I simply don't have the time or the patience for it. I need her—and those boxes—gone, so the next task is to move this along quickly and then head next door to see if I can borrow a ladder.

'How are things at the beauty salon? Are you busy?' I enquire, when she eventually pulls herself together and walks through to join me.

That topic will keep her going for the next thirty minutes,

or so, and then she'll be eager to get back home. Time may roll on, but regrettably, some things never change.

'Did Alice manage to catch you?'

I sidle up to Dad as he stands, his hands clasped around the broom handle, surveying his handiwork with a sense of satisfaction. The garden is now looking as neat as the boarding facilities. There are still a couple of areas that need a few weeds pulled. And there's a massive pile of general garden debris to be burnt, but I'm impressed.

'Yes, but she didn't stay long. It's quiet here today. No Rufus, even?' I know his owner has an arthritic knee and Rufus comes to stay when the walks become a problem.

'I'm dog-free while I move on to tackle stage two. Sorting out the house will mean a quick lick of paint throughout. I also need to get rid of that stale, doggy smell. It's time to throw open the windows and air it all out.'

Everyone copes with the aftermath of grief in their own way. The wonderful thing about animals is that they don't talk, well not in terms of human language. What's the point in answering well-meaning questions like, 'How are you doing today, Eddie?' when the answer doesn't change? 'Missing me wife and nothing will ever be the same again.'

'I'm not taking any bookings for the next couple of weeks,' he explains. 'I've told everyone there will be a grand reopening. You weren't the only one who noticed I wasn't managing things very well and a few of my customers have been in touch with encouraging messages of support.'

'That's wonderful news, Dad. I'm so proud of you.'

'You are?'

'I am.'

'Good. So now you can stop worrying about me.' He grins and I raise my hand to give him a high five. Dad is making it clear he can manage without my help, not least because he feels I have a lot to sort out for myself. I will admit I haven't made an awful lot of progress, but every time I make a start I get interrupted.

'James from next door is going to give me a hand with the painting. I wanted to ask you what you thought is a fair hourly rate to pay him. He's been grateful to earn a bit of cash helping out with the dog-walking the last couple of weeks and I didn't want to leave him in the lurch.'

When I left for London, James was a lad, playing with his toys. Now he's a strong and capable young man, looking for opportunities to grow his dreams.

'Ask him what he'd be happy to accept. He's not a boy any longer.'

Dad nods appreciatively.

'Anyway,' I continue, 'I wondered if you fancied a little walk down to the cove? I'll buy you lunch and a pint in The Lark and Lantern, afterwards.'

Dad gives me a knowing smile. 'Ah, you're putting your face out there to get it over and done with. Well, a quick trip to the pub should catch a lot of people on a Sunday. I need a shower and a change of clothes first, to make myself presentable.'

'I'll put this lot back in the shed while I'm waiting.'

'Can't remember the last time I had a pub lunch,' Dad half-whispers, talking to himself as he begins walking back up the path to the house. 'It's good to have me daughter back.'

I stare after him, thinking about what Mrs Moyle was

saying earlier on. Dad isn't old, but he was looking older than his years for a while there. It's good to see a bit of a spark lighting him up again.

As I begin clearing up, a voice calls out.

'Hey there, Kerra!'

Straightening up, I turn and to my utter surprise, Uncle Alistair swings open the gate. He only lives about a ten-minute drive away but far enough that it isn't a coincidence he's here. Given that Alice only left about fifteen minutes ago, I guess a text only takes a couple of seconds to do the rounds and it must have been a shocker.

Walking towards me, he gives me a welcoming smile and closes in to wrap his arms around me.

'How's my favourite niece doing these days?'

'Good, thank you, Uncle Alistair. And you?'

'Doing fine. It's great to have you back, Kerra, and Auntie Marge sends her love. You've been missed, for sure.'

'You know me, I always needed a challenge and having achieved what I set out to do, I now have a new one.'

He beams at me and his delight is genuine.

'Are you referring to your dad, or the cottage?'

I know he's been worried about his brother. They're always falling out over something, because having worked together for so many years there were good days and bad days. And differences of opinion. But family means a lot to them both because Granddad Harry instilled that belief in them.

'A little of both, I think. Although Dad would say I'm my own biggest challenge until I decide what I'm going to do next. But I'm in no hurry.'

'Is he doing better now?' My uncle's question is direct and I can hear the tension in his voice.

'He is. Are the two of you speaking at the moment?'

Uncle Alistair looks around cagily, then throws his head back and laughs, lowering his voice. 'No. I overstepped the mark, apparently, keeping on at him to come back to work. I meant well, but I was heavy-handed, Kerra, I will admit that. But I could see this wasn't right for him. I haven't been here for months because he made it clear I wasn't welcome, but it's all looking in rather good shape.'

'He's turned the corner. Maybe if he can get things sorted, I'll be able to convince him to find someone to run the kennels for him.'

Nettie Pentreath—of course! Mrs Moyle, you might have something, there. It's a thought, anyway, and it puts a little smile on my face. Uncle Alistair stares down at me and I can see a sense of relief as he steps back. It's clear he thinks it's a good idea, too.

'It's a bit of a risk, because you know how easy it is to offend him, but let's be honest, it's the sensible thing to do. He needs to get back to doing something he loves and he can't tell me he doesn't miss working with his hands. Look, I'd best disappear as it's still awkward between us. You and I will catch up properly before too long. I only wanted to let you know that if *you* need anything, anything at all, you know where to come. And it's always in confidence.'

With that he turns on his heels and hurries away. *Oh Alice, what have you been saying to worry Uncle Alistair enough to head straight over to offer his help?* Life is about more than a few possessions and if she doesn't start seeing beyond that shiny veneer which can be so misleading, she's going to miss out on the things that really matter in life.

8. Really Feeling That Country Vibe

When Dad reappears, I'm relieved to see that he has no idea Uncle Alistair was here and he's in a jovial mood. Aside from the fact he's badly in need of a haircut, he's made a real effort and is wearing what he calls his *Sunday best*. That means a pale blue shirt, a tidy jumper and a freshly ironed pair of jeans—all without a dog hair in sight.

'My goodness, I'm honoured,' I say approvingly. 'I hardly recognise you.'

He scowls. 'That's enough of that, young lady. Now, what is it that you want to tell me?'

There's no fooling him.

'We can discuss that in detail, over lunch. You don't think you're the only one who has been busy, do you?'

We set off on the downhill trek to the beautiful and mesmerising Penvennan Cove.

'Are the boxes sorted then?' he enquires.

'No. I've decided to put most of them in the loft, once I can get my hands on a ladder. They're in the way and I want to sort out some bits of furniture. I'm sure Drew will give me a hand moving them, but when I knocked just now, he wasn't in.'

The road running through Penvennan village is narrow in parts, but there are places to pass, cut back into the often wild-looking banks. Everything grows so quickly and it's a constant battle for the local authorities to keep it under control. It's not a through-road, as it simply takes you up to the headland and there's only one turn-off, which leads down to the cove itself. The fact that's the only access at least ensures it's pretty well maintained.

The moment we turn the corner, the vista in front of us instantly brings me to a halt.

'Oh Dad, why on earth did I wait to take the walk? Just seeing that view fills my heart with joy. Look at it!'

A pale blue ribbon of sky meets almost seamlessly on the horizon with a sea that barely shows a ripple. Only the water lapping gently against the sandy shoreline beyond the cobbled expanse, has those little cresting, foamy white tips.

'It's impossible to tire of that view, lovely. It warms my heart to know it's the same for you, still.'

We link arms and I hope it's not because Dad feels his legs need steadying, but because with cars parked both sides and an intermittent pavement, it's easier to walk down the middle of the road. It's rather uneven and easy to slip where there are pockets of loose surface gravel and grit, which accumulate because of the downhill gradient. It's even worse in the rain. He seems fine and there's a lightness in his step that wasn't there the last time I came home for a visit.

'Shall we head for the beach first?'

I nod my head, too busy to respond as my eyes reacquaint themselves with the tiny details that are like a road map to me. The rustic, white-washed stonework of the little row of fishermen's cottages are so small it makes Pedrevan seem spacious. Originally, they were all two rooms up and two down, with a coal house on the back and a toilet at the end of the garden. Most have been extended now, of course, and only a couple are still owned by working fishermen.

We walk on past the little newsagent's, probably one of the tiniest shops in existence, but it serves its purpose. Then, taking the prime corner spot, the pride of the village— Pascoe's Café and Bakery. Although that was Grandma's maiden name, it's pretty common around here, and as far as I'm aware there's no family connection.

After that, all that stands between the beach and the buildings is the big square with a barely adequate parking area for permit holders only and the small, council-owned car park. It's impossible to get a place there unless it's in the very early hours of the morning. Even then, if the tide is in the chance is that there will be a few surfers' vans parked up. There was a barrier once to stop people staying overnight, but it was damaged and has never been replaced.

Beyond that, before the sheer rock face of the headland looms up like a monolith, is a rusty old boat and car repair workshop, belonging to Dad's neighbour, Tom. The access for boats isn't good, so the only marine trade he really gets is for the two-man fishing boats. There is passing trade from the odd holidaymaker who ends up clipping the small boat they're towing, or their trailer, in their eagerness to get down to the slipway.

Scanning back around, Dad follows my gaze and our eyes alight on the steep path as it wends its way up behind the cottages, to Lanryon. The old church has always sent a shiver through me. Standing tall, from a distance the grey, stone form resembles a face with a pointed head, like a witch's hat. The double doors are made of solid, Cornish oak and are so dark they look like a big, gaping hole—a mouth screaming out to sea as it calls the souls of drowning sailors to it. Like it called my granddad. There's a reason why it's not popular for weddings and it isn't just the steep, uneven path as it snakes up the hillside.

It's funny, but I'm only now picking up on the raucous calls of the seagulls circling overhead, as I stare up with unease. They scare me; always have done. I try hard not to think of Granddad, his tiny boat smashing up against the rocks and that the last sound he heard was probably the crashing of the waves and the screeching of the gulls.

'Come on, lovely,' Dad's voice brings me back to the present. 'I don't know about you, but I'm starving.'

Pulling my arm into him, he gives it a squeeze, as we retrace our steps to walk past the café and turn into the pub car park, which is already half-full.

'We should have reserved a table. Oh, there's Drew.'

Sure enough, Drew is propping up the end of the packed bar and he waves out.

'I'll get the drinks in Dad. Why don't you see if you can organise us a table?' He grins back at me.

'No problem, lovely. It's not what you know, but who you know. Do you think Drew would like to join us?'

'I'll talk him into it. Work your magic and see if you can get us a booth in the annexe, will you? At least it's a little quieter in there.'

Dad gives me a thumbs up and I head off in Drew's direction.

'I had a feeling I might find you in here when I couldn't

get an answer. I'm in need of a ladder and was hoping you could help. Did you pop in for a drink, or are you eating?'

He smiles gratefully. 'I'm always up for a roast lunch and I was rather hoping someone would ask me to join them. There aren't any tables for one, you'll notice.'

Drew looks pleased and I'm more than happy because it means I can bring up the topic of our joint project. I lean into the bar, checking who is serving.

'Hey, Kerra, I wondered when you'd get a chance to pop in. It's good to see you. What would you like to drink?'

'Hi Polly, it's great to finally be home again. A pint of the usual for Dad and a half for me, please. You've had some work done since I was last here, I see. It's all looking very upmarket and what a difference it makes.'

Polly grabs a pint mug and pulls down hard on the pump handle.

'We're hoping for a busy season to help pay for the refurbishment. It was looking dark and dingy. The new theme was my idea.'

It was tired and very dated, as are many old pubs. But a good paint through in a very pale bluey-grey, with pristine white ceilings and a dark navy, flecked carpet, it certainly feels a lot bigger. The heavy, dark-wood fixtures and fittings have been painted and distressed, which has made a huge difference to the overall ambience. Large pieces of driftwood are displayed like pieces of art and it's a refreshing take on a nautical theme.

'Loving that picture gallery, too.' I lean in closer as the noise around us is growing. 'You've done a great job. It can't have been easy convincing Sam, but it needed doing.'

It's been just Polly and her dad here for as long as I can

remember. When we were at school she did once tell me that her mum didn't live with them any longer, but even my dad can't recall ever seeing her around. I always thought that was rather sad for Polly not having her mum in her life, but Sam is a wonderful man and he has been both a mum and a dad to her.

Polly beams back at me. 'Oh, you know him. He made a bit of noise, but mainly over the cost. I told him straight that we'd never do more than break even if something didn't change. That made him sit up and listen. Now, when the numbers are up and you hear him talking, you'd think it was his idea from the start! The old photos do look good, don't they? I bought the frames at the big car boot sale up at Leath's farm. A bit of white paint and a rub of wax to distress them and now it's a real talking point.'

Dad appears on the other side of the bar and raises his arm to catch my attention.

'Well, it looks amazing and even the old furniture has come up a treat. Oh, Drew, we have a table.' I nudge his arm, as I pick up the drinks. 'Follow me. Maybe we can have a proper catch up sometime soon, Polly. It's been too long.'

As we head past the bar and out into the corridor, I glance at the mass of old photos going way back. So many of them are imprinted on my mind, as this represents the history of the cove.

Dad's already seated in the corner booth and I flop down next to him, grateful to hand over the pint glass. As Drew settles in, we chink glasses.

'To progress,' I propose the toast. 'This is rather

unexpected to see The Lark and Lantern brought up to date. Very boutique-hotel style, if I do say so.'

'I liked the old style,' Dad replies, and Drew looks at me hesitantly.

'Better get used to a lot more changes, Dad,' I reply.

He looks from me to Drew and back again. 'What are you two plotting?'

'Over to you,' I say, looking firmly in Drew's direction. 'It was your idea.'

An hour and a half later, after a delicious roast beef dinner with all the trimmings, followed by a couple of scoops of organic, clotted cream ice cream from Leath's farm, Drew and I head out. We leave Dad chatting away to some old friends, putting the world to rights.

We seem to have convinced him that joining forces to renovate the two cottages together, makes sound financial sense. I was expecting him to have reservations about such a bold venture but having sown the seed, at least he was prepared. Drew's enthusiasm clinched it, though.

'Thanks for your patience talking Dad through it all, Drew. I knew he'd come around. His whole life has changed dramatically in the last twelve months and it is a lot to cope with. I understand how unsettling it is for him but standing still isn't an option. The pub is a great example of that. What an improvement.'

'It sure is. I'd noticed visitors walk in, take a glance around and head straight back out, before. It seems more welcoming now and less daunting when it's obvious it's full of locals in the quieter season. Anyway, I'm glad it went well with your dad. You said you're in need of a ladder?'

'Oh, yes. I want to move those boxes up into the loft. I've decided there's little point in unpacking stuff for the sake of it.'

'Sure. Do you want a hand?'

We're within ten metres of the cottages and I'm shocked when I spot a man peering in through my sitting room window. Suddenly, another guy appears from around the side of the property.

Picking up the pace, I call out, 'Can I help you?'

Drew is close on my heels. I don't know who they are, but they aren't locals and they don't look friendly. Both are tall and quite stout, wearing black trousers and plain black T-shirts, which strikes me as a little odd. However, one of them has a sleeve tattoo on his right arm from wrist to elbow and that I'm most certainly going to remember.

'We're looking for Mr Mills. Is he home?' The guy who had his head up against my window to look inside replies, making it sound more like an accusation than a question.

'Mr Mills doesn't live here anymore,' Drew responds, stepping into the space between the man and me.

The two men are now standing side by side, staring rather menacingly at Drew. I touch his arm, moving alongside him to try to diffuse the situation.

'I own this cottage and can confirm that Mr Mills no longer lives here.'

'Do you have a forwarding address for him?'

I press Drew's arm, as I can see he's annoyed at the curt response.

'And you are?'

The two guys look at each other and one of them shrugs his shoulders.

'Business acquaintances,' the other guy replies.

'I'm sure he'll be in touch with you, then. He was a tenant here and now he's gone. Excuse me.'

Grabbing the key from my bag, I literally push past them. Drew steps to one side, indicating for them to leave. I don't know about him, but I'm a little rattled. So much so, that my hand shakes a little as I try to insert the key in the lock.

Eventually it opens and I turn to watch the men as they walk off down the street and climb into a black Range Rover.

'Have you ever seen either of them hanging around here before?' I ask Drew, as we watch them drive off.

'No, and if I see them again, I'll call the police. We should have taken a note of the number plate. Are you alright?'

I nod. 'I'm fine, it was a little intimidating, that's all. I did think it was strange that Mr Mills never provided a forwarding address, particularly as he hasn't redirected his post. I just pop it back in the box with *no longer at this address* written across the envelopes. Hopefully, now they're aware that he no longer lives here, they won't waste their time coming back again. Is there any chance you could fetch that ladder and give me a hand lifting the boxes into the loft?'

'Of course. Lock the door and I'll bring them around to the back.'

He's only gone a few minutes, but I feel a little spooked by what just happened. I never had problems with Mr Mills and he always paid on time. Tegan would have said if he'd left the cottage in a mess, so I assume she just did a standard clean through. But those men don't look the sort to give up easily. For some reason, I feel they didn't believe me. They were threatening, if not verbally but with their body language.

Drew raps on the back door and it is with relief I open up. He looks at me intently.

'Everything alright inside?'

'Yes. Fine. Come on in and thanks for helping out.'

'My pleasure, Kerra. If you ever feel unsafe or have a problem, whatever time of the day, or night, I'll give you my number. Oh, and I need your email address as I've just had a revised quote back from the builders.'

'Great. Can you give me a bottom-line figure?'

I hold the door open as he eases the bulky stepladders inside.

'Sixty-two thousand all-in, which includes a top-of-the-range kitchen with all the latest equipment. Choice of three high-gloss finishes.'

His eyes study my face.

'Perfect,' I confirm, then proceed to scrunch up my face a little. 'I know I said I was happy to go with it as is, but I've had a thought. I rather like what they've done at the pub with that shabby chic, country style. I don't do fussy, but somehow I'm not quite seeing glossy minimalist here, and I think I'd like a bit of a cosier feel for the finishes in the kitchen.'

'Contemporary country is very popular. That chalk finish comes in a whole variety of colours and you could team it with solid wood worktops if you want that timeless, traditional look.'

Drew doesn't seem at all put out, which is good. I've

lived the ultra-modern, high-gloss, loft-style apartment life and the longer I'm here, the more I'm yearning for home comforts. Maybe because I don't have any at all, at the moment. Or maybe this is the new me, the one who really is settling down long-term and wants to fill the cottage with furniture you can sink into. Grandma made this cottage homely. There wasn't anything inside it that you felt you couldn't touch or wasn't practical. Coming home, she'd told me once, should feel like getting a hug.

'I think that's the way to go. My uncle makes bespoke kitchens. He owns Shaw & Sons Joinery and I'd rather like to put the work his way. I'm happy to pay extra, as you'll need to liaise with him with regard to a delivery date, but presumably your builder could still do the installation, so it doesn't mess things up too much. What do you think?'

'I've heard of them and they have a great reputation. It's not a problem to switch suppliers. So, we really are going to do this, then?'

I hand him my phone. 'Pop your number in and I'll text you my email address. My mind was made up the moment I saw the plans.'

9. The Paint Run

'Morning, Tegan. I hope you had a relaxing Sunday. I was just wondering if you needed any help this week?'

'Like you don't have enough to do, so you're looking for work?' The amusement in her voice tells me she's not fooled.

'I told you that I owe you and I meant it. If you're stuck, I want to know. Aside from doing a base coat in the main bedroom before I decide on the final colour scheme, I've nothing planned. I've made a decision to have some major building work done, though. It's going to get very messy before it begins to take shape. There's no point touching the downstairs at all, until the worst of it is out the way and that's going to take several months. I'll be in need of a distraction and I'm more than happy to do a bit of cleaning, or whatever. Admin is my strongpoint, too—I love a spreadsheet.'

I throw that last bit in with a lift in my voice, hopefully making it sound like an afterthought.

'No one has phoned in so far to say they're sick, so fingers crossed this coming week should run smoothly. Weekdays are usually fine, as the appointments are nicely spread out.

As for Saturdays, well, it's always crazy. If all the staff are in, then it's something like the clean bedding doesn't get delivered in time, or one of the minibuses breaks down. Or a visitor's dog has chewed a carpet and the minute the cleaner arrives they're expected to sort it out.'

'That's hardly fair, Tegan.'

'I know, but we have to be flexible with the holiday rental properties, because in the eyes of the customer the person walking through the door represents the owner.'

'Your contract covers more than a straightforward clean?'

'In theory it's an in and out service. Most properties have a management company who sort the big things, like a water leak and they carry out regular checks, naturally. But take the Saturday before last, for example. A front door key had snapped off inside the lock and while it wasn't strictly our problem, once the visitors drove off, I can't tell my member of staff to ignore it. Kate was stuck there for a couple of hours, as the owner wasn't answering her phone and the management company said they'd send a locksmith. They did, but that was two hours later.'

That's ridiculous.

'What happened about the rest of her work for the day?'

'I drove back to clean another two flats in the same building to cover her, while Kate waited around and then I took the spare keys and dropped them in to Hawthorn's, in town, who look after the property.'

'And you charged them for your time, petrol and inconvenience?'

'N... no. It's a goodwill thing, if annoying.'

I gasp, exasperated. There's no point in going any further

with this now, but Tegan really does need some help or she's going to lose money, if she hasn't already.

'You've gone very quiet. That wasn't the right answer, was it?' She sounds subdued.

'I appreciate it's not an easy situation but it really isn't your problem. Especially when it ends up costing you money, because it's nothing at all to do with the service you're providing.'

Tegan frowns. 'But how do we get around a situation like that?'

'I'm afraid that's for the client to sort out, Tegan, and you need to make your staff aware of that fact.'

'You've made your point. And it's a valid one. Maybe that's why everything feels like it's going downhill because we're working harder than ever but seeing little profit. And I'm drowning in paperwork, as that was Pete's strong point, not mine.'

'Listen, I don't want you to worry about anything. Pick a day, whichever suits you best, and we'll put our heads together to get things back on track. I can help with that and once everyone is clear that there are set procedures in place to handle the grey areas, it will be less disruptive.'

Tegan takes a deep breath in before answering. 'You make it sound so simple, Kerra. Thank you. I just hope I have what it takes to see it through, because I have my doubts. We finish by 1 p.m. each day doing the non-commercial cleaning, so I'm available every afternoon. But I can't take advantage of your business experience for free, that would be wrong of me.'

Ah, genuinely good people always have a conscience and principles, don't they? Tegan has been my eyes and ears here for the past few years. She underestimates how invaluable and important that was to me, but I don't want to offend her.

'Well, I have a rather pressing need, myself. I want to get hold of some secondhand furniture and have a go at upcycling.'

'Ooh,' her voice picks up. 'There are a few places we can visit and the minibuses really come in handy for collecting big items. It's a deal, then. Shall we make a start this afternoon?'

The first part of my master plan to help out my old friend is about to begin. The second part is going to take a while longer, but it will be worth the wait.

'Shaw & Sons, how can I help?'

'Uncle Alistair, it's Kerra.'

'Well, this is a surprise. Oh, don't tell me that Eddie caught sight of us talking in the garden?'

'No,' I laugh, 'nothing like that. I'm going to be having some building work done at the cottage. The architect is my neighbour, Drew Matthews, I don't know if you've met him?'

'Can't say I have. That's not the one with the *girlfriend*, is it?'

I roll my eyes. 'He has a girlfriend, but she's not local.'

'Ah, I've heard Alice mention her, or rather her absence. So she does exist?'

'Drew will introduce me to her when she visits next. Anyway, he's project managing the work. I'm not sure which building company he's using, but I'd love you to make the kitchen units. Drew and I will work out the design over the next couple of weeks and by then he'll be able to give you an idea of the timescale involved.'

'I can give you a bit of a discount as you're family, but custom isn't cheap, Kerra. I'm not trying to put you off, but on top of the building work this will set you back a fair chunk of money.'

Goodness. Is every single thing I do here going to come under scrutiny going forward?

'It's fine, Uncle Alistair, really it is. Having had a new kitchen installed in my London apartment only eighteen months ago, I have a rough idea and I have it covered.'

Ooh, that makes me cringe a little. I hope he doesn't think I'm showing off. I figure it's good to put a little work his way and I know he genuinely means well, thinking I might over-stretch myself.

'I assumed most ordinary people working in London rented. The prices are ludicrous, apparently.'

He's not being nosy, but I don't want to back myself into a corner here.

'They are, but I was lucky to get onto the property ladder when I did.' Good deflect, Kerra, I tell myself.

'Prices can go up and down, though.'

Hmm.

'Yes, that's true. I've rented it out for a year, though, and it's going to make me a nice little profit.'

'I'm glad things are working out for you, Kerra. Sorry if you felt I was overstepping the mark and poking my nose in, but when Alice said you didn't have anything much—well, you know what she's like. I thought it was a bit strange, but if you're doing major building works then you're going to be camping out for a while, I suspect.'

Finally! 'Having seen what they've done to the pub, I'm thinking of going all Annie Sloan and chalk paint. In fact, I'm out and about with Tegan this afternoon to look for furniture I can experiment on.'

'Ha! Love it! We carry a lot of that colour range and if you pop onto our website there are a few examples of kitchens we've done in that style over the last couple of years.'

'Thanks, Uncle Alistair. I'll check them out. And Drew will be in touch very soon. Bye for now.'

I might just have sorted the little problem of tittle-tattle Alice, too. When she learns that I have plans for extensive renovation work in mind it should put a stop to the curiosity over my current living conditions. My goodness, it's not even 10 a.m. and things are beginning to come together quite nicely. What's next?

As if on cue, the doorbell rings and it's Dad.

'Hey lovely, I've come to cut the grass. I won't disturb you and I'll use the side entrance to save tramping through. Everything alright this morning?'

'Fine. I need to pop out and get some paint and a few things. Oh, there is a quick question I have about Mr Mills. Did you ever have much to do with him?'

Dad rubs his chin, giving it some thought, but his face is curiously blank.

'I don't think anyone had much to do with him. He was in sales, I believe. Delivered cars, as there was a different vehicle parked outside the cottage every couple of days. He used those trade plates, so maybe he worked for one of the online dealers. I'm not even sure he had a car of his own, come to think of it. He doesn't owe you any rent money, does he?'

'No. Nothing like that. It's just that two guys were here yesterday, looking for him. I explained he doesn't live here anymore. Curiously, Drew didn't seem to have anything to do with him, either.'

Dad shrugs and then turns to start emptying the boot of his car. 'I'll take the cuttings back to mine for the compost heap, lovely. It'll be looking nice and neat when you get back.'

'Thanks, Dad. Having a one-hundred-and-fifty-feet-long garden is wonderful until it comes to cutting the grass and pulling the weeds. It's much appreciated. See you later.'

Grabbing my bag, I drive into Polreweek, which is this side of St Austell. It takes about half an hour, but there's a big DIY store on the industrial estate and in less than half the time it takes to get there, I manage to fill their largest trolley.

Paint. Tick. Brushes. Tick. Masking tape. Tick. Brush cleaner. Tick. Dust sheets. Tick. Wax. Tick. What else do I need? Oh, sandpaper. Maybe I should take a look at those handheld sanding machines, which might be good for getting off old varnish.

Sauntering along the display of more than a dozen different machines, which all seem to do the same thing, a familiar face looms up in front of me.

'Now you're the last person I expected to bump into, Kerra Shaw. How are you?'

Nettie Pentreath was one of Mum's closest friends. The last time I saw her was at the funeral and we didn't really get a chance to chat. We hug and she pats my back, sharing a moment. When we pull away, I give her a weak smile.

'Life goes on. But I've moved into Pedrevan Cottage now—hence the paint.'

She gazes down at the heavily laden trolley in awe.

'Enough to keep you busy for a bit, in there.'

'You can say that again. Funnily enough, Mrs Moyle was talking about you the other day. I hear you're semi-retired now.'

'I am. Sort of. I work one day a week at the vet's to get me out of the house for a bit. I do miss the company, I will say.'

There's a hesitancy to her words, as her eyes flick over my face.

'Between you and me, I have a hobby. One that generates an income, but it's not common knowledge.'

I wait, thinking she's going to tell all, but that's it. I guess I can sympathise with that desire to hold back a little. You never know who might be listening, even the other side of some racking. Besides, this is my chance to offer an open invitation and I've been mulling over how best to engineer crossing paths with her.

'Well, next time you're passing my door, do pop in for a proper chat. I'd love to catch up.'

'I will, I promise. It's good to see you, Kerra. Take care of yourself.'

Mum relied upon Nettie quite a bit when my parents made the decision to move from their first home together in the village of Tremont, back to within a stone's throw of where Mum was born. The house is called Green Acre, but they both hated the name. It was built on just over an acre of land that was formerly used as a market garden. A developer bought the plot and built a typical Sixties-style house with large rooms and big, panoramic windows looking out across the garden. It was perfect for Mum's business venture and they were delighted when the change of use was eventually rubber-stamped. Dad was on board because he knew it was her dream, but his day job was working in the family business, in between having explosive arguments with Uncle Alistair.

Mum couldn't have set up the business without Nettie's help. She worked full-time at the vet's surgery then, but she'd appear to walk the dogs first thing and early evening, and spent hours here most weekends. It wasn't because she needed the money, she just enjoyed the company of the dogs and her best friend.

I thought that maybe Nettie and Dad would comfort each other after Mum's long illness, but instead it was obvious to me that they had drifted apart. Maybe this new hobby Nettie has, fills the void for her. Each to their own, as Mum would have said.

As I stand in the queue waiting to pay, I consider how everyone's life has moved on. Dad is now sorting himself out and Nettie seems content, but does she miss being involved in something that was a large part of her life? The unknown is whether Dad and Nettie fell out over something after Mum's passing. If they did, then maybe Mrs Moyle thinks it's time their paths crossed again. I don't know for sure and that means I need to proceed very carefully. It's a puzzle, but I suspect at some point Mrs Moyle will drop another hint. She's not one to hold back for long when she's got something on her mind and, clearly, she does. But I'm delighted that Nettie seemed keen to call in and that's a start.

I hope this queue speeds up a bit as it's going to be tight to grab a sandwich before Tegan arrives. Still, I'm excited about this afternoon and I think Tegan is going to enjoy it, too.

10. A Different Mindset

'How good are you at bartering?' Tegan throws at me. I assume she's joking, but one glance in her direction and I can see it's a serious question.

'Can't say I've ever bartered, but I know how to negotiate a contract.'

She laughs. 'There is no rule book, this is role-playing. The seller needs to feel they are the ultimate winner. To get to that point, one of us has to play the good cop, and the other one the bad cop. Get it?'

Jeez, I just want to buy some secondhand furniture, which is going to be a fraction of the price of anything new and better quality. Considering most of the items in here were made to last, it's a win-win situation. Ironically, things have gone full circle with more people valuing handcrafted, bespoke items rather than less durable, mass-produced things.

However, I thought this was going to be a fun and an easy shopping experience, and now it's beginning to sound like hard work.

'Can I be the good cop? I'm going to find it hard to barter as this stuff is cheap, Tegan. None of these stallholders are making a fortune here, are they?'

Tegan gives me a scathing look.

'Everything you see is priced at least twenty-five per cent higher than they expect to sell it for. Tourists don't always haggle, but locals know the score. It's the way it works, and everyone ends up happy. It sounds like you're going to be a pushover, so good cop it is, but take your direction from me. Pick out something you like and enthuse over it. That gets them on your side—they love a serious purchaser. Then I'll talk them down.'

Goodness, there isn't much I'm going to have to teach Tegan to get her business operating more efficiently. This woman is a shark and she's in for the kill. Why on earth she sees this exercise in a totally different light to her own business, when her clients have been taking advantage of her, makes no sense at all.

'Oh! Oh! I need that!' I say, pointing across the room at the most amazing wall cabinet. It's about a metre square and twenty centimetres deep, so has endless possibilities. Made out of solid pine and with a glass door that has the cutest lock, it even has a little bit of woodworm. I'm in love.

'Calm down, Kerra,' Tegan leans in to whisper in my ear.

'What a shame it has woodworm,' she declares rather loudly. I reach out to look at the price tag. At only £150, it's a steal.

The woman standing behind the tiny counter in the corner concession of what is the ground floor of an old warehouse, looks unfazed.

'Yes, but isn't it amazing? It's been treated, so it's fine and it gives this piece such character.'

I'm thinking the same thing, and fighting with myself not

to jump in and say it's sold. Tegan keeps giving me the evil eye, as if to say, 'don't you dare!'

'I know what you mean,' she muses, directing her words at me. 'However, I do prefer that cabinet we saw earlier, Kerra. This one is rather large.'

And perfect for the bathroom, kitchen, or on the staircase wall as a display cabinet. I need it. I simply must have it.

'Hmm.' Pretending that my interest is waning is ridiculous. I'll be gutted if we walk out without it and at that price, I can't see the point in haggling. Tegan can see I'm weakening.

'It's too much,' she declares. 'Let's go for the other one, it was more affordable,' and with that she begins to turn away, as if the negotiations are over.

'One-thirty?' The woman throws out there.

'One-twenty and it's a deal,' Tegan counters.

'Done.'

As we walk away carrying this beautiful piece of furniture between us, I'm dumbfounded.

'Tegan, it was worth paying the full price. This isn't an item either of us will ever see again. It's unique. It will be a talking point, wherever I put it in the cottage.'

She shakes her head sadly.

'You're used to silly London prices. You need to watch more TV, Kerra. Antique dealers make a fortune scouting around places like this. They don't just double the prices they pay, they quadruple them and more. But here you are buying at source. The stallholder probably only paid fifty quid for this in the first place. And I thought you were the astute businesswoman. I can't wait to take you to a car boot sale,' she laughs.

Our next bargain is a set of four wooden stools that, apparently, came out of the science lab of a local school. Dented and dinged, worn with age, they are gorgeous.

Then I see the rattan egg chair. There isn't any age to it and it's in pristine condition, nice enough to think it might have been a display piece. It's unusual, as items like this are often fussy, with overtly high backs. Or they have intricate designs woven into them. This one is in a chunky, pale grey weave. After sinking down into it, I can see it needs a more substantial cushion to replace the thin foam pad, but you can curl up inside it. When I slide down a little, I can comfortably rest my head on the back edge and instantly imagine myself on the new decking, gazing out over the garden. It's a pity there is only the one, because I'd love to buy a set of these.

'Now I'm surprised you like that. It doesn't scream country-style to me, at all,' Tegan screws up her face.

'But it's so comfortable. If I add a big, fluffy, cushion in a pretty design, it would look lovely in the corner of any room. I could happily sit and read for an hour or two in this.'

Of course, the moment I stop speaking Tegan stares at me intently, and I leave her to barter.

Travelling back to the cottage, we're both in high spirits. It occurs to me that I haven't had this much fun in a very long time, and I feel a ridiculous level of excitement about my haul. By comparison, the sofa I purchased for the apartment cost me almost five thousand pounds and I didn't even get a buzz from it. And yet, here I am, impatient to begin rolling up my sleeves to start work on this lot.

Ten years ago, I wouldn't have appreciated any of this

and now here I am, like a magpie grabbing treasures with which to surround myself. After losing someone you love, you find yourself looking at your life in a different way. Who, or what, puts a smile on your face when you are having a bad day? The answer, for me, was very little when I was in London—aside from Sy. Surrounding myself with people and things I feel some sort of connection with is making me feel positive about the future. It's helping to create a sense of belonging and maybe it never was about fitting in, at all, but accepting who I am without apology.

Gosh, it's only taken me twenty-nine years to realise that and I thought I was a fast learner.

'Hi, Polly, thank you so much for popping in. I see you've come equipped.'

She's carrying a large jute bag, slung over her shoulder.

'My pleasure, Kerra. I thought I'd bring a few things I use to make the job easier. It wasn't lost on Dad how impressed you were by the new décor at the pub and that was a bit of a confidence boost for me. I needed it, as you can imagine the mixed reaction it received at first. He still has moments when he wavers over whether it was the right thing to do, even now. Especially when the older clients have a moan.'

'Everyone has an opinion, but these days people's expectations are higher. Lots of visitors will be used to wine bars and boutique, or industrial, settings. I like that blend of character and cosy contemporary you've managed to achieve. People stay longer if the ambience is welcoming.

You did a brilliant job, so great that it's sort of inspired what I want to do here. Anyway, come on through.'

In the sitting room most of the floor is now covered with two large dust sheets.

'I think I have everything I need, but I'd really appreciate your advice before I make a start. I don't want to risk messing it up as this is a first for me.'

She slides the bag off her shoulder and places it on the floor, slipping off her hoodie. There's a slight chill in the air today, as the breeze is blowing in off the sea.

'Can I make you a drink? Hot, cold?'

'No, I'm good thank you. I have about an hour, as Dad has to head off to the wholesaler's. Some interesting pieces you have here. What's the overall plan?'

Yanking a small scrunchy out of my pocket, I scoop my hair back and tie it into a tight ponytail.

'The plans for the cottage are to extend the ground floor and make it all open plan. There will be a wall of glass doors to the rear, opening out onto a large decking area.'

Polly looks impressed, if a little surprised.

'While I want to have that sense of space, I'm keen to soften the look without cluttering it up. My uncle is going to make the kitchen units and I'm thinking Shaker-style, with a muted, pale grey, chalk paint finish and white quartz worktops. Then a dark grey, slate floor.'

Polly claps her hands together as she raises them to her mouth, excitedly.

'Gosh, Kerra, it's going to look absolutely stunning!'

'While it's going through the planning process, I intend to start work on the furniture. I want to add a little character by having a go at upcycling a few things. I've brought very little with me, so I'm starting from scratch.'

'Well, I love the pieces you've chosen. Is the idea to paint everything?'

'The egg chair I think I'll leave for the moment, as it might go into one of the bedrooms as it is. If I have it down here, I'm thinking of keeping everything white, so I'd probably spray it.'

She nods. 'I think that's wise if you don't want it to look too fussy, to be honest. A dark, slate floor is going to contrast nicely. What's going to be the focal point of the room? Please say it's going to be a huge table.'

You can tell Polly studied interior design at college. But with the long hours she works alongside her dad in the pub, if he was paying someone I suspect they'd struggle to make a profit on top of their other staffing costs. She's never resented it, but I'm glad he let her show off her natural flair for design. Maybe it was his way of ensuring she continues to stay.

I smile. 'A huuuuge table and an eclectic collection of chairs, painted white, of course. I'm going for comfort over style, but hope to combine the two. It depends on what pieces I can find.'

'Sounds good. Okay, so what's your main concern? I see you have a nifty little hand-sander there. No steel wool, though.'

She dips into her bag, pulling out a small box.

'This is the finest grade. Not only does it clean up the surface, but often it will take off just enough shine to save having to sand an item. If you decide to paint the egg chair, for instance, I'd give it a going over with this and then I'd spray it with a can of matt paint. Don't pick up eggshell by mistake, as you'll hate the shine.'

Polly bends, opening up her bag and grabbing a few more items to stack them in the crook of her arm.

'Here you go. Brushes are great, but for larger, flat surfaces a roller is perfect. These four-inch ones come with two different heads—one for emulsion paint and one for woodwork finishes, which is the smooth one. But I often use the fluffy one as then you don't get that totally flat look, but it gives it a slightly mottled appearance. I think it would be perfect for those stools. I love that they aren't all exactly the same, just similar styles.'

'Yes, I rather liked that, too.'

Polly won't let me pay her for the little stash of goodies and even though time is short, we prep one of the stools and she gives me a demonstration. I discover that thin coats ensure a better finish than being heavy-handed, as if the paint gets knocked, she explains, it tends to chip off in one piece and exposes the original wood.

'I can't thank you enough, Polly. Maybe you, me and Tegan can get together one evening? I know it isn't easy for you, but if you have a night off when you aren't doing anything it would give me an excuse to get the recipe book out and don an apron. I'm sure I can't have forgotten everything Mum taught me.'

She gives me a grateful smile. 'I'd love that, I really would. Thank you. And both your mum and your grandma would have loved the way you're planning on updating the cottage. Good luck and be bold. Remember, there's no mistake that a little paint-stripper can't handle.'

As she steps out through the front door, Drew is walking towards us.

'Hi, ladies. Am I interrupting?'

'No,' Polly confirms, 'I have to get back to the pub. I'll catch up with you very soon, Kerra. Bye for now.'

As I wave her off, Drew steps inside.

'Goodness, you don't hang around, do you? This lot is going to keep you busy for a little while.'

Drew surveys the contents of what is now my workshop.

'I love a challenge.'

'Well, I haven't come to stop you working, but I wanted to let you know that I have the detailed breakdown of the revised figures and I'll be emailing them across shortly. I've taken out the cost of the kitchen units and worktops but left in the appliances.'

'Remind me about the flooring. Wasn't it a high-gloss, natural stone tile?'

'Yes. Why?'

'Thinking about it, a slate floor would work better with the bespoke cabinets in here.'

Drew's brow wrinkles as he stops to consider my proposal. 'It might cost a little more; I don't know for sure until I find a source and get a quote. Leave it with me. In the grand scheme of things, it's a minor change and the labour to lay the floor is the same. Anyway, I must get back, as I have another meeting with the planning officer shortly, to put in both application packs. We've been liaising for months as I've adjusted the basic plan and he said it's unlikely there will be objections because no one overlooks this plot. You were the only potential threat and now that's out the window. Hopefully, six weeks and we'll get the go-ahead, as the builders are pressing me and threatening to put the start date back.'

'You have a start date?'

'End of May, with completion by mid-July, latest. You know how clogged up the road gets in August and they've been trying to steer me into postponing it until the autumn. But now, well, there's no need to hold back. I'll send you the payment schedule, as well. There's a document listing the terms of business with the contract. Any questions, just shout.'

I expected no less than a totally professional set up and Drew hasn't disappointed me. It's obvious he's in a rush to get off to his meeting as I see him out, but I'm still taking in the happy news. The quicker they start, the quicker they finish.

'Which company are you using?'

'Treloar's Building Limited, they're well thought of in the area. I've been to their offices a few times discussing the proposed plans in detail before we got to the quotation stage. They also took me on a tour of two large extensions they've recently completed, and their work is top-class.'

My heart sinks. Treloar's—why, oh why? The image that instantly pops into my head takes me back to senior school. I'm fifteen years old and Ross Treloar's mouth is pressed up against mine, turning my legs to jelly. My first kiss.

Damn it, though. This could get a little awkward.

MAY

11. The Calm Before the Storm

'Bit of a last-minute change of plan, I'm afraid,' Drew says, sounding terribly apologetic as he strides past Tegan.

She pushes the front door shut behind him, casting me a nervous glance. It's the last Friday in May and we've nearly finished emptying the entire ground floor, which included rolling up carpets and underlay ready for the skip. The kitchen looks sad, empty units with only the white goods in situ. We are now in the process of setting up a temporary kitchen in the small box room, upstairs.

'The builders are starting on Monday as planned, but one of their guys is going to do a couple of runs to drop off some lengths of pipe over the weekend. Unfortunately, I won't be here to help, as Felicity isn't feeling very well. I'm heading straight up to be with her. It's some sort of 'flu thing and she's home alone. I'm not much of a nurse, but at least I can fetch and carry.'

'Poor Felicity. Just tell me what you need me to do and then forget about things here.'

I think both Tegan and I feared that he was going to say there's been a hold-up. If I thought my living conditions have been tough so far, setting up camp upstairs takes it to a whole new level, so a delay is unthinkable.

'Deliveries I can cope with, but a delayed start now would feel like a total disaster.'

'I didn't mean to panic you, Kerra, but I am sorry about the timing of this. I wanted to be here in case there are any questions, but if anything crops up please ring me. Here's a key for the double gates at the side; I'll contact the site foreman now to let him know I won't be around. Tell the driver this is a spare key for them to keep at the office. If you don't mind checking he locks it before he leaves that would be great, as I won't be back until late Sunday night.'

Drew is running through a mental list, but he's flustered and obviously concerned he'll forget something important. 'Oh, and there are also two skips being delivered tomorrow morning and there are a stack of cones in my front garden. Someone will be here first thing to supervise the drop and make sure the roadside lights are working. I'll cone off the area outside Tigry Cottage when I leave shortly. If at some point today you can find a parking space further along the road, don't forget to leave enough space for the builders to access both skips from each end. I think that's everything, but I feel really bad dumping this on you.'

'Drew, just go. It's no big deal and everything will be fine. Drive safely and I hope it all goes well with Felicity.'

When he's gone, Tegan turns to face me.

'Ah, he's such a sweet guy! Pete was like that, he'd do anything for me,' she heaves a sigh.

Losing a parent is hard, but I guess when you lose a spouse, as time goes on what you are left with is a sense of loneliness, as well as loss. And that's the stage Tegan is at right now.

'I've never found anyone who ticked all the boxes,' I confide in her.

She starts laughing. 'Ticked all the boxes? Oh, Kerra, you've never been in love then. Your heart tells you what you want, not what you necessarily need. I'm not perfect and neither was Pete, but we changed each other in subtle ways that made each of us a better person. My problem is that some of the strengths he had, are the ones I simply can't grasp. I feel like half a person now and that's why you're having to help me out. It's rather pathetic, isn't it?'

Is that truly what Tegan believes?

'Listen, lady. You are a one-woman band when it comes to running your business and you should be proud of yourself. We've made a start by reviewing your charges and negotiating a wider window between guests leaving and arriving on changeover days. When that kicks in, in the autumn, you will notice a big difference. Plus, your clients now understand that if they don't respond immediately to problems your cleaners walk into, then you will levy a fixed fee. If you want to stay in business you have to make a profit, because you aren't a charity.'

It sounds harsh, but it's the truth.

'It has already begun to make a difference, Kerra. I don't know anyone else who could have sorted all of that out for me so quickly and is also willing to strip beds and clean toilets. And we've had some laughs along the way like old times, haven't we?'

That's a bit of an understatement. A couple of weeks ago I

managed to lock myself out of a bijou little bungalow, when I popped outside to put some rubbish in the bin. I had no idea the door locked automatically. I found myself standing in the pouring rain, hair wrapped up in a scarf and sporting a pair of bright yellow, rubber gloves. Without my phone I couldn't even call for help, so I did the only thing possible. I wheeled the bin around to the rear of the property to get a boost up to climb in through the bathroom window. Elegant it most certainly wasn't, and I was mortified when Tegan turned up at a point where I'd gotten a bit stuck. Apparently, the elderly neighbour next door had spotted my dilemma and given her a call.

'Sy arrives tomorrow and I can't wait to introduce you to him. He was my right-hand man and he's also a workflow management specialist, which is exactly what you need.'

'I know you said I should pick his brains while he's here, but if the solution isn't a simple one, I'll flounder. He's used to dealing with professionals, Kerra, and he's going to see right through me.'

'What precisely do you think he will see, Tegan? You've succeeded in setting up a business, which you are actively managing and are looking for ways to become more efficient. In the early years it's a struggle, that's par for the course. It's all about constantly refining the way you do things and learning lessons as you go along. Sy might have a smart title, but basically what he does isn't rocket science, it's about standing back and seeing the bigger picture to identify what needs tweaking. You work hard, you're a problem solver and you manage a team of people in an operation that is spread out over a large area. That's no mean feat, lady.'

This is personal, because facing up to the fact that change

is inevitable is sending her into a panic and I understand that feeling. Her business has grown too large for one person to control and Pete isn't there any more to pick up the slack. Tegan's cleaners are a credit to her and the lady who drives the other minibus has worked for her from the start. But Pete put in a lot of hours on evenings and weekends, sorting the paperwork and doing the drop offs when Tegan had to step in and cover for absences. As things stand, she simply can't afford to employ someone to do what he did for free. And that's why things are beginning to unravel. She spends her time firefighting and bit by bit she's beginning to lose the battle.

Once Sy is here and they start talking, I think she'll quickly see that the ideas he'll put forward will be both practical and effective. When it comes to streamlining an operation, he can't resist a challenge and when he sees the potential for growth, I think he'll be excited.

'I believe you make your own luck in this life, Tegan, and that means tackling the problems as they arise. It might involve a bit of delicate manoeuvring and maybe a little shove, here and there, to achieve the end goal but I'm convinced it's going to be well worth the effort.' She's listening intently and I can she's coming around.

What I don't mention is that it could also solve the problems of two people I care about, who are both struggling. Sy is growing unhappier by the day, that's very clear. The burning question is whether it's going to be possible to take the city out of the man, even if I succeed in taking the man out of the city.

Could Sy adjust to bracing sea walks and see that as a substitute for the twinkling bright lights of theatreland? I genuinely believe he clings onto his old ways out of habit and the fact he jumped at the offer to venture down here is meaningful. I'm going to give this little plan my best shot, because I sense that Sy is teetering on the edge of walking out. He isn't a quitter and something like that would be a blot on his CV, a red flag for future employers. Helping Tegan by coming up with an action plan will not only help her, but also boost his confidence. He could so easily set up a consultancy and it might remind him that life exists outside of London, too.

'Sy is a real pro, but he also has a good heart—he loves to feel needed. I think the two of you will get on very well and you'll soon see there's nothing at all to worry about. On a practical level you have nothing to lose, but a lot to gain—believe me.'

I'm nervous, as this afternoon is Dad's grand relaunch of Home from Home. Thankfully, the sun is putting in an appearance again, after a bit of a wet start to the day. Still, the garden looks fresher for it. I'm off to collect a batch of Mrs Moyle's homemade cakes before heading over to the house.

The shop is busy today and I'm delighted to see that my order is ready and waiting. Mrs Moyle points to a stack of trays sitting on the end of the counter and I give her a thumbs up.

A queue of five people stand in a line, snaking back into the chilled goods aisle, all with baskets filled to the brim. Mrs Moyle would never hurry a customer and the lady at the head of the queue is at pains to tell the entire shop about the problems she's having with her boiler. Sy would be appalled, but no one minds waiting. This is the true definition of a convenience store—all the basic items you need within easy walking distance of your home. And it's the hub of this little community. People are happy enough to stand around chatting, if only to catch up on the latest news—well, some might call it gossip. Many of the older inhabitants pop in daily, just for a bit of company and they might only be buying a carton of milk, but it gets them out of the house and that's important. A village without a shop is like a community without a heart. And that's the sort of service money can't buy.

Throwing a quick 'thank you, Mrs Moyle' over my shoulder, I carry the stack of trays out to the car and head off to Dad's. As I pull up he's tying a welcome banner to the five-bar gate. He's already hammered a stake into the ground with a sign saying 'parking' and a big arrow directing people to the next turning on the left, which is the area beyond the main kennels. I lift out the trays and young James races over to take them from me, then I jump back into the car to go and park up.

Sauntering up through the gardens from the orchard reminds me how large a plot it is and how much work is involved throughout the summer months to keep the garden under control. I wonder if Dad really will be able to cope if business takes off again. With only James to help with the dog-walking, he's going to be stretching himself pretty thin. I've had to back off, as Dad seems adamant that he has it all under control, but I keep wondering about Nettie; I haven't written off that idea just yet. It's not my place to interfere, but his situation isn't that dissimilar to Tegan's. It all rests on their shoulders and it's a lot of pressure. What if he's ill, or wants to take a day off? Running a business requires drive and motivation, whereas I fear that Dad is simply trying to prove something. That's touching, but if his heart isn't really in it, then that doesn't bode well for the long-term future. Even if he feels he's honouring Mum's memory.

That's another reason why I can't wait for Sy to arrive, as I really value his opinion. He's staying at Dad's, as there's barely room for me to sleep at Pedrevan Cottage, given that things are now shoved in everywhere. The middle bedroom is supposed to be a sitting room, but it's also home for my new purchases. And as for the temporary kitchen, well it's tiny. Anyway, I'm hoping Dad will enjoy Sy's company and maybe open up to him a little during the week he's here. In return, Sy is going to be helping out and getting his first hands-on experience of dog-walking. And wearing wellies. And getting up close and personal with nature. It's going to be sink or swim, but I have a good feeling about it.

'Here she is, then,' Dad's neighbour, Tom, calls out as soon as he spots me. His wife, Georgia, waves out.

'Just in time to help with displaying the cakes, Kerra,' she joins in. 'Arranging things in a pretty fashion isn't my strong point, I'm afraid. I'm a bit clumsy at times.'

The pair of them express a giggle, and I can't help thinking that this is probably the most fun they've had in a long while.

'What do you think of the bunting?' Tom asks tentatively.

'You did an amazing job, Tom,' I gush, and his face colours-up.

He's tall and lanky, with big hands and strong arms

because of all that hammer-wielding in his workshop at the cove. Georgia, by contrast, barely reaches his shoulder. Given their physical differences, though, they seem to instinctively pre-empt each other's actions and it's lovely to watch.

'What can I do?'

'If you can help me assemble these fiddly cake stands, that would be lovely. Our James has gone to fetch the glasses and your cousin, Alice, is in the kitchen making up jugs of lemonade.'

I'm surprised that Alice would take a half-day off work simply to give a hand; maybe I'm being a tad mean-spirited, but it is unusual. Unless it was my aunt, or my uncle, who suggested it. It would be a little awkward for either of them to come along and support Dad without being invited, but Alice is always welcome, and they know that.

'That's very kind of her. These are a bit fiddly, aren't they?'

The clock is ticking and we have just under half an hour now to get everything ready. Dad appears, carrying the box of advertising materials I had printed up with the new logo. He took a bit of convincing, but when it arrived I could see he was pleased. After all the effort he's put in, I thought it would give him a boost—and it has.

'Where should we put these, lovely?' he asks.

'Everywhere. A big pile on the cake and drinks table, for starters. Put some on the long window ledges inside the kennels. As people are walking around they can pick them up. Do the inserts inside detail the new pricing structure?'

'Yep. Did 'em myself last night.'

'Well done. I think you should put a large pile on a small

table up by the five-bar gate for walk-ins, too. Actually, I'll sort that if you put some on the side for me.'

James appears and I make space on the table for the tray of glasses; behind him, Alice is very carefully carrying a full jug in each hand.

'Let me take those off you.' I jump forward. She's wearing heels on a block-paver path with a gentle slope, and it isn't the most even of surfaces.

'Thanks, Kerra. I can't walk on the grass because I keep sinking in.' With that, she stares down at my feet, frowning. 'I've never been able to carry off flat shoes. They make your legs look shapeless, don't they?'

It wouldn't have sounded quite so bad if she'd said, 'one's legs' and I try not to take it personally.

Even Georgia takes a quick peek and then she stares back at Alice's feet in disbelief. I can't help thinking that Alice is the one who looks silly, not me. Then I feel guilty as she is lending a hand and that's good of her.

As Alice turns to retrace her wobbly steps back up to the house, she almost loses her footing and James jumps in to offer his arm.

'I'll collect the other jugs once I've sorted these leaflets, Alice. Why don't you stay and help Georgia with the cakes?' I suggest.

She doesn't seem put out, but I can't help noticing that as she steps forward onto the springy turf, she ends up kicking off her shoes out of pure frustration.

'James, could you have a look and see if you can find Alice some alternative footwear, please?' I ask and he nods.

I know for a fact the only thing Dad is likely to have hanging around will be a pair of wellies. This is going to be fun as they won't be pink, purple or sparkly, and they definitely don't make anyone's legs look slimmer—but they are much more practical than a pair of five-inch, spiky heels.

As I head towards the gate I hear the clang of the latch when it swings shut, and look up to see Sy standing there beaming at me.

'What on earth? I wasn't expecting you until tomorrow!'

I fling my arms around him and we dance around together on the spot.

'Slight change of plan. It's been the week from hell and some.'

I pull away from him, being careful not to drop the handful of leaflets I'm desperately trying to hold onto, and he gives me a shake of his head.

'Don't even ask! Anyway, I've arrived in time for the party and I'm looking forward to giving a hand.'

Hot on his heels, three of Dad's regular clients arrive in a jolly mood, dogs in tow. A quick glimpse along the road confirms that a few more furry friends are on their way.

'Hi everyone. Dad, your models are arriving,' I call out. 'Sy, can you hold these for me?' I stuff the leaflets into his hands, as he stands back rather awkwardly.

Rufus is jumping around and making his presence felt, but the other two dogs are also determined not to be left out. I end up having to crouch down to scratch ears and ruffle coats, to calm them down. Sy glances at me, appalled at the flurry of wagging tails and grasping paws vying for attention.

'See what little darlings they are?' I comment but he takes another step backwards. 'It's important to say hello and acknowledge their presence. No one likes to be ignored.'

Sy frowns as Dad approaches to lead the little party down to the kennels. As Sy and I head inside I can see he's wondering what he's let himself in for.

'Listen, you don't need to be scared of them. Just relax, let the dogs hear your voice and if they jump around, a few pats on the back will soon settle them down. Animals give their love without reservation and they're a darn sight easier to deal with than people.'

'I'll take your word for it.' He doesn't sound convinced.

'We'll sort your room out a bit later, if that's alright with you. I'll help you fetch up your bags at the same time. It's all about to kick off here and we're expecting quite a crowd. Can you help me carry this little table outside? The weather forecast is good, but I'm hoping that breeze doesn't pick up, as that could make things a bit tricky. Maybe I'll find a large stone to anchor the leaflets, just in case. Oh, it's so good to have you here, I'm only sorry it's not possible for you to stay with me in the cottage. And I can't wait for you to meet Tegan.' There's little I can do to hide my excitement and a feeling of relief that he seems very happy to be here.

In fact, Sy throws himself into everything as the afternoon goes on and even ends up taking potential new clients on a tour of the facilities. The cakes are a big hit and although Alice is not amused by her replacement footwear, to be honest, no one even notices.

Judging by the turnout, there's a bright future ahead with some new clients lining up to join the old regulars. There are a lot of elderly people who have always used the kennels as a way of having a doggy break and retirees who enjoy regular holidays abroad. And people who came here to live the dream but take frequent trips to visit family. Being busy will really help to stop Dad slipping back into his bad habits and even Rufus seemed perky when he settled into his old home. I just hope he's not expecting to see Mum turning up at some point. Shutting everything down for a few weeks was so the right thing to do; it was akin to pressing a reset button. Even Dad looked relieved that his first canine visitors seem to accept that things are finally back to normal. Well, the new normal from here on in, hopefully.

12. Introductions

Sy is totally shocked when, eventually, I swing open the front door to Pedrevan Cottage and he steps inside. There are several seconds of silence as he scans the bare, drab-looking room.

'It's a quaint little cottage from the outside but, Kerra, how can you possibly live like this?'

It's true that Sy is a man who is used to a comfortable standard of living and the term *roughing it* isn't even in his vocabulary. I bet he's never been camping or sampled the delights of sleeping in a caravan. But this is the reality of my life for the next couple of months.

The doors to the dining room and kitchen are open and he stares through into the gloom, his expression frozen.

'I know it all looks rather grim right now, but my mother was born and brought up here, and it was my grandparents' home until they died. Drew is away this weekend, but when he's back I'll get him to show you the plans. Seriously, Sy, it's going to end up looking like something out of a magazine!'

His expression is like a still shot from a *Wallace and Gromit* film—you know the one—teeth gritted together and lips curled back into a fake smile, which ends up looking like an uncomfortable grimace.

'Come on, let's sit out in the garden, it's going to be a lovely evening, but you will need that jumper. It's through here.'

Even switching on the light in the dining room doesn't do much to brighten things up.

He seems happier outside, though, and the moment we're seated I can see something is troubling him.

'I'm done with it, Kerra,' he blurts out and I glance at him, horrified. 'Losing one's temper in front of everyone isn't exactly the way I'd planned to leave but at least I know there's no going back.' He smiles weakly in an attempt to shrug off the enormity of what he's done.

'Oh, no—I feared that might have been the case.' I let out a loud, heartfelt sigh. 'It just restricts your options in terms of jumping straight back into something.'

The way he's slumped in the chair shows how dejected he feels.

'I know. At least a few days away will allow it all to sink in, but I'm well aware that it was a stupid thing to do. Living off my savings while I sort myself out isn't exactly a plan, but it's all I have for now. I'll be lucky if anyone will consider taking me on, but when I go back maybe I can call in a favour. You won't believe how my phone was pinging with text messages all the way here and I haven't had the heart to look at them. You know what they say, bad news travels fast.'

And rumours spread quickly in business circles, even in London.

'Dad's looking forward to having you here to help out for a bit and he'll enjoy the company. If you want to extend your stay, he really does rattle around in that house on his own. But I suppose you're tied to the house share.'

I'm trying so hard to be low-key, but Sy will need to let things calm down before he starts approaching anyone about a job. He's staring blankly out at the garden, his thoughts, no doubt, churning.

'To be honest I feel I made a right fool of myself and I'm embarrassed about it. Maybe I'm the one who needs to cool off. But the changes being made aren't going down well with the customers and people are cancelling their subscriptions. I guess I could ask Karl if he can advertise for a new tenant to take over my room. The rent is fair and it's a nice house with great facilities. But how much help I can be to your dad is questionable.' At least his smile is genuine now and the fact that he hasn't dismissed the idea out of hand is cheering.

'Anyone can walk a dog, so you'll be fine and he will really appreciate any assistance you can give him. When he discovers you can cook, too, he'll be over the moon.' That elicits a belly laugh. 'Your offer to talk to Tegan and see if you can come up with any useful suggestions to improve her business set-up might open up an opportunity for you to do a little consultancy work. And even if you go back into employment, at least it will show there was no break in your work continuity.'

Sy looks at me, amazed. 'Clever you. I guess I won't be putting dog-walking on my CV, then?'

'You'd be helping someone out who really is in need and that'll boost your spirits, anyway.'

Guess there'll be three of us to cater for tonight, then.

I walk off, phone in hand, to invite Tegan over for supper and a glass of wine. I don't mention that Sy is already here.

After Tegan admitted she's feeling nervous about meeting

him, it seems the kindest way to get that initial introduction over and done with. Then I ring the Chinese takeaway and place an order for collection at eight-thirty. They don't deliver, but that suits me fine. It's only ten minutes away, and that's not too long to leave Sy and Tegan alone together, but long enough to get some general conversation flowing.

Sy has settled into one of the two garden chairs and I go back inside to bring down the egg chair. It's more bulky than heavy, but as soon as I start easing it through the back door, Sy jumps up to clear a space.

'Here, let me help you.'

Ding-dong.

'I'm good Sy, but can you get that? It's probably Tegan.'

I've told him a little bit about her situation, explaining that emotionally she's extremely fragile. What I love about Sy is that he's a thoughtful guy: sensitive, funny and he doesn't take himself too seriously. He understands precisely why I'm so worried about her and how precarious her situation is, feeling alone and lonely. Not everyone is capable of being empathetic and I believe those who can, do so because they carry old hurts. And Sy has been hurt many times over in his quest to find someone with whom he can trust his heart. Fortunately, Tegan's not his type and that's crucial, because sex and business is like oil and water—not a good mix. The one concern I have is that Tegan seriously underestimates her abilities and that innate lack of self-confidence could mess things up if she can't relax around him.

When I re-arrange the three chairs in a semi-circle and reposition the candles on the tray that I managed to rescue from one of the boxes before Drew put them up in the attic, it looks cosy. Note to self: I really need to do some more shopping, even if I'll struggle to fit things in—this is bordering on ridiculous. Dad already thinks I should stay at his while the work is being done, but in all honesty, I'd end up interfering, as he put it. I'm better off focusing on the cottage and there will be enough going on here to keep me distracted. Drew is the project manager, but this cottage is my new baby and it's all I've got right now to satisfy my creativity.

Listening to the low mumble of voices, I can't hear what either Sy or Tegan are saying as they make their way out into the garden to join me.

When Tegan steps down onto the patio, although she's smiling, I can see that she's a little unnerved as I approach to give her a hug.

'Hi Tegan. Sy, can you do me a favour and pop up to the small bedroom, please? There's a pile of plates on top of a little table and a tray of cutlery. We'll need the usual and a couple of serving spoons.'

Tegan looks from Sy to me and back again, rather nervously. As soon as he's out of earshot, I move closer, lowering my voice.

'Sy arrived just as Dad's party was kicking off and he was brilliant. In fact, we'd have struggled without him there. But we're shattered after clearing up. I thought it might be nice to have a quiet little supper together, I hope that's okay?'

She gives me an obliging smile, which is reassuring.

'I was just surprised to see him. He seems very nice,' she replies softly.

'I need to head out to pick up the takeaway. I'll be as quick as I can. Maybe ask Sy to uncork the wine—there's a bottle of red on the windowsill in the kitchen, alongside the corkscrew and some glasses. There's also a bottle of white in the fridge if anyone fancies that. Thanks, Tegan. I'm sure he'll explain that his plans have changed and he'll be staying for a little while. It means a lot to me that Sy feels welcome, because he's a good friend. I feel bad that he can't stay here as originally planned and this isn't exactly a comfortable setting to welcome him.'

I can see Tegan understands my dilemma and she gives me an affirming nod.

'Don't worry, I'm sure he understands and keep heart— you won't be living like this forever.'

It's a cheerful thought and one I need to keep reminding myself of, as there are moments when I wonder what the heck I've gotten myself into. I reach out to give her shoulder a grateful squeeze and then turn on my heels. Tonight is simply about welcoming Sy, and breaking the ice, and you can't get more low-key than this. A little wine and some food, a few laughs and, fingers crossed, we'll be off to a perfect start.

'Sorry guys, they were queuing out the door. Tegan, can you do the honours while I pop upstairs and wash my hands?'

She jumps up to grab the carrier bag of food and, glancing at her face, I'm relieved to see that she's looking surprisingly relaxed in Sy's company.

When I return, they've improvised and look extremely pleased with themselves. The dishes are set out on the tray, which is now elevated, having been placed on two, upside down flowerpots from a stack at the end of the garden. The candles have been lined up along the edge of the patio and the flickering light is enough to light our buffet table. I'm so hungry, the smell makes my stomach rumble in anticipation.

'Dig in, guys,' I remark, breaking out into a big smile. 'Now this is what I call al fresco dining.'

They both start laughing conspiratorially and as they glance at each other, even in the twilight I can see that playful spark of interest between them. Oh no... this isn't what I think it is—is it? If so, it's bad news, really bad. Sy's relationships never last and this could ruin everything. I try my best to quash a rising sense of panic, though it's obvious that they're much too busy locking eyes to notice my reaction.

This is one complication I didn't foresee. Tegan is nothing at all like Sy's usual love interests. She is most definitely not the sort of woman who wouldn't dream of leaving the house unless she was all glammed up and as for being the centre of attention, that's her worst nightmare!

The only slight consolation I can grab right now, is that at least the ambience is pleasant as darkness begins to descend around us. Far from being awkward, as I'd feared, the conversation is filled with that easy banter between two people who are getting to know each other and enjoying the process. As I sit there, eating and feeling a little like a spare part, to my surprise, Ripley suddenly trots out of the shadows and into view. She sits in the middle of the lawn, bathed in the little pool of moonlight, miaowing. Which is a first for her. Up to now all she's allowed me is fleeting glimpses as she darted from place to place. The fork in my hand clatters against the plate as I realise she has no idea what's going on.

'Oh no! Drew didn't give me a key for Tigry Cottage and

I'm supposed to be cat-sitting. In the rush for him to get off, we both forgot about Ripley.' Sy and Tegan stop talking and stare at me as I jump up out of my seat, berating myself for the oversight. Drew was in a bit of a panic at the time, but I should have engaged my brain and given thought to poor Ripley.

Raiding the fridge, I return with a plastic plate bearing little cubes of cheese and some shredded ham. Tegan is already on her knees reassuring our little visitor, who is clearly loving having her back stroked. As I walk up to them, I see that Ripley is a Bengal. Her cinnamon-coloured coat has those tell-tale, beautiful ringed markings. Curiously, the tip of her tail is pure white, with a tiny dark centre, like a bullseye, as she whips it back and forth.

'Shall I search around for something to put some water in?' Sy offers, which surprises me, and I can't help wondering whether he's trying to impress Tegan.

'That would be great, thanks. Poor little thing, I suspect she's apprehensive about what's going on. And on Monday it's going to get a lot worse as there will be a small digger here when they start moving the drains.'

As amenable as Ripley is, it takes a couple of hours of fussing to entice her inside the cottage and onto the little pile of blankets Sy and Tegan sculpt into a nest. Ripley has turned out to be a little star and at least it put a halt to all the starry-eyed glances. I text Drew to let him know that she's safely curled up for the night, as I don't want him panicking when he remembers we both forgot about her.

It's funny how Ripley has only been skulking around in the shadows up to now, but as soon as she realised supper wasn't coming, she was prepared to drop her guard. I guess we all need the reassurance of a good meal in our stomachs and a safe place to lay our heads when we're tired. Or does she think Drew has abandoned her and making new friends is simply a matter of survival?

Watching Sy sitting on the floor next to Tegan, happily stroking Ripley as she purrs contentedly, I wonder if it's the same for him? Feeling uncertain about his imminent future, he has no choice but to consider another option. One that could, potentially, feel like a lifeline. And in a way, isn't it the same for Tegan? What's the worst that can happen? Nothing is ever guaranteed and it's not in Sy's nature to be the heartbreaker, so why am I worried? Maybe a little fun will lift them both up and if it comes to nothing, then that's life. They move on, but in between could be that wonderful phase where everything looks a little brighter. Oh well, the best laid plans and all that. I'd better give Dad a quick call and explain that my little plan to get these two working together is kicking in earlier than expected.

13. The Fun Begins

Ding-dong. Ding-dong.

The guy standing at my door is probably in his early twenties and if he bumped into a brick wall, the wall might well come off the worse for it.

'Morning Mrs, sorry to disturb you. I've come to collect a key for the side entrance to next door. I'm dropping off a bundle of soil pipes.'

'Are you the guy waiting for the skips to be delivered, too?' I enquire, slipping the key off the hook and handing it over.

'Nope. Don't know anything about that. I'll be back tomorrow with another load, though.'

'That's fine. Mr Matthews asked if you could make sure you lock the gates up afterwards and the key has to go back to the office. Oh, and there's a cinnamon-coloured cat named Ripley, who lives next door, if you can keep an eye out for her I'd be grateful.'

'Thanks, and I'll bear that in mind, Mrs, for sure. The boss has just pulled up.' He waves out and I crane my neck to look over his shoulder. 'He'll know what's happening about the skips.'

Beyond the cones Drew put out yesterday, I spot a white

van pulling into the small lay-by on the opposite side of the road. The driver isn't in a hurry to get out and I decide to hang around, in case he needs anything.

Watching the young guy unlock the gates, it strikes me that I must look all of my nearly thirty years and maybe a few more. He was addressing me in the same way that workmen always talked to my mum. Age is only a number, I console myself. He's bursting with energy and muscle, and at a guess I'd say he's twenty, maybe twenty-one at a push. Ten years makes a big difference. You experience a lot of life as you hurtle through that next decade and before you know it, life is etching your face with fine little lines that seem to appear overnight. Character, they call it, but in my case long nights staring at a computer screen and screwing up my forehead haven't done me any favours.

Honestly though, I can say that I've felt more relaxed this past few weeks than I've felt for several years. It's funny how life can begin to feel more like a treadmill than a path, and we don't even notice it happening.

The man finally climbs out of the van parked opposite, clipboard in hand, and the moment he looks in my direction, my stomach lurches. He strides forward eagerly, until he's within earshot.

'I didn't dare believe the rumours, but you're back!'

Ross is smiling broadly at me, as my legs begin to wobble, and I find myself leaning up against the door frame for a bit of extra support. For some stupid reason time seems to slow down as he walks the last few steps up the path towards me. Gone is the shoulder-length, curly hair I remember. It's still long on the top but shaved up the back and sides; he now wears a full beard, kept closely cropped but a little longer than merely a couple of days' stubble. It suits him, in fact he's even more gorgeous than I remember, and I can't take my eyes off him. Why, oh why, has he always had this devastating effect on me? It wasn't cool as a teen but it's absolutely ridiculous for a woman of my age. Plastering on what I hope is a nonchalant smile, I take a slow, deep, breath before replying.

'You still work for the family business, then.' I hoped it would sound very matter-of-fact. However, my attempts to calm myself down are not working and to my horror, there's a slight breathlessness to my voice. My pulse is racing and the sound of my heartbeat is filling my ears with a loud drumming sound. How utterly humiliating. Get a grip, woman!

He's standing less than eighteen inches away from me now, as if he's expecting me to invite him in. Those dark brown eyes hold a tantalisingly teasing smile. Oh, grow up, Kerra, you're not a hormonal teen anymore, staring into the eyes of the boy who fills your dreams. The one who broke every girl's heart whose path he crossed. Doing my best to ignore the undeniable charm he still exudes, I rein in my thoughts as he begins talking.

'I do. Except that I'm the man in charge, now. My father retired early and my parents bought a villa in Spain.'

I'm thrown when he looks away and I notice a nervous little tick tugging at his right eyelid; I'd forgotten how those dark lashes look against his cheek when he lowers his gaze. But Ross, nervous—that's a first. Is he, too, feeling a little disturbed by our encounter? I wonder. As he raises his left hand to slide a pen under the clip on the board he's holding, I notice he isn't wearing a wedding ring. I know he is married, because both Mum and Tegan mentioned it at the time. They didn't say very much because no one from the village was on the guest list, apparently, and all of the talk centred around that.

He might have had a major problem committing to just one person when we were in our teens but seeing him up close again reminds me exactly why he was my first kiss. There's an inherent warmth in his smile and, somehow, he has that annoying ability to make you believe it's just for you. Well, it worked when I was young, but I refuse to let it rattle me now. He's probably thinking about the big fat cheque that will be winging its way to him before too long.

'Drew said the skips are arriving this morning?' My voice is level, belying the fact that my pulse is still racing and it's beginning to make me feel a tad light-headed.

Ross nods. 'Yes. I'm a little early, though.' He sounds genuinely apologetic.

That's awkward because I don't want to appear rude, and common courtesy would be to invite him in. But the shock I'm feeling at seeing him again makes me want to slam the door shut and run away. Never in my wildest imaginings did I think I'd feel so... vulnerable and exposed as I do right now. *Keep calm, Kerra*, I instruct myself. *It's time to put the armour back on. You can do this, you've done it many times before in a business situation, so you know it works. Don't let anyone see your weak spots and play you for a fool.*

'I'd ask you in for a drink, but everything is stripped bare ready for Monday. It's going to be fun managing without a proper kitchen,' I bemoan. I hope that came out sounding plausible and not like the trifling excuse it is, but I'm floundering.

'Oh, I'm fine, but I'd love a quick look around, if that's alright.'

Forcing my legs to take my weight so I can step aside, I try not to sag as we pass within inches of each other. Or catch my breath as I see that he still has that little swagger in his step. Even as a young man he always had a sense of confidence about him that was so appealing and exciting. He has a joy for life, like a spark he can't contain and it's mesmerising.

'You're doing the right thing, extending out,' he comments, scanning around the shell of the room. 'I expect it's hard for you though, given the family history attached to the property. But times change and after life in London, well, you'll be wanting something a bit special.'

As he turns to look at me, his eyes search my face and I wonder what he's thinking. When he begins speaking again, this time there's a softness to his voice that catches me unawares.

'Few come back for the right reasons, Kerra, but putting family first is admirable.'

Get a grip, woman—if you can't pull yourself together then you'd better make a quick exit.

'Oh,' I blurt out, glancing down at my watch. 'I didn't realise it was that time already.' I sound and look a little flustered, which—ironically—makes it seem all the more realistic. Turning on my heels and grabbing my bag, I hope he'll think I'm eager to leave because I'm late. 'I'm helping Tegan out today and she'll be wondering where I am. Can you check the other guy remembers to lock up the side gates before he leaves, please?'

A look of confusion flashes over Ross's face, but it's

momentary. 'Of course. Sorry, I didn't mean to hold you up; it's just that... well, it's good to see you again.'

I'm out through the front door the moment he stops speaking, leaving him no choice but to follow me outside. Slamming it shut and locking up, I turn to give him a fleeting, almost dismissive smile.

'Same here, Ross. Guess I'll see you around, then.' Miraculously, it comes out sounding suitably light and breezy.

Seconds later I'm driving away, beads of nervous sweat now beginning to gather on my top lip as I steady my breathing. Either I came across as rather dismissive, or he saw through me and I made a total fool of myself. I groan out loud. Why can I still see that sexy, boyish charm in him?

'Nostalgia!' I declare, making myself jump, as the solitary word shoots out of my mouth at quite a volume. 'It's just nostalgia. He reminds you of your youth and that exhilarating phase as you stood on the threshold of adulthood.'

That explains it, then. For one moment there I half-feared the old crush hadn't totally disappeared. I mean, that would be utterly ridiculous, wouldn't it?

'Are you okay?' Tegan asks, looking concerned.

'Yes, why?'

'You're looking a bit flushed and I wasn't expecting you for another hour, at least. But I'm ready.'

I promised Tegan I'd give her a hand with the holiday lets up at Treeve Perran. With a full complement of cleaners today, she's fitting in what she calls a deep clean. Being a complex attached to a working farm means after a rainy spell there's a lot of mud gets tramped around the outside and the windows get dirty very quickly.

'Come on, I'll explain on the way.'

As Tegan indicates to pull out after we've settled into the minibus, she says, 'As we're early, shall we take a stroll around the car boot sale over at Leath's farm?'

'Great idea!'

After my first foray into upcycling I've caught the bug but having spent so much time with Tegan I haven't had a chance to source any more items.

'What's going on at yours today, then?'

'I bumped into Ross Treloar. I left him waiting around for the skips to be delivered.'

'Gosh, I haven't crossed paths with him for a while. He didn't say something to upset you, did he? I've always found him rather pleasant to talk to, but he doesn't have much to do with the village these days. Funnily enough, it was his firm who built the little complex up at Treeve Perran. I just assumed one of the larger companies would be doing your extension. I suppose that ramps up the cost though, and it's nice to support local businesses.'

Judging by her reaction so far, Tegan has no idea at all that Ross was my first crush and I'd like to keep it that way.

'I'm fine with that, but I am getting anxious about seeing the cottage pulled apart. Camping out upstairs isn't the best and I needed to get away. I'm not putting you out, am I?'

'No, not at all. Just grateful you can give me a hand. So how is Ross doing?'

Her eyes are firmly on the road ahead, but she turns for a brief second to glance my way.

'He didn't really say. Ross arrived just as I was about to

leave. I can't remember whether it was you, or Mum, who told me that he got married a few years ago but he didn't mention that. Ross just said that his parents now live in Spain and he's running the company.'

I'm hoping Tegan will continue the conversation, but we lapse into silence, meaning that I have to pick it back up somehow.

'I don't even know where he lives, these days. I suspect he's done very well for himself, having taken over the business,' I add, trying my best to make it sound like a casual remark.

'Ross's marriage didn't last too long. He owns Treylya up on the headland—I assumed you knew that. He hasn't lived there for, I don't know, at least two years as that's when he started letting it out. I don't deal with him direct, of course, only the letting agency who are a national company. It must cost him a fair bit, but he might have more than one let. His divorce was long-winded and messy. There's a flat above the Treloar's offices, but I can't really see him living there. The last time I saw him was at least eighteen months ago; he said he was looking at a fixer-upper over in Trehoweth.'

Rather disappointingly, that seems to be the sum total of Tegan's knowledge.

'Maybe settling down isn't his thing. Some men are like that.' Why am I pursuing this?

'Oh, the problem wasn't with him, it was Bailey. They had the lavish wedding and he was besotted, so we were all waiting for the next announcement about their first arrival. I don't really listen to the tittle-tattle that does the rounds, but the bust-up was very public. She had a problem with credit cards and racked up a lot of debt in his name before Ross discovered how bad it was. I think his parents helped bail him out, as at one point it looked like he'd lose the house. He had it built for her and it cost him a small fortune, that's why the finish is a bit over the top.'

I'm stunned. The property is amazing, and I assumed it was built by some wealthy person who had more money than sense. Ross will never recoup the building costs if he tries to sell it.

'It was a bad time,' Tegan continues. 'He could have chosen anyone but...' She tails off.

'But?'

'I don't know the details of what happened, of course— none of us do, not really—but his parents always aspired to something better. They worked hard and deserved the rewards they got. Joining the country club set, though, well—it's a different world. But it was the world they wanted for Ross.'

What's Tegan trying to say? 'You think he married her to please them?'

'Oh no, he was captivated by her. She was one of those women who seem to get what they want without much effort, you know, people fawn over them because they're so perfect. That sounds awful, but you know what I mean. She's glamorous and stylish. But his parents pushed them together, there's no doubt of that. He liked her because she was different, and she stood out. Maybe it was because she didn't chase after him, and he found that refreshing. Once his parents joined the golf club they were mixing with a very different circle of friends and his dad became a local councillor. Ross was dragged into that and the whole socialising thing. I never got the impression he was entirely comfortable with it, though.'

'And then it all went wrong. I wonder if that's why his parents moved to Spain?'

As Tegan eases the minibus over the uneven field to park up, I reach for the grab handle overhead to steady myself.

'Wow—that hadn't occurred to me before, but you could be right, Kerra. It was very embarrassing all round and I was disappointed for Ross. He's always been the odd one out, since he was a kid, hasn't he? The lads at school were jealous of him, all the girls wanted to date him and he was top of the class. I bet even now he brightens the day of every female customer he visits, married or single, because he's good to look at and utterly charming. But I wonder how that makes him feel? He worked hard from a young age because his parents constantly pushed him. Second place was never good enough for them and that can't have been easy. At least now he can be his own man.'

I'd never thought about what life was like from Ross's point of view before. It's easy to think he enjoyed being popular, but what if that wasn't the case? My head is in a spin and I have to stop this because it's not a healthy obsession. You never forget your secret first love, but when it's all in your head that's rather pathetic, isn't it?

Tegan turns off the engine, undoes her seat belt and steps out onto the grass. I still haven't moved a muscle, though. Seconds later, she swings open the passenger door.

'Come on. We have about half an hour and I know what you're like. It won't be long enough to look at everything, so we're going to have to pick up the pace.'

*

It's a gruelling couple of hours and my triceps are already killing me, as we had to really scrub the windows. The strong winds that sweep across Rosveth moor blow the dusty dirt off the fields everywhere and the recent rain made it stick like glue.

'Will Sy really be able to help me?' Tegan asks, biting her lip.

I can see it's a mounting dilemma for her and I don't want to allude to what I witnessed going on between them last night. I have to be very careful what I say here.

'He knows his stuff, Tegan. The real question is, where do you see yourself in say five, or ten years' time? Still firefighting and rolling up your sleeves? Or employing a team of people who report to you as you steer the whole thing forward profitably?'

She stops what she's doing to look at me and swallows slowly, as if there's a huge lump stuck in her throat.

'I don't know how to run it any differently than I do now. There isn't time to think about tomorrow, let alone the future.'

'That's precisely my point. When I needed help to grow my business, I sought advice from people I knew could give me answers. Sy is one of those people and he's offering his help. Grab the opportunity to spend some time with him this week and see where it goes. He's going to be here for a while and maybe the two of you can come to some sort of financial arrangement if you want to enlist his help implementing any changes.'

Having started this, I can hardly do an about turn now and try to keep them apart. I am concerned about pushing them together, obviously, but opportunities like this don't come along very often.

She's gone very quiet and when I glance her way I notice she swipes the back of her hand across her eyes.

'Hey, come on. I know how hard this is but we'll sort it out.' Throwing my arms around her shoulders, I give her a comforting hug.

'I feel lost without Pete, Kerra. Even after all this time. It's like a piece of me is missing and without it I will always feel incomplete.'

'I know. But Pete wouldn't want you giving up on anything.'

Tegan pulls away from me.

'Laughing and joking with Sy last night made me feel guilty. Like I was doing something wrong.'

Oh, how my heart constricts as I see the pain reflected in her eyes.

'We both know that's not the case, Tegan. Life goes on and you can't avoid change. It's time to accept that, my dear friend.'

Tegan gives me such a sad, acknowledging look in return that words fail me. We continue working in companionable silence until each of the units is up to her high standards. It occurs to me that burying herself in her work is probably the only way Tegan can get a grip on her life, as if it's her penance. It gives her time to sift through the thoughts running through her head and I wonder if the reality is that she's still only living one day at a time. That has to change.

As we finish up, I can feel that her spirits have lifted.

'Please tell me you charge extra for a deep clean?' I ask, as we head off on the late-afternoon staff pick-up run.

For once, she beams back at me: 'I do!'

There's hope for her yet.

14. Bonding

Heading back home, I'm achy and tired. I get Tegan to drop me off at the shop as I want to ask Mrs Moyle if she has any idea which cat food Drew buys for Ripley. She doesn't bat an eyelid and leads me straight over to the pet food section.

'She likes these pouches and those are her favourite treats. They're expensive, mind you, being dried chicken, but I get them in specially. I didn't think my other customers would pay that sort of money, I mean, three pounds for a small tube and they are light as a feather. But it isn't only Drew who buys them, so I'm not complaining.'

'Did Mr Mills ever shop in here?' I ask, as an aside, as I follow her back to the till.

'No. But then he was away a lot and it was often difficult to tell when he was home. It's funny you should mention it, though, as there was a man in here asking after him.'

'Tall, black T-shirt and trousers, with a big tattoo on his right arm going from his wrist up to his elbow?'

She walks back around the counter, tilting her head to one side for a moment.

'Yes, that's him. And the way he spoke, sounded like a thug to me.'

I couldn't have put it any more succinctly myself. 'Yes.'

'I told him I have better things to do than poke my nose into other people's business. He didn't stay long.'

'He was hanging around the cottage with another guy. It spooked me a little. I don't think he believed me when I said Mr Mills had moved on.'

'I'll get Arthur to keep an eye out. There isn't much he can't see from his chair in front of the window. Pop your number down and I'll put it in my phone. If Arthur spots anyone snooping around, we'll let you know.'

She searches around for a piece of paper and a pen, sliding it across the counter.

'Thank you, I'd appreciate that.'

Arthur is Mrs Moyle's *other half*, as she calls him. They live above the shop, which doesn't make life easy for him, as he has a back problem and walks with the aid of two sticks. He spends a lot of time sitting in his armchair, watching the world go by and I often wonder what the street looks like from up there. He wouldn't even need to crane his neck to see the cottages, albeit two large skips are now partially obscuring the view of the frontages. As the shop is on the same side of the road as Dad's property, that won't be in his line of vision, but the general coming and going of passing cars might make a vehicle stand out if it drove by on a regular basis.

'I bumped into Nettie when I was buying some paint over at Polreweek. She looks well. She didn't ask about Dad and that surprised me a little.'

Mrs Moyle doesn't stop what she's doing, or even look up.

'It strikes me as sad that she and your dad have lost touch.'

If I'm going to ask the question it's now, or never.

'Mrs Moyle, I don't suppose you know if the two of them fell out at all?'

'Can't say I heard anything about a disagreement, Kerra. Your dad retreated into his shell, we all saw that, and I think Nettie felt she had no choice but to leave him be. The trouble is, time creeps by and then it's awkward, isn't it? It's not like either of them would cross paths these days, as she doesn't have any real reason to drive this far into the village.'

The vet's surgery is one of the first properties as you enter Penvennan and it stands alone. Formerly a residential property with a large garden, it was converted into offices a long time ago. Aside from a few trees around the boundary, most of the grounds were turned into a large car park. With that, Mrs Moyle gives me a pointed look and I nod appreciatively.

'Well, I invited her to call in to Pedrevan and she promised she would. Maybe, when she does put in an appearance, we can pop across to Dad's.'

'That's a great idea, Kerra. I'm sure Nettie will be delighted to see the kennels being run like a proper business again.'

I can't help chuckling to myself as I walk back home. Something is telling me that there's more to this than Mrs Moyle is letting on. Clearly, she thinks I'm capable of handling this—as long as I can figure it out, of course.

'Miaow, miaow, miaow.' Ripley is sitting on the doorstep, calling out to me as I walk towards her.

'Hi Ripley. Look, this is for you!' I rustle the bag in front of her and as I pop the key in the door, she winds herself around my feet. 'Careful, I don't want to end up stepping on your tail.'

It seems we are now officially best friends and it is rather nice having her around. She follows me inside, but heads straight for the back door.

'You want to go out again?' I ask and she sits there, miaowing as if she's responding to me. It's comical.

As I walk across and go to unlock the door, there it is, lying prostrate on the paving slab—a dead mouse.

'Oh. Oh… good girl,' I enthuse, bending down to stroke her back and she purrs, contentedly. 'That deserves a treat, Ripley.'

Poor mouse. I mean, I know I don't want them running around inside the cottage, but I'd rather it was alive and doing what mice do. And now I have the horrible job of having to dispose of it. It doesn't feel right tossing it into the dustbin and I might end up having to bury the poor thing.

Ripley is delighted to tuck into a few cubes of her favourite dried chicken, as I pull the rubber gloves from my cleaning kit.

'Once I've attended to my little surprise, I'm going to have an early night, I think,' I inform her, but she doesn't look up. 'I'll whack a frozen pizza in the oven and then I'm going to laze out on the bed and begin drawing up a plan for my gorgeous new kitchen. Care to join me?'

It turns out that I don't have a choice, as Ripley ignores her nest downstairs and spends the night on my bed. At five in the morning a movement disturbs me. Ripley raises herself up and does a big stretch, arching her back and then sneezing once. And then she starts talking to me. I knew Bengals were vocal cats, but Ripley really does hold some rather intense conversations. It was obvious there was no way she was going to be ignored and once I was awake, there was little point in going back to bed.

Ding-dong, ding-dong.

I quickly run the roller over the last third of the top of the pine cabinet, unwilling to stop mid-section.

Ding-dong. Ding-dong.

'I'm coming,' I yell out, ripping off the disposable gloves and striding forward.

'Morning, Mrs. Sorry to bother you, but as there's no one in next door I thought it best to mention there's a ladder leaning up against your fence. Down in the bottom corner. It wasn't there yesterday when I dropped off my first load.'

His frown is concerning.

'Really? Let me grab a key and perhaps you can show me?'

I'm thrown and I glance around, checking to see where Ripley is before remembering she went back upstairs an hour ago and hasn't resurfaced. I lock the front door and hurry to catch up with the driver.

'I'm Kerra, by the way.'

'Mark,' he says, with an acknowledging nod. 'I checked around and the shed looks okay, and as far as I can see, no one's tampered with the windows or doors. All the pipes are still there. You'd have heard a fair bit of noise if anyone was trying to steal something, but it struck me as odd. Has anyone else been here?'

As we head around the side and I follow him down the

path, I'm dismayed to spot a ladder leaning up against the fence, as he said.

'Not as far as I know. I was out until late afternoon and then I spent the evening upstairs working in the front bedroom; I didn't hear a thing. When I left in the morning though, your boss was still here. Would he have had any reason to check out my garden and maybe forgot to put it away afterwards?'

Mark shrugs his shoulders. 'Can't see why. That big patch at the bottom is thick with brambles and woody shrubs. He'd be more likely to want to inspect the back of the cottage where the extension is going, and he could just have walked around the side of your place. I'm pretty sure he wouldn't leave a ladder out in plain view, anyway.'

Alarm bells start to ring inside my head.

'Well, thanks for alerting me, Mark. Fortunately, my neighbour is due back this evening.'

'I suppose some kids could have climbed over the fence to see what's going on. No harm done, but I'll move that ladder now and lay it down behind the shed, I think. At least it will be out of sight.'

'Appreciated, thanks.'

'It's a nice spot here. And quiet, too. I'll be making two trips today and I won't forget to lock those gates.'

We walk back around to the front and he drops the tailgate of the lorry as I let myself in. Ripley is sitting by the back door and immediately begins talking to me. I open the door, thinking she wants to go out, but she doesn't move, just sits there unblinking.

'I'm not good with cat-speak. Sorry, was it because I left

without saying goodbye? You weren't around, but I'm back now.'

Traipsing into the sitting room, I don another pair of disposable gloves and pick up the roller once more. Minutes later my phone pings and I immediately grab it without thinking, having to quickly wipe off a big smear of white undercoat from the side. Sy was giving Dad a hand this morning, then Tegan was picking him up to take him back to her place for lunch. Well, a working lunch, as they put it. I hope nothing has gone wrong but staring down I see the text is from Drew.

> Sorry, Kerra, but I can't get back until mid-afternoon tomorrow at the earliest. I'm taking Felicity to the doctor's first thing as it looks like she has a chest infection. I'm just a phone call away if you need me and thanks so much for sorting out Ripley. Can't believe I forgot about her, but I know she's in good hands.

I exhale sharply. It would have been a real comfort with Drew back tonight, after the ladder incident.

'Guess it's going to be just us again, Ripley.'

She's not overly impressed with the bare concrete floor and has now curled up on her makeshift nest.

'Never mind, one more night and Drew will be home and things will be back to normal. Well, the new normal for a while, which is going to mean lots of noise, builders and mess. Anyway, we can look after each other, can't we? It might be a long night, though, if there's as much as a leaf rustling out there.'

With the undercoat finished, I decide to stop for a cup of coffee while it's drying. Gazing out over the garden as I wait for the kettle to boil, it strikes me that it isn't that easy for someone to climb over the back fence. For a start, it's a good two metres high and there's trellis work on top with a variety of climbers woven through it; and it extends along the entire length of both gardens. The other side is quite a drop, as the bank slopes down to a small stream. Besides, if someone wants to steal the materials they're delivering next door, there isn't much I can do about it. It wouldn't be worth putting myself, or Ripley, at risk. I push all thoughts aside and let the caffeine hit act as a pick-me-up.

Three hours and two top-coats later, I stand back and gaze at my upcycled cabinet with a real sense of pride.

'What do you think, Ripley?' I ask. She looks up at me and yawns lazily. Then she puts her head back down on her paws for a moment before it shoots back up, ears perked and twitching.

Ding-dong. Ding-dong.

Really? Again? What now?

Swinging open the door with a decidedly resigned look on my face, my first thought is that I don't need to be told every single time Mark drops something off. But the face staring back at me isn't Mark's. It's Ross I see standing before me.

'Oh. Hi.'

'Morning, Kerra,' he coughs to clear his throat, 'Mark rang in to say we might have a problem.'

'A problem?' I realise I'm peering at him around the edge of the door and I stand back, opening it a little wider.

'We've had a few incidents recently with thieves following

our more remote deliveries. We don't expect it in residential areas, but with these two cottages backing onto woodland, Mark suggested I call in and check it out for myself.'

He waves the key to the side gates in front of me, rather awkwardly.

'Great.' My throat has gone dry and all I can think about is how my hair looks. Is he asking for my permission? I thought that was the whole point of having a key and I look at him rather blankly.

'I'd um... appreciate it if you had a moment to show me the exact position of the ladder.'

'Is that important?' I ask, trying my best not to look flustered as those gorgeous eyes stare into mine. I feel like I'm sinking fast.

Ross takes a deep breath and squares his shoulders as he looks at me, wrinkling his brow.

'We take the matter of security very seriously, Kerra. This is our problem and I'm here to make sure we do everything we can not to inconvenience you as the homeowner. Drew is still away, I gather?'

Of course. Ross is simply exercising due diligence and he's going to wonder why I'm being a tad unhelpful.

'Yes. I was expecting him back tonight, but he's been delayed. I'm painting,' I reply, feeling the need to explain myself.

Ross gives me an apologetic look and peers over my shoulder.

'I can wait if you're in the middle of something,' he offers. 'I'm just making sure my guys have everything they need and it's all in order for them to begin work tomorrow bright and early.'

'Um... give me a few seconds. I'll just get rid of these,' I say, holding up my paint-splattered gloves rather lamely and with that I shut the door.

Leaning back against it, I groan inwardly. *Pull yourself together, Kerra.* Yanking off the gloves, I roll them into a ball and take a moment to compose myself.

'Ripley, if you need to go out, now's your chance, as this might take a few minutes.' I head through to open the back door and she looks at me, then slowly eases herself up. After a big stretch she saunters out through to the patio as if time is of no importance. Turning the key in the lock, I pull the scrunchy off my ponytail. Running my hands through my hair to catch any strays, I redo it. A couple of strides, two deep breaths and I'm ready to face Ross.

'Sorry about that,' I say brightly, as I fling open the front door once more. 'I'm looking after Ripley while Drew is away. I had to shoo her out the back door as I don't really like her following me out to the front in case she runs into the road. It's difficult with no cat flap.'

He relaxes his initial look of bewilderment, as I slam the door behind me.

'You think this might be linked to other thefts?'

Ross shrugs his shoulders. 'Maybe, but I won't lie, it is odd; Mark mentioned it in passing and I thought it best to check it out right away. Thefts tend to occur in spates, when a gang infiltrate an area. There's always a market for building supplies and it's often hard to determine what might be nicked, as opposed to what is surplus to requirements. Smaller builders and DIYers often sell off leftover stuff.'

He unlocks the gates and we walk through to the rear of Tigry Cottage. There is quite a stack of various supplies now, mostly long lengths of terracotta-coloured pipes and two round, black plastic barrels with connectors coming off them. There are also two large plastic bags full of pipe fittings and a huge, open bag filled to the brim with chippings.

'We have a good team, so don't be anxious about tomorrow. Besides, I'll be keeping a close eye on everything.' Ross is attempting to put me at ease. Am I a tad disappointed it's not merely an excuse to see me again? Of course not, that would be ridiculous. Well, at least thinking I'm stressing over uninvited visitors is some sort of explanation for my erratic behaviour just now.

'Thanks, Ross. The ladder was about here, as if someone had been peering over into my garden.'

Looking down at the grass beneath our feet, Ross swipes the toe of his boot over a depression in the ground and then another similar one, close by.

He frowns.

'What are you thinking?' I ask, worried that he isn't just dismissing this lightly.

Scanning around, he's deep in thought. 'Well, there's no way anyone could pass anything at all over the fence to the rear of your property because the shrubs are too dense. Even on this side, the height and the steep drop the other side rules that out. With the tall trees in the gardens of the detached houses either side of the cottages, it does mean you aren't overlooked. If someone was scouting around looking for the easiest way out, maybe across the rear of your property makes sense.'

'Surely, all they need to do is cut the padlock on Drew's gates, though? It's the most direct route.'

Ross isn't really listening as he walks around, inspecting the grass beneath his feet.

'It's trampled here, probably by more than one person,' he mutters, almost to himself. 'Mark wouldn't have had a reason to walk this far down.'

It's true. The last ten metres of Drew's garden is given over to a vegetable patch and a herb garden.

'It might be our footprints, when we were standing here earlier and Mark came back afterwards to move the ladder,' I confirm.

'Hmm. Some of this was made by more than one person wearing lighter footwear though; look at how the grass is really flattened in this area, but none of it is churned up. I can clearly see where Mark's boots have trodden.' I hate to agree, but he has a point.

I follow Ross as he walks back up to the gates and stands for a moment, scanning around.

'I suspect that the proximity to the shop would make anyone nervous about using this as an exit to carry things out to a waiting vehicle.'

'Even when the shop is shut, there's often a light on in the flat above until quite late and the drive is in range of the streetlight over there, too,' I add.

'I'm afraid your side access is the best bet. It's that bit further away and late at night, unless the light in your sitting room or the front bedroom is on, it's pretty much in shadow I would have thought.'

Now I'm concerned.

Ross shuts the gates and re-attaches the padlock.

'Let's take a quick look around the side of your place.'

As we walk up the path and pass in front of the sitting

room window, I see that Ross isn't happy. Ripley suddenly appears, eager to make her presence known and I stoop to smooth her back.

'It's okay, Ripley. We're just checking everything out.'

Ross starts laughing as Ripley begins one of her little conversations.

'She doesn't like strangers,' I explain, 'it unsettles her.'

'None of us like strangers if they're not invited,' Ross replies, raising an eyebrow as he looks at me meaningfully. 'Look, I'd be much happier if there was a lockable gate here. The laurel hedge running along the side boundary is pretty much impenetrable, but anyone could wander around to the back. For someone on their own, that's not good. And, if I'm being honest, I'd have a security light here, on this corner as a deterrent.'

'I hadn't given it much thought, I will be honest.' Then I think of the two guys who were here looking for Mr Mills. Ross is right.

'Is that something your guys could sort out for me?'

Ripley is now sitting on the path, watching us as if she's following our conversation.

'Of course. I hope you don't think I'm poking my nose in, but if I lived here this would be one of the first things I'd address. I'll ring the police station when I get back and let them know we think someone's been snooping around.' He yanks out his wallet, pulling out a business card. 'Any problems tonight, give me a call. My mobile number is on the back. I'm about a twenty-five-minute drive away.'

As I reach out to take it from him our eyes linger on each other for a few, brief moments. I should invite him in for a coffee but the thought of standing around making polite conversation is too much for me. I can't trust myself to stay calm and in control. That thought is as tantalising as it is embarrassing.

'Thank you, Ross,' I reply, my voice steady and reflecting my gratitude.

'My pleasure, Kerra. I'll get someone onto this little job as quickly as possible. I ought to take your number, too, in case I need to contact you. I left my phone in the car, so would you mind writing it down for me?'

There it is again, that nervous little twitch at the side of his eye as he smiles at me.

I go back inside, searching around in my handbag for a pen, but can't find one. Instead I grab one of my old business cards and take it back to Ross, who is patiently waiting on the doorstep.

'Great,' he pops it into his back pocket, and we stand looking at each other. I hesitate for a split second over whether, or not, to invite him in and briefly wonder if that's what he was hoping I'd do. Ross interprets the silence as a hint to head off. He throws a cheery, 'See you soon,' over his shoulder, leaving me to suppress an excited little shudder. If I was the sort to throw caution to the wind... if only.

15. Night Terrors

'I'm in trouble.'

Sy stops, mid-throw, in his attempt to skim a flat pebble across the water for what feels like the hundredth time.

'Now that's a worrying look I don't recall having seen before.'

As I lower my eyes, my body language is the only response he needs. I stand here watching him without even registering the beauty around me, or his growing annoyance at his lack of skill, which—under normal circumstances—would have me laughing out loud.

'Well? Are you going to just stand there gazing out over the water, or are you going to tell me what's on your mind?'

I shrug my shoulders. Sy turns to throw the last stone in the little pile we'd gathered, with determination. Like the others, it bounces once on the rippling surface beyond the foamy crests of the incoming waves and then promptly sinks without trace.

'Come on, let's walk and talk. I'm fed up of making a fool of myself, even though there aren't many people around.'

That raises a smile. I turn to cast my eyes along the full length of Penvennan Cove, and see he's right. There are merely a handful of people out for a stroll and I know I can speak freely. The one person in the whole wide world I can be totally frank with right now is Sy. If I don't share this, he'll pick up on it at some point, anyway and at least he's neutral.

We saunter along and I can feel his eyes on me, watching and waiting.

'There's a certain someone, from my past... someone who has this er... *effect* on me.'

That sounds pathetic.

'What sort of effect?'

'I spend more time gazing at him, than I do listening to what he's saying,' I admit, as I burst out laughing. 'Oh, that makes me sound so shallow!'

'And that's so not like you. What has gotten into you, Kerra?'

I thought Sy would see the funny side of this, but he doesn't sound at all amused. He sounds shocked.

'Look, I can't help it. It's not by choice. It's just that years ago, you know what it's like. First crush and all that. Admiring someone from afar, then they sort of worm their way into your head and become that impossible dream. The one where everything is perfect, which—of course—bears no resemblance at all to reality.'

'Are we talking fantasy here?' Now he sounds scandalised.

'No! He's just... there's something about him that makes me feel nervous. Unsure of myself. Like turning back the clock and suddenly I'm that painfully shy, young girl all over again.'

'That sounds suspiciously like infatuation to me. Is this unrequited love, or is it purely a physical thing?'

Now I'm shocked that Sy should interpret it that way. It sounds harsh. But the truth is that I don't know what it is, only that it's unnerving.

'It makes me feel uncomfortable around him, that's all, and the chances are that he's going to be around a fair bit. How do I handle it? It all feels rather silly.'

Now Sy starts to laugh, his eyes opening wide. He stares at me in disbelief as we draw to a halt. 'I've witnessed you cutting someone down with one purposeful, withering glance. This is hilarious! It's physical and you can't bring yourself to admit that. The number of times you've lectured me about lust versus love, well, this is karma. Perhaps now you'll understand that you have to fancy someone before you can fall in love with them. Love is the thing that grows over time, lust is the thing that tempts you to hang around long enough to find out if it has a chance of going anywhere.'

I stare at him, narrowing my eyes as I consider whether he could be right. We've wandered back up the beach to the long, stone wall that separates it from the car park. I hoist myself up and sit with my legs dangling. Above me the seagulls are wheeling and circling, their raucous squeals like a constant backing track.

Sy settles down next to me.

'You're wrong. I know the difference, of course I do. I've had lots of relationships.'

'And none of them lasted,' he points out.

'I could say the same for you.'

He shrugs his shoulders. 'We're a sad pair, aren't we? But at least I keep trying whereas you, well, you've given up. Until now, it seems.'

'No. This is just nerves, and stupid memories raking up childish dreams of falling in love at first sight and living happily ever after. However, I can't say I know many people who are living the fairytale, so that tells me everything I need to know.'

We're silent for a while, listening to the gentle lapping of the water which is low on the beach.

'Well, I wouldn't dismiss it out of hand, Kerra,' he replies soberly. 'Not much rattles you and clearly, this is posing a real problem. Whoever it is, he's just a guy, like any other and before long he'll say or do something to make you see him in another light. I doubt any man alive could live up to your expectations.'

Now I'm offended. 'I'm not prepared to settle. I've experienced the spongers, the chauvinists, the guys who think you are their property. You name it, I have the T-shirt and that's why no one has lasted the course.'

'Yet.'

'Enough of this, how did it go with Tegan?'

Sy isn't prepared for that and the look on his face quickly changes. He squints, staring out to sea and trying to focus on a boat way in the distance.

'We covered quite a bit,' he replies, sounding very business-like. 'She gave me a quick overview but I'm going to accompany her on her rounds on Tuesday morning and Saturday afternoon. I promised your dad I'd help him reorganise some of the furniture in the house tomorrow and wash through the kennels.'

My jaw drops.

'Dad moving furniture around—I don't believe it.'

'Over breakfast, we got talking about the work you're

having done here. That led to Eddie giving me the tour and it's a big house. I asked if he had any plans for it and he scratched his head and then, you know what I'm like, I threw in a couple of suggestions.'

Sy is one of those guys who likes everything just so and he has annoyed me in the past by re-arranging some of the items in my apartment when my back was turned. But that's why he's so good at his job, because it's all about attention to detail and I always forgave him.

'Well, that's not quite what I was expecting, but well done you. It's a topic I daren't mention. How did the walk go this morning?'

Sy shakes his head. 'I know the dog-walking idea is a great way to help out and it's supposed to relax me at the same time, but they're crazy things. They jump around all the time and get all muddy. I have no idea what they're thinking and the big one, Rufus? He's nuts.'

'And adorable. His owner is elderly, so Rufus is a frequent visitor when he needs to run off a little steam. He's a dog who loves everyone. Just relax a little, Sy, and enjoy it.'

Sy tilts his head in my direction.

'Even Ripley avoids me; she ran off as soon as I arrived. Animals just aren't my thing.'

'Now that's not true, she's just standing guard at the moment. We think someone climbed over Drew's gate yesterday to look around, possibly with a view to stealing some of the supplies the builders have already dropped off.'

He shoots me a pinched look.

'Drew's back tonight, though, isn't he?'

'No, it's tomorrow now.'

'You're not seriously going to sleep there alone tonight, are you?'

'I'll have Ripley for company. There isn't enough material of value there to warrant the risk and I'm sure it will be fine. I am going to have a side gate installed and a security light, though, at the front.'

'It's a pity you can't just sleep over at your Dad's.'

'That wouldn't be fair on Ripley, as I can't lock her out and I can't exactly lock her in, either. I seriously doubt she's ever set foot in the kennels before and the last thing she needs now is more stress.'

'I could come and sleep over, tonight.'

'In what is now a junk room piled high with furniture?' I laugh. 'If they do come back, I promise not to rush out and try to tackle them. It's not worth getting hurt for the sake of replacing a few lengths of plastic pipe.'

'Well, ring me if you change your mind.'

'I have the builder's number as well, so I'm covered—technically the stuff belongs to them, after all. Stop worrying about me. I will say, you are looking a lot more relaxed than when you first arrived.'

He screws up his face a little. 'Hmm. It's not quite as bad as I thought it would be, here in the wilds but I need to think about longer-term options. I can't wait to get down to the detail with Tegan, I will be honest—my mind is going off in all directions. Your dad isn't quite so easy, and I can see why you're worried. There is no way he could cope by himself if the kennels were full. The problem is that he's convinced he can.'

'I know. I just needed confirmation that I wasn't simply

being overprotective. And I'm not sure what I'm going to do about it.'

'From what I've seen, Kerra, you have no choice but to wait until he asks for your help. I can see now where you get that fierce determination of yours from and while it's an admirable quality, enviable even, it's not easy to battle against.'

'My mum knew exactly how to deal with it and I fear that's what he needs. Someone he'll listen to without being on the defensive.'

Hearing Sy agreeing with me is worrying; I was so hoping he'd say I was being paranoid.

'I could sit here all day just listening to the sounds of the birds and the water. There's something so relaxing about it and yet it's noisy in its own way. You must have missed this, at times.'

I close my eyes for a few brief moments.

'The truth is that as a child I took it for granted. No matter what the weather, we always came to the beach to marvel at the wonders of nature; whether it was sunny and happy, or stormy and angry, this was my playground.'

'And now?'

'Now it feels comforting. Every little sound invokes a memory, though, and there are moments when it's bitter-sweet.'

It's just after 2 a.m. when my phone kicks into life, waking both Ripley and me. I don't recognise the number and I hesitate for a moment before answering it.

'Hello?' Even whispering, it sounds loud in the encompassing darkness.

'Kerra, it's Mrs Moyle. Arthur's been up all night and he woke me up to say he thinks he saw someone in your front garden. He wasn't sure and we've both been peering out the window for the last five minutes, watching. I'm wondering if it was a shadow from the laurel bushes waving about, as the wind has picked up a little. I didn't know what to do. Do you think it's worth calling the police? I mean, Arthur's in a lot of pain and I'm not saying he's imagining it, but the painkillers he's taking are strong.' She sounds rather agitated and I do my best to remain calm.

'Thank you for the heads up, but I'll take it from here. Ross Treloar gave me his number in case there was a problem. I'll call him right away, so please don't worry. There isn't very much to steal, and it probably was just the bushes waving about and casting a shadow.' I try my best to diffuse her concern, but fear sends a chill running through me.

I put Ross's number on speed dial earlier, hoping I wouldn't have to use it and when he answers he sounds sleepy.

'I think there's someone in the garden.'

His response is immediate and instantly he's wide awake.

'I'm close by. Do not look out of the window.'

What do I do? I jump straight out of bed, pull on some jeans and a jumper, then I crouch down as I enter the second bedroom. Gingerly raising my head up an inch or two above the windowsill, I peer out. Ripley unexpectedly leaps up next to me, making me jump and I fall back.

'Ripley, down here, there's a good girl,' I whisper, clicking my fingers to attract her attention but it's obvious she has spotted something. She moves her head, her ears perk up and the fur on her back begins to stand up. Then a low growling sound starts to rumble through her. Whether that can be heard from outside I don't know, but her silhouette is unmistakable and she's on the defence. If she's going to draw attention this is probably going to be my best chance of catching a glimpse of whoever it is, as moonlight bathes the far end of the garden.

Working my way across to the side of the window on my hands and knees, I ease myself up in line with the edge of the curtain for cover. Taking a deep breath and hoping there is nothing to see other than another animal maybe, I peer out. Ripley is now pacing back and forth on the windowsill, becoming even more vocal and the growl has turned into a drawn-out whining sound. It's beginning to set my nerves on edge as her agitation grows. And then I see the shape, crouched down in the bushes about halfway down the garden. I immediately duck back out of sight, my heart now literally pounding in my chest.

We're safe, I keep repeating over and over in my head, thinking there never was a time I felt threatened inside my own home when I lived in London. This is crazy and unbelievable. That horrible sense of vulnerability doesn't sit well with me. They're probably disappointed there isn't enough of a haul next door to warrant taking a risk. However, I'm scared to go downstairs to investigate further, which is silly. The doors are locked, and if they've been keeping watch they'll have seen lights going on and off, whereas next door has been in total darkness all evening. I'd hear the sound of breaking glass, anyway, if they tried to force an entry. *Come on, Kerra, you're letting your imagination get the better of you. Pinching something from a garden is one thing, but robbing a house is another. Besides, Ross is on his way.*

Suddenly, Ripley leaps down onto the floor with a heavy thud and races out of the room. I can't even keep up with her. Rushing back into my bedroom, I grab the tube of treats.

'Ripley, Ripley, treats!' I whisper, keeping my voice as low as possible. Rattling the tube as I walk, I hope she'll come running back to me, but she doesn't. I suspect she's staring out through the pane of glass in the back door and if I walk through into the sitting room, the person in the garden will probably be able to see me.

Creeping around the edge of the room, I hope I blend into the shadows. Thankfully, only the kitchen door is open, and I lean my back up against the narrow section of wall next to the dining room door.

'Ripley,' I hiss, 'treats.'

She emits a loud, high-pitched miaow in between a low, rumbling growl as she paces back and forth.

I pop the lid off the tube—the pop alone was enough to bring her running earlier on. Now, she's too intent on standing guard to take any notice of what I'm doing. Desperately ramming the lid back on, I pop it off in quick succession several times. Finally, she comes to investigate.

Now I'm shivering, although it isn't really cold in here, but at least Ripley's next to me, head bent as she tucks into the small pile of treats. Even so, every few seconds she turns her head nervously, to look over her shoulder. I tip a pile of the cubes into my hand and lay one in front of her every time she looks like she's going to turn tail and run off again.

Smoothing her coat to calm her, even the texture of her fur is different as it refuses to lay flat. She's on edge, in fight or flight mode. It feels like forever as I sit here, determined not to let her out of my sight when, finally, there's a tap on the door and as I look up, Ross's face appears at the sitting room window.

Jumping up, I rush to the front door. A sense of relief floods through me as I fling it open but Ripley is spooked and clatters up the stairs as if she's being chased.

'Thank you for coming, thank you!' I blurt out and Ross steps forward, placing his arms around me reassuringly. Pushing the door shut with his foot, he guides me back into the sitting room as my body begins to shake.

'It's all clear now. You're safe, Kerra.' He's talking at normal volume, but his words seem to shatter the silence. I step away from him, glancing around the darkened room and my eyes are immediately drawn out through to the moonlit garden.

'It's all clear?' I felt his heart pounding in his chest just then and I realise he's a little breathless. We're both in shock.

'Is there any chance of a strong coffee? I think we've earned one.'

'Of course. Sorry. I've been crouched on the floor for what seems like an eternity. I'll admit I was terrified and poor Ripley, her fur was standing on end. She's been extremely vocal.'

'Well, my presence succeeded in scaring them off. There were two of them, but they split up and ran off in different directions. I have no idea where they were parked. How did you know someone was out there?'

I stare at Ross blankly, as I struggle to take it all in. My head is now reeling, knowing there were two of them. It's not simply a coincidence.

'Mrs Moyle rang me. Arthur was having a bad night and happened to be looking out the window. He thought he saw someone loitering by the bushes. You managed to get here very quickly, Ross. It felt like forever, but it must have been what, less than fifteen minutes, tops?'

He follows me upstairs into the temporary kitchen. What I spotted before I turned away from him was a look of hesitancy on his face.

'I rang the station in Polreweek and talked to the sergeant. Shortly afterwards Clem rang me.'

'It wouldn't have been much of a stretch of the imagination to guess that our former school mate would end up being a policeman when he grew up, would it?' I reflect. Even at a young age Clem was a people-watcher, always standing back to see how things played out rather than rushing in.

'I knew something was up, because he wasn't even on duty. I don't want to worry you unduly, but he asked if I knew a former tenant here, a Mr Mills. That's the first time I'd even heard that name mentioned. What exactly do you know about him?'

Well, that's not quite the response I was expecting.

'Not much.' That's the truth, as the letting agency handled everything for me. 'But how did you get here so quickly?'

He shifts his weight rather awkwardly from one foot to the other.

'I've been parked up in the lay-by opposite since about

eleven, keeping watch. Annoyingly, I fell asleep and your call woke me with a start. I headed for the lane a bit further along and approached the garden from the back, as I knew they wouldn't expect that. It's not an easy route but I was able to climb up, high enough to get a look. Neither of them was showing any interest at all in what was in the garden of Tigry Cottage. I made a noise and that's when they scattered.'

I pause, kettle in hand, and Ross leans forward to take it from me.

'I'll finish this off. You go and sit down. Um... *is* there somewhere to sit down?'

'The bedroom at the front. I'll check on Ripley. She's probably scared witless at the moment, poor thing, as she couldn't understand why I wouldn't let her out.'

'It seems that Drew has one feisty little feline there, who thinks she is a guard dog,' Ross replies with a nervous little chuckle in his voice. The adrenaline is probably still pumping around his body too, I realise, as I wrap my arms around myself in an effort to stop them from trembling.

16. Waiting for the World to Wake Up

If anyone had told me I'd end up out here on the patio, with Ross sitting next to me and waiting for dawn to break, I wouldn't have believed them. After lying on the bed drinking coffee and talking about the building work as a distraction, it was clear neither of us was going to get any sleep. I grabbed some throws and here we are, passing a couple of hours until Ross's foreman, Will, arrives.

As the dark, menacing shadows of the night gradually fade, so too does that intense feeling of danger. Once the birds begin to stir, it isn't long before a much calmer Ripley joins us.

'You're a beauty, aren't you?' Ross mutters, reaching down as she saunters straight up to him for a smooth. She twists and turns in a zigzag pattern after each stroke, wanting more.

'I'm going to miss my little shadow when Drew gets back,' I tell him. 'I don't know what I would have done without her to distract me.'

A little posse of birds swoop across the garden, settling noisily in the bushes at the bottom and begin squabbling.

Maybe they're fighting over some juicy insects, or just a favourite place to perch. Ripley stops, head erect, and seconds later races off to cause yet another disturbance, as they scatter noisily.

'You didn't finish telling me what Clem said when you went to the station.'

Ross eases himself back into his seat, half-turning to face me as I stifle a yawn.

'He couldn't divulge any specific information, but it seems Mr Mills is *of interest* to them.' He raises his eyebrows, eyes widening as his tone changes and he tries to mimic Clem's voice. 'His exact words were "We are pursuing a line of enquiry" and he made it sound like something you'd hear on one of those crime watch programmes.' It makes me laugh.

'You could simply have phoned to tell me that and been done with it. Instead you came back to stand guard. I'm terribly grateful you did, Ross, but why? Would you really have slept in the van all night long?'

'We've known each other since we were little kids, Kerra. Of course I'm going to look out for you in a situation like this and, believe it or not, Clem is usually a man of even fewer words. He said enough for me to understand that he didn't think it was a great idea for you to be here on your own. Especially overnight, without any additional security measures in place and with no one home next door.

'The guy I've arranged to fit your gate will pop in some time this morning, but the earliest I can get an electrician here is tomorrow. When he's installed the light with the motion sensor at the front, I thought I'd have him rig up some temporary ones across the back of both properties.

They'll all come on automatically if anything moves within range of them, which includes animals of course, but it is a good security measure. There's no point in making it easy for a couple of chancers. If you're asleep it shouldn't wake you, but it would send them running for cover. What do you think?'

'Well, I'm extremely grateful to Clem as he needn't have done that, and to you, Ross, for being willing to sacrifice a night's sleep in a comfy bed.'

He gives me an artful smile. 'I can sleep anywhere, so it's not a big deal, really. I was lying in bed thinking about you...' There's a slight pause. 'I mean, your situation. The more I thought about what Clem had said, the more I realised there was a real underlying concern in his tone.'

Ross is embarrassed now, because was that a telling little slip there? Would he really have lain there thinking of me? Little goose bumps begin to creep down my back as a thrill runs through my veins, triggering all sorts of reactions. I never forgot Ross, but is it possible Ross never forgot me? Really? He never gave me any reason to have any hope at all.

My legs begin to feel a little shaky; it's probably tiredness, so I nod, marvelling at the fact that I'm suddenly seeing Ross in an entirely different light. Gone is that carefree, slightly overconfident youth; sitting next to me is a man who steps up and takes charge. I like that. But old memories run through my mind on action replay. As a girl blossoming into a young woman, I'd needed to feel I was attractive. Ross wasn't the only one who didn't quite fit in at school and I guess I was feeling left out. I wanted him to notice me in the way my friends made him notice them. I knew he was alone in the empty classroom that day, because I'd been watching him. When I breezed through the door and drew to a halt, he'd frozen for a moment, unable to take his eyes off me. Retrieving his sports bag he'd looked guilty, as if I'd caught him doing something he shouldn't have been doing.

'Hey, Kerra,' he'd said.

'Hi Ross.' My voice had sounded confident that day, although it was just bravado. Panicking when I realised I had no reason at all to be in there, I'd yanked the bag off my shoulder and reached inside to pull out an exercise book. Heading in his direction to place it on the teacher's desk, as he walked past me I turned. Our faces were mere inches away from each other when he came to an abrupt halt.

I'd held my breath for a second and he'd leant in to kiss me. Except that he hadn't—it was all in my head.

It was only ever in my head.

Ross had simply turned to look at me in a way he'd never done before, hesitating and then I ran off, realising it wasn't going to happen. Disappointment had flooded through me, closely followed by a sense of confusion. He'd wanted to kiss me, almost as badly as I'd wanted to feel his lips on mine. The way he looked at me with such longing, left me in no doubt about that at all. He hadn't been toying with me though, he just wasn't sure what my reaction would be. It's funny how that never was the way I chose to remember it—until now. A part of me needed to believe my version because love hurts. And the pain is agonisingly real.

'You're a good man, Ross.' The words that just popped into my head slip between my lips with a softness I wasn't expecting, and I can see he's a little surprised. He looks away, staring down at his feet for a few moments.

'I um... always felt I made a bit of a fool of myself whenever I was around you, Kerra. We were young, of course, and you were the serious one in the group we hung around with. I could never quite work out what you were thinking.'

'I was shy, that's all, and desperate to hide that fact. It was just easier to say nothing, than speak out and draw attention to myself. I saw things differently from most of the people around me and I never knew why. Some things seemed so pointless, when there was so much to learn.'

Glancing at him, I see a little twinkle of amusement reflected back at me.

'I wish I'd known that back then,' he replies. 'I mistook shy for disapproving and I was a bit of a hothead at times, I knew that. With my father constantly criticising me I always felt I had something to prove. Well, not to everyone, just people I admired. What I saw in you was that you dared to be different.'

I flash him a look of amusement. 'You mean I wasn't too worried about being popular?'

He laughs. 'Maybe you were more popular than you realised.' Ross raises his eyebrows and I feel my cheeks growing hotter by the second.

'I'm sorry that life has been tough for you these past few years.' Why is it that when you're struggling for words you end up saying the exact thing you didn't want to bring up?

He looks down at the floor, drawing his feet back and adjusting his position.

'You heard about the divorce, then.'

I tilt my head, unable to hide how crushed I feel for what he's been through and not wanting him to see that. It occurs to me that for virtually the whole of his life people have taken note of everything he's done, mainly because he's one of those interesting people. The sort who attract attention without having to try. At least I managed to get away from the spotlight for a while and that has allowed me to gain a sense of perspective. When you're different in some way, you stand out—whether you want to or not. It throws up a range of emotions that some people simply can't understand. All you long for is to blend in and yet you end up being the focus of attention because people are naturally curious. And some are judgemental, maybe even a little jealous. Others can be downright mean.

'It was mentioned in passing, that's all.' I can't bring myself to admit that I asked Tegan about him, but I also don't want to imply it's still a hot topic of conversation.

'It, um, was one big mess. In all honesty, I was a mess for a while there, too. It was hard to see the effect it had on my parents when their son's failing marriage turned into the talking point of every little huddle. They kept their heads held high, but it was a front and it knocked them. Mixing in the same circle as Bailey's parents, people took sides and, well, the truth has more than one version, I've come to discover. Several, depending on who you hear it from.'

His words sound hollow, almost devoid of emotion—he feels he messed up and he's disappointed in himself. I can't even read the expression on Ross's face right now and I remain still, not wishing to distract him.

'There were a few people who believed I had it coming. People who thought I'd had everything handed to me on a plate from day one, being the boss's son and all that. You know, moving away from the village and living in a big house. And my father always driving a flash car. A lot of it was just for show. I didn't have a choice in the matter, and you know he never made life easy for me. When he and my mother flew off to start their retirement in Spain, his parting words were harsh. He said, "Let's see if you can avoid messing this up" and I realised nothing I do will ever be good enough for him. At least now I don't have him constantly looking over my shoulder anymore. When I moved to Trehoweth it was the right thing to do. It's far enough away, but not too far if you know what I mean. Outside of work my life is now quiet, devoid of any drama, let's say.'

A stab of pain shoots through my heart as I reach out to touch his arm.

'One thing that running away to London taught me, Ross, is that even when you disappear among a city full of strangers, it doesn't change how you feel deep down inside. It isn't visibility, or the lack of it, that shapes us. It's one's life experiences and the same applies to failure and success. If you are ambitious and driven, there is no such thing as a quiet life.'

Ross raises his head and glances my way, nodding his head in agreement.

'I think you're right. Maybe I'm hiding, but it works for me. But you are a success. Even Treloar's is on The Happy Hive website. Those reviews really matter.'

'How did you find out?'

'The business card you gave me with your email address on the back was a bit of a giveaway.'

I smile, fleetingly.

'Now that I'm home for good if people knew I was behind that, to some it would instantly become a barrier. It would make me the odd one out, all over again. Ironically, if I'd failed then I'd be on the receiving end of a lot of sympathy, which is often easier to handle. Having all this work done to the cottage is going to get people asking questions, but that doesn't mean I have to justify myself, or how I'm able to afford it. I'm finally accepting that it doesn't matter what outsiders think, only those close to me.'

Ross pauses for a moment, deep in thought.

'Thanks for listening Kerra, and for understanding. It's good to be able to catch up after all this time. Another half an hour and I'll ring Will to let him know I'm here with the key. I'll hang around for a bit as I'm going to arrange for a lockable container to be delivered, but I need to give Drew a call about that, first.'

'And then you'll head for home and get some sleep?'

He gives a throaty laugh.

'Maybe. And you?'

'I'll be ferrying endless trays of tea back and forth; you know what builders are like. You have to keep them sweet. But in between I'll take myself upstairs and lie on the bed for a while. I suspect my little companion will be with me. All this excitement is a lot to handle.'

'It's not the best start, but hopefully it will be onwards and upwards from here.'

Actually, aside from feeling petrified at one point, it's been a memorable night in more ways than one. And surprising.

17. The Good, the Bad and the Simply Beautiful

'Morning, Kerra. Ross has just filled me in on what's been going on. I wanted to check that you really are okay. I was shocked, so I can only imagine what it must have been like for you being there on your own.'

'I'm fine. Besides, I had Ripley and Ross, of course.' I'm trying to make light of it as I don't want Drew feeling guilty for not being around.

'I didn't realise you and Ross were old friends. You never mentioned that.'

'We went to school together, that's all. A group of us caught the same bus there and back every day. Ross wasn't always with us as sometimes his father would give him a lift. During the school holidays we'd often meet up and head down to the cove. It was just hanging out, as kids tend to do.'

'Well, it was good of him to step up and I'm glad he took Clem's words seriously. The extra security measures should do the trick but, heck, I wish I'd been there. I'm just relieved to know that he was looking out for you.'

'Me, too,' I reply, trying to keep it light. 'How's Felicity doing?'

'She had a rough night again, but the tablets should start to kick in soon. I'm just doing a quick supermarket run before I head back to pack up my things. I'll be home late afternoon.'

'You're not rushing back on my account, are you? Ripley and I are fine, really,' I reassure him.

'No. Felicity's mum has decided to come and stay with her for a bit. It would be awkward if I was around.'

I can hear the disappointment in his voice.

'Ah, right. Well, I guess I'll see you later then. Pop in for a coffee if you have time.'

'Will do. It's tough being here and then heading for home, alone. Every time I'm with her it gives me hope, though. Makes me sound needy, doesn't it?'

'No. Not at all, Drew. Having a special connection with someone isn't something that can be turned off and on, like a switch. Hang in there, there's always hope.'

Goodness, where on earth did that come from?

It looks like a bomb has exploded as I stare out of the kitchen window. After three beautifully sunny days, two days of non-stop rain hasn't helped the situation. Gone is my tidy little patio and part of the leafy green hedge separating the two gardens. Instead, there is now a quagmire of ugly brown dirt and Drew's half is even worse. There's a mountain of sand, industrial-size bags of gravel, various pieces of large machinery locked up inside a compound of metal fencing, and a walk-in, lockable container.

I look down at Ripley as she sits on the windowsill next to me.

'What are we going to do?' I ask, out loud. She looks up at me and emits one solitary, drawn-out miaow. The cat equivalent of 'I have no idea', I should imagine. 'At least the sky is clear and if we're lucky the sun will be back today to dry it out a bit.'

It's been a gruelling week in many ways, but you can't make a cake without breaking a few eggs, as they say. Then I turn full circle and a little tingle of excitement courses through me. The whole of the downstairs is now open plan and ignoring the fine, gritty layer of dust that covers everything, and which no amount of cleaning will eradicate, I couldn't be happier.

'No walls,' I declare, as my eyes glance up at the newly plasterboarded ceiling.

Ding-dong. Ding-dong.

As I head for the front door my footsteps echo around the hollow space rather satisfyingly and seconds later Tegan steps inside, immediately uttering an explosive, 'A-maz-ing!'

'It is, isn't it? The steelwork is up, the plasterboard ceiling is ready to be skimmed and they've done a tidy job of taking down the walls.' I cringe a little at the sound of that gritty crunch underfoot, as we walk towards the rear of the cottage.

Tegan stares out glumly at the mud pile. 'Oh,' she shrugs, as she takes in the devastation. 'They've made a heck of a lot of progress in five days, but poor you.'

'I know. At least the plastic sheeting they put up at the top of the stairs has helped contain the dust a little. The next job is laying the footings for the extension. I can't wait until they get to the stage where they can pour the new concrete floor and seal it. Until then, I just have to suck it up and try not to let it bother me.'

'It is sad that you've lost your little sanctuary outside,' she commiserates. 'But what a difference already. I know it all looks rather ugly, but it's a good-size space even as it stands. Imagine when the extension is up and with the glass wall it's going to be so much lighter and brighter.'

Tegan, Ripley and I stand in a line in front of the back door, watching as a guy climbs onto the digger and it kicks into life.

'There will be more skip changes today as they are clearing out a lot of those woody shrubs at the bottom, for me. It's a big area down there and will make up for what I'm losing with the extension.'

'Miaow,' Ripley endorses and Tegan and I both look down at her, smiling.

'And she's still here with you, I see,' Tegan says, stooping to stroke her back, affectionately.

Glancing at Ripley and then back at Tegan, I can't hide my sense of exasperation.

'Drew isn't happy about it, but what can I do? I stopped putting food down for her the day he arrived back, but she pops in to his to clear her bowl and then heads straight back here. He's done everything he can think of to tempt her to stay, but she treats his place like a café and then insists on sitting on my doorstep, miaowing until I let her in. I'm thinking of putting food down for her again, as sometimes she just sits looking at me, wailing.'

Tegan shrugs. We both know cats do whatever they want. 'Talking of cafés, are you ready for breakfast?'

'And some. I haven't had a chance to speak to Sy yet this morning—is he joining us?'

'Sadly, no. He's dog-walking with your dad first thing and then giving a hand cleaning the kennels for a couple of hours before I pick him up. Are you sure you don't mind helping Kate, while Sy shadows me later today? Well, I say that term loosely, as he says he's prepared to roll up his sleeves and help out.'

'And he will. It's fine, really. I'm looking forward to a day away from the noise and the chaos. Sorry Ripley, it means you're going to have to find somewhere to curl up for a few hours,' I inform her. 'Or maybe you could make today the day that you go back home to Drew.'

She stares at me with those innocent, mesmerisingly luminous, green eyes of hers, as if she isn't causing me a lot of anxiety at the moment. Drew really is very upset about it and I feel awful, as if I'm purposely trying to steal her away from him.

I grab my bag and she follows us out through the front door without making a sound. We watch as she saunters along the front path, disappearing beneath the laurel hedge next to my sturdy, new side gate.

'It doesn't look promising, does it?' Tegan says. 'I think she intends to find somewhere to curl up until you get back. It's awkward and I can understand Drew feeling miffed about it because she is a beauty.'

'Ripley gets me up at least twice every night, expecting to be let out. And in between she sits outside the front door, wailing when she wants to come back in. I don't like to ignore her in case she disturbs anyone. I'm sure the Moyles can hear her and Arthur is a light sleeper anyway.'

Tegan shakes her head, sadly, and we turn to head off down to the cove.

'Was she as much trouble for Drew?'

'Well, no. He'd let her out the once, apparently, as he installed a cat flap in the side of the shed. Ripley has a rather nice little cat nest inside. I didn't know that, of course, because he forgot to mention it. When he was away, I was at her beck and call. I was really glad of her company, so I'm not complaining but it never crossed my mind she'd want to stay permanently.'

'A precedence has been set, now. She might go back to him once the work is finished and things settle down, I suppose.'

'I hope so, as I feel it's entirely my fault for having spoiled her but she was such a brave little thing.'

'How's Drew's girlfriend doing?'

'Improving with the antibiotics, apparently. She rings him quite a bit. Her mum is staying with her. There's so much going on here and it's not as if he could bring her back with him, although I suspect he'd have loved that.'

'Any more news about Mr Mills? Or your nocturnal visitors?'

'No. It's gone very quiet. The lighting Ross had installed picks up any movement within close range of the rear of the cottages. My side entrance now lights up like a Christmas tree at night, whenever Ripley walks around the side.'

'And how is Ross?' She casts me a sideways glance as we head towards Pascoe's Café and Bakery. The smell of bacon frying hits my nose and my mouth begins to water.

'I haven't really had a chance to talk to him since the weekend.'

'Ah yes, the night the two of you spent together.'

'Tegan!' I exclaim, as she holds open the door to the bustling coffee shop. She's laughing, of course, and I know she's only playing around with me. But Ross stepped in when I was in dire need of help and I will never forget that.

'It's on me this morning. Bacon sandwich, or pancakes?' she asks, scanning the menu on the huge chalkboard wall behind the counter.

'Surprise me. I'm feeling rather cavalier today.'

When she joins me at a table tucked away in the corner, I can see there's something on her mind. I gaze at her, shrugging my shoulders. 'What?'

'It's time for you to come clean about Ross.'

I look at her, a sense of confusion washing over me.

'And don't pretend you don't know what I'm on about, Kerra. I'm a bit disappointed in you, to be frank. Don't you trust me enough to tell me what's going on?'

I swallow hard, my throat dry. The waitress arrives with a tray, placing two cups of coffee and two glasses of water in front of us. I down half of my glass of water in one go before facing Tegan's questioning eyes.

'It's all a bit something and nothing after all these years. Being fifteen years old and watching the one guy you want to notice you, noticing everyone else but not you, it leaves a scar.'

Tegan slaps her hand to her mouth. 'Oh, Kerra. I never realised. Honestly, you hid that well. All those years you were away and you never once asked me about him.'

'I didn't have to; you kept me up to date with all the news and Ross was big news, at times. Until he got married and then you stopped mentioning him. I assumed he was happy.'

She looks at me, shocked. 'Oh. I guess I did. But you never showed any interest in him, at all!'

'Self-preservation. I didn't feel attractive back then. I was shy and awkward. It was easier to pretend I didn't care, and that I didn't have any feelings for him.'

'Ross was in awe of you, we could all see that.'

Was he, I wonder, or is Tegan just being kind?

'Why is this the first I'm hearing about this? If I had no idea you liked him, I'm pretty damned sure he would have felt the same way. You were very cool and a bit... hmm... how can I put this? Dismissive around him. But then, you didn't really approve of all that flirtatious stuff going on back then, did you? Most of the girls were after him because didn't we all long to be able to say we had a boyfriend?'

'Yes, well, not all of us were of a mind to throw ourselves at him.'

She starts laughing. 'He couldn't help being popular and so totally gorgeous he made most of the girls' hearts flutter.'

'But not yours?'

Tegan smiles. 'I had my sights set on someone else. It just took a few years for me to get up the courage to get friendly with Pete. But it's sad to discover you hid how you felt from me, too. Your bestie.'

'I thought it was simply a phase.'

'He was head and shoulders above the rest; all the other boys were show-offs but Ross, well, he was more mature for his age. "Intense" springs to mind. Just because all the girls were falling over him, doesn't mean to say he encouraged it. As far as I'm aware he only dated a couple of girls while we were at school. I don't think his parents would have welcomed anyone from our little group into their home, anyway. Not good enough, I'm afraid. Well, except for one and she wasn't interested. Or so I thought.'

I stare back at her as she looks at me, her eyes widening.

'What are you implying?' I ask, a little bewildered.

'I'm pretty sure he would have asked you out regardless of whether it upset his parents or not, if only you'd relaxed a little and joined in. The poor guy isn't a mind-reader, Kerra. There were times even I felt that you hung out because it was what everyone did, not because you wanted to. You had better things to do and I got that. If I'd had your brain power, I'd have spent my time on the computer, too.'

I was the nerd who tried so hard to fit in, but never did and Tegan is right. Ish. I hung around in the hopes that one day Ross would single me out.

'Now you're home for good, did you secretly hope your paths would cross and one look at him would confirm he was never good enough for you, anyway? I can't see you falling for anyone who hasn't got what it takes to make a marriage work. You're not wired that way. It's all or nothing with you, isn't it?'

I breathe a little sigh of relief at Tegan's interpretation of my interest.

'Anyone who jumps into a marriage without really knowing the other person is asking for trouble. And not a good judge of character.'

'Ah, that's a bit mean, Kerra. If you'd been here at the time you'd understand. Personally, I think it's all a bit sad to see a man searching for something and never finding it.'

'Searching for what, exactly?' I ask, surprised at the change in Tegan's tone.

'Validation, I think. For all his success, most of his life it's been thrown back at him by his father as not enough. That's a travesty and I feel sorry for Ross. He deserves a chance to grab some happiness for himself.'

My hunger seems to disappear as her words sink in. Did Ross think I disapproved of him? My heart feels heavy in my chest to think that my act of self-preservation might have been misinterpreted, all those years ago.

The car boot sale is busy, and it's already been going for a couple of hours.

'Right, we have an hour and ten minutes before I'm due to pick up Sy and you head out with Kate. Is there something in particular that you're looking for?' Tegan asks as we approach the first aisle.

'Anything that catches my eye, really.'

She looks at me, lifting one eyebrow and giving me that look of hers. 'As long as you haggle.'

I'm buzzing—I find this all so exciting because you never know what dusty treasures are waiting to be discovered.

Since Sy suggested I use one of Dad's garages as a workshop and storage area, I no longer have to think twice for fear of running out of space. And I can take over the second garage, if necessary. I kicked myself for not thinking of it before. Over the course of a couple of evenings, Sy helped me carry the items I've lovingly worked on along to Dad's and now my second bedroom is clutter-free. At least it's somewhere to sit and eat, as I have a set of four dining chairs in there that I'll be upcycling ready for use in my new kitchen and a small coffee table. But psychologically it has made a huge difference, as I'm not confined to the main bedroom anymore. Admittedly, it does feel a little like being a student again and living in a first floor flat, but at least there's some semblance of order.

'I've decided I'm going French country style upstairs and I've ordered a new bed, some bedside tables and a large wardrobe. It has a very simple take on what is an old romantic style, with sweeping curves and the white, matt finish I love. Contemporary country is the term, I believe.'

'But you already have a new bed,' Tegan points out.

'I know, but it's not the look I want. Dad's going to have it for one of his bedrooms. Now I know where I'm going with the general theme, what I need next are a few unusual, decorative items.'

She shrugs her shoulders.

'Well, have a good look around. Let me know if you see something you fancy and then leave it to me.'

I end up walking on ahead of Tegan, doubling back to point things out to her that are simply must-haves. She pops back to the minibus with a wall-mounted, metal candle holder, when my eyes alight on the globes. Like a moth to the proverbial flame I head straight over to them. There are two, fourteen-inch high, white, ball-shaped objects with an opening at the top, above which is a little handle. As I reach out to pick one up, the lady behind the trestle table sidles up to me.

'Gorgeous night lights, aren't they?'

I run my hands over the metal fretwork, where tiny leaves have been punched out creating an intricate design. 'They're stunning. Do you only have the two?' If Tegan was here she'd be jumping in to take over right now.

'Hey there, Kerra, fancy seeing you here.' Nettie strolls

up, carrying two takeaway coffees in a cardboard tray and offers one to the woman in front of me. 'Sissy, this is Eddie and Meryn's daughter. You know, Home from Home—the kennels.' She turns back to me. 'Sissy is my good friend and neighbour; they don't get much better.'

The dark-haired woman smiles good-naturedly. 'She only says that because I let her take my dog, Willow, for walks.'

'Well, it's lovely to meet you, Sissy.'

'Sissy has a small shop in the arcade in Polreweek, called The Design Cave.'

'I thought everything on this table looked brand new,' I reply. 'You have some lovely items.'

Nettie scrunches up her forehead. 'It's sad when they hike up the business rates and the only way to make ends meet is to spend weekends at car boot sales to boost your income. Looks like you have a sale here, though, Sissy,' she laughs.

'How many did you want?' Sissy enquires, answering my question. We haven't discussed price and nothing is labelled.

'Well, I'll take both of these,' I confirm, wishing Tegan was here. 'How much are they?'

'As you're a friend of Nettie's I can do those for twenty pounds each, is that okay?' Sissy glances at me nervously, and it's clear I'm not the only one who doesn't enjoy this form of buying and selling.

'I don't suppose you have another eight of them?' I enquire.

Nettie almost drops her coffee as Sissy's face breaks out into a huge smile.

'I most certainly do, but I only have the two with me today.'

'Great. That's perfect. Here you go,' I pull out two,

twenty-pound notes and thrust them at her as Nettie goes in search of some carrier bags. 'Is it possible to collect the others from your shop, if I pop into Polreweek one day during the week? I'd love to come and have a look around, as there's still quite a bit I need to furnish the cottage.'

'Here,' Sissy says, handing me a card. 'The address is on the back. It's just a case of collecting the stock from my lock-up facility, so any day from Tuesday onwards?'

'Great, thank you so much!'

Nettie hands over the two bags just as Tegan arrives wearing a slight frown of annoyance, no doubt wondering why I didn't wait for her to come back before striking a deal. Fortunately, she simply acknowledges Nettie and Sissy.

'See you on Wednesday, then,' I call out, as Tegan and I bid them goodbye.

'Wednesday?' she asks, when we're out of earshot.

'I've bought another eight of these.'

'Eight? You bought ten of the same thing?' She looks at me as if I've lost my mind.

'This purchase has made my entire day sparkle,' I declare. And it has. This magpie is already imagining her new treasures in situ, as she lazes back in the egg chair surrounded by the flickering candlelight from ten beautiful globes.

'This is ghastly, isn't it?' Drew declares, sounding more than a little cheesed-off. It's been a long and tiring day all round and this feels like the final straw.

We are each nursing a mug of hot chocolate and gazing out over what is now virtually one conjoined mud pit.

Well, that's a bit of an exaggeration, because on my side at least there is still a patch of grass that hasn't been churned up by the tracks of the digger or trampled by muddy workmen's boots.

'I'm used to traipsing around building sites,' Drew points out, 'but usually I'm the one who gets to go home to a nice, clean environment. We're crazy living here while the work is being done, you do know that?'

From this vantage point, down near the newly cleared patch on the edge of what little lawn remains, the beautiful stonework of the cottages is the only saving grace. They now look like one property, with almost a quarter of the hedging between the two gardens having been ripped out and only a few courses of the new concrete block wall for the extension, in situ.

'My offer still stands,' I casually throw out there. 'The cash could be in your bank account tomorrow and you could find somewhere comfortable to stay while you sort things out. It would just mean knocking down that little bit of wall they built yesterday, and the cement is hardly dry. Easy. A few small revisions to the plans and job done.'

He hesitates for one second as if he's giving it some consideration, before he begins speaking. 'Sorry to disappoint you, Kerra, but Felicity is head over heels in love with how it's going to look once it's finished. I'm here to stay, as tempting as your offer sounds right now.'

I thought he was going to say that she was head over heels in love with him and will be moving in once it's all finished. It would be nice to think that was actually the case, as with Ripley turning her back on him, poor Drew now has no one to keep him company. Except me, of course.

'Well, get used to the mess and the chaos, then,' I banter, 'because this is only the start of it.' It is rather a pity, though. It could be my dream property with all the space I'd ever need. But, after recent events, my mindset is changing a little. A woman on her own in a sleepy, rather sheltered, rural location is a very different proposition to living alone in a luxury apartment on the third floor of a prestigious building, which has a concierge.

'Actually, I'd miss having a neighbour on my doorstep. Even one who is cross with me because he thinks I've enticed his cat away by giving them too many chicken treats.'

Drew puts his head back and begins to laugh, good-naturedly.

'Do you know what I think is really behind this thing with Ripley?'

I pause, looking at him with interest. 'What?'

'Ripley thinks *you* need protecting. She's not at all concerned about me, even though I've done nothing but worship her since the day I brought her home.' He's purposely trying to make me feel bad, but I can see from the little glint in his eye that he knows there is nothing at all we can do about it. Cats are a law unto themselves.

Hmm. 'You could be right there. She does alert me whenever anyone is about to ring the doorbell and she wasn't happy when those men were in the garden. Ripley wasn't turning tail and running away from them, but she seemed eager to get out there, as if she wanted to chase them off. And I am sorry that this is so unfair on you, Drew, as I know you're missing her. When all this mess is gone and things settle down, she might suddenly return home.'

He doesn't look convinced.

'I noticed her going in and out of the shed while you were out today. I put a big bowl of her favourite biscuits in there and some water. At least if we're both out, then she has somewhere to go. I guess I'm just going to have to learn to live with her decision. I've heard her out the front miaowing in the early hours, waiting for you to let her back in, the little minx. She's lucky you aren't a heavy sleeper.' He grins at me, shrugging his shoulders in acceptance.

'Ah, Drew, that's really kind of you. Look, have you ever thought about getting a dog? They're much less fickle and brilliant company. You probably paid a lot for Ripley, so think about it and if you decide it's a good idea, I'll happily pay for a new little companion for you. It's the very least I can do.'

'A dog? It's not something I'd considered but it's a thought. There's no point in thinking about it at the moment, though, as you know how tough it is living out of two rooms upstairs.'

'How are you managing when it comes to cooking facilities?' I ask, already fed up having to use a free-standing cooker that has now been pulled into the middle of what was the old kitchen.

'It's difficult. Funny you should mention it, because when I was in the shed I took a look at my gas barbecue. There is almost a full container of Calor gas in there, too. It's just a pity there's nowhere safe to put it out here.'

We exchange meaningful glances.

'Are you thinking what I'm thinking?' I ask.

'Mmm, maybe if we could turn this little bit of grass

into a seating area and tidy it up, we could do the cooking over there against the back fence now one half of it has been cleared out. All we'd need is a garden table and chairs, something a bit more comfortable than these wooden ones, and mealtimes would be sorted. We could take it in turns to do the cooking. I've got one of those cheap gazebos folded up in the shed and it's virtually brand new. Even if it was raining it would give some cover.'

'I think that's a brilliant idea,' I reply, my spirits lifting at the thought of having somewhere decent to sit and eat on glorious evenings like tonight. Hopefully, there will be many more to come as summer approaches.

'Leave it with me. It'll require a bit of prepping, as the dirt where they dug the old bushes out will need compacting and levelling, or we'll end up traipsing it everywhere when we're cooking. If I address that tomorrow morning, we could fire up the grill and celebrate with a late lunch. Sy's decided to extend his stay a bit, hasn't he? We can turn it into a little welcoming party.'

'Yes, he has. That's a great idea. I'll invite Tegan, too. Dad will probably prefer a trip to the pub on a Sunday, as it gives him a chance to grab a pint or two with his mates.'

I pick up my phone and begin looking at garden furniture. The internet is slow as the signal isn't great this far from the cottage, but eventually I find something suitable.

'What do you think? Eight chairs, with reasonably comfortable looking seat pads and a nice table. If I order in one hour and thirty-eight minutes it could be here tomorrow morning.'

Drew's face instantly brightens. 'I'll go halves.'

'No, I'll get this. You sort something to stand the barbecue on. There, that's ordered. Here's to our first outdoor dining experience tomorrow, then.'

We clink mugs and suddenly instead of mourning the loss of two tidy and respectable gardens, we're both looking forward to turning this little spot into a temporary oasis.

18. The Garden Party

Itake Rufus's lead from Sy and hand Bertie over to him. He's a very cute-looking, miniature Schnauzer and although he has a tendency to stop every few yards with monotonous regularity, he doesn't yank and he doesn't jump up. It's not his style. Instead he will stop abruptly and there's no moving him. He'll sit there, one paw half-hanging in the air and those cute little eyes pleading with you until you hunker down to make a fuss of him. Then he's off again. Occasionally, if it starts to rain, he'll stop mid-walk and you have to carry him for a bit, which is hilarious. He stands there with all four legs locked rigid and you instantly know he's not impressed by the weather.

'Thanks. Rufus is all over the place for me, isn't he?' Sy isn't complaining, just puzzling over why the moment I take control, Rufus calms down.

'In all honesty, it's your nervousness that unsettles him. He doesn't feel safe with you,' I laugh.

'He probably isn't,' Sy admits. 'Bertie is a lot easier.'

'As a puppy, his owner took him to dog-training classes and that makes a huge difference. But Rufus is just a big, lovable and enthusiastic dog who wants to explore. That's not wrong and a firm grasp on the lead lets him know how far he can go. It's that simple.'

Once we get past the turning down to the cove, we start to climb as we head up into the forest and the dogs love being able to bound around unfettered. We walk on for a while and it's good to gulp in the slightly salty air, reminding us that beyond the tall trees to the right-hand side the land falls away quite sharply down to the sea.

'I'm grateful to both you and Eddie, Kerra. Inviting me down here for a short break is one thing, but I didn't mean to lay my problems on your shoulders,' Sy's voice breaks the silence between us.

'You haven't. Dad needs a man around he can talk to and I knew the two of you would get on. He appreciates someone with a practical mind. And you were doing me a favour, anyway. How was your stint with Tegan yesterday?'

'That woman is amazing. We started off by dropping six of her staff at four different locations, then she drove back here. I gave her a hand cleaning the house up on the headland.' We stop for a moment to catch our breath and Sy points to Treylya, which is just about visible through the mass of tree trunks. 'It's a beautiful house but every bedroom had been used and those shiny floor tiles take a lot of buffing. What does the name mean?'

I stare up at the house for a moment.

'To change, as in the wind or the current, I think. From the tip of the headland you can see in two different directions. Depending on the weather, sometimes if you look down you can spot the turbulence in the water where the current from east to west meets the strong winds coming around the bay.

I've been up there with Tegan and it's a two-man job, for sure. Where did you go next?'

'There was quite a lot of ferrying people around because the other minibus was busy. It's a logistical nightmare at times and there is a lot of wasted mileage.'

'So, what's the plan? Is there a better way of organising things?'

He lapses into silence for a few minutes.

'I have a couple of ideas but they need costing out. I'll thrash out the finer details over the next week or two.'

'Does that mean Tegan is open to working closely with you?'

'She seems keen. The main problem, as far as I can see, is how spread out the properties are. I'm afraid the answer might increase costs to begin with, but on the other hand it would allow Tegan to take on more properties and end up improving the overall profit margin.'

I'd suspected as much. 'If it's going to require an influx of cash to kick-start things then I'd love to help. Tegan never talks about money and it's not a topic I've managed to raise for fear of offending her. But this wouldn't be business, she's a friend and I don't want her borrowing money and having to shell out interest she can't afford.'

'I'll bear that in mind but it's hard for anyone to borrow from someone they know. It's like admitting defeat, in a way. But I suspect you're right and it's going to be about watching every penny.'

The good news is that Sy's gut instincts are telling him the business has a future.

'Maybe this is the silver lining to your little cloud. I'm sure there are lots of small businesses in similar situations, who require a trouble shooter. Once you've sorted Tegan out, I doubt we'll need to look very far to find your next client.'

'That's enough of that. Any action plan is likely to take quite a while to implement and I'm not convinced the country scene is a good fit for me, longer-term. Look at the state I'm in. I've had more mud on me in this last ten days than I've had in my entire life.'

I glance down as his grimy wellie boots and the mud splashes on his trousers from where Rufus has run through areas of soft mud and then come back to jump up on Sy, to share his enthusiasm.

'It's just a bit of mud, stop being so dramatic. Anyway, I must get back as I have a delivery coming ready for the barbecue this afternoon. Drew is laying some sort of temporary patio area and my job is to pretty it up. I'm in charge of assembling the furniture and hopefully the boxes are there ready and waiting for me.'

'Don't think that I don't know what you're doing. You'll go to any lengths to make me feel at home here, won't you?'

I give Sy an overtly innocent look, as if I have no idea what he's talking about. Without warning, Rufus comes bounding back once again, ignoring me and honing in on Sy to get his attention.

'See, even Rufus wants you to stay.'

'Enough, now. I get the message. But I am kinda missing London—the parties, the theatre. Going cold turkey on anything in life is a bit of a shock to the system.'

'Oh, we have plenty to rival that. We have the Biodome Project and you can visit a real tin mine. And we have the tall ships—you haven't seen anything yet.'

Sy looks at me without blinking. 'Sounds fascinating,' he replies, his voice deadpan. Guess I have a little convincing still to do, but the fact he's keen to assist Tegan if they can agree a plan of action, is a great start.

We head back to Dad's and as we approach the cottage I'm surprised to see a white van double-parked in front of the skips.

'Looks like your delivery has arrived, Kerra. Give me Rufus's lead, I can manage the two of them for this short distance. See you later.'

Crossing over, I'm shocked to see Drew and Ross helping the driver offload some lengths of decking.

'What's all this?' I ask, expecting to see nice, neat boxes with pictures of garden chairs on the front.

'Oh, your delivery is already round the back,' Drew replies. 'Ross had some old decking going spare and thought it would be a quick and easy solution. He's brought a machine that will compact the soil more effectively than any quick fix I could have come up with.'

'Oh, well, that's great. Thanks, Ross. I'll unlock the side gate and get the kettle on, then.' Ross gives me a broad smile and I try hard not to stare at him. He's wearing an old T-shirt and ripped jeans. No one should look that good in clothes fit for the rag bag—it should be against the law, I half-smile to myself as I head inside.

Drew and Ross immediately set to work. They carry everything they need across from the shed and then Ross shows Drew how to use the whacker, as Ross referred to a rather noisy, thumping machine. Once the earth in front of the fence has been flattened, they carry some buckets of gravel across and then repeat the process.

'I think that's a pretty good job,' Drew says, clearly delighted with the result.

It takes them another hour and a half to create what I'm reliably informed is a floating deck. It's three metres by four and all they did was to lay the old lengths of decking upside down on the grass vertically, then screw sturdy looking battens on the back at twelve-inch intervals. Two men, two drills and three of us to flip it over and get it into position. Job done.

In between passing things and generally doing what I can to help, Tegan arrives and offers to peel some potatoes for me. She heads inside and my next task is to unpack the boxes and begin assembling the garden furniture.

Ross reappears after putting away the tools and locking the shed back up.

'I see you've got the table done and half of the chairs, Kerra. Do you want a hand while Drew sorts out the barbecue?' He's standing with his hands on his hips and his legs astride. He really enjoys rolling up his sleeves and getting stuck in. I wondered how he kept so fit, or maybe he lives in the gym when he isn't working.

'If you like. Or you could just make yourself a coffee and sit for a bit. Tegan is inside and she'll show you where everything is if you need a break.'

He barely broke a sweat, I noticed, when they were assembling the decking. I couldn't help my eyes glancing over at him from time to time. He has this intense look whenever he's doing anything, like he's totally in the zone and oblivious to anything else going on around him.

'I know how fiddly this sort of job is and you've got the biggest part out of the way. The sooner it's done, the sooner we eat.'

Well, I'm not going to refuse a little help as this is a tedious job, to say the least. It's all screws, washers and nuts, and a fiddly Allen key—those annoying little metal bars with the bent end that you seem to have to turn forever and a day. It becomes a bit of a race, as we both start assembling at the same time. As my fingers are smaller I win the first round and I'm on to my next chair before Ross stands to grab the final box.

He clears his throat as he settles back down again. 'You haven't mentioned a significant other and you don't wear a wedding ring, I see. Is Sy...'

I realise he's stopped what he's doing and is staring at me intently, awaiting my response. The conversation I had with Tegan at the café pops into my head, but I quickly push it away. Looking across at him, I raise my eyebrows in an attempt to stop myself from automatically frowning and making those ugly, unflattering little lines even worse.

'Oh, no. Sy and I aren't, I mean, Sy worked for me. We've always been great friends outside of work but...' Instinctively my eyes stray across to the other side of the garden, where Tegan is now helping Drew to clean out the barbecue.

'Tegan? You've swapped sides?'

I burst out laughing. 'I haven't totally given up on men—yet. No, I think although Sy is just helping Tegan to streamline her business, I sense there's a little something going on between them. It's probably a bit of harmless flirtation, that's all. But as for me, well, the last thing I need right now is some complicated relationship that requires a lot of work. This is a point in my life where I'm free of any constraints for the first time and I'm going to make the most of it.'

Great, Kerra, you sound convincing. I mean, it's the truth after all.

'It's funny, you always were different to the other girls, Kerra. Some can't see past a ring on their finger and a man on their arm. I didn't think I had what it takes to settle down and, given what happened, I was probably right about that. Having been through it, it's not something I'll be jumping into again. You're right, it does make life complicated and there's a lot to be said for being on your own.'

'Well, that's a sad statement, if ever I heard one,' Tegan's voice pipes up as she saunters over, catching the tail end of our conversation. She's been watching us with interest.

Ross and I exchange a brief smile. 'Well, you probably couldn't avoid overhearing at least some of the rumours, Tegan, so you know I'm right.'

Tegan chews on her lip. 'Maybe you just chose the wrong one, Ross,' she replies sadly. 'It happens. But when it works out there is nothing better, I promise you.' Oh, Tegan, please leave it alone.

As if on cue, Drew rescues us. 'Can someone unlock the side gate for Sy, please? He's been trying to attract your attention for the last couple of minutes.' From his vantage point at the end of the garden, Sy is in his line of sight but our chatter obliterated his attempts to call out. I head straight around the side, pulling the key from my pocket.

'Sorry, Sy. We're just finishing off assembling the chairs. Is that the meat?'

'Yes. Eddie said he'll call in later on his way back from the pub. He pulled a load of lettuce leaves and some radishes from the garden. Oh, and there are a few tomatoes in there, too.'

'Perfect.'

'Shall I head in and get the salad ready up in the little kitchen while you guys set up the table and chairs?'

'That's great, if you don't mind. Tegan peeled some potatoes ready to roast in the oven for convenience. We're using disposables today as there's no way we'll be able to cope with the dishes upstairs.'

'I'll give you a hand,' Sy offers, flashing Tegan a warm smile.

'Thank you. Come on then. Drew,' she calls out, 'where do you want me to stash this?'

'Take it inside and I'll come and sort it out once I'm done here, thanks Tegan.'

That leaves Ross and me to assemble the last two chairs and begin carrying them over to the deck. At one point he leans into me, his voice low.

'I think you're right. There's a definite little spark going on there between Sy and Tegan. It's good to see, because I've thought for a while that she's struggling on her own and that's not what Pete would have wanted for her.'

Placing the chairs on the deck, we exchange a look. 'Well, Sy is here for a while and he's going to help her get the business back on track. Loneliness is a terrible thing, but often it's companionship people are looking for,' I reflect.

'You think it's too soon for Tegan to get involved with someone?'

'It's not that. Pete helped her set up the business and when it comes to making the necessary changes I just wonder if, well, if she might end up wanting to shoot the messenger.'

'Well, I think she's ready for change and she can't do that on her own. Do you ever get lonely, Kerra?'

'Sometimes, although I do enjoy my own company and I know that sounds awful, but it's the truth. However, that night you arrived at my door I will be very honest and say you did look rather like a knight in shining armour to me. Having a man in one's life can be useful at times.'

He chuckles. 'Yeah, guess we do have our uses. Occasionally.'

'How about you?'

'I keep busy in, and out, of work, so I don't really notice. It's great not being pulled into a constant round of arguments over not a lot, so what's to miss? I run, I like to paint and I do Tai Chi. I also help out at the Penvennan Amateur Dramatics club making some of the scenery for the stage. They usually put on a play in the summer and a pantomime over the Christmas and New Year period.'

That's a surprise.

'What do you do in your spare time? Um, can we move this between us, or should I call Drew over?' Ross indicates for me to check the weight of the table. With the chairs all set, we're nearly there.

'No, it's fine. Spare time? In the past I spent most of my time working and online. Now, it's getting the inside of this place all sorted because a house doesn't furnish itself. I'm giving Tegan a hand, too, just until things are running a little smoother for her. Then, I'm not quite sure what comes next. I thought I'd be helping Dad out, but that doesn't seem to be the case.'

'You'll be looking for a hobby, then.'

'I'm not sure I'm the hobby type.'

We lower the table onto the decking area and Ross leans on it, his hands palm down as he looks across at me.

'No. I didn't think you were.'

I don't know what to make of that and can't think of a suitable response.

'You're a doer, Kerra,' he continues, 'and finding something to pass the time isn't really you, is it?'

Oh. Well, I suppose he's right.

'Maybe what you need is a distraction.' His smile changes into something else and I realise he's flirting with me. Oh heck! Now I really am in trouble.

19. Doing What Friends Do Best

Admittedly, some of the chicken is a little charred, but the steaks are cooked to perfection and the afternoon seems to slide away from us with ease. As we sit chatting and bantering, there's a real air of camaraderie among our little gathering. Tegan, Ross and I might have been born in the village, but we haven't been closely involved in each other's lives, on a regular basis, for years. It's great to be able to take time out to get reacquainted, which means Drew and Sy don't feel like outsiders, merely part of a group of friends enjoying a leisurely meal and catching up.

Then it's time to play a few games, as you do. Charades is great fun, as is wearing sticky notes plastered onto our foreheads and guessing which celebrity we are, from the clues the others give us. It's a light-hearted, lazy Sunday afternoon. One that will stick in our memories for a long time to come and raise a smile. No one seems to find it rather bizarre that we're sitting in the middle of a building site and it does feel like a little oasis among the chaos.

It's Drew's turn to choose and Tegan suggests we re-enact that scene from the film *Notting Hill* – the one where a group of friends are sitting around the dinner table and there's one chocolate brownie left. Except that we aren't fighting over the last chocolate brownie on the plate, but the last of Mrs Moyle's saffron buns. I think it's fair to say it's a prize worthy of fighting for and everyone looks at Drew to decide on the challenge.

'Guess it has to be airing one of those awful moments in life that you will never forget, no matter how hard you try,' he declares and we all roll our eyes.

Drew scans around the table looking for someone to go first. Without any hesitation whatsoever, Tegan jumps straight in.

'I think I have this. I will say, upfront, that no names will be mentioned in the telling of this story…' She pauses for effect, waggling her finger at us and we all sit up, intrigued.

'Get on with it, then,' Drew demands, adding a mock seriousness to the proceedings.

'It was, note I say *was*, one of my biggest rental properties and it was off season. The owners didn't visit very often and they'd ordered a stack of new bedding to be delivered direct to the property. They asked if I could get someone to take delivery and check everything was there. On the day, I received a text from the courier saying they were an hour away and I headed straight over to the house. Letting myself in, I wandered around doing a general check, as we were due to do a deep clean later that week. When I opened the door to the master bedroom, let's just say the bed was not empty and I don't know who was more shocked, the couple intent on enjoying a leisurely, romantic afternoon, or me.'

Tegan does her best impression of someone in shock, then raises her hands to her eyes as if trying to shield herself from the memory. It's hilarious, but she then holds one hand up in the air, looking around the table.

'Stay with me, the worst is yet to come. The man who had literally *risen* to the occasion,' Tegan coughs, trying hard to suppress a grin, 'was the owner. He was wearing nothing more than a studded collar and a leash and his rather attractive partner had tied him to the headboard. Of course, he had absolutely no idea his wife had arranged for me to pop in and we all froze in horror. Now I don't accept bribes and I had to make that very clear when, a few minutes later, he joined me in the sitting room. However, I do have a code of practice. A client's business is confidential and whatever happens on their property is also confidential. Unfortunately, shortly afterwards I had to hand the cleaning of the property over to another company due to staffing issues.'

Eyebrows have been raised and there's a little ripple of laughter. How do you un-see something like that?

'Good try, Tegan, but I think I have a story to top that,' Ross says, sounding extremely confident.

We all look at him a little surprised, as that's going to take some beating. It must have been a truly shocking moment for Tegan.

'I think most people around this table are aware I'm divorced. My ex decided to go on a huge spending spree. And I mean HUGE. There wasn't a designer label that didn't come up on the stack of credit card bills I ended up having to sort out.'

Suddenly, everyone is silent and no one moves a muscle as we're all a little on edge, wondering where this is going next.

'There were several overnight stays at the Savoy Hotel in London and as Bailey spent a lot of time shopping in Harrods, I thought little of it. Until I found out that she had been having an affair with one of the caddies at Polreweek golf club. It seems if you're going to sleep with someone eleven years your junior, a stylish setting lends an air of acceptability to it. The shocker was that Bailey didn't think it was at all unreasonable to expect me to pay for their little excursions.'

We're all left speechless. Drew finally lets out a, 'Jeez, that's...' He can't even finish his sentence.

'It's appalling,' I throw in, breaking the awkward hush that has fallen over us all. Ross, I can see, is simply amused.

'Now that deserves the last bun, surely?' he states, glancing at Drew for confirmation.

'Hmm... close call. I think we should vote on it,' Drew suggests, clearly feeling very uncomfortable.

'Um... don't we all get a chance to opt in?' Sy pipes up and I turn to look at him, thinking he's joking, then I see that he isn't. Well, I think I know pretty much everything there is to know about him and I can't think of anything to trump Ross's incredibly frank admission.

Drew nods. 'Go ahead, but you've got tough competition,' he warns.

'I was eight years old when my heart was well and truly broken by the funniest, cutest girl in the entire world. Her name was Wendy, and I was hopelessly in love with her. She dumped me for a boy whose father owned the local bakery. In fairness to her, he did make the best cupcakes any of us had ever tasted and, in hindsight, I can see the temptation. But the real tragedy of the story is that it made me very aware of my emotions and that has carried with me throughout my entire life, so far.

'Now my family aren't particularly emotional people.

Maybe I wouldn't have been if I hadn't been totally traumatised at such a tender age. But wind forward and I'm now an adult, living at home to save money as I've just started my first job. I meet a wonderful young woman and instantly fall in love, but after a while she says I'm too serious. Apparently, she just wants to have a little fun and it's the start of a pattern I can't seem to break.'

It's a sterling performance, as his voice dips and even breaks a little as if he's truly devastated. It is hard not to laugh, as Sy has this very natural tendency to be dramatic, as a part of his inherent sense of humour.

'It's sad,' Ross interjects, sounding truly sympathetic, 'but isn't falling in and out of love, to varying degrees, what happens to everyone until they find the right one? I'm sorry, Sy, but it is the last saffron bun we are fighting for here and I still think I'm in the lead.'

Ross's eyes sparkle with amusement. I guess you only really know you're finally over something terrible that happens to you, if you can laugh about it afterwards. And he is laughing. Good on him.

'Excuse me,' Sy immediately jumps back in, 'I haven't finished. There's more to this story. Two years later, at the tender age of twenty, and another broken heart later, my father takes me to one side and says that it's not manly to be so openly emotional and he accuses me of being a closet homosexual. And that's why I can't, according to him, make a relationship work.'

Slam dunk! And there's the winner.

'No!' Tegan is horrified. 'That's an awful thing for a parent to say to their offspring, Sy. What was your response?'

Sy's smile begins to slip.

'If it were true, then I'd be loud and proud—why not? What hurt, was the fact that he thought I was different and not in a way he could accept. Then I packed my bags and headed off to London and I haven't spoken to him since. My mother has, on several occasions, tried to reach out to me but the fact that, at the time, she stood there without saying a word—well, that's hard to forgive.'

We're all sitting here stunned and I get the feeling this is the first time he's talked about this to anyone. The silence hangs awkwardly around us for a few seconds. Then Drew pushes the plate bearing the last saffron bun across to Sy, who instantly beams.

'Sorry, Ross.' Sy holds his hand in the air and Ross high-five's him. 'That was a bit unfair of me. This just seemed like a safe place to finally let it go.'

It's a humbling moment for us all.

'A deserved winner, hands down, mate.'

'I'm a sensitive guy—what's the term, something about being in touch with one's feminine side?' Sy jokes and he stares directly across at me, as if he's trying to assess my reaction. I'm just sad he hasn't felt able to talk about it until now.

'That's where the problem lies,' I throw in. 'Feminine and masculine energy isn't gender related. We each have both to varying degrees, that's all. And do you know something, Sy? I can honestly say you are the only close male friend I have, and I never gave thought to why that was, before. I guess it's because I really admire any man who can express his emotions and isn't afraid to show them. As I'm not afraid to flex my muscles and stand my ground when I'm fighting for something I believe in. It's the same thing, isn't it?'

'I totally agree.' Tegan is quick to pick up on it. 'My Pete was a man who wasn't afraid to show his emotions and share his feelings. When I was growing up, my father wasn't very expressive and it's only since he retired that he's realised what he's missed out on. We've succeeded in turning him into a hugger, at last. It's changed him in ways that have surprised us all. There were things we'd never discuss with him before and now he's more receptive and understanding.'

Gosh, what a bonding session this has turned out to be.

'I think this calls for a topping up of glasses and a toast,' I say and both Ross and Drew grab the open bottles of wine and do the honours. Everyone raises their hands to meet in the centre of the table as I begin speaking.

'To honesty and friendship; to good times with good people who understand that the bumps in life are what make us stronger. To us all!'

When it quietens back down, both Drew and I look at each other and nod. He goes first.

'I think it's only fair that we all participate, even though the winner was deserving of the trophy. For my part, my gut-wrenching moment, let's call it, was probably last night. I was chatting with Kerra and I told her that my girlfriend, Felicity, is in love with the plans for Tigry Cottage. Oh, she is, but it seems that she's no longer in love with me and yet I'm having trouble accepting that fact.'

I gulp, uncomfortably, feeling his pain.

'Oh, Drew. I'm so sorry. When something like that happens it takes a while to get your head around it.'

He gives me a weak smile of thanks. 'I didn't have the heart to hear myself say it out loud when we were chatting as that would have made it real, but hey, there are worse things in life and today is a new day. At least it's no longer a secret now and there's enough going on here to keep me from dwelling on it.'

Now all eyes are on me. I swallow hard.

'Here we go… I've spent the last six months telling myself I was coming home because my dad was struggling in the aftermath of Mum's death. But that's only partly true. I woke up one morning in a cold sweat, worried sick that the livelihood of a group of wonderful people was dependent upon me and suddenly I didn't want to do it anymore. The life I had, wasn't the life I wanted. And what was even worse, I had no idea what I did want. And that's why I came home, to try to find myself again.'

A lone voice rises up from behind me.

'There's no better reason for coming back, lovely.'

Dad is walking towards us, having let himself in, and I rush over to give him a hug.

Ross immediately jumps up. 'I'll get you a beer, Eddie. It's good to see you.'

'You, too, Ross—it's been quite a while. Before I sit myself down, this game is over, isn't it?'

'Dad, while I'm sure everyone here would love to hear your most embarrassing moment, a daughter has to draw a line somewhere.'

He isn't at all offended when everyone starts laughing. Late into the evening Dad starts off the singing with some of Mum's favourite sea shanties. For many years, Dad was a member of a local group who gathered together in the pub every Tuesday night, for a pint and a singalong. Mum usually went with him and she told me once that it reminded her of her childhood, as my granddad was a fisherman. What's amazing about tonight is that everyone is happy to join in, even if it's just for the chorus. Ripley isn't too impressed by all the noise, of course, and disappeared beneath the laurel hedge hours ago.

Sitting back and gazing at the smiling faces around the table, what I find amazing is that considering Sy loves the anonymity of London life, he's doing a jolly good impersonation of someone who is feeling quite at home. At home in a little village in Cornwall.

Ripley's ears start twitching and seconds later the doorbell rings, twice in quick succession. Swinging open the door, it's Nettie.

'What a lovely surprise! I'm really glad you stopped by. Come on in. Sorry about the mess.'

Nettie looks around, her reaction one of disbelief.

'Wow. No wonder you're on the lookout for furniture and things. I had to pop into the vet's to sort out my schedule for next month. I only work one day a week, but it's rarely the same day and I thought, well, as I'm on your doorstep I'll see if I can catch you. I wasn't expecting to see this, though.'

I talk her through the plans but today there's a jack hammer going again, as they're breaking up some concrete they found beneath the old patio. It's hard to hear yourself think at times.

'Look, it's rather noisy. Why don't we head over the road to Dad's and we can have a coffee in the orchard? It'll be a lot pleasanter than here.'

'Sounds great,' Nettie says, seemingly not fazed by the thought. Maybe she and Dad haven't had a falling out, then.

'Ripley, Ripley,' I call out, picking up my bag and waiting for her to sidle downstairs.

'Ah, you have a cat and he... she is gorgeous. A Bengal, isn't it?'

'Yes. She is quite a little diva, I will say, and very talkative. Particularly at 3 a.m. in the morning. But she actually belongs to my neighbour, although it appears that for the time being she's decided this is her home.'

Nettie shakes her head, laughing. 'Sounds about right for a Bengal. All cats are independent by nature, but Bengals— well, they are tigers and no one tells a tiger what to do.'

'Perhaps over coffee you can share your knowledge, as any tips I can glean would be most appreciated. Dogs I can handle, cats are a little more of an unknown.'

Ripley follows us out and heads off in the direction of her favourite spot.

'I'm going to be sorting out a cat flap, very soon. Unfortunately, the only place that will work is in the panel next to the front door. When the renovations are finished the back will be all glass.'

'You do know they're climbers and they love to get up high?' Nettie tells me, as we head over to Dad's place. 'If you leave a small top window open, she will come in and out that way. We had one client whose Bengal used the upstairs bathroom as their way in. Seriously, that involved jumping up from a sloping roof at first floor level. But it only works if it's a top opening window, as it is a bit of a security risk. They also like water, so watch out whenever you are running a bath, as it's not unknown for a Bengal to jump in. Always run the cold first, just in case.'

Nettie has worked in a vet's office for years and I often wondered why she didn't continue her studies rather than settling for being an assistant, as she loves working with animals.

'Hi Dad.' He looks up as I swing open the gate.

'Well, I never. Nettie, my dear, it's good to see you. I was just having a wander around the garden, reminiscing about the old days and you step through the gate. You, me and Meryn, we were always on the go, weren't we?'

Nettie walks over to give Dad a hug. 'There was always work to be done, Eddie. Fond memories all round, for sure.'

'Right, I'll put the kettle on.'

'We'll give you a hand,' I offer, as we follow Dad up to the house.

Less than ten minutes later, Drew comes looking for me and we've only just settled ourselves down at the table beneath the big old apple tree.

'Sorry to interrupt, guys. We have a little problem, Kerra.'

I look at him, bemused. 'A little problem?'

'Um, well, it's more of an unfortunate accident, really. Can you come and take a quick look?'

'Of course. I'll be as quick as I can, Nettie. I'm sure you two have enough to catch up on until I get back.'

'I'll give Nettie the tour. Take your time, lovely,' Dad replies and I feel like I'm being dismissed.

As Drew and I head back, I fleetingly wonder if fate has decided to step in. There is absolutely no way I could have engineered Dad and Nettie sitting down to have a quiet cup of tea together. Glancing up at the sky and the little fluffy clouds as they drift by aimlessly, I can't help thinking that this is too much of a coincidence. Is it possible that Mum had a hand in this? Well, you never know for sure, do you?

20. Yo! Ho! Ho! The Treasure Chest

As we step out through the back door of Pedrevan, three men are standing in the far corner of my garden and no one is working. Looking beyond them, I'm shocked.

'OMG! Granddad's old shed. I thought he'd taken that down years ago,' I exclaim, hurrying forward.

'You weren't the only one who was surprised to see it there. One of the workers, Bill, used a saw to chop down that diseased tree trunk as it was in the way. It didn't quite fall where he expected it to and in among all those laurel bushes that's what took the brunt.'

The tree trunk is lying at a forty-five-degree angle and the splintered roof of the old shed pokes up either side of it, rising out of the mass of greenery like a fork.

'Sorry, Mrs.' Bill's a lovely man, a gentle giant and I'm only glad that hulking great tree trunk didn't fall back on him.

'Hey, it's not a problem. I'm simply surprised it's still standing.'

'Well, it weren't really. Just held up by the boxes inside it, I should imagine, as most of the exterior is rotten. Stacks of old crates in there, it seems. We haven't touched anything, as we didn't know what to do for the best.'

Drew edges around to the side, pushing into the bushes to get a better look.

'You're right, Bill. It's listing to one side. Just take it down as safely as possible.'

'I'm so sorry. I thought it was long gone. I do remember Granddad using it when I was very small, mainly for his fishing stuff, I believe. Do you think any of the contents are salvageable?'

Bill scratches his head. 'Maybe. It might be easier if I use a chainsaw and get this tree trunk out of the way first. Then we can get that roof off before it falls in any further. We can drag the crates out then, so you can decide whether it's all stuff for the skip, or not.'

'Thanks, Bill. Sorry to have added to your workload.'

As Drew and I leave them to it and head back inside, I give him a bit of a guilty look. 'Bet you wish I hadn't tacked this little job on, now. But I wanted to get the mess out of the way in one go. I can't believe how much it's opened up the garden but Granddad's old shed, who would've thought? Do you fancy a cuppa?'

'Aren't you in a hurry to get back to the tea party?'

'No. I think Dad and Nettie will enjoy a little time reminiscing.'

Drew gives me a knowing look. 'Are you plotting something? I bet you are. I'll tell you what, if you can give me half an hour of your time, we could pop into mine and go through the final set of plans for your kitchen. I promised Alistair I'd get those to him ASAP.'

Oh, my beautiful new kitchen—we are inching ever closer!

'Lead on, this is exciting. I can't wait to see the final version because it's all starting to feel very real.'

Drew bursts out laughing as he turns to scan around when Bill starts up the chainsaw.

'Oh, it's real, alright.'

'I might need some headache tablets, later. But first, I'm sorry to hear things aren't going well between you and Felicity. Is it really over?'

'I guess. It was my fault. She's pretty stressed out right now and a simple conversation turned into a bit of an argument and then, to my horror, I sort of gave her an ultimatum.'

He stops for a moment, bowing his head slightly and I can see he's angry with himself.

'I said if she really loved me she'd walk away from it all and join me here. Like a fresh start. Then she went off on one about family meaning something and raised the fact that I rarely visit my parents, so I couldn't be expected to understand. She said she didn't want to be with someone who didn't share the same values.'

'Ouch. I'm sure she didn't mean it like that. We all say the worst things when we're at the end of our tether.'

'I know, but I pushed her too far and there was no coming back from it.'

I reach out and place a hand on his shoulder, for comfort.

'Something tells me it isn't over, Drew. Just give her some time and space to work through her problems. She'll reach a conclusion and then you'll know for sure what the future holds.'

'Well, she's blocked me on her phone, so I guess you're

right. But I can't imagine my life going forward without her in it.'

At this rate the village is in danger of turning into a lonely-hearts club. *There's a lesson to be learnt here, Kerra and it's to speak your truth. Yep, easier said, than done though.*

'Sorry, that took longer than anticipated, Dad. And I've missed Nettie.'

Dad is in the garden pulling weeds and he straightens to give me a beaming smile.

'She hung on as long as she could but had to get back to walk her neighbour's dog. The lady works and Nettie plays dog-sitter.'

He looks and sounds very upbeat.

'How are things with her?'

Am I imagining it, or is Dad looking a little flushed?

'Fine, it seems. Keeping busy. What was the problem over at yours?'

Um… that's it? It's obvious he's not going to tell me anything else and maybe it was a mistake not heading back sooner.

'Did you know there was an old shed still standing, down in the far corner? Well, it's hardly standing now as they've taken most of it down.'

'What, in the wilderness?'

That makes me smile and I nod. 'Yes. I'm quite excited about it, actually. They're about to pull a whole stack of wooden crates out so they can level the rest of the area. Why don't you pop back with me and have a look?'

James appears, sauntering down the path with his hands stuffed into his pockets.

'Hey Kerra, Eddie. What's happening?'

He's such a cheerful young man and seems to be getting through his teen years without any real angst. I've never seen him walking around with any friends, though.

'More of the same,' I reply. 'Dust, dirt and mess.'

We exchange smiles.

Dad stoops to pick up the bucket of weeds. 'I'm just going to head over to Kerra's to take a look at something, then we'll do the first walk when I get back?'

'Fair enough. I'll hang around here. Maybe make a start on the sweeping up. See you in a bit, then.'

I follow Dad and wait for him to empty the bucket into the composter and off we go.

'Nettie is happy working part-time, now?' I enquire gently.

'Yes, or so she says. She told me she keeps busy and she still does the amateur dramatics thing. She's writing a play at the moment.'

'She writes?' I'm gobsmacked.

'Seems so. It surprised me, too.'

As we approach the skips in front of the cottage there's a changeover going on and it's blocking the entire road. We walk around the idling lorry, just as the driver begins the lift. As I turn to walk up the path, I notice a man standing alongside the laurel hedge, peering down through the side gate. He didn't hear our approach above the noise of the engine. Fortunately, it's locked as the builders use Drew's side entrance for access because it's wider.

'Can I help you?'

When he turns around, startled, I see it's one of the men from the other day.

'I've come to see Mr Mills.'

'I told you when you were here before, Mr Mills was a tenant, and he no longer lives here. Do I need to call the police?'

Dad immediately jumps in. 'This is private property and you're trespassing.'

Yanking my phone out of the back pocket of my jeans, I begin tapping at the screen.

'Just checking, in case he came back.' The guy isn't fazed, it seems, and sounds rather underwhelmed by my threat until I hold the phone up to my ear.

'I'll be off then,' he says, as he turns and walks past us without another glance.

We watch as he heads off down the road, but today there's no sign of a black Range Rover and he simply keeps walking until he's out of sight. This is really weird.

'I don't like the look of him. If he comes by again, Kerra, you ring the police first and me next. Right?'

'Okay, Dad. Now I have the gate and the security lights all round it's not a problem though. I think he got the message this time. Come on, let's check out the shed.'

Unlocking the side gate, I'm careful to lock it straight back up and this incident acts as a reminder that I need to make sure I do that every single time.

'Oh my,' Dad exclaims. 'What a good job they've done of clearing that corner.'

There are three guys working on it now and they've

stacked the crates on a bare patch of earth next to the barbecue.

'Great job, guys. Thanks so much.'

'We wanted to finish loading up the skips so it made sense to get it cleared as quickly as we could. The boss will be around later and he wouldn't have been too happy if we'd left it in a mess,' Bill explains.

Dad is already dipping into the crates.

'Oh.' Bill points to the decking. 'There were some fishing rods in a bag. It's a bit musty, but I put it over there in case anyone trod on it and broke 'em. It's not often you come across things like that.'

'Ah, appreciated. I'm hoping there are a few little things I can rescue. Granddad was a fisherman most of his life and even after he retired he'd go out hand line fishing, in his little boat.'

'There's a metal box full of reels here, lovely,' Dad calls over his shoulder and I'm straight there.

'What a find!'

'Well, you don't see many of these around anymore. I bet those rods are collectibles, too, if they aren't broken. And look at this,' Dad exclaims, as he pulls a large metal object from another of the crates.

'What is it? Some sort of lamp?'

'It's a Davy lamp and there are a few others here, as well. There are a number of old tin miners still alive who had one of these back in the day.'

'What a totally unexpected surprise. I wasn't sure what I was going to use the pine wall cabinet for, but I do now.'

'That's a nice thought, Kerra. He was a grand old man

and his heart was in the right place. He doted on your mum and in his eyes she couldn't do a thing wrong.'

I stare at Dad, raising an eyebrow. 'Just like me,' and he laughs.

Oh Dad. What am I going to do about you? I half-hoped you'd reach out to Nettie for a little help as a start. Perhaps she'd realise how much she missed the kennels and offer to run it for you. Uncle Alistair is gutted that his attempt to lure you back has come between you both. I think it's because you can't admit to yourself that's what you really want to do. But with Nettie seemingly content with her life the way it is now, I've drawn a total blank. Mrs Moyle doesn't often get it wrong, but it seems in this instance her radar was way off. As was mine. Unless I've missed something.

Ding-dong.

'Hi Ross, come in. How are you?'

It's almost eight o'clock and he's the last person I expected to see, but a welcome sight, for sure. My mood immediately brightens, despite the haze of tiredness that surrounds me.

'Good, thanks. I heard about the accident with the shed and I wanted to check you're happy with how it was handled. Bill's retiring at the end of the month and he feels bad he made such a stupid mistake.'

'I'm the one who should be apologising for not giving Bill any warning it might still be there. I just assumed it had been taken down at some point. Thank goodness no one was hurt, that's all that matters. And I'm delighted with some of the things we found inside—it means a lot to me that they could rescue them.'

'Inside?'

Ross follows me out through to the garden and I can see from the look on his face he's pleased with what they've done. It's transformed the garden and there's a clear view right down to the back fence now.

'It's really opened it up. What are your plans for the garden once the building work is done?'

'Funny you should ask that question as I have an idea, but I'm not sure how practical it is. Anyway, do you have time to stop for a drink, or were you on your way home?'

Ross looks at me and his face softens, his eyes crinkling up as he smiles. Behind that there is a genuine warmth and it makes my heart skip a beat. He was looking for an excuse to call in because he needed some company. And he chose to come here.

'Perfect. It's been a long day and a stressful drive back, so a drink would go down well. I'd kill for a coffee.'

'Give me five, then I'll join you.'

Ross turns and walks on down the garden as I go back inside. When I return he's inspecting the fence and I set the tray down on the patio table. Lighting the candles in my gorgeous metal globes, they cover the tabletop in a myriad of tiny leaves. I can't wait to collect the others as they are going to look amazing lined-up outside the glass exterior to the cottage.

'Saffron bun?' I call out to Ross and he heads straight back to me.

'Don't mind if I do,' he says with a grin and I know we're both thinking about the little garden party.

'I was deserving of the prize that day, but you surprised me, Kerra.'

LINN B HALTON

He takes a seat, half the bun already gone in one bite.
'Did I?'

'You've always been a woman on a mission. Even at school you were head down and into something or other. You weren't like the other girls. There was something very different about the way you looked at things.'

It's cosy in this corner and as the light continues to fade, so does the ugliness of the raw dirt around us. But it still feels strange, sitting here with Ross and I can't help that little frisson of happiness from welling up inside of me.

'Mum used to say to me that there was nothing wrong with being a square peg in a round hole. She said life would be boring if everyone was the same but, in general, people don't quite see it that way. And now I'm back here, I want to fit in more than ever.'

He finishes his bun, chewing for a moment as his eyes scan my face.

'You meant what you said, then? That you're trying to find yourself?'

He's puzzled and I can see why.

'Since I started work, the number of days my hands haven't touched a keyboard wouldn't take me out of two digits, tops. Since I've been here all I've done is online shopping. It's like work no longer exists for me. But what do I do once the renovations are done?'

'What do you want to do?'

I heave a sigh. 'I have no idea, but I want it to mean something. Not in terms of achievement but making a difference. But my skills are what they are, and I can't change that.'

We sit for a while and as the night shadows creep upon

us, the candlelight comes into its own. The world is a softer place in the flickering light.

'This is so out of character for you. However, I wouldn't worry about it. Regard it as downtime that you've earned, and it would be hell having to hold down a busy day job and cope with all this upheaval. So, the garden. Ask away.'

He leans back in his chair, stretching out his arms until his muscles strain against his shirt, and then links his hands behind his head. It's good to see him looking more relaxed, as when he first arrived he was so tense. I could sense that. We all have good days and bad days, but when you're on your own it's hard to go back home to an empty house when what you need is a little company.

'I had this crazy idea. I haven't mentioned it to Drew because he's still a little up and down over the Felicity thing. She rang him yesterday when I was signing off the plans for the kitchen. I don't think it's totally over, but he excused himself to take the call and when he returned he was visibly upset.'

'That's a shame. Sometimes a clean break is best.' The way he says that makes me want to ask the question, because he's inferring his break with Bailey wasn't straightforward. I assumed it was, but it's none of my business.

'Possibly. Anyway, I'm still not sure what to do about my home office. Well, assuming I find myself something I want to do online, of course. At this rate I could be asking Dad to give me a job.'

Ross finishes his coffee and turns his head, shaking it slightly. 'No, you won't.'

'I'm thinking about having a bespoke office built here, at the end of the garden. What do you think?'

Ross looks rather taken aback.

'It's a good idea. Just a pity you didn't think about it earlier, given we have all the heavy equipment on site. Once the two gardens are separate again, your side access is very restricted.'

'I was thinking of something that arrives on the back of a lorry, you know in kit form. Like a posh shed, but I'm not sure what the planning requirements are.'

'There's a height limit for the roof, but it's four metres at the ridge line if the building is more than two-point-five metres from the fence. You've plenty of space for a nice size garden room that would fall within permitted development rights. If you are seriously considering doing this, it would save quite a bit of upheaval and cost, if we laid the concrete slab and ran the power cables down while we're here.'

My eyes light up. 'It's do-able then? I can have my little office in the garden?'

Ross looks at me, cocking his head to one side, smiling. 'You can have anything you want, Kerra. And I'm game for anything that gives me an excuse to keep coming back here. But I think it's about time you paid me a visit instead, at The Forge, what do you think?'

It's all I can do to stop myself from asking whether it's a date, but that's just the devil in me coming out.

21. Big Plans

I wave at Sissy, who is busy serving a customer as I step through the door to The Design Cave. A little bell tinkles and it's a nice touch. In fact, although it's one of the smallest shops in the arcade, it's one of those places you walk into and feel you've been transported to another place. There is so much stock in here you have to tread warily, but everything is interesting, and it smells heavenly. Mainly due to the expensive candles, but goodness you get what you pay for because the scents hit your nose instantly.

I go over to the counter to grab one of the net bags and begin shopping.

'I have your order all ready, I'll be with you in a moment, Kerra.' Sissy acknowledges me, and I put up my hand to let her know I'm not in a hurry.

As I browse, I find myself filling the bag rather quickly.

It isn't long before the tinkling of the bell lets me know that Sissy's customer has left, even though I'm the other side of the central display that blocks my view. Making my way back over to the counter, Sissy is apologetic.

'Sorry about the wait,' she says. 'Goodness, that's a basket-full.'

'And it's heavy,' I laugh. 'I'd like that little cabinet as well.

The problem is that I'm parked on the other side of town as it's heaving out there today.'

'It's market day,' Sissy commiserates. I'd totally forgotten that. 'I could deliver it all, if you like? Those night lights are quite bulky and you'd only be able to carry two at a time. It would have to be this evening, though, as it's just me and I always think it looks bad if people shut up shop. You know, that little handwritten sign that says gone to lunch, or back soon. So unprofessional.'

As I listen and Sissy begins scanning the items, I'm still glancing around. There's so much to see and I don't want to miss a thing.

'Is that what I think it is?' I point to an item standing against the wall to my left. Partially obscured by a pile of throws and some cushions, it's a cute piece of furniture. If I'm not mistaken it's in a very similar style to the range I've ordered for the bedroom. The legs have the same graceful sweep to them.

'It's an end-of-bed chaise, you know, for the extra pillows you don't use at night.'

'Sold! It's just what I've been looking for.'

Sissy beams. 'My goodness, maybe I should slow down a little,' she laughs, 'you might end up buying an entire van load before I've finished ringing this lot up. I am very grateful for the custom, Kerra. If you write down your address I'll pop everything round to you about six-thirty this evening? Delivery is free.'

'That's very kind of you, thanks so much, Sissy. You have a great eye and there are some lovely pieces here. I'll definitely be calling in again.'

Walking back to the car my phone kicks into life; it's Dad.

'Hey, how's your day going? Everything under control?' My voice is upbeat after a little retail therapy.

'It most certainly is,' he replies and he sounds unusually bright.

'Well, tell me all about it, then.'

'I had lunch with Nettie down at The Lark and Lantern. It seems she's not too busy to fit in a few hours here and there at the kennels, after all.'

Scrunching up my eyes I utter a silent *yes* and the smile that follows couldn't possibly get any bigger.

'Oh Dad, that's wonderful news!'

'I know you've been worried, but I'm only taking on as much as I can handle. With Nettie's help it will help me cope with the really busy periods.'

It's a huge relief, because I don't know how long Sy is going to stay. And while James is a great help, it's just a little cash in his pocket as and when he has the time to spare.

'Well, it will be nice for you to have Nettie around again. I'm just about to drive back from Polreweek. If you have time later, pop over for a coffee.'

'I can't today. Sy and I have cleared out the smallest bedroom. I'm having a bit of new carpet put down.'

That's what I love about Sy, he inspires people to confront change head on and that's a real gift. He still hasn't responded to the text I sent him yesterday, just checking in on him, but I know what he's like when he's head down working. I find myself taking the slightly longer route home with the intention of stopping off at Tegan's place. She might be out and about, of course, but it's worth a shot. I even surprise myself when I realise I'm humming as I drive along.

As I turn into Tegan's road, her house is on the right and my eyes scan around for a parking place. Few of the terraced cottages have off-road parking and it's always a nightmare to find a spot. As I slow, I see a couple walking hand in hand along the pavement on the other side of the road. Suddenly they stop, and she turns into him as he inclines his head to kiss her. Aww… as a silhouette they look perfect.

As I slowly drive by they break apart, after lingering for several seconds, and it's Sy I'm staring at as he gazes down at Tegan. My foot instantly hits the accelerator. The last time I saw Tegan kissing a man, it was Pete and that sends a little wave of unease through me. When two people come together there are so many factors that need to slot into place to make it work. I realise that at the moment they are both in a vulnerable position but what if that makes them cling to each other like a lifeline? Is it enough to guarantee they won't end up breaking each other's hearts? I could never forgive myself if either of them got hurt because of my intervention.

When Sissy pulls up in the lay-by opposite, I'm on my hands and knees weeding the front garden.

'Sorry I'm a bit late. I had a customer come in literally two minutes before closing and it was a big sale. What a day it's been today—I can't believe my luck!'

Sissy's face is flushed with excitement.

I smile back at her. 'Selling isn't luck, it's down to all your hard work. You've turned that little shop into a cave of treasures and it's a delight to step inside.'

She looks back at me, but her smile has disappeared. 'Hard work alone doesn't guarantee anything, I've found.'

'I'm really sorry to hear that, Sissy.'

'Still, today has been a good one and it was enough to buy me another month.' As soon as she finishes speaking, I can see that she's embarrassed. 'Oh dear, I didn't mean to… I'll start carrying everything in. It's a truly beautiful cottage you have here.'

'Just wait until you get inside,' I laugh, and she looks at me quizzically. 'I'll give you a hand.'

Sissy swings open the rear doors and nimbly levers herself up into the back, untying a strap which is anchoring the chaise. As she slides it along to the rear doors and jumps down, we each take an end. I nod and we lift in unison.

'This is nice and solid. I've just ordered some bedroom furniture and it could be from the same range. French Elite, isn't it?'

'Yes, it is—what a coincidence.'

'I certainly didn't see this piece when I was looking online. I wonder what else I missed.'

We stop to look both ways, waiting for a car to pass before hurrying across the road and manoeuvring between the two skips.

'It's a wide range and they do dining room furniture and dressers, as well as bedroom furniture,' Sissy replies.

'Oh, I'll just grab my key. We've had a couple of dodgy-looking characters hanging around, so I keep the front door locked at all times.'

A look of surprise flashes over her face as we lower the bench to the ground. I pop the key in the door.

'Safety first, I always say. The day after I took over the lease on the shop I arrived early morning to find someone had broken in through the back. I wasn't open for business at that stage and nothing had been unpacked. They must have thought their luck was in, as everything was all in nice little boxes that were easy to transport. Thankfully, the intruders were disturbed, so they weren't able to steal all of my stock, but they grabbed a fair bit before getting away. Unfortunately, I had an insurance quote all sorted but forgot to finalise it. It was a double hit, as I had to pay for the back door to be replaced, too. Lesson learnt, but it was a tough one.'

I shake my head sadly.

'Thieves have no conscience at all, and it isn't just the cost, it makes you feel vulnerable. I've recently had to have security lights and a gate with a big padlock installed because of prowlers. That was a horrible start for you, though.'

Sissy's eyes have opened wide as I back into the sitting room and she gazes around at the empty shell.

'Goodness me. This was not at all what I was expecting.'

I grin back at her.

'What, a cavernous, empty hole, or the thick layer of gritty dust?'

She starts laughing. 'Both! I presume this needs to go upstairs? I'm a bit taller than you, so it might be best if you go up backwards and I'll grab this end, so I can take the weight.'

'Are you sure you don't mind? It's too awkward to do it

on my own, but I could wait and get one of the builders to give me a hand tomorrow.'

'Oh no, I'm stronger than I look. I move wardrobes on my own, so this is nothing.'

'You sell wardrobes?'

I shuffle backwards and take a first cautious step up.

'I have in the past. Unfortunately, the new shop severely restricts what I can display, but I have a big lock-up facility. Some of my old customers still buy direct from me. I store lots of things there as I buy and sell old furniture, too— that's how it all began.'

The conversation stops as we negotiate the plastic sheeting and the very tight turn at the top of the stairs. It's obvious that Sissy has done this before, many times, and after a few concise instructions we're on the landing, tipping the chaise on its end and easing it through into the master bedroom at the front.

'What a lovely room,' Sissy remarks. 'For a cottage it's a good size and having two windows makes it so light.'

'The new bed will go in the same position but I'm adding matching bedside tables and a triple wardrobe over there.'

Sissy frowns. 'I hate to tell you, but you won't get the triple around that tight turn at the top of the stairs, Kerra. It's a massive piece of furniture and although the doors and legs come off, the entire frame is in one piece. It's a two-man job just to lift it and you'd need a lot more headroom on the landing to get it over the bannister rail.'

I look at her, crestfallen. Why didn't I think about that?

'I wish I'd bumped into you before I'd placed the order. What am I going to do?'

'Give them a ring and explain your dilemma. Maybe

give them the dimensions and ask them to check with the delivery guys—they'll know if it's do-able, or not. You could change it for two doubles, instead. If you move the bed over there, this entire wall opposite the windows could house the wardrobes, with a drawer unit in between.'

She's right. The bonus is that I'd gain a little extra hanging space, too.

'What a brilliant idea, Sissy. Do you have the sizes of this range on your website?'

Her face falls.

'I don't have a website yet, I'm afraid. The chaise is the only stock item I keep, mainly because it's small enough to fit in the shop and it's a good example of the range. Come to think of it, I do have one of the bow-fronted chest of drawers in the lock-up. I ordered it in for someone and they changed their mind. I'm pretty sure it's the large one with seven drawers, but I'd need to check as it could be the five-drawer one.'

What's the point of having stock in a lock-up facility when it's not on display either in a retail outlet, or online. That makes no sense at all.

'It's a bit of a cheek, but could I possibly come and take a peek at it? I loved the shape of it, but the drawer sizes looked a bit small and I wondered if it was more of a decorative piece, than a fully functional storage item. And, as you can see, I'm badly in need of storage.'

'If you're free now, we'll grab the rest of your items and I could run you over there. It's only fifteen minutes away.'

'Now I've seen the quality of the finish, I think I want to carry the look throughout the upstairs and I'd much rather purchase locally.'

'Let's fetch the rest of the items and head over to the lock-up, then. This is going to look amazing when it's finished, Kerra.'

I like Sissy, she isn't a pushy salesperson, but she knows what she's talking about. And now I have the problem of sorting out that beast of a wardrobe—but if it wasn't for Sissy that could have been a very expensive problem. Once they'd taken it apart to try to get it upstairs, I'd have been left with a piece of furniture I couldn't use.

22. The Devil is in the Detail

'That accent wall is looking good, Kerra. You do have a big blob of paint in your hair, though.'

I smile up at Tegan as she looks down at me from the ladder. For much of the last hour she's been humming softly to herself as she rollers the ceiling, and I can't recall the last time I heard her do that. I mean sing. And I know the reason why, but she's saying nothing.

'That final coat makes a huge difference. I was a bit worried painting three walls and the ceiling white would make it look a bit stark, but this soft clover colour on the window wall really softens the overall look.'

Standing back to gaze around, I think we've done a sterling job. Miraculously, we've managed to keep the beautiful, stripped pine floorboards protected and paint-free. It's much easier now the bulky bed frame has gone to Dad's, but it's not much fun sleeping on the floor on a mattress sitting on top of a sheet of polythene. Together with my temporary wardrobe, which is still only a collection of cardboard garment carriers, it does feel like one step forward and two steps back. But at least it's easier to slide the mattress around as we paint.

'When is the furniture arriving?' Tegan asks.

'On Saturday. And that reminds me, I need to make a quick call.'

I place the brush back in the tray and pull the phone out of my pocket.

'Hi, Sissy. It's Kerra. I've had confirmation that the triple wardrobe has been taken off the delivery. I didn't reorder a replacement from them, so could you add two more doubles to the list I gave you? Do you want me to pay over the phone, or is it better if I pop in later this afternoon?'

'Of course, I can. Thank you, Kerra and whichever is easiest for you. I'm serving someone at the moment, but I could ring you back shortly to save you a trip.'

'No, don't worry, I'll pop in around four. I wanted to have a quick chat about something else, anyway. See you in a bit.'

I let out a satisfied sigh.

'Problems?'

'No. Not now, anyway. Rather stupidly, I ordered the wrong size wardrobe. Did I tell you that I've found the perfect table for the new extension?'

'You have? You went shopping without me?' Tegan pouts.

'Not really shopping, as such. You know that nice little furniture shop in the arcade in Polreweek? They have a storage facility up on the trading estate and sell secondhand furniture from there, too.'

'I bet you didn't barter,' Tegan laughs, and it comes out as a disapproving snort.

'No. I didn't on this occasion,' I reply firmly. 'Sissy is Nettie's neighbour and her prices are reasonable. The Design Cave was burgled on the day she moved in and that's not an easy start for any small business. After the problems I've had here, it struck a chord with me.'

Tegan looks at me sheepishly.

'What is it?'

'I know the shop. Rumours were rife about the break-in at the time. Her landlord isn't the nicest of guys and it was such a coincidence it happened on the day most of her stock was delivered. The police were involved, but their investigations didn't come to anything.'

Tegan doesn't usually pay much heed to what she hears on the grapevine, but it seems she has her own suspicions about it.

'Sissy said they were disturbed, or they'd have gotten away with the lot.'

Tegan frowns. 'Maybe, unless that was a part of the plan. It all seemed too coincidental, the fact they used a small van. Not too big to attract attention late in the evening, but big enough to look like someone was dropping off the last few things. Unfortunately, it gave them a nice little haul, though, and goods that would have been easy to sell on. People don't realise that a lot of small businesses start out in debt and it's tough living from month to month, worrying over whether you'll be able to pay the bills. I know that only too well.'

Could this be the opportunity I've been looking for to ease into that awkward conversation about money? 'It happens, but it's hard to accept when it's someone's livelihood on the line. But changing the subject ever so slightly, I am looking for projects to invest in, Tegan. Not necessarily something I'd have to get hands-on with.'

She gives me a stern look. 'I'm not looking for handouts,

Kerra. I know you mean well, and it touches my heart, but I can sort this myself. Really. I'm so grateful to you for introducing me to Sy. I'm very confident that between us we'll come up with the right plan of action.'

We? I should feel happy she sounds so positive, but a part of me can't help wondering whether her emotions are making her see things in a rosy light. One that doesn't reflect the reality of the situation. Maybe she doesn't yet understand that making big changes requires funding.

'An investment isn't a handout, Tegan, believe me. But the offer stands. And how is it going with Sy?'

Her frown doesn't turn into a smile.

'Fine. Why?' The way she said that made it sound like what she really wanted to say was that it's none of my business.

'I was just wondering. You were a little anxious about it at the start.'

'The business needs a shake-up and I need advice. What else can I say? Anyway, I think it's time we had a break, as I'm in need of a strong cup of coffee.'

I guess the conversation ends here then, but the moment Tegan heads off, I give Sy a call.

'Hi stranger, how's it going?'

'Hectic. How about you?'

'Same here. I'm brewing some ideas for a new project. Talking of projects, how is yours progressing? Tegan isn't giving much away—should I take that as a good sign?' I ask, sounding upbeat.

Normally Sy and I often interrupt each other when we're sharing work stuff but this time there's a lull before he responds.

'We're getting there.'

That's it?

'Good. Great, in fact. Is there anything I can do to help?'

'No. You know what it's like, we're fine-tuning the plan and it takes a while to get there.'

'Well, shout if you need anything. Anything at all.'

So neither of them want to talk to me about what's going on. Is that a good, or a bad thing? I wonder.

'Sorry I'm late. I took a wrong turn.' I apologise, rather embarrassed and feeling more than a little hot and bothered. My shortcut ended up taking me around in a huge circle when I hit an unexpected diversion. It turned into the journey from hell, because some of those lanes are very narrow and twice I had to reverse back when a stream of cars came towards me.

Ross stands there, door ajar, smiling at me. 'I was beginning to think I'd been stood up.'

As my eyes travel over his face, I notice his mouth twitches and realise he's teasing me.

'You obviously haven't had to manage living on a building site with limited facilities. The prospect of a meal cooked by someone else and sitting at a dining table in a civilised manner, is hard to resist,' I reply, continuing the banter. 'There was no way I was not going to turn up.'

He laughs, indicating for me to go on through. 'It wasn't the thought of spending some time in my scintillating company, then?'

'Is that the best you can do? You know that the charm

thing doesn't work on me. But when it comes to a decent meal, I'm never going to refuse.'

His face falls, feigning disappointment, before breaking out into a big grin.

'It never did, I mean, work on you. Anyway, I thought food was the way to a man's heart, not a woman's,' he replies.

'Well, I'm starving as all I've eaten since breakfast is two apples.'

'In that case, make yourself comfortable while I dish up. I have a range of soft drinks, but if you're in the mood for wine I could run you home later then pop you back early tomorrow to collect your car,' Ross calls out, disappearing through a doorway into what I assume is the kitchen. Ooh, awkward.

'Water will be fine, but thanks for the offer. If Dad doesn't see my car parked up before he turns in for the night, he'd only panic,' I call out.

The smells beginning to waft into the sitting room make my stomach start to rumble. Circling around, I realise this is a far cry from the very modern Treylya up on the headland. Modest and manly, springs to mind. The flagstone floor is typical of a barn conversion, but it's lovely to see a good-sized log burner, as in winter it must be a little cold underfoot.

'Just waiting for the veggies, two more minutes.' Ross's voice filters into the room.

'No hurry, I'm having a nose around. Shout if you need any help.'

Three of the stone walls have been left exposed and only

the fireplace wall has been plastered. The fireplace isn't original, but reclaimed stone has been used and it blends in well. Either side of it the walls are entirely taken up with shelves, jam-packed with books.

'This is quite a library you have here. I didn't know you were an avid reader,' I shout over my shoulder.

'There's a lot you don't know about me, as I can say the same about you.'

Ross has reappeared and is leaning against the door jamb, a tea towel slung over his shoulder. Somehow, he can make even a slouch look sexy. 'Dinner is served. Come this way.'

'This wasn't originally a forge, though, was it?' I ask, thinking back to my childhood. I clearly remember trips with Dad to Trehoweth wharf to watch the fishing boats unloading. None of the properties really come to mind, although the overall impression is that not a lot has changed.

'No. The barn was used to dry out the fishing nets and store the lobster pots, back in the day. It was converted into two residential properties in the eighties. When I bought it, it was tired, but the shell was still good, and the roof had been replaced. It just needed a rewire, bit of plastering, new windows, new kitchen and bathroom—the usual.'

'Well, you've done a great job. And this is a good size for a kitchen/diner.'

You can tell when someone is in the business as the layout works.

'There's a downstairs cloakroom and a utility through there. The difficulty with a barn conversion is that it's long and narrow. And there's no garden, except for a tiny courtyard at the back. But it suits me. Anyway, sit, eat— can't keep a hungry woman waiting.'

He throws the tea towel on the countertop as I take a seat and wait until he joins me.

'You might like this; it's elderflower and pomegranate with a splash of carbonated water.' He places a jug on the table between us, then immediately starts tucking in.

'The lemon sole is fresh from this morning's catch,' Ross informs me.

It does look wonderful, the fleshy fish cooked in a little butter and sitting on top of a bed of julienne vegetables. I'm impressed.

It feels a little surreal to be here, opposite Ross, and I suddenly feel a little self-conscious.

'You don't like it?' He looks across at me and I immediately shake my head.

'No, it smells great and it looks lovely. It's just that I'm realising what coming home means. Everything seems to trigger a memory.'

'I forgot the parsley.' He leaps to his feet and returns with a small dish. All I can do is stare at him. Ross cooking for me. That was never in any of my daydreams.

'What sort of memories?' he asks.

'Just random things.'

'And the bread!' Once again, he leaps up and returns, carrying a chopping board with slices of rosemary ciabatta on it. 'Hopefully it's still warm, sorry.'

He seems on edge.

'Ross, is there anything wrong?'

He lifts the jug, filling our glasses and I sit back, watching his every move.

'This is a first,' he says, apologetically. 'I'm a little out of practice.'

'A first?'

'For us. In the old days I'd never have dared to ask you out. Not that I'm saying this is a date, or anything, as we're just old friends. But I'm not in the habit of inviting anyone back here and cooking for a guest is nerve-wracking.'

He raises his glass and I raise mine. The heat level in the room is climbing and we're both feeling it.

'To old friends and one who turns out to be a very good cook,' I quip, as we chink.

'And new beginnings.' As Ross lowers his glass, he looks directly at me for a second, as if he's mulling over his words. I wish I knew what he was thinking, deep down inside.

He begins eating in earnest and I'm left hanging, not sure what to say, so I follow suit. If I don't eat something soon, I feel as if I might faint, but whether that's from an adrenaline rush, or hunger, I'm not sure.

'Ah, I see what you mean about the courtyard. But it is cosy and very private.' It runs the length of both properties but it's barely two-metres wide. The rear wall is at least two-and-a-half-metres high, as it retains a large bank with some overhanging shrubs.

'I keep meaning to add a few potted plants or something, but I don't use it much.'

There's only a small bistro table, two chairs and a water butt.

'It's a great place to sit and read, although it does need a little colour to brighten it up.'

The chairs scrape on the stone floor as we settle ourselves down to sit and drink our coffee.

'That was a lovely meal, Ross, thank you. I'm tired of barbecue food, I will admit, but don't tell Drew.'

'You're not tiring of being back?' The glance he gives me is a hesitant one.

'No. I'll be glad when the work is finished, of course. At least I now have a little online project to play around with which might, or might not, turn into something. We'll see. It gives me something different to do and I can head upstairs for a few hours to lose myself. I just can't bear not being productive. It's how I'm wired, unfortunately.'

'That makes two of us, then. I've had to learn how to relax and it doesn't come easy, even now. I work late most nights and, if we're busy, I put in a couple of hours at the weekend. Just checking everything is running smoothly. I have site managers and foremen, but old habits die hard and I like to show my face.'

'You said you paint? That's quite a surprise.'

'Yeah, I dabble. It's a bit hit and miss at times, but cathartic and it passes a few hours on a Sunday.'

'And Tai Chi, wasn't it?'

'When things got on top of me, Yvonne, Gawen's wife over at Treeve Perran, suggested I go along to a class with her. I was sceptical, I will admit, but I go most weeks and it helped me through some tough times.'

I'm surprised he's so willing to talk about it. And now he's looking at me as if it's my turn. We're trading confidences, one at a time. I guess beneath it all we're both cautious people and this is no longer idle banter.

'Earlier on you said you could never figure out what I was thinking. I was angsting over the fact that small talk was beyond me and I'd probably never get a boyfriend.'

Ross looks surprised. 'Well, that's rather unexpected. Everyone knew you'd make a success of whatever you chose to do and you came across as very cool and collected. Nothing I did ever seemed to impress you, I remember.' As I begin to sip my coffee, he chuckles to himself, a fleeting thought flashing through his mind.

'Heck, I remember once I wanted to kiss you,' he declares, and I quickly swallow before I choke. 'But you gave me the look, the one you're so good at, and it put me firmly in my place. No one messed with Kerra, you weren't a flirt.'

As I put my mug down it clatters on the tabletop.

I laugh. 'I wasn't being cool back then, I was wondering what was wrong with *me*.'

'You did know I found you very attractive?' Ross declares and his voice softens.

My mouth goes dry, but I daren't pick up the mug again as my hand wouldn't be steady. *Tell him the truth, Kerra*, that little voice inside my head is yelling at me. But I can't.

'Did you? Why didn't you say something?' The surprise in my tone is real.

'All the boys wanted to catch your eye, but you were kinda scary, not easy to approach. At that age most of us were full of hot air and not a lot else, so it was tough trying to figure out how to gain your attention.'

His amusement is clear as he thinks back, surprisingly fondly of those days, it seems.

'I often wondered if you'd stayed here whether, as I matured, you'd have looked at me in a different light. I grew up quickly once I started working for my father, I had no choice. He doesn't suffer fools gladly. And now you're back, but I'm no better off. I might have grown up, but I'm mightily messed up when it comes to relationships.'

Say it. Say it now.

'There's nothing wrong with being cautious, Ross. When you like someone, the fear is always there that they'll reject you. Was I the only girl you didn't kiss in our year?' I ask, laughing.

He looks bemused, pausing for thought. 'Possibly. In fairness to me, I didn't instigate a lot of it—I was on the receiving end most of the time.'

'Maybe you should have kissed me that day, you know, in the classroom.'

His head tilts back and his expression changes. 'You wanted me to?'

I nod and he shakes his head. 'What a fool I was.'

'And how rejected I felt.'

He rubs both of his eyes with the heels of his hands and when he lowers them the look is one of amusement. And then he leans forward across the little bistro table.

'We could remedy that,' he whispers. And we do.

It might not be my first kiss, but it's my first non-fantasy kiss with Ross and it's well worth the wait.

Last night I was elated but this morning my emotions are in freefall. I'm not ready for this new development with Ross. What goes on inside my head is one thing, but the reality is much more complicated than that. I've walked away from my old life to start over again and I have nowhere to run and hide if things go wrong, because this is my safe zone.

He's obviously lonely and what if we rush into this and end up regretting it? It would be devastating. Snatching up my phone, I stab at the buttons.

'Tegan, it's Kerra.'

'Hi, what's up? It's a bit early for you to be ringing. Those guys aren't back, are they?'

'No. Nothing like that. Where are you now? Are you driving?'

'Yes. I'm on my way to the warehouse to pick up some cleaning supplies. Why?'

'Can I meet you somewhere for a quick chat? There's been a development and I'm in a bit of a quandary. I'd really value your opinion.'

'Of course. Look, I'm only a few minutes away from The Rocks. I'll head there now and meet you in the lay-by, is that okay?'

'Perfect, see you in about five minutes and thanks.'

I try to pull my thoughts together as I drive, but the same phrase keeps going around and around inside my head. Just because you want something doesn't mean to say that it's good for you. Of course, the moment I pull up alongside Tegan's van and she hops out to meet me, I blurt it out.

'I kissed Ross.'

I look around nervously. There are two other cars parked a few metres away but I notice there's a woman sitting in one of them with the window wound down.

'Come on, let's take the trail.'

It's been many years since I drove across to one of our old haunts. I remember borrowing Mum's car and sitting behind the steering wheel quite proudly, as Tegan searched for something to blast out on the radio.

The track down to The Rocks is narrow and quite steep, steeper than I remembered. But nostalgia floods over me as we cautiously make our way down. The beach is tiny but there are two people walking their dogs. It's not a popular or well-known destination, as the sandy patches surrounding several mounds of towering rock are small and there's a lot of seaweed washed up on the narrow shoreline.

'You kissed Ross, you say? He didn't kiss you?'

'We kissed each other.'

'Um, so you're saying it was a mistake?'

'No. I wanted to. And so did he.'

A little frown furrows her brow. 'I thought you'd decided he was a bit of a disaster zone. I think the words you used were that he was a bad judge of character, given his disastrous marriage and divorce.'

'I did but that was then, and things have moved on.'

'Obviously. And where did this kiss take place, might I ask?'

'At his place. Last night. He made me dinner.'

Tegan's eyes spring open wide.

'You're seeing each other?' Her reaction is understandable, I suppose, given our previous conversation. 'If people see you together, this will be big news. You're prepared for that, are you?'

I let out a huge sigh, my feet idly scuffing at the sandy floor.

'Clearly you are,' she labours, 'if you're happy to spend time alone with him.'

I glance at her, a little surprised to hear there's an edge to her tone. Is it disapproval? I turn away, staring out across the ribbon of blue water ebbing and flowing.

'There's enough tittle-tattle being talked about me right now and this could be the thing that makes my future here untenable,' I admit.

'Look, you hid your feelings so well and for so long that I can understand how overwhelming this might be, but I know you. Kerra Shaw doesn't make snap decisions and she doesn't like other people knowing her business. People will begin to see as plainly as I do right now that you're in love with Ross.'

I roll my eyes and push my head back, staring up at the soft blue sky above us and those fluffy, marshmallow-white clouds.

'I've kept my feelings buried for what feels like forever because I had no idea he was interested in me. Now is not the time for me to—'

'—loosen up? Take a risk and see what happens? And for the first time in your life stop caring about what other people think?'

I guess I deserve that.

'I took a risk coming back here and putting myself in the limelight,' I reply.

'This is different and you know it, Kerra. That's why we're here talking about it, right now. You are clever, focused and you have a big heart, but you seem incapable of putting your trust in someone unless you are in total control.'

'What if Ross is merely looking for a distraction? Imagine how humiliating it would be if word gets out and people make a big deal of it, like they do, and then things fizzle out between us?'

'Are you worried about your reputation, being labelled as one of Ross's exes, or how to carry on if your heart gets broken? If it's either of the first two, then I'm disappointed in you. If it's the latter then I'm sad, because allowing yourself to love someone is all about trust. You can't hedge your bets. This isn't some business deal you're considering, Kerra. You're scared Ross will let you down, but what if he doesn't? He's probably experiencing a similar level of anxiety after what he's been through. It's unlikely that either of you is going to want to flaunt your blossoming romance in front of everybody, is it? No one knows what goes on behind closed doors, Kerra, remember that.'

Either Tegan is very astute and good at thinking on her feet, or those words have been floating around inside her head for a while. A part of me can't help wondering whether she's talking about me, or herself. Is that why she sounds so angry?

'You think it's no one's business but ours, even though my dad might not take it well? He has a lot of respect for Ross, but he fell out with Ross's father when he tried to stop the change of use going through for the dog kennels.'

'Oh my, I'd forgotten all about that. And yes, I do. Anyway, I'm sorry but I must get on as I have a massive to-do list. And I'm having one of those grumpy days, so I apologise if I sounded a little short with you there.'

I step forward to give her a hug.

'Thank you for dropping everything for me. And I'm here for you, Tegan, always. I understand that some things aren't easy to talk about, but when you're ready you know where to come, my friend.'

She nods, then heads off in the direction of the incline. Suddenly, Tegan stops, turning back to glance briefly at me.

'If this gets out you do know it will be the talk of not just the village, but the entire area? I mean, you're so... cool, calm and collected and he's so...' She struggles to finish her sentence. 'So, fiery. Passionate. If you're really worried it's going to be short-lived then it's decision time, because it isn't going to be easy to keep this a secret.'

Is she saying I'm cold or calculating? Or both?

We climb back up the trail in silence and I stand next to her car ready to wave her off. The mood between us is fraught with tension. Slamming the door shut, Tegan winds down the window.

'Just be careful,' she says. 'I'm being honest with you, Kerra, because it's time to face your fears. I've been there and I'm coming through it, but it hurts like hell and if the decisions are easy then you're only chipping away at the edges and avoiding the real issue.'

'That took courage and I appreciate it. I've decided not to mention this to anyone else, including Sy. His focus is on the work you two are doing and I don't want to be a distraction.'

'He won't hear it from me, Kerra, I promise. Sorry to cut and run. Give it some thought, and you know where to find me if you need to talk.'

As I watch her pull away, I think about the way Ross's arms wrapped around me as we stood in the hallway. And the undeniable passion as we kissed goodnight and I knew he didn't want me to leave. I didn't want to leave, either, but Tegan is right—I've never been the sort to act on impulse. My life is here now, and I'm adamant that my love life is not fair game for the gossips.

I'm not only thinking of myself, but of the effect on Ross, too. He's been through so much and he's being equally as careful as I am. However, I fear we might both have thrown caution to the wind last night if it wasn't for the fact that Dad would have been worried sick if I hadn't arrived home. I couldn't exactly phone him and say I was having a sleepover and ask him to let Ripley in, could I? The anonymity of London has never felt so appealing as it does right now.

Ross Treloar, you have a lot to answer for, but you do cook a damn fine meal and that kiss delivered and some. But is that enough for me to risk everything?

JULY

23. Revelations

It's been a hectic few weeks. Life is good and I've been head down working while everything in the cottage finally takes shape around me. After showing Sissy a demo of the sort of website I could build for her, three weeks ago we shook hands on a deal. The contract has been signed and she's in the process of looking for bigger premises. With a thirty per cent share in return for my investment, I'll provide all the training and IT support she needs for the online shop, but she'll run the business day-to-day. Sissy has the vision, she just didn't have the capital, or the volume of sales and I'm more than happy for her to bounce ideas off me whenever required.

Now she has the funds to move forward, I have no doubt at all the website will soon begin to generate a reasonable income. We've already done a mail shot to her database of customers, offering them a discount on their first online order. My next job is to make a quick phone call as what Sissy needs now is an assistant and I've told her that I know just the person. Trawling through my contacts, I give Logan a call.

'Hi there, Kerra. I hope you're not having problems with the internet.'

I laugh. 'No. It's perfectly fine, although I will need to talk to you about a possible booster, as Treloar's will be building me a little office in the garden once the main work here is finished. Actually, I was ringing to see if Sienna has had any luck finding a new job with more hours?'

'Not as yet, although she does have an interview for something the week after next. Why?'

'Well, I've gone into partnership with a woman named Sissy Warren. At the moment she has a little shop in the arcade in Polreweek, called The Design Cave. Do you know it?'

'I don't, but Sienna might.'

'Well, aside from setting up an online store, the business is going to move to larger premises nearby. Sissy needs an assistant to help set up the office and general things like ordering stock and invoicing. I mentioned that I might know someone who was looking for a job with flexible working hours. Do you think it might be worth Sienna and Sissy having a chat?'

'I'm sure Sienna would be delighted. She's looking for something more challenging now, but with the flexibility to work around the school run when it's her turn.'

'Great, I'll text you Sissy's number then and you can pass that on.'

'Thanks for thinking of Sienna, Kerra, it's very kind of you. I was going to drop in to see how you were doing, you know, what with the latest news on the grapevine.'

'What news is this? I've been glued to my keyboard getting the website up and running so I haven't been out and about much. Who's talking and about what?'

'The news about Mr Mills. I heard it from one of my customers in the village.'

'He's back?'

'No. He's in police custody, apparently. Something to do with selling stolen cars and they're gearing up for a big investigation. Some nasty people involved, apparently, so be vigilant and if you notice anything suspicious, ring the police.'

My stomach turns over as I recall the men who were hanging around.

'Thanks, Logan. I appreciate the tip off. I'll, um, send you that contact number, then. Speak soon.' I am shocked by the news but at least I can stop worrying now, I tell myself firmly. After all, it's unlikely I'll get any more unwelcome visitors now they know the police are on to them.

After dropping Sissy a quick email to let her know Sienna will be giving her a call, I'm keen to finish up a few odds and ends when I hear Dad's voice calling up the stairs.

'Only me. Do you have five minutes?'

'Yes, come on up.'

When Dad appears I notice he's had his hair cut and he's looking rather smart, but he's wearing a frown and it's clear something has upset him.

'Is this about Mr Mills?'

'You heard, then? I just got off the phone with Alistair.'

I move some papers off the seat alongside my desk and Dad sits down with a thump.

'Uncle Alistair?'

'Yes. About Alice's careless comments. I'm fuming. I bet you are, too!'

I shrug my shoulders, looking at him quite blankly.

'That girl has a nasty habit of saying the first thing that comes into her head. I doubt she meant to link you to him and his shady dealings, but you know what it's like. And now some people are putting two and two together and...' Dad tails off, angrily.

'What exactly did she say?'

'Something along the lines of she hopes people don't think you were involved in the scam, given how much money you're piling into this place.'

I'm rendered speechless, as Dad shakes his head and grunts. 'I advised Alistair to have a firm word with her and I went a bit far, Kerra. I told him you don't go flaunting your success, but I doubt anyone else we know is likely to become a millionaire unless they win the lottery.'

I feel my whole body deflate, as I let out the breath I've been holding in.

'Oh Dad, that's bad, that's very bad. I wish you hadn't said that. I don't care what people think, but it's easier to fit in when you don't stand out, if you know what I mean. You're right, Alice was just being... Alice, but imagine what she'll be saying if Uncle Alistair repeats that to her.'

As he looks at me his expression is one of remorse. 'It was wrong, I knew that the minute the words popped out of my mouth. But Alice needs to be put in her place once and for all and, damn it, I'm proud of what you've achieved. I'm sure as hell not going to stand back and let the rumour mill cast doubts on my daughter's integrity.'

There's a little rap on the door and Will's head appears around the side of it.

'I'm very sorry to disturb you, Kerra, but I can't find Drew and we're just about to install the kitchen cabinets. There's a problem as it appears the run is out by a couple of hundred millimetres and the worktop doesn't fit.'

He looks at me gingerly and then across at Dad, observing our grim expressions. 'If you're busy right now, we can start unpacking the wall units while we wait.'

'No, I'm just going,' Dad says, as he eases himself up off the chair. 'Sorry, lovely, I'll see you later.' Dad places his hand on my shoulder to give it a comforting squeeze on his way out.

Will is standing there not quite sure what to do, or say, but his men are waiting and I can't hold things up now.

'Right. I'm all yours,' I say to Will, as brightly as I can. I woke up buzzing with optimism this morning but that feeling has already dissipated. Something is telling me that it isn't about to get any better.

There's a problem with the kitchen units, but in the grand scheme of things it seems too trivial to get upset about. I leave Will to come up with a solution, even though I can see he doesn't agree with my decision. But I really don't want him ringing Uncle Alistair and getting him on site to point out the mistake.

Making my way back upstairs, I know it's going to be impossible to focus on work, as my head is all over the place. The cottage might have been a temporary home to a criminal, but how was I to know that?

When word of this reaches Tegan's ears she'll wonder

why I haven't called her. But after a few rings her phone goes straight to voicemail, yet again. Guess I'd better try Sy, even though he's been very quiet, recently.

'It's only me,' I say as casually as I can. 'How are things going?'

'Good. Busy. Sorry, I keep meaning to ring you and then something else crops up.' I can hear the guilt in Sy's voice. Dad mentioned to me recently that Sy heads out as soon as the morning dog-walking session is done and often doesn't return until quite late.

'Sy, what's going on and why are you avoiding me?'

The line goes ominously silent for a few seconds, before he emits a soft groan.

'I'm moving out of your Dad's place.'

'You're going back to London?' I ask, my voice tinged with apprehension. I'm not sure he's ready to go back and mend fences yet.

'No. Working with Tegan is going to command all my attention from here on in if we're going to do this properly.'

'That's great!' I enthuse. Things must be going well, then. Thank goodness something is, as I'm not sure I could take any more bad news today.

'So why are you moving out of Dad's place? He'll understand, but he really enjoys your company.'

When Sy begins speaking again his tone is apologetic.

'I'm moving in with Tegan.'

'You're WHAT?' Am I the only one who can hear alarm bells ringing, because they're so loud I'm sure they can't just be inside my head. This is so wrong.

'Don't panic,' Sy immediately jumps in. 'It makes sense. I'm helping her get everything sorted so she can run a paperless office. We're scanning in all the contracts and organising what records she does have on the computer and it's time-consuming. And we've been running a targeted advertising campaign linked to a couple of the letting companies' websites. As we expand those areas we'll be taking on new staff and costing out alternative methods of transport.'

He isn't simply brainstorming this, it's a firm plan he's outlining and, clearly, they are both on board with it. I knew there was something big on Tegan's mind that day I told her about Ross, but not this and that's why Sy has been hiding himself away.

'But that's going to cost quite a bit. It's money Tegan doesn't have, Sy, and shouldn't you be giving at least a little thought to what you're going to be doing next? It's wonderful that you're able to help her out, but what happens when the plan is in place and it's time to move on?'

He clears his throat, hesitantly. 'We're going into partnership. I'm using my nest egg to buy into the business. Permanently. A new tenant is taking over my lease on the house share and I'll be popping back to pack up my things sometime next week, probably.'

I'm floored. 'So, you're going to be living *and* working together? Sy, that's too much, too soon. What if you have a falling out? I know it solves two major problems in one, but come on, even you must see it's a monumental step for you both.'

'We're being practical,' he replies rather tersely. 'There's a lot of work ahead of us but the figures stack up.'

I slap the palm of my hand against my forehead.

'And you've fallen for each other, so life seems rosy.'

Argh, that sounded rather glib. It's too late to talk him out of this now and that's why they've been avoiding me. They knew I'd suggest they take it slowly.

'Oh, Sy.' The words slip from between my lips and I can't hide a sense of exasperation. 'I know you only have the best of intentions and this is partly my fault, I should have seen this coming. But—'

'But what? I've never been more certain about anything in my whole life. Ever. Tegan feels the same way, too. So why can't you just be happy for us? Why assume it's going to go wrong?'

Where do I start. Do I mention all his past disappointments? Or that being together 24/7 isn't the best idea when you've only known each other for a couple of months? What if Tegan feels conflicted as they grow closer; is she really ready to move on emotionally? Working together is hard for any couple, but more so in their case as the pressure is on. Failure could mean losing everything. It's a recipe for disaster if ever there was one.

'I'm sorry, Sy. It's just that… we know it isn't easy running a business, especially when it's one that is struggling to survive. But a new relationship—that's a whole different thing. It grows slowly as you get to know each other and the time apart is crucial to that process. You need space to be able to step back and see things clearly. That old saying absence makes the heart grow fonder sounds trite, but there's a fundamental truth to it. A little distance allows you to gauge your true feelings. Why don't you stay at Dad's for a while longer? What difference would a month or two make?'

I hold my breath, awaiting his response.

'I'm disappointed, Kerra, because I really hoped you'd

trust that I would never take a risk if I thought for one second Tegan would end up getting hurt. You think I'm going to mess this up, don't you?'

Tears begin to well-up behind my eyelids as I suck in a deep breath to calm myself. I remember Tegan telling me that I don't *trust* anyone unless I'm in control.

'No, you're wrong about that, Sy. I was the one who brought the two of you together. I'm just asking you to exercise a little caution here and tread lightly. Coping with one major upheaval in life is a challenge for anyone. But here you are—new home, new job, new relationship... can't you see that's overload? And for Tegan, like it or not, Pete played a big part in the business, so there will be moments when she'll be ultra-sensitive. Maybe over things that are rather trivial, but not too insignificant to trigger a reaction.'

'You don't think I'm aware of that? Or is it that you don't think I can handle it?' He's offended and that wasn't my intention.

'Of course not. If you weren't such a genuinely kind and caring person, I wouldn't have introduced you two in the first place. All I'm saying is that we all need something to cling onto, something familiar that helps to ground us in moments when we hit the bumps in the road. There is no avoiding them, Sy. What happens when the pressure begins to build, and you need a little break from each other?'

It sounds harsh, but ever since I've known Sy I'm the one he turns to and now I've upset him. And Tegan, well, she has her parents, but I wonder what their view is of what's going on and how happy she would be to run to them if she has a problem. At the moment, I seriously doubt she'd come knocking on my door.

I half-fear the line will suddenly disconnect as the seconds pass but when Sy begins speaking again he sounds calmer.

'This is different, Kerra. That's why Tegan hasn't said anything to you. We've spent hours talking it through, believe me. I know it sounds crazy, but it feels right. Do we edge forward half expecting to fail, or do we see this as an opportunity to turn our lives around and grab some happiness? Don't you see that neither Tegan, nor I, have anything left that represents that comfort zone? This is probably the most honest way for two people to come together, because you're right—we're putting everything on the line.'

It's a humbling confession and my heart feels heavy that my initial reaction was one of fear and doubt. Life has taught me to tread warily and hold back, and I'm wondering now if that's not always a good thing.

'If there is anything at all I can do to help the two of you, I'm here no matter what you need. Whether it's time, money or just a listening ear.'

'That's all we wanted to hear you say, Kerra, but we've got this. I must go. I'm heading back to break the news to Eddie. I'm sure he'll be fine with it now Nettie is helping out and I have a feeling it won't come as a total surprise to him, anyway. We'll speak soon, I promise. Tegan will be relieved we've talked, as she's worried sick what you'll think. But please believe me when I say we are going to make this work.'

'I'm happy for you guys, I really am. Oh, I forget the reason for making the call. Can you tell Tegan that Mr Mills has been arrested for some dodgy dealings to do with cars? Rumours are beginning to circulate but let her know I'm aware of them and tell her not to let it worry her. Maybe she can call in next time she's passing, and I'll explain what happened.'

'Oh, that's a surprise. I'm sure she will, now that you finally know the truth. Thanks, Kerra.'

I've been so caught up with my own affairs, I ignored that niggling little worry in the pit of my stomach and it was wrong of me. And now I'm merely an observer, as my two best friends are coping with the seemingly impossible. How could I let this happen?

24. The Morning After the Night Before

The sound of the doorbell disturbs my worrisome thoughts. I'm half-expecting to see a police officer, as it's been a week and I've heard nothing further. Instead, Ross is standing in front of me and he immediately launches into a little speech.

'I probably shouldn't have come, but I wanted to check you are happy with the way the guys left the garden after signing off the job yesterday.'

As I step back and he follows me through into the light, bright space, I can see that's not the only reason he's here. I half-smile to myself, as I bite my lip for fear of looking a little smug.

'Perfectly happy,' I beam at him, as his eyes search mine.

'If we'd been drinking last night, Kerra, then I would have said it was one of those things. But it wasn't, was it?'

A warm glow begins to radiate out from my core, as I get a flashback from last night. I don't think either of us was really surprised we ended up in bed together after yet another romantic dinner at The Forge.

It's just after 7 a.m. on a Saturday morning and there's little sign of movement outside. I haven't even had a cup of coffee yet, but it's clear Ross has been up a while.

'No. It wasn't. What we do about it is another thing entirely, though. People notice everything that happens around here, Ross, and we both know that. I bet Arthur saw you arrive just now and I've no doubt he's called Mrs Moyle to the window.'

'So, I'm popping in to inform you that there's still no news regarding your garden office. I can't book in the installation until I have a firm date. More importantly, what are the chances that anyone who knows you saw you arriving, or leaving, The Forge, last night?'

It was our fourth dinner date. But what happened between us was a turning point and I can see he's on edge.

'Pretty slim, I hope, but we need to be careful. Given all the ongoing speculation about this thing with Mr Mills, people's eyes are everywhere. I can't believe anyone who knows me would seriously consider I knew what was going on, but word travels far and wide, as we know.'

Ross's smile is tinged with relief. Did he think I'd be regretful this morning?

'Okay. Point taken.'

'So, when you're here we keep it purely professional,' I reply firmly.

'And when we're at mine we...' He steps forward, gazing into my eyes and I smile back up at him.

'We're two people who don't have to worry about what happens outside of The Forge.'

As Ross's lips seek out mine, I just want to sink into him.

Throwing my arms around his shoulders, I feel like a girl again. I've imagined this time and time again, but even in my dreams it was never this good.

'If this turns out to be a fleeting thing,' I half-whisper into his neck, 'I wouldn't want it to spoil our friendship going forward. Or involve the people we care about. Things get complicated then and yet, if we were strangers who had just started seeing each other it wouldn't be a big deal. No one seems at all concerned about Sy and Tegan, except me, of course. And that's because I'd hate to see either of them get hurt.'

'I understand,' he sighs. 'Hopefully, my place can be our little sanctuary, then. I can't pretend I haven't been scarred by what I've been through, Kerra. Let's take this one step at a time—no pressure, no expectations. And now I really must go, because it will look odd if I stay for too long.'

I lean my forehead against his.

'It's a pity we didn't take advantage of our youth, Ross. As adults it changes everything and look at us, worrying about what people will think. We didn't care way back then. It was all about the fear of rejection, wasn't it?'

Ross smiles down at me.

'Different things matter when you're older. And that's village life for you, anyway. It's why I moved away when I split up with Bailey. It's not far, but it's far enough to feel I have room to breathe and I'm away from prying eyes and loose tongues. You're welcome at The Forge at any time— day, or night. But I have a lot of respect for your dad and I always had the feeling he wasn't too impressed by my family.'

'I'm all grown up now, Ross, and what I do is my business,' I reply emphatically.

'I know, but I wouldn't want to upset him and I know you don't, either. Anyway, I must go. I've asked Will if one of the carpenters can install a cat flap for you. It's on me.'

'Just in case I don't make it home one night?' I enquire, shaking my head as he grins back at me cheekily.

Ross plants a kiss on my forehead and his arms circle around my waist as he pulls me into him. I don't resist and our lips touch for the merest of seconds. We want to linger, but we both know we can't.

As Ross hurries off to start his working day, I think about Dad. Oh dear. Dad sensed I had a thing for Ross when I was at school. He was always a little wary of him because Ross's father had this way of making people feel they were beneath him and his family. It was worse after the big planning application row, when Ross's father lodged an objection. Mum sensed how I felt, of course, but she wouldn't have said anything, and my pride alone wouldn't have allowed me to talk about it. But mums have a way of noticing the small things, and in those days, Ross's family lived in the big house on the outskirts of the village. We all hung around together, albeit some more comfortable as a part of the group, than others.

When his parents moved into a much bigger property up near Rosveth moor, that all changed. I think Dad was relieved Ross wasn't around anymore. Mum could see my disappointment, though, as my path rarely crossed with him from that point onwards. By the time I left for London, I'd heard that Ross had been seeing someone for a while and

I'd long accepted the inevitable. I might have been heartbroken, but I wasn't about to share that fact with anyone.

I have no idea what Dad's reaction would be if he knew. I know most parents live in hope of their offspring finding someone suitable to settle down with. Dad is quite a traditional man in many ways, and I don't think he'd approve of the whispers if it got out that Ross and I are casually involved. All I can hope is that he doesn't notice a change in me, because it's been a long time since I've had any romantic excitement in my life. Or good sex, come to that.

Drew's jaw drops as I catch him up on the latest news after yet another visit to spend time with Felicity.

'Stolen vehicles? And all of this was going on right here and I had absolutely no idea. It's a wonder the police haven't interviewed me, yet. But in all honesty, I sort of assumed he worked in the motor trade delivering secondhand cars. He had those trade plates they use and he must have travelled some distance, because he wasn't home every night. But he was one of those guys you don't really notice because he didn't go out of his way to speak.'

It seems no one really knew anything about him and Dad pretty much said the same.

'Well, I knew less than you did, but when the police rang to ask a few questions, I was able to give them his bank details and they were going to talk to the letting agency, next. He would have had references, so either he's not very bright, or maybe he isn't a hardened criminal at all. Some people find themselves getting caught up in things because of their situation. I guess we won't know unless the investigations succeed in uncovering all the facts.'

I'm over the shock of it now and having braved a visit to Mrs Moyle, her tirade about Alice's careless talk took me by surprise. Knowing Mrs Moyle won't stand to hear anyone speculating over such a ridiculous rumour has made me feel a lot better. It's Dad I feel sorry for, because he just wants an easy life and here I am, unwittingly causing all sorts of problems. And that's without anyone knowing about my involvement with Ross.

'So, are you pleased with the final result?' Drew gazes around, taking in what has been a solid week's work and the completion of the project.

'Pleased? I'm thrilled. And you?'

He scrunches up his face. 'Wishing I'd gone with the slate floor, too, but Felicity fell in love with the travertine and I haven't given up all hope of tempting her back here. This week was amazing and she needed the break from work.'

Felicity. On. Off. On. Off.

'I did wonder how it was going but assumed no news was good news.'

'Sorry. I should have messaged you. I was in constant contact with the guys over the mess up with the cabinets. It wasn't down to Treloar, you do know that? I was disappointed Will didn't get someone from your uncle's company to sort it out.'

'He did suggest that, but I'm avoiding my cousin, Alice, and the last thing I wanted was my uncle here. Ross's carpenter did a brilliant job making it work.'

'But it cost you a new worktop, Kerra, and that wasn't cheap.'

'Sometimes it's not about the money. Uncle Alistair would love Dad to go back and work in the family business again. I know it's unlikely, but it's in his blood, woodworking. If things at the kennels don't work out, I don't want anything to come between them. Alice made a few unfortunate comments in the shop and she went too far. I'm sure she doesn't believe I knew about Mr Mills' illegal business, but Dad is angry. Uncle Alistair is embarrassed by her behaviour, so I don't want it blowing up into a big thing. Family means something, even when they do wrong and it's a case of the least said the better, right now.'

Drew crosses his arms in front of him, turning to stare out at the garden through the beautiful wall of glass.

'I know the feeling—dealing with fallout from family rows is a minefield. Felicity is so miserable at work and yet she can't walk away. Her brother has made a couple of really bad decisions and she feels it would be disloyal to turn her back on the business when things are starting to go wrong. Felicity loves me as much as I love her, but she says she owes it to her dad to support her brother. All I can do is be there when she needs a shoulder to cry on, in the hope that at some point she will be able to make the break.'

I nod in agreement. 'It's hard to sit back and wait for things to play out, isn't it? Dad won't let me forgive Alice, unless she apologises for what she said. I don't think she meant it nastily; she just speaks without thinking.'

Drew looks at me sadly. 'I've been here a while, Kerra, and I can tell you that it's a bit more than that. She's jealous of you, the fact that you had the guts to move away and prove yourself. Then you come back home for good, and everyone is in awe of what you're doing. You could so easily have sold this place and it would probably have ended up as someone's second home.'

It's a sad thought, but a valid one and it won't have gone unnoticed.

'*Emmets* don't realise they are pricing locals out of the area by buying a second home here. And with investors buying up properties to let out, it means the younger generation can't afford to get on the property ladder. I'm sure Alice is disappointed she still has to live with her parents. But even the tiny, old fisherman's cottages go for extortionate prices because they're in a prime location and often have sea views. Long term, it's the local businesses that will suffer if they aren't in a position to hand down their legacy to the next generation.'

'I know I was guilty of buying into that dream myself,' Drew acknowledges. 'But I didn't realise the impact on the local community, at that time. Strangely enough, ending up living here on a permanent basis was the best thing that's happened to me and I don't feel quite so bad, now. It's obvious as each day passes that you're very happy to be back here for good and that has surprised quite a lot of people.'

I hope no one thinks I'm like Ross's parents, who cut off their old friends as soon as the business took off. I'm proud of my roots and the links my family have here.

'Selling up was never an option for me. I rented this out simply because I didn't want the place to deteriorate. My mum would have approved of the work that's been done here; my dad, well, he's not one for change. A little old cottage is just that to him and he doesn't see the need for extra space and all this glass. If he was being honest with me, he'd probably say it was a waste of money. But this, now, is my home forever. I have a few things that have been handed down to me that belong here, and it means more than all the expensive stuff I left behind at my apartment in London. And now I'm working with Sissy, life couldn't get any better because I've made a start and I'm back in business. I hope to find some more investment opportunities locally, that could end up making a difference.'

Drew gives me a look.

'What's up?'

'Nothing. It all sounds great. And I'm glad you're pleased with the end result here. Ross certainly delivered. Another week and the landscape gardeners will have the new fencing up and the lawns laid. We can put the barbecue away.'

He looks directly at me when he mentions Ross's name, but I ignore it.

'I'm thinking of inviting Felicity down once the final clean through has been done. I want her to see that I kept to the plan—our plan.'

Life is nothing without hope, I reflect.

'That's a great idea. Keep heart, Drew. When you love someone, giving up is never really an option, is it—but admitting that could break your heart forever.'

'I knew it!' Drew blurts out. 'Your secret about Ross is safe with me, Kerra. You are so right, but few people can appreciate that fact.'

My heart skips a beat for a moment, as I realise that while I might be able to fool a lot of people, it's hard to fool someone who is in a similar position.

'Come on, let's head around to mine. I have a bottle of white wine chilling and I want to show off my kitchen.'

Ripley suddenly appears and Drew's face lights up.

'Hey, look who's here. You're invited too, Ripley. I still have some treats in the cupboard.'

She hesitates as we step through the doors onto the newly laid patio and I wait patiently while she makes up her mind.

'I'm counting to three,' I inform her. 'After that it's the cat flap for you lady, if you change your mind. One... two...' She runs out and I lock up, but she doesn't follow me around to Drew's.

'She's still keeping guard for you,' he comments, as I follow him inside.

'Yes. And she has a mind of her own. Wow,' I gasp, 'I didn't realise they were finished in here, too. It's wonderful. Felicity is going to love it.'

Every surface is bright and shiny—that chic, glossy, contemporary look that reminds me of London living. Old buildings with sparkling new interiors and clean lines. Drew pulls out one of the tall chairs and I take a seat at the island.

'She will. I still have two rooms to sort out upstairs, but I'm dragging my feet until she's here. When is your new office being delivered?'

'We're still awaiting confirmation. Until then, Treloar's can't even give me an indication of when they could install it.'

'I'm sure Ross will be keeping you updated on a regular basis,' he says, giving me a knowing wink.

I ignore his comment as if it didn't register. 'The traffic is crazy out there and the parking situation gets worse every year. Did you see there were visitors double-parking in the lay-by yesterday?'

'I know, I heard the honking of horns as it was hard

for anyone to get past. Goodness knows what's going to happen when the low-loader arrives on Monday morning to take the heavy equipment away. The skips will go, too, so we'll be back to fighting for a parking space outside our own homes again.'

Ross didn't mention clearing the site. How much longer will he have an excuse to call in, I wonder? A week at most? It's funny, but when the work started all I could dream of was the day Pedrevan became all mine again and now it feels a little hollow.

'Why the sad look?'

I shrug my shoulders. 'I guess I can't really believe we're nearly there.'

'Aren't you excited about emptying out the stuff you've stored over at your dad's? It's the fun bit putting the final look together.'

He hands me a glass. Drew is right, it calls for a celebration so why don't I feel enthused?

'I guess it is. Anyway, let's toast to one hugely successful project and to the brilliant architect of it all!'

25. The Empty Place at the Table

'This was such a great idea of yours, Tegan, and thank you all for coming to help out. I'm keeping my fingers crossed it ends up looking styled and not like a random collection of items I simply fell in love with.'

The unwrapping has begun, and Tegan gives me a beaming smile as Sissy, Polly and I get stuck in.

'You have some lovely things here and I know it looks like a lot, but this is a huge space,' Polly says encouragingly.

'Let's get the table in situ first, ladies, shall we?' Sissy suggests. 'It's going to take all of us to manoeuvre it into position. I'll grab some felt pads for the legs in case we end up having to slide it. This slate floor is stunning.'

As we pull off the bubble wrap protecting the top of the table, I glance around, thinking it is everything I hoped for and more.

'Okay, ladies. Tilting on the count of three, while I put on the pads.' Sissy is good at organising people and it shows. We tilt as we're told and then the big lift begins.

'Who knew these old pine tables were so heavy?' Tegan exclaims as we shuffle along.

'Keep going, keep going. Another half-a-metre towards the doors, Kerra?'

'Yep. Perfect. Right here!'

It's funny how quickly the memory of builders traipsing in and out fades with each item of furniture we put in place. It's the point where a shell finally becomes a home.

'Where is this small display case going, Kerra?'

'On the wall just inside the porch. There are two of Granddad's old lamps to go in there. I think they're in the box on the top, the one marked fragile. I'll grab Sissy's drill and a raw plug if you can hang on a moment.'

Tegan and I are carrying an oversized mirror into the dining area ready to lift it onto the wall mountings.

'I've got it,' Sissy calls out.

Polly is busy unwrapping the upcycled dining chairs and placing them around the table. I toyed with painting them grey instead of white, but I'm glad I didn't, as the white keeps it simple.

'It's coming together ladies and looking good.'

The doorbell chimes and Polly flings it open.

'The food has arrived,' she calls out over her shoulder, as Dad and Sy make their way through with their hands full. They both stop and stare.

'Well I never! I can't even believe it's the same place.' Dad sounds surprised and yet he's seen the work as it progressed. His eyes alight on the large display cabinet on the wall which houses Mum's treasured glassware, handed down to her from Grandma. And then back at the little cabinet with Granddad's lamps. 'You did it, Kerra, and you're right— Mum would love it!'

★

'How's it going Tegan? I heard on the grapevine that you're recruiting. Business must be good.' Polly reaches out for another slice of pizza. She turns briefly towards Sy, before looking back at Tegan, whose cheeks are now blazing.

'Well, we've been really busy and it's already beginning to pay off,' she replies. 'We're working long days, but I can't remember the last time I put on my rubber gloves and got hands on. I never realised how important it was to keep on top of the paperwork. As for actively seeking new business, well, I didn't have a clue, but I do now. We desperately need to take on more cleaners and quickly.'

Tegan turns to look at Sy, giving him a huge smile.

'We're not just looking for people on the doorstep but further afield, too, if you hear of anyone looking for a part-time job,' Sy adds. 'We prefer them to have their own transport and they get paid mileage, but we are buddying up people to car-share in the more remote areas, as well.'

'You two have done well in a short space of time and I'm glad it's all working out. Guess sometimes it takes a little thinking outside the box to change things up,' Dad says, looking in my direction. 'I still can't get over the transformation, but it wasn't something I could ever have imagined. It just looked like a great big cavern to me and now, here we all are, sitting around an old-fashioned pine table like friends and family used to do, years ago.'

Polly is sitting next to Dad and she turns to face him, her voice empathetic. 'Life is all about change today, Eddie. Some of the old ways simply don't work anymore.'

He nods his head sadly. 'Your dad was telling me he's having to face some tough decisions about the future of the pub. It's a sorry state of affairs when you can't make a decent living, even though you work every hour God gives.'

Polly told me earlier that they're still hoping this will turn out to be a bumper season and not simply cover the costs of upgrading the interior.

'You've both put a lot into that place,' Dad acknowledges.

'It's a worry,' Polly agrees, 'but there are options to explore, so I'm not panicking just yet. But it gets to him sometimes and we all know the feeling.'

There's a lull in conversation while Tegan refills the coffee cups.

'You'll be missing all the company,' Sy says, turning to me.

I look at him, surprised. Has Tegan broken our confidence and talked to him about Ross?

'The landscapers will be here for a few days, yet. And Treloar's will be back to install an office in the garden, but I still don't have a delivery date.'

Studying his face, to my immense relief I can see my suspicions are unfounded. He's just making conversation.

'That's a shame. I bet you can't wait to get things all set up properly now that you're back to work with a vengeance.'

He glances across at Sissy, who breaks out into a smile.

'Kerra has made my head spin with it all. I can't believe how quickly she set up the online shop and I'm already struggling to keep up with the orders. But my new assistant is joining me the week after next and it will be a huge relief.'

'I'm so glad you and Sienna hit it off, Sissy. I think the

two of you will work very well together and she has a lot of enthusiasm.'

Ripley appears and decides to join in on the conversation with a loud tirade of miaows. Everyone stops to look at her. She's a little indignant, probably because when she retired upstairs there wasn't a stick of furniture in here. And now it's full of people and things. She walks off, tail erect, to begin investigating her new surroundings. She's still very vocal, expressing her opinion as a low grumbling sound I haven't heard before.

'Poor Ripley, it's been one thing after another. I hope she approves of the changes,' Dad says, trying not to laugh at her. 'She's probably wondering where her supper is and why she wasn't invited to the party.'

Miaow. Miaow. Miaow.

'Okay. I'm on it. I didn't forget you and I have some chicken ready and waiting.'

As I get up and head over to the fridge, I wish that I could pick up the phone and ask Ross to join us. I know it would make eyebrows rise, though, and not least Dad's.

Sissy saunters up with a stack of plates and starts loading up the dishwasher.

'Don't forget that I'm not chained to the cottage anymore, so I'll give a hand packing up those orders until Sienna starts,' I remind her.

She closes the dishwasher door and turns to look at me, her eyes twinkling.

'I have some good news I've been dying to share with you. We are now officially one of the main UK stockists for the French Elite range. Their representative will be paying our new premises a visit as soon as we're ready to start setting up.'

Sissy is a rather reserved person by nature, but as I turn to face her it's obvious that she's finding it difficult to contain her delight. Delight, no doubt tinged with relief.

'Well done, you! This is a huge deal and it's going to make all the difference.'

I know how disappointed she would have been if she hadn't been able to pull it off. She's so eager to prove herself and she's certainly done that, alright.

'If I can get similar deals set up with the local companies I use for soft furnishings and ornamental pieces, we'd be virtually a one-stop shop holding stock on sale or return. All we'd need to add is a range of country-style wallpapers, and a good selection of table lamps, and we will be able to display everything as individually styled rooms. What do you think?'

'I think The Design Cave is going to do us proud, Sissy.'

'Well, it seems to be taking flight and that's down to you, Kerra. You've broken my run of bad luck and now nothing is going to stop me making the dream happen.'

I can't help but glance back at the others, as their loud chatter and peals of laughter fills the air. I feel so very grateful for tonight. It has been chaotic, but now things are settling down I know I made the right decision. To see Dad looking so animated and content, Sy and Tegan holding hands beneath the table, and Sissy finally feeling validated, is truly wonderful. As for Polly, well, the battle continues at The Lark and Lantern but she isn't giving up without a fight.

★

'I really missed you, tonight,' I whisper into the phone.

I always told myself I would never be the sort of woman who clung on to a man. And I can't believe I've just said that to Ross.

'Me, too. It's tough not being able to call in to see you whenever I want. We're so busy, though, and I seem to be travelling further and further afield to look at potential jobs. I'm exhausted and had to resort to takeaway fish and chips tonight.'

That makes me smile. 'Aww… there was a bit of a takeaway fest here, too. It was the unpacking party. Dad and Sy did the food run and now they've all gone I'm feeling lonely.'

'But happy, I hope? Does it feel like home?'

'It does. There isn't one single thing I'd change. It's weird to finally feel settled and to be able to focus on the next part of my life.'

I can hear Ross groan a little as he stretches and then he drops the phone, a range of disparate little sounds filling my ear for a moment or two.

'Sorry, that was clumsy of me. I'm not in the best of moods, I'm afraid.'

'Would it help to talk about whatever it is that's gone wrong? It's not like you to sound so dejected.'

'It's just family stuff,' Ross admits, his voice sounding subdued. 'My father tries to dabble when he's bored and at the moment, he's a little restless. He thinks it's time we expanded the territory we cover and he's talking about setting up a second office. I've told him straight I don't have the time to do that and he's talking about flying back to start making things happen, effectively forcing my hand.'

Ross is well respected by both his employees and his customers, so if he has his reservations, there's a solid reasoning behind it.

'But I thought he'd retired?'

'Well, supposedly, but he didn't hand over the business as such. It's still in my parents' names, but I'm the managing director. He'll always call the shots, though. He wants to take on self-employed contractors and have someone in the second office running the paperwork and the work schedules. But the reason the business does well is because that's not the way we operate. The guys who work for us are a team.'

Ross is right; reputation and standing in the community counts for a lot in this part of the world.

'And you aren't comfortable to be a part of the changes he wants to make.'

'My worry is that the guys we employ now will see it as a threat to their future. They know the standard required and I make sure they get a fair wage out of it. We don't need to advertise because our reputation for quality and reliability ensures the work keeps coming in. Contractors don't have that same level of loyalty and that's a fact. If something doesn't work out for them, they move on and often at short notice. You can't guarantee reliability with schedules if there's a chance a contractor will drop the job he's on because someone else offers him a higher rate, for example. Anyway, hopefully my mother will find something else to distract him. She has no intention of coming back to the UK for anything more than a fleeting visit.'

His voice sounds devoid of emotion because I'm beginning to see that Ross regards that as a form of weakness. But I know that deep down inside he'll be feeling angry, knowing there is little he can do to influence his father.

'It would be a big step for him to come back, even temporarily, so try not to let this stress you out. Cross that bridge if it happens.'

'I know you're right. Anyway, never mind all that—when are you going to visit me next?' His mood instantly changes, and I can hear the smile in his voice.

'I'm working on it. The Design Cave website has been incredibly successful and I need to support Sissy in any way I can until Sienna joins the team. Ironically, now I've finished unpacking, I'll be spending all my free time packing up items to send out. It's only temporary, though and I'm sure I will be able to grab at least one evening off.'

'Make it sooner rather than later, won't you?' There's a longing in his voice that I recognise only too well.

What I want is to jump in my car and drive over there right now, but Ripley is watching and patiently waiting for me to put down the phone and head upstairs to bed.

'I will. I intend to work fast. Sleep well, Ross.'

As we disconnect, I wonder what my little feline companion will think when the time comes that I sleep overnight at The Forge for the first time. I've set up her food station, so she has two different bowls of dry food and biscuits, and a little plug-in water fountain.

'If I wasn't here,' I address her in all seriousness, 'you'd make your way upstairs to bed on your own, you little minx, wouldn't you?'

Ripley simply continues to stare at me, sitting there so

prim and proper with her back straight and her tail curled around her paws.

Miaow, miaow, miaow... she begins, sounding rather doleful and she doesn't stop until I get up.

Is life conspiring against Ross and me, I wonder? Were we only ever destined to be people whose lives touched briefly as they pass by? Ross was key in turning Pedrevan into the sort of place I could never walk away from. In a strange way is that giving me a message loud and clear that I need to get him out of my system and move on? He lives alone and is happy to do so. Am I prepared to settle for a relationship that is conducted in secrecy because I value my privacy? And who knows when, or if, Ross will ever be ready to fully commit to someone? Could I see him moving in here? The mere thought of that makes me laugh out loud.

My head is telling me one thing, my heart another. Why can't I have it all? The home, the man of my dreams and the ability to use the nest egg I have sitting in the bank to make it count for something.

26. Night Owls

It's just after midnight and yet here I am, still tossing and turning. Ripley keeps jumping on and off the bed, and it's clear she's unsettled. She's been through a lot since she took up residence here and tonight was the final straw, it seems. Not only was the house crowded with people, but suddenly the vast empty room is full of strange items invading her territory.

She keeps going downstairs to have yet another sniff around, but each time I can hear her down there wailing pitifully. It has set me on edge and I've given up on sleep, so I grab my phone to surf for advice. Maybe there's something I can do to ease her through this period until she can adjust to the new norm. To my surprise, I notice that Ross is online.

Hey, can't you sleep, either?

No. Family stuff whirling around inside my head. How about you?

Ripley is acting a bit weird and keeps howling.

Is it unsettling you?

I should brush it off, but I'd be lying if I said it wasn't.

A little.

Well, I can't have that. Is there any food left after your little party?

Yes, but it's the middle of the night, remember?

I'll be discreet and park around the corner.

You're crazy.

No, just hungry and maybe Ripley will settle down for me.

Without any warning she jumps up on the bed again and, staring straight at me as if she's passing on a message, she begins one of her long conversations. I wish I knew what she was trying to tell me, because clearly it's important to her.

Thanks, Ross. Maybe we all need a little company tonight for whatever reason.

He sends me a smiley emoji and I throw down my phone, patting my lap to encourage Ripley to settle down. She launches herself forward, landing on me rather heavily and I begin smoothing her back.

'Come on, everything is going to be fine. I know there was a lot going on here tonight, but this is it now. Our home.

No more mess, no more strange items suddenly appearing without warning. You're such a brave girl and there's no need to be scared.'

Those gorgeous cat eyes don't blink as she stares up at me and even keeping my voice soft and low to console her, it's several minutes before she is relaxed enough to curl up. While I wait for Ross to arrive, I jump online again and read a few articles about cats and their sense of smell.

I know they mark their territory by leaving scent trails and rubbing against their human family is a part of that, too. The smells transfer and that's important to make them feel safe. But most of the furniture we brought in tonight had been stored in one of Dad's garages and maybe there were mice in there. If that's what she's picking up, it makes sense that she'll be hyped-up as it will put her into hunting mode.

'You poor thing,' I whisper, running my hand along her jawline and up over her ears. She starts to purr and rolls over onto her side, finally chilled enough to stretch out.

Easing myself off the bed, I run my hands through my hair, gazing down at my less-than-glamorous, baggy T-shirt. It's very warm tonight again and I'm sure I can find something a little more flattering to wear without looking like I've fussed over my appearance. However, the thought of a few unexpected hours with Ross feels decadent—let's just hope we don't regret it. Peering out into the street, though, the only lights that are visible are the streetlamps and it seems everyone is asleep except me. Even Ripley is now softly snoring away as if she doesn't have a care in the world.

*

I leap into Ross's arms and as our cheeks touch, I draw back. 'Your face is bristly,' I laugh.

'I just threw on some clothes, imagining you here with Ripley constantly wailing in the background. Where is she?'

'Asleep on the bed. Sorry, I dragged you here for nothing, as she eventually ran out of steam.'

Ross places his fingers under my chin, tipping my head back a little so he can look down into my eyes.

'I wouldn't say it was for nothing, but feed me first. Then I have a couple of ideas about how we can pass a sleepless night. It seems a pity to waste all that wired energy when it can be used to good effect.'

I shake my head at him, pulling away. 'You are incorrigible.'

'I know, but you're such a temptation.'

Ross follows me through into the kitchen, but we don't turn on any lights. Outside a half-moon casts its light through the wall of glass, bathing the room in a soft glow.

'It really has come together well, now the furniture is in. It's a great look and I love the table.'

I nod, indicating for Ross to take a seat, as I pull two platters from the fridge and place them in front of him. He eases back the clingfilm covering, grabbing a slice of cold pizza and I follow his lead. Now he's here everything seems different. I'm relaxed and content in a way I didn't feel earlier on. I've lived alone for a long time and now I have Ripley, she's good company but this is more than that, it's a sense of completeness.

'What?' Ross pauses for a second, before pushing the last bit of pizza into his mouth.

'I'm glad you decided to come over.'

He grins at me. 'To be honest, when you rang me after the party it was hard not to come straight here. You sounded… I don't know, like you didn't want to be alone after your guests left.'

'I was missing you and the fact that you weren't here to join in felt wrong, somehow. Something was missing and it was you.'

He breathes out slowly and there is a heaviness attached to it.

'It's hard creeping around like this when our emotions are so full-on. But—'

I jump in, finishing Ross's sentence. 'But this is no one's business, but ours.'

Ross looks at me wearily.

'I'm not just thinking of my situation, Kerra, but of your reputation. When it comes to maintaining a relationship, I'm regarded as a bit of a disaster area and I am, I've proven that. It would be nice to continue to keep out of the limelight for a while on the personal front, and yet I want to be around you all the time. I feel bad that I can't make any promises because I've learnt to my cost that rushing into something is foolhardy. But I don't want you to feel that I'm using you. Or that what we're feeling right now isn't real.'

I reach out across the table to place my hand on his. His words mirror my own thoughts exactly and it's a relief.

'I understand, really I do. I'm fine with taking things slow unless you—'

'Did you hear that?' Ross freezes, raising a finger to his lips.

I pause, listening. 'What?' I whisper, my skin suddenly feeling clammy.

Ross turns his gaze towards the garden and we sit very still. I hold my breath hoping there's nothing to see.

'Stay where you are,' he mutters softly, easing himself off the chair but keeping his body low. 'Is the side gate locked?'

'Yes.'

'I'm going to head out the front and find a way around to the back. It might take a few minutes but promise me you'll stay here.'

He fixes me with a stare and I nod my head reluctantly.

'Go careful,' I murmur, but he's already merging into the shadows behind me.

Without any appreciable sound, Ripley appears alongside me and the last thing I want now is for her to start making a noise, so I grab a piece of breaded chicken off the platter. Slowly leaning to one side, I break it into small pieces, talking softly to her.

'There you go. Good girl. We need to be quiet.'

She looks at me as if she's about to start talking, so I run my hand down her back, reassuringly and she puts her head down to sniff my little offering. It's tempting enough for her to crouch down and begin nibbling away.

My head instinctively turns back towards the glass doors, but anything beyond the patio area is in heavy shadow. The breeze has definitely picked up and I wonder if what Ross heard was something at the bottom of the garden falling over. I still haven't cleared the massive stacks of old, clay pots from the shed. It seemed a pity to dispose of them, as once the landscapers have finished their work, I intend to use some of them.

Ripley stops eating and her ears prick up.

'It's only the breeze coming in off the sea. Good girl. Want some more chicken?'

And then I hear it, too. A clatter, like a falling stone. Ripley let's out a solitary miaow, as if she's warning me something isn't right. If I continue to sit here she's only going to get more vocal, so I slither off the chair, keeping as low to the ground as I can while making my way over to the stairs. Then I clamber up two steps at a time, heading straight for the back bedroom and she's close behind me.

Peeking gingerly around the partially pulled curtains, Ross is clambering over the fence at the bottom of the garden and then I see a shape, like a blur, heading towards the barbecue area. Seconds later Ross has almost caught up and he takes a flying leap in the air, ending up in a mound on the floor.

Rushing back downstairs, my hands are trembling as I scrabble to unlock the sliding doors. I run outside, oblivious to the fact that my feet are bare and the ground is still uneven.

'Don't even think about it,' Ross's voice is low, but angry, as he kneels over the shape lying prostrate on the floor. As he stands, he literally drags the person upright, both of his hands gripping the back of his top so he can't escape his grasp.

'Alright,' the guy replies, stumbling to his feet and raising both hands up in submission.

'Let's get back inside, Kerra. This is going to take some explaining.'

My heart is pounding in my chest and I run on ahead, sliding the doors back wide enough for Ross to drag the man inside. As soon as they cross the threshold, I close the doors and lock them, then head over to turn on the light.

'Mr Mills!' I exclaim, totally shocked. 'What are you doing here? I thought you were in police custody.'

I walk over to Ross and touch his arm lightly, encouraging him to let go of our interloper. 'He's not going anywhere, Ross. He's very shaken. Sit down and I'll put the kettle on.'

Ross's jaw is clenched and his eyes are almost black, the pupils are so dilated. We're all struggling a little to adjust to the sudden brightness of the lights overhead, but it only takes seconds for his grip to loosen. He pulls out a chair, indicating for Mr Mills to sit down. Which he does, gratefully.

I make three cups of strong tea, simply because Dad once told me it was a good remedy if someone has had a shock. My hands are still shaking a little as I load the tray and carry it across. Ross is sitting opposite our uninvited guest, who still hasn't uttered a single word.

'Drink this, it will calm your nerves. I want to know exactly what you're doing in my garden at this unearthly hour.' As I place a mug in front of him, he can tell from my tone that I want answers.

'And we want the truth. I'm sure the police would be very curious to know, too,' Ross adds.

Mr Mills clears his throat. Without any warning at all, Ripley clatters down the stairs as if her tail is on fire and begins wailing at Mr Mills. So that's why she's been acting so strangely tonight.

Walking across to Ripley, I pick her up in my arms and smooth her until she's quiet. Then I set her back down, but instead of coming closer to sniff around, she runs away and settles herself down about halfway up the stairs. She's spooked but a lot less agitated than she has been.

'You're frightening my cat,' I explain. 'It might be better if you take off your hoodie.'

He does as instructed, his T-shirt beneath clinging to him as he's drenched in sweat. He sits there looking down at his hands as he flexes his fingers.

'I didn't mean to scare you Ms Shaw, really I didn't. I'm in trouble and I left something here that I need to get my hands on.'

Casting a glance his way, I can't help frowning. If I'd come across anything at all of his, I would most certainly have put it to one side regardless of the fact I have no forwarding address.

'What sort of something?'

'I left a small package here, hidden among the pots stacked up against the old shed. Proof that I was tricked into doing something illegal.'

Ross narrows his eyes as he leans forward to stare at Mr Mills. 'I think you'd better start at the beginning, don't you?'

He nods, grabbing the mug of tea and taking a big swig, even though it's still quite hot.

'I came here to start over again. I'm a trawlerman by trade and I got sick. That meant no pay and me wife ended up leaving me for someone else. After I recovered, it was clear my days on board were over. I found myself what I thought was a nice little job working for a small Manchester-based firm, who were looking for van drivers to cover the whole of the south west. Mainly house clearances, moving stock about and doing runs to storage facilities, that sort of thing.

Seemed perfect for me and less demanding than a life at sea.'

Ross doesn't look impressed.

'Get on with it,' he says pointedly.

'I rented the cottage and settled in. Me first trip was on an evening. It wasn't a bother and it was easy enough. I had to pick up someone who had a key to this shop and the boxes were there ready and waiting for us. It took about an hour, in and out. They said to take the van home and I parked it out there, in the lay-by. This guy appeared the next morning and he pulled out his phone. He had photos that identified me carrying the boxes out through the back of the shop. Turns out it wasn't a job at all, but they faked a break-in and it was stealing. I was given instructions on where to drop the van and then he said they'd be in touch.'

I look at him, horrified. Ross isn't that easily convinced.

'But the guy had a key?'

'Yes, sir, he did, but the goods didn't belong to the owner of that key. After I left, they smashed in the door to make it look like a break-in. I swear I had no idea what we were doing was illegal. After that it was made clear to me that I was on the books and if I didn't comply then the photos would find their way into the hands of the police.'

Ross's head goes back and he stares down his nose at Mr Mills, deciding whether or not to believe him.

'Where was this?'

'Was it the arcade in Polreweek?' I interrupt.

Mr Mills nods his head, a look of surprise flashing over his face.

'Ross, I believe what he's saying. The day Sissy moved into The Design Cave, someone broke in and stole a lot of her stock. It hadn't even been unpacked, as the shop wasn't open.'

'That was it—The Design Cave. Nice little place, I remember thinking. Someone had recently painted through; you could still smell it but there wasn't much on display. I assumed the old tenants were moving out and getting it ready for the new people.'

'The impression we're under is that it's about stolen cars. What has this got to do with it?'

At least Ross is calmer now and Mr Mills doesn't look quite so intimidated.

'A guy in my old local set me up with a man named Rod, who phoned me about the van driving job. I'd been in and out of hospital as I'd had pneumonia and a collapsed lung. As things picked up, I was desperate for money, so I lied and told him that I was working out my notice on the trawler. I received a letter confirming my start date, where to go to pick up the van and the details of that first job.'

'That's it? You left a letter here and that's your proof?' Ross scowls.

'No. Not quite. The break-in was a way of having something they could hold over me and what they really wanted was a driver to transport cars around the country. I kept a record of every vehicle they got me to pick up and drop off. They gave me a set of trade plates to use, so it all looked above board, but I had my doubts about whether the number plates on the cars were real. Someone rang to tell me the pick-up and drop-off details and I was paid cash each time.'

Ross shakes his head in disbelief. 'You went along with it?'

Mr Mills closes his eyes for a few seconds. 'I had no choice. They aren't exactly the type of people you can just walk away from. I didn't know what to do, so I did as I was told. When I was served notice on this place, it sort of shocked me into doing something. My sister offered to put me up and I thought that if I just upped and left, I'd be safe there. Turns out I wasn't, and they even tracked down my wife, who I haven't seen in months, and paid her a visit. She wants a divorce but is expecting me to sort it all out. I don't have a clue what to do and I sure as hell can't afford to get a solicitor involved. She told them what they wanted to know and probably felt I had it coming. I was lucky; I missed them by half an hour and when my sister described the two men who were asking about me, I went straight to the police.'

I'm appalled and I can see that Ross is thinking about the guys who were hanging around here. Mr Mills isn't exaggerating, because they were intimidating.

'I couldn't believe it when I saw how much work had been done here. All the overgrown shrubs cleared and the shed gone. I started going through the stacks of pots, but they've been sorted and the package I left isn't there now.'

I think back to the day Ross's guys took the shed apart and put it in the skip. There was stuff everywhere, as not all of it was contained in wooden crates. Dad and I sorted through it as best we could, but some of it was mouldy. We were keen to get rid of as much as we could while we had the opportunity.

'Was it in an envelope?'

Mr Mills shakes his head. 'No. I put it in an old tin I picked up in a secondhand shop. It was one of those tea caddies people used to have in sets. Blue and white, it was.

I wrapped it all in a polythene bag first, just to be safe.' He laughs to himself. 'Safe, eh? Those pots hadn't been disturbed for years. I've cooperated with the police every step of the way, but the contents of that tin could save me serving a prison sentence.'

Ross looks directly at me, frowning. 'Does it ring a bell, Kerra?'

I shrug. 'There were lots of tins of all shapes and sizes, most of them housing screws and bits of fishing stuff. I gave a whole load of it to Bill, as he's a keen fisherman and I just kept a few bits to remind me of Granddad. One of his rods and a couple of reels. But Dad was sorting through, too, and if it didn't rattle he might just have assumed it was empty.'

'Who's Bill?' Mr Mills asks.

'One of the guys who worked on the site. He's just retired. I'll pop round to see him this morning and ask him if it's among the stuff he has,' Ross confirms.

'I never thought in a million years that I'd get myself into this sort of trouble. Or find myself living in constant fear and having to keep looking over my shoulder.'

'Yes, well it's a pity you didn't give any thought to Ms Shaw's safety. Those thugs weren't just watching the cottage in case you came back, they decided to make their presence felt.'

Mr Mill's face freezes. 'I assumed they were only watching me. That's partly why I came back at night to grab my stash, as I thought the less you know, the better. I had no idea I'd put you in danger.'

His concern and regret seem genuine enough and Ross, too, can see that.

'There's no point in calling the police, Ross. If you're

happy to pop in to Bill later this morning, I'll check the attic, in case it was thrown into one of the boxes that Drew put up there for me. Give me a contact number, Mr Mills and I do hope we can track it down. People like that have no idea what the consequences are of their actions on hard-working people trying to make a decent living. A new business was almost stopped in its tracks the night that stock was stolen. It was nothing to them, of course, just a means to an end and a bit of extra cash in their pockets. But one woman has had to struggle every single day since, just to keep going.'

There's no more we can do right now, so I head off to get a pen and paper.

When Ross closes the door behind Mr Mills, he turns around to face me, frowning. I can see he's still in two minds about whether we should inform the police.

'I believe what he said and that he acted out of desperation. It doesn't excuse what he did, but at least he's doing what he can now to help the police gather as much information as possible. Let's hope we can find that tin. If you hadn't raced over here, I have no idea how I would have coped with this and Ripley, bless her, must have sensed he was out there. He might have been lurking all evening, waiting for the lights to go off.'

'It certainly isn't the night I had in mind for us,' Ross says, heaving a tired sigh. 'As long as you feel we did the right thing, that's all that matters. I don't know about you, but I'm exhausted and ready for bed.'

I step forward and he throws his arms around my shoulders, tilting his head to rest it against mine.

'My first sleepover and it's going to be just that,' he groans.

SEPTEMBER

27. Autumnal Chills

'Morning, it's a bit nippy, but look at that sky.' I lay the secateurs down on the wall as I stop to speak to Dad and Nettie. Between them, they're juggling four very energetic and excited dogs who all want to say hello.

'It's such a bonus and the array of colours as the leaves begin to turn makes walking a real pleasure. You're doing a grand job there, Kerra,' Nettie replies.

'Now that the landscaping at the back is bedding in nicely, it's time to give the front a little trim for the autumn. Another twenty minutes and I'm off to The Design Cave. Will you guys be able to make it on Friday?'

Dad and Nettie glance at each other, nodding in agreement. 'Try keeping us away,' Dad says, giving me a wink. 'Everyone will be there to check it out, you mark my words.'

'Sissy has been overwhelmed by the wave of support she's had since the truth came out about the robbery. Folk had no idea she wasn't insured at the time, or that some of the rumours about it being an inside job were spread by her dodgy landlord, to deflect from his part in it. Even if people only come along for a free glass of wine and a posh canapé, hopefully some of them will be tempted to open their wallets.'

'Will everything be ready in time?' Dad asks rather casually, but his eyes narrow a little. 'Is there anything we can do to help?'

'We've all been working non-stop, but the end is in sight now. We hope to finish off the last few bits of painting today, now that the room displays are all set up. We're running ahead of target and the only concern is ensuring we don't over, or under order on the food and drink, after the massive leaflet drop.'

'If that's the only panic, you'll be doing well,' Nettie adds, sounding impressed.

'How are things at the kennels? Sorry I haven't had much time to pop in lately. I feel like a bad daughter when I only live a stone's throw away.'

'As long as you're happy and things are going well with you, I'm happy. I don't know what I'd do without Nettie here, I will admit, but things are beginning to quieten down a little now. We had a bit of bad news, though. Bertie's owner died yesterday and a relative rang to ask if I could possibly find a permanent home for him.'

'Oh, Dad. I didn't realise the situation was that bad. And poor Bertie. He's such a cute little character and so full of energy.'

'Well, if you could spread the word, that would be great and hopefully we'll find a suitable home for him. I'd keep him with me permanently, but it wouldn't be fair on Bertie. He deserves to be the centre of attention.'

Dad's right and if I didn't have Ripley, I'd take him myself. Dogs require more attention than cats, I reflect, although

Bengals might be the exception that proves the rule. On one hand Ripley is content to do her own thing, but on the other she is very territorial. A right little diva, for sure.

'We'd best get off as these guys are all impatient to be let off their leads. See you on Friday, if not before, lovely.'

I watch as Dad and Nettie walk off down the road together. It's coat weather, but as they increase their pace to keep up with the dogs, it will be hot work. There's a lot of laughter and banter between the two of them as they walk away, which is good to see. Mum wouldn't want Dad to become a hermit and he's comfortable with Nettie around.

'Are you speaking to me, still?'

Lost in thought, I didn't see Alice approaching and it's an effort to shake off an instant frown at the sound of her voice. It's been a couple of months since we last crossed paths and I can't even imagine what she's doing here.

'I don't think we have very much to say to each other, do you?'

I focus on snipping away at the shrub in front of me, which I only know as a red robin as I'm not really a gardener. But I know enough to understand a good trim encourages new growth in the spring. Anyway, eye contact isn't necessary to continue this conversation, and I hope my body language, too, conveys the fact that I'm too busy for idle chatter.

'Dad suggested I pop in to see you,' she says lamely.

The truth is that I don't care to hear anything Alice has to say. I continue working in silence.

'It was lucky Ross managed to track down the stuff Mr Mills left behind, wasn't it? Uncle Eddie told Dad all about it. It must have been scary for you when those guys were hanging around.'

Reluctantly, I stop what I'm doing to look directly at her.

'What do you want, Alice? I need to get this finished before I head out for the day. Just say whatever it is and leave me in peace.'

She wasn't expecting that and her face falls. Is she turning her attention to Ross, now, I wonder? I mean, seriously— why is she so interested in what's going on in my life, all the time?

'Look, I'm sorry if I said anything out of place. I never meant to imply that you knew what Mr Mills was involved in.'

'Which part of what you said made that clear? It certainly wasn't throwing in the bit about how much money I was *suddenly* spending on the cottage.'

Her eyes start to blaze. 'I didn't say that! I said... well, I think I said you might be a bit worried about what people might think, given how much the work was costing.'

I fix my gaze on her, as the words coming out of her mouth begin to sink in and she blinks, rapidly in succession.

'But I didn't mean it like that. I was just thinking out loud.'

'It's called gossiping, Alice, and some people believe everything they hear because they don't have the common sense to think for themselves. If you don't know the facts, you're better off saying nothing. Remember that in future, because if I hear you've been talking about me again, we're done.'

With that, I close the secateurs, grab the black sack of garden debris and turn away from her. Maybe that was a little harsh, but I meant every word I said. Heading inside and slamming the door behind me, I walk through to the kitchen to wash my hands. A few minutes later the doorbell springs into life. Glancing at the clock, I'm conscious that I still need to change and get my things together, so I hope it isn't Ross. I haven't seen him for a few days and I don't know if I'd have the heart to send him on his way when I miss him so much.

'Alice,' I blurt out in surprise, as she stares back at me tearfully. I'm angry with her, but she's family, I remind myself. 'I didn't mean to be quite so blunt with you. You'd better come in for a moment.'

Great. Just what I need now, a guilt trip.

'It's not your fault. Sometimes I say the first thing that comes into my head. I've always been like that.'

She follows me through to the kitchen and stops, slowly twirling around to take in the changes.

'Oh, Kerra—this is fabulous—the furniture looks amazing! Why am I not surprised?' A minute or two passes, before she begins speaking again. 'Do you think it's true that some people are born to be successful?'

She turns to face me and it's a serious question.

'That's a curious thing to say, Alice,' I reply. I stop to consider my answer. 'I think people who work hard are more likely to be successful when it comes to achieving their goals. But success can be measured in many different ways.'

'It's just that, at school the standing joke was that you had all the brains and I had—' she comes to an abrupt halt, looking mortified.

'The beauty. You are beautiful, Alice, that's a fact, but it was a mean thing to say to you and it simply isn't true.

You have the skills to make someone feel better about themselves. We all get days when we look in the mirror and wish we had a magic wand. After a visit to you, a client walks away from the salon with their confidence boosted. At school there was a lot of jealousy, you know that, and insecure people picking on others to make themselves feel superior. It makes me feel sad you've never forgotten it, though. That's not good for your self-esteem.'

'But you are the clever one, Kerra and I always wished I was more like you. I just wanted you to know that I really didn't mean to cause trouble and you were right to say what you did. I need to stop and think things through first. Like just now.'

She gives me a weak smile and I can't stop myself from letting out a little laugh. It was a classic when it comes to her throwaway comments, which often leave people speechless.

'We both work hard at what we do, Alice,' I reply warmly. 'Please don't undersell yourself, or your skills. I couldn't do what you do. In fact, I wonder if you could do me a big favour?'

'Anything, anything at all,' she replies, her smile growing.

'Sissy, Sienna and I are all running out of steam on the run-up to the big opening on Friday and it shows.' I run my hands through my hair, which seems to have a life of its own these days due to lack of maintenance. 'We're all a bit anxious about how the launch will go and I think a little pampering might help boost our morale. What do you think?'

Alice raises an eyebrow. 'Seriously? Are you talking makeovers here?'

I nod and her face lights up. 'Leave it to me; I'm sure I can get a few hours off work. I figure it will take about an hour each, to get hair and make-up done. What time is the official opening?'

'Noon. What if I make sure we're all at The Design Cave for eight o'clock?'

'Perfect. And it's my treat, Kerra. I'll bring all my stuff. Now, I've probably made you late, but tell Sissy and Sienna that I'll more than make it up to them on Friday.'

Alice steps forward to throw her arms around me and it's the first time we've hugged in a long while. It's horrifying to think she was having problems with some of the other kids at school and I hadn't noticed. That was remiss of me and I intend to make up for the oversight. I guess I'm not ready to give up on my cousin just yet.

Anyway, Sissy and Sienna are going to be thrilled when I share the news. To be honest, I'm way overdue for a makeover myself and if there's anyone I'd trust to do that, it's Alice.

When I'm wrapped in Ross's arms in the semi-darkness, all my worries slip away as if they count for nothing. Except one.

'You're not stressing over Ripley, are you?' Ross shifts his position, pulling me even closer.

'I'm trying my best not to,' I declare, groaning. 'She has everything she needs but I guess the test is what she has to say when I drive home in the morning.'

Pulling away to ease myself up onto my elbow, I gaze down at his shadowy face.

'You don't think she'll refuse to use the cat flap and sit outside wailing all night, do you?'

'Well, I sincerely hope not. They'd all be curious as to why your car isn't there.' He's joking but it's true.

I collapse back onto the bed, trying not to imagine the worst-case scenario. I picture Drew being woken up and going out to investigate, then tapping on Dad's door to see if he knows where I am.

'Oh Ross, there's no point trying to kid myself. I'm only going to lie here worrying.'

It's a horrible way to end what was an impromptu visit that led to a rash decision to stay the night. But talking on the phone earlier, we were both miserable and missing each other.

'If you go back, we go together. There's no way I'm going to let you drive home alone at this time of the morning. Besides, Ripley is a clever cat and she won't waste her energy when there's no one around to listen. I bet she's curled up on your bed now, fast asleep. She might have a bit of a moan in the morning, but there's a price to be paid by people who sneak out of their houses under cover of darkness.'

I grab a pillow and lob it at him, and he starts laughing.

'Sorry, I deserved that. But I'm sure everything is fine. If it wasn't, your phone would be ringing.'

He has a point. I do feel guilty, but I don't want to leave. He was really down when I arrived, and it was obvious he needed to talk. So, I let him. His father has no idea how much pressure he puts on Ross, even from a distance. It's unfair when the business is doing so well, but some people are never satisfied. They have this way of undermining your achievements, so they always have the upper hand. That thought reminds me of poor Alice.

'Alice popped round to see me and she said something that made me stop and think.'

'She did?'

I frown. Does Alice always get that reaction?

'We'd been avoiding each other and now we've cleared the air. She asked whether I thought that some people were born to be successful. What do you think?'

'That's a bit heavyweight.' I watch as he takes a moment to consider his answer. 'Is this the fate versus free will question?'

I shrug my shoulders. 'Perhaps, I suppose it depends on how you look at things.'

'My take on it is that when an opportunity arises it's up to the individual to grab it. Then it's all about hard work, making good decisions and dedication. Maybe fate might be at play when it comes to buying a winning lottery ticket, but it's still down to that person to decide whether they change one life, or many. Some fritter it all away and end up back where they started. And many people would put that down to bad luck, but I believe you make your own luck.'

Do I say what's really on my mind?

'I agree, but I learnt the hard way that success alone doesn't bring happiness, or a sense of fulfilment. So this isn't just about work, is it?'

'Ah, you're talking about a balanced life and the dream of having it all. You're asking the wrong person, in that case.' He trawls a finger along my arm, growing impatient for the conversation to be over, given that we're both wide awake now. But that's my point. Ross never talks about the future, unless it's connected to work.

Damn it, Alice—the first really sensible question you ask and it highlights the one big difference between Ross and me. I'm not working to prove anything, I'm over that and it's about recycling, really. Maintaining my nest egg because I worked damned hard to get it, while using it carefully to support people who deserve a little help. Ross is caught in that trap of feeling what he's achieved still isn't enough. I'd hoped that because he'd settled here, at The Forge, it meant he wasn't just hiding away, but was rejecting the life that Treylya represents. That his ex and his family represent.

'A frown like that doesn't suit you, Kerra,' he says, dragging me away from my thoughts. 'You worry too much. Me, I like to grab my moments of happiness whenever I can.'

He pulls me on top of him and as our lips touch everything whirling around inside my head evaporates as easily as a smoke trail. My body feels alive in a way it doesn't when I'm not with Ross and I decide I deserve a few hours of make-believe. Real life is a battle and it's all about remaining optimistic. No one knows what tomorrow will bring—actually, it's today now, anyway.

28. TGI Friday

'Have you ever tried false eyelashes?' Alice asks
Sienna, who shakes her head. She's still taking in the
transformation after having her hair restyled.

'No. Well, I did once buy a pair, but couldn't get them to
stay on. Kerra, what do you think Logan and the boys will
think of my new look?'

'It fabulous and once your make-up is done, I think you'll
stop them all in their tracks,' I reply as Sissy and I exchange
a discreet smile. Sienna often looks a little tired, but even
though it's been an exhausting couple of weeks, her eyes are
shining as she stares back at herself in the mirror.

'I can't wait to see what Alice does to you two,' she
giggles.

'It will only take me ten minutes to apply Sienna's make-
up, so you'd better decide who is going next.'

We both move closer to watch Alice in action, hoping to
pick up a few useful tips.

'I think you should go next, as it was your idea,' Sissy
nudges me, sporting a roguish smile. 'I want to do a final
walkaround and check the cleaners didn't disturb anything.
Then I'll begin setting out the glasses on the welcome table.
You can put your feet up, Kerra, while you wait.'

'How many people do you think will turn up?' Alice asks. She stubs a small brush onto a large palette, then dusts it off on the back of her hand before applying it in deft strokes above Sienna's left eye.

'It's hard to tell, but friends, family and local suppliers should generate at least thirty to forty people. As long as when a real customer arrives there are a few bodies milling around, we'll be happy. It's always a gamble, but we had three thousand leaflets distributed through letter boxes and as inserts in local free papers over a wide area. It's been advertised everywhere and we're hoping the curiosity factor alone will attract some footfall.'

'She knows what she's doing,' Sienna adds, sounding more confident than I feel right now. 'And this was a great idea, Kerra. Gone is the tired mum and now I'm looking at someone people might actually approach to help them make a purchase,' she laughs. 'It's amazing, Alice. Thank you so much. I am nervous about the event, as I've never done anything like this before, but at least I look the part, now. You're next, Kerra.'

'The food is going to run out very soon at this rate,' Sissy leans in to whisper in my ear, flashing me a look of concern. I'm momentarily distracted, still unable to believe how Alice turned her mop of hair into a mass of shiny curls.

The place is heaving with a huge number of people, which is brilliant, but we've only been open for forty-five minutes and we don't close until five.

'I know and I'm on it. I've just phoned the caterers and explained our dilemma. They're limited in what they can supply as a lot of their stuff is cooked to order from frozen.' She grimaces as we both scan around. All the advertising invited customers to join us for a glass of wine and canapés. 'Two of their staff are on the way over and they said not to panic. I tracked down Dad and he's gone to pick up some more boxes of wine.'

Sienna is at the till and calls out for Sissy, raising her hand in the air in case she can't hear her over the general background noise.

'You deal with that and I'll enlist some help, then get back to wandering around and generally answering questions. Don't worry, it's going to be fine.'

Well, I hope it is. People are buying, but lots are browsing and the longer they stay, the more likely they are to commit. I spot Sy and march forward purposefully, hoping no one stops me as I'm a woman on a mission.

'Thank you for coming. I hate to ask, but could you lend a hand?'

He can see I'm a little panicked.

'Just tell me what you want me to do and consider it done. Tegan's around, too, but she's shopping at the moment,' he grins. 'For real. Love the new look, it suits you.'

That raises a smile and I lean in to give him a grateful hug. I've missed our chats, but I know how wholeheartedly he throws himself into a project and the current one is so much more than that.

'We're nearly out of food already and the caterers are coming to bail us out. I'm not sure what they're going to need, maybe another table set up. There's one in the stockroom. It's through the kitchen. If you can sort them out when they arrive, that would be a lifesaver.'

'No problem. Tegan and I have your back. Someone over there is trying to attract your attention; go on. We'll catch up later.'

The woman in question is frantically waving at me, dragging her husband in tow.

'Kerra, Kerra! We didn't know you were involved in this venture—it's thrilling to see our daughter's cushions here on display. We're so proud of what she's achieved, and this means a lot to her.'

Mr and Mrs Mullins no longer live in the village, but their daughter, Trina, runs her own little business from home.

'Thank you for coming. Sissy is the brains and I'm just giving a little hand. How is Trina?'

'Good. She'll be along later with some friends, as we all want to support this new venture. It's very busy at the desk and I wanted to know if the room displays only come as a package? We've fallen in love with the purple room, but there's only one wardrobe in it and we'd need two. And another chest of drawers.'

'It's laid out to give you a general idea of the look you can achieve, but you can mix and match anything at all. Let me get you one of our order forms and a pen, they're over here. You can either list the items you want to buy, or tick one of the colour boxes—for instance, purple, and then in the comments box alongside write down anything extra you wish to order that isn't on show, or anything you don't want included.'

'That's a much simpler way of operating.'

It was meant to be, but the queue at the desk is getting longer, so I grab a handful of pens and forms. Leaving them to it, I launch myself into the crowd to make an announcement.

'If you'd rather not wait while we're so busy,' I inform those around me, 'you can hand in your completed order form when you're done. We'll ring you within the next forty-eight hours to take your payment over the phone and give you a delivery date.'

Time to think on your feet, Kerra but you'd better head straight over to Sissy next, as we don't want to look like we can't cope. Hands are thrust in my direction as the handout begins.

'You can leave completed forms at the desk, then continue browsing,' I keep repeating, so the word will spread. 'Here you go, thank you. We really appreciate your support.'

Sissy hurries over.

'Great idea,' she mouths, following my example.

It doesn't take long to work our way around the unit and the only people heading to the till now, it appears, are those buying small items they can pick and carry. At least it takes the pressure off Sienna, who was beginning to look panic-stricken.

The caterers are back and they're engaged in conversation with Sy. He looks in my direction, inclining his head, and I stride over to thank the two women who are obviously keen to start setting up.

'We think the table should go here, if that's okay with you. We can lay out some platters and then start making up some finger food. We have various fillings for little vol-au-vent cases, and a selection of cold meats and cheeses, which we'll pair with a range of Cornish relishes and pop onto bite-sized crackers.'

'Thank you so much for coming to our rescue—it's much appreciated. If you have any business cards, please feel free to display them on the table for people to pick up. I'll leave you in Sy's capable hands, then.'

Tegan appears at my side to give me a quick hug. 'I won't stop you, but this is amazing and I love the new hairstyle. I'm going to help your dad carry in the wine supplies.'

As her arms slip from around me, something catches my eye. It's an engagement ring and it's new.

'What an unbelievable day,' Sissy exclaims, sounding as exhausted as she looks. We are all equally as shattered, as I gaze around the gathering in the kitchen.

'I didn't think people were going to leave,' I say, still reeling from the sheer numbers we had through the door.

We ended up staying open an extra hour, because we couldn't exactly kick out potential customers who came to support us.

'I thought the locals would pop in for a quick look around and a free drink, but it was like a social event.' Dad glances down at his watch. 'We'd best get off, as James is keeping an eye at the kennels and will be wondering where we are.'

Rising up out of my seat to see him and Nettie off, I follow them out.

'Thanks so much, both of you. Nettie, you were amazing jumping on the till to give Sienna a hand while she wrapped items.'

Hugging them both, I feel a little tearful. Not because Sissy's day went so well, but because we couldn't have managed without their help.

'It was fun,' Nettie replies warmly. 'Now it's time to get yourself home and into a hot, relaxing bath.'

Ah. That's exactly the sort of thing my mum would have said.

'I will, promise.'

As I unlock the door, Nettie stoops to pick up several completed order forms that have been pushed back through the letterbox. She hands them to me, fanning them out.

'Looks like a good result, anyway. The till didn't stop ringing and you have stacks of these.'

I bite my lip. 'Yes, and we've processed quite a few, already. Let's hope our suppliers can handle the demand.'

'There are worse problems to worry over and you'll sort people out, I know that,' Dad says, giving me one of his customary winks.

'I know. Take care, you two. I'm going to have a thank you party at mine on Sunday for everyone who was good enough to come to our rescue today. It's the least I can do. Bye for now.'

Taking the forms, I lay them on top of the unprocessed pile lying next to the till.

'Do you think our profit from today will cover the hospitality costs?' Sissy calls out, as she approaches, but she's smiling.

'Several times over, I hope. There's a lot here, Sissy and I don't think either of us was expecting this level of response.'

She nods. 'I've already been on to the suppliers and warned them that some big orders are coming their way. Sienna and I will start working through these first thing tomorrow, if that's okay with you.'

I turn to look at her. 'Sissy, you're the boss. This is your business. I'm here to add whatever value I can. If you need to bounce ideas off me, or you want some hands-on help,

I'm here. But you steer this ship, lady, and you have a good eye when it comes to buying. That's why we're staring at a whole stack of orders.'

Sissy looks at me, bouncing those curls around as she laughs.

'Is this really me?' she asks.

'Well, it's a new you and I like it. You look happy.'

'I am. And while I'm loath to admit it, I'm loving this curly thing. I've already booked in an appointment for a trim in six weeks with Alice. She knows her stuff.'

'That's lovely to hear, Sissy. Alice did us proud today and, given the turnout, I'm so glad we set time aside for it. We looked the business, didn't we?'

'We most certainly did. You know, I think I'll take these forms home with me. I'm too excited to sleep. As soon as I have some firm figures, I'll email you.'

'Please do. Right, let's get everyone moving.'

Sitting here eating freshly heated Cornish pasties with Sy and Tegan, feels like old times. Although, it was usually barbecue food, but that's already beginning to feel like a distant memory now.

'I'm going to invite everyone who helped out today over on Sunday, as a thank you. You'll come, won't you?'

'Try stopping us,' Sy instantly replies and Tegan nods enthusiastically. 'We've been going through much the same thing as you with the changes to the business. It takes up every second of every day, but when the results start to show it makes it all worthwhile, doesn't it?'

It's so hard not to mention that engagement ring.

'It does. Sissy is up and running now. I'm trying to imagine Logan's reaction when Sienna walked through the door. She's a dead ringer for Cate Blanchett and I don't know why I didn't see that before.'

'Oh, she is! I couldn't quite put my finger on it—but, yes,' Tegan interrupts. As she raises her mug of coffee to her mouth, that ring flashes at me again. I feel sad that they don't want to share their news and yet these two people are my closest and dearest friends.

The doorbell goes and Sy jumps up.

'I'll get it,' he says, looking purposefully at Tegan, which I pretend I don't notice as he turns to walk away.

Tegan clears her throat.

'I know you saw it straight away. We've agonised over telling you, because we knew you had a lot on your plate with the launch and getting this place finished off. And that you'd stress over it.'

'You thought I wouldn't be happy for you two?'

She shakes her head, eyes wide. 'No. It wasn't that. It was a big step for us both, and we need to let it sink in a bit first, before we share the news. No one knows, not even my parents, as they're in Italy on holiday at the moment. It wouldn't be fair to spring it on them. I keep telling myself that Pete would understand. If it had been the other way around, I would have wanted him to find someone to spend the rest of his life with. But that doesn't stop me feeling guilty and Sy, lovely Sy, understands that.'

Fate presented the opportunity; Sy and Tegan made it happen.

'I couldn't be happier—'

'Look who called in,' Sy announces, as Ross follows a few paces behind him looking a little put out.

'Sorry, am I interrupting something?' He takes one look at me and I can see by his reaction the new hairstyle is a shock and he's momentarily distracted. 'I um... I wanted to let Kerra know there's still no delivery date for her office. Sorry, Kerra—but I'm on it.'

Sy and Tegan freeze, as does Ross, and they glance at each other uneasily. It's blatantly obvious to me that Tegan has shared what I told her with Sy, and given their reaction, Ross is now aware that they know about us.

'You'd better sit down, Ross. Tegan and Sy have some wonderful news. Are you hungry? I'll just pop another pasty in the oven while they bring you up to date.'

I'm exhausted and too tired to tread on eggshells, so I leave them to talk while I faff around in the kitchen. Sy and Tegan seem relaxed, as I listen to them telling Ross about their partnership and the fact that the news of their engagement is still a secret.

'Well, I'm delighted,' I add, as I sit back down, avoiding Ross's intense gaze. My hair is different, but everyone said the sleeker style suits me. It's probably the first time he's seen me wearing full make-up, though. Or maybe that wasn't what threw him, but the fact that I have company.

'We thought you might think it was a bit too soon, Kerra. But when you know, you know. The only drawback is the house. There are too many memories there and we think it's best if we rent it out, so we're house-hunting.'

'Buying or renting?' Ross asks rather curiously.

'Renting to start with, as we're ploughing everything into

expanding the business. We want to err on the cautious side and have a safety net.'

'It's tempting for small businesses to overextend themselves and we don't want to fall into that trap,' Sy explains.

'I only ask because I've decided to move back into Treylya.'

Tegan looks at me and then at Ross in surprise. 'But I thought you weren't renting it out anymore because you were going to sell it?'

Well, it's all news to me and I'm in shock. I can't believe it hasn't come up in conversation, given how many hours we've spent together. Ross talks about the business and his parents all the time but when it comes to his own plans he's a closed book.

'I'm going to do a swap and rent out The Forge, instead. It won't affect your weekly cleaning contract for Treylya, Tegan. It's a tough decision for me and a longer-term let to someone I know means I'd happily accept a lower rental. You're welcome to come and take a look around the place. It's not huge, but it has a nice feel to it.'

I know. And Ross said I was welcome there any time of the day, or night. That was a hollow offer then.

Tegan's eyes stray my way, but I jump up, hurrying across to check the oven and grab an extra plate. I'm reeling. Treylya of all places? I get that it's none of my business if he wants to sell it, but to live there? Is this because his father is coming back, and he thinks The Forge isn't impressive enough as a home? I'm gutted.

'That could be a great solution for us, Ross. What do you think, Tegan?'

She looks at Sy enthusiastically, and I sit here thinking this has nothing at all to do with me and yet my stomach is in knots. I look at Ross, unable to hide my disappointment, but he seems oblivious as he tucks into his pasty.

'Text me when it's convenient and we'll pop over to check it out. It's rather exciting,' Tegan replies, between mouthfuls of food.

When a chunk of crumbly pastry drops down onto her top they all laugh, but I can't. If all Ross cares about is proving to his family he's maintaining their standards, then we're never going to be on the same page. Or end up living together under the same roof.

29. A Listening Ear

'What have I missed besides this new, sleek look of yours—which I'm totally loving,' Drew remarks, as he stretches his legs out in front of him on the decking. 'I feel like I've been on a jolly, rather than at a conference. It's probably one of the most lively, and fun ones, I've ever attended.' He sounds upbeat, as if he's had a good time and I'm glad of that.

'Where do I start?' My tone sounds as jaded as I feel.

'Sounds bad. I'm guessing launch day didn't have quite the buzz you were hoping for?'

My chin slumps down onto my chest as I let out the biggest of sighs and I can feel him watching me, concerned.

'No, not at all. We were overwhelmed by the response, in fact. Our little celebration turned into quite a gathering and it'll take a day or two to process all the orders. The party will probably end up costing three times as much as we'd budgeted for when we tally up the wine and food. But the number of people we got through the door, and the way word has spread, means Sissy might have to think about taking on another part-time person.'

'That's all good then, so why the big sigh and the long face?'

Ripley puts in a brief appearance, presenting herself alongside Drew and waiting to be smoothed. His hand instinctively runs along her back and she begins purring. After a few moments she walks off, tail in the air as if she hasn't a care in the world.

I want a cat's life, I decide. Sleep, eat, have people fawn over you, put the world to rights in cat talk and pretend you can't understand when anyone talks back. Sounds like heaven to me.

'I threw Ross out last night and told him to stay away.'

'Why? What on earth brought that on?'

'He's moving back to Treylya.'

Drew frowns. 'So… that's a bad thing?'

'He didn't tell me. He announced it when Sy and Tegan were here last night, after the launch. And now they're thinking of renting The Forge from him.'

I can see Drew doesn't understand, but it's a tricky situation and I can't deal with my churning emotions right now.

'Well, that's an unexpected development, Kerra, and I'm sorry to hear it.'

I'm only grateful Drew wasn't around to hear us rowing in the garden after Sy and Tegan left. Ross's parting comments are still ringing in my ears: 'When you're done judging me and are prepared to sit down and talk, let me know. I've been honest from the start and yet you still don't trust me and I can't figure out why.'

Does he even know what honesty means when it comes to emotions? I feel I've been manipulated. He agreed to keep our affair—or whatever it is that we have going on—quiet, until we figured out how we felt. Was it out of respect for me, or my dad, or to avoid speculation because of his own agenda? He needs a partner on his arm who will be happy to fall in line with his future aspirations and maybe he's beginning to realise that isn't me. And the fact that his parents would be horrified if they knew with whom he was spending his time.

'Kerra, are you alright?'

'Sorry, I'm still tired after yesterday. Anyway, the brilliant news is that Sy and Tegan are engaged. It's a secret, well, until tomorrow, as I'm having a little do and you must come. It's to thank everyone who helped out at the launch, but I suggested to Sy and Tegan that we expand the guest list a little and it would be an ideal time to share their news. They're keeping it all low-key, which is understandable, not least because Tegan's parents are away. It's difficult when you don't have a big family network around you, but they have plenty of friends.'

Drew nods, understanding that their situation is a tough one.

'Under the circumstances, that's only natural. But as for Ross, he's a good man, Kerra. Did you hear him out?'

I turn to look at Drew, surprised by his reaction.

'Don't look at me like that. I'm not just sticking up for him, because I don't know exactly what happened, but I've seen the way you two are whenever you're around each other. You're a strong woman, Kerra, but don't confuse stubbornness with strength.'

I look at him, rather dismayed.

'I'm not stubborn, I simply recognise it when someone acts like they want to be in a relationship but aren't prepared to commit properly. In my book, that makes them users.'

Drew draws back a little, almost as if I'd just thrown something at him. 'Ouch! Well, I don't know what he said, but it didn't do him any favours. As far as I can see, you've been very careful to keep it all behind closed doors, too.'

'Just as well, then, wasn't it?' I reply caustically.

'Okay. I'll leave it there. All I'm saying is that I think the two of you are good together.'

On some levels, yes, on others—no.

'Life's too short to waste it on people who say one thing and do another. So, what's the latest with Felicity?'

He instantly perks up, shifting around in his seat.

'She's on her way here, as we speak. Another hour, maybe. She's going back early on Monday morning. We'd love it if you'd join us for a drink this evening so you can get to know her.'

This is a huge deal.

'Oh, Drew. I'm so pleased for you. The timing couldn't be more perfect, because you can introduce her to everyone at the party.'

'She isn't aware that Ripley doesn't live here anymore, though. I should have told her before, but there was so much going on. Do you think cats remember people from their past? I mean, Felicity knew her as a tiny kitten.'

'You know Ripley. She has a mind of her own, anyway. Felicity might be able to tempt her back. Especially now my garden intruders are all either in custody, or out on bail and unlikely to put in an appearance.'

There's a huge sense of relief that accompanies the thought that I finally feel safe here. But I can't pretend I wouldn't be gutted to lose my trusty companion. The truth about cats is that they choose where they want to live and with whom, so it's entirely up to Ripley.

'I'm not so sure about that. There was this instant connection between the two of you and nothing has changed.'

I think about Ripley wailing in the early hours of the morning because she'd prefer me to let her out the front door, rather than use the cat flap next to it. But I also think about that warm, purring, fur ball curled up on the bed, cuddling my feet. And the feeling of knowing that I'm not home alone.

'It's been comforting knowing Ripley was watching out for me and you're right, I would miss her. But everything she does is for a reason.'

I don't add that if she hops back over the fence for good, it might be to convince Felicity this is where she belongs. I wonder why Ripley let me down when it comes to Ross, though. She's all over him whenever he's here. Why didn't she sense he only ever had one agenda and that was his own? It's gutting.

The thing about a village and last-minute get-togethers, is that everyone mucks in. After a chilly start, the sun is out and as noon approaches, we slide back the glass doors and it's party time. I've been working non-stop in the kitchen since eight o'clock this morning. Mrs Moyle has been back and forth to the shop so many times to collect things I need, that she's now keeping a running tally and I'll settle up with her tomorrow.

Arthur is content to sit in a sunny corner of the garden next to the barbecue, which Drew is in the process of firing up. I notice that Felicity is busy erecting a table to use as a prep area once the burgers and sausages are flying off the grill. I wave out to her and she waves back, stopping to say something to Drew before heading inside.

After she arrived last night, the three of us sat in Drew's garden talking for several hours until I could no longer keep my eyes open. The impression I'd formed of Felicity from my chats with Drew, was coloured by a feeling that she was messing him around, by dipping in and out of his life. Instead, it's clear that she adores him and that's why she was prepared to let him go.

The battle she's fighting has been a long one and that's the dilemma. If you believe what you are doing is right, at what point do you give in, because that means it's all been for nothing. I recognised that innate strength, the willpower which is like a survival instinct and it's something that you are blessed—although some might say cursed—to be born with. And then I understood that Drew wasn't hanging in there because he was a lovesick guy, willing to accept whatever treatment was handed out to him, but he was simply supporting Felicity until it was over.

She approaches, smiling.

'Hey, Felicity. Mrs Moyle will bring across a range of sauces and condiments shortly. The buns are in the tall larder unit over there, when you need them. Paper napkins and plates are in the cupboard next to the sink unit and you'll find cutlery in the drawer above.'

'Thanks, Kerra. It won't take long to get organised once the charcoal is ready. One thing Drew is good at, is barbecuing. Well, he designs a pretty good extension, too,' she says, proudly.

I like that she seems very relaxed to be here and is taking everything in her stride. I wondered if she'd be concerned about my friendship with Drew, but that's not the case at all. The doorbell rings and Felicity turns on her heels, 'I've got it.'

Seconds later Dad and Nettie appear, with Bertie on a lead.

'Sorry we're late, lovely, but we were settling in our little guest.'

'Who's this?' Felicity says, kneeling down to introduce herself to an excited little bundle of fur.

'His name is Bertie,' Nettie says.

'Felicity, this is my dad, Eddie, and Nettie is an old friend. Dad runs the kennels opposite. Little Bertie is staying for a while as his owner died recently. He's been a constant guest over the last year or so.'

'He's so cute. Miniature Schnauzers have such a lovely nature, in general. Happy dogs, for sure.'

'We didn't want to leave him as soon as he arrived, so is it okay if we take him out into the garden? Is Ripley about?' Nettie enquires.

'She's upstairs, on the bed. I doubt we'll see her for a few hours yet.'

'I'll take Bertie outside, if you like,' Felicity offers.

'Thank you. I brought a dog bowl and I'll fill it with water for him. The poor little guy senses this isn't the usual stay. It's sad there wasn't a family member who could take him, but we'll spoil him until he's rehomed.'

'Aww... you're so cute, Bertie,' Felicity croons to him

softly, as she takes his lead from Nettie. 'You are going to make some lucky family very happy indeed.'

Felicity walks him down to the bottom of the garden before undoing his lead and Bertie immediately trots over to meet Arthur.

'How lovely that we get to meet Felicity, at last. That's another rumour now firmly put to bed.'

Nettie looks at Dad questioningly.

'No one thought she really existed,' he explains in a hushed tone and Nettie shakes her head sadly.

'What can we do to help?' she asks, turning in my direction.

I raise an arm to brush my hair aside with the back of my hand, as I pause to think. What hasn't been done?

'Oh, yes. If you can look for some glass jugs and start making up pitchers of soft drinks. There are some large bottles of fizzy water in the larder unit, lots of ice cubes ready in the freezer and plenty of frozen summer fruits. Dad, can you ask Drew if it's okay to grab some mint from his herb garden, please? I think we'll set the drinks up in here on the table. There's wine and beer, too.'

'On it,' Dad says, hurrying outside to go in search of Drew and say a general hello to everyone.

The sound of the front door opening confirms Mrs Moyle is back and behind her, Sy and Tegan are followed by Alice, Uncle Alistair and Auntie Marge.

Everyone is smiling and happy, but standing here I've never felt so alone. It's like life is happening all around me, but I'm numb and going through the motions. I'm used to gritting my teeth when times are tough and putting on a fake smile. Ploughing forward, desperately hoping everything will turn out fine if I just keep working at it, is what I'm good at. But look at Felicity, a kindred soul it turns out, and her situation. Maybe sometimes inner strength and determination isn't enough. We can control ourselves and our own actions, but not those of others.

Mrs Moyle sets down two full carrier bags and walks across to stand next to me.

'Are you okay, Kerra? This is so kind of you. I was thinking about Sy and Tegan. I brought over the biggest cake left on the shelf. It's chocolate, and that always goes down well, doesn't it? I found a few decorations, just some little roses made out of white icing, but I thought it might be a nice touch to make it a bit special. It's my treat.'

She slides her arm around my waist, giving me a squeeze and something tells me it hasn't gone unnoticed that Ross isn't here.

'It's a lovely thought, thank you. They'll be delighted.'

'People who give out good karma get it back, my dear. Mark my words. Your turn will come.'

She walks off and I make a concerted effort to stop feeling maudlin. How often have I had a setback, only to discover down the line that everything happens for a reason? Some things aren't meant to be, and you can kick, scream, and shout all you want but it won't change anything. As my mum always said, if something is meant for you it won't pass you by.

It's time to stop feeling sorry for yourself, Kerra, that little voice inside my head says with conviction. I take a moment to gaze out across the garden. People are laughing and chattering away quite happily. Sy and Tegan do the rounds, as everyone takes turns to congratulate them. They might only have known each other for a few months, but they inspire hope because when something is right, it's easy to take that leap of faith. But Sy has no history here and with what Tegan has been through, it would take a cold heart indeed not to be cheering her on. And me? Well, I feel like I'm living under a magnifying glass, while people wait with bated breath to see what I'm going to do next; and then judge me for it. Is that paranoia?

30. Do Cats Have a Sixth Sense?

As people continue to arrive the atmosphere has a happy buzz to it. Sissy appears with Sienna, Logan and their lovely boys—Oscar and Caden. Ironically, neither Tegan nor Sy have any family here. Tegan's brother still isn't speaking to her, apparently, but they've always had that sort of relationship. Sy hasn't spoken to his family in a long time, of course, but I doubt that will change any time soon. But there are enough people here who are thrilled to hear their news and it means a lot to them.

Ripley put in one, very brief appearance earlier on and ran off when someone bumped into a chair and it hit the deck with a bang. Bertie's presence didn't seem to upset her, in any way. But then she was out most of the night on mouse alert and I think her problem is that she doesn't like noise. Or people invading her space when there isn't even anything in it for her. They're all too busy talking to stop and fuss over her. But she's clever enough to know that they won't stay forever and she'll no doubt saunter back when the evening chill begins to set in and people head for home.

'I hear the launch at The Design Cave went well.' Uncle Alistair appears next to me and I turn to smile at him and

Auntie Marge, giving them each a hug. 'It did. And what do you think of the hair?' I ask, twisting my head and marvelling that it's still beautifully straight.

'You look lovely, Kerra,' Auntie Marge replies, with genuine affection. She's a sweet woman, the sort who is the backbone of the family because she keeps everything running smoothly. She's not a party sort of person, so I'm delighted Uncle Alistair talked her into coming.

'Alice also did Sissy's hair, and even she will admit that was a challenge. And Sienna's, over there.' I link arms with Auntie Marge and lead her to one side so she can catch a glimpse of Sienna's new look.

'Oh my—you all look so stylish. Alice keeps on at me to let her do my hair, but I don't bother with it very much as I seldom go out. You know me, I'm either stuck in the office sorting the accounts, working on our veggie plot, or in the kitchen cooking.'

I'm edging her away from Uncle Alistair for a reason.

'Auntie Marge, about Alice… she's brilliant at what she does and I don't think she gets the kudos she deserves.'

'Because she doesn't have a head for business, you mean?'

I nod and we exchange an acknowledging glance.

'Yes.'

'It's no secret that your uncle and I were hoping she'd take an interest in the office side of things. It's funny, though, how from an early age Alice just loved sparkly things and dressing up. She hated getting her hands dirty in the garden when I made her help me do the weeding and she never was a *head in a book* type of girl, as you were.'

'Hmm, well, I used to drive Mum mad at times. I always had an excuse not to help around the house and Dad would tell her that my schoolwork had to come first. We're a bit of a driven family, aren't we?'

I can see she understands where I'm heading.

'She's been unsettled since you've been back, Kerra, and it worries your uncle and me. Alice has always felt she lives in your shadow.'

'I didn't realise that until the other day, when Alice admitted she was being picked on at school. I had no idea people were being mean to her and I feel bad. She works hard at a job she loves doing and I admire her for that. It was remiss of me not to acknowledge that and support her. But I will be, in future.'

Auntie Marge nestles my arm closer to her.

'Your dear mum would have loved all this,' she enthuses, scanning around. 'She always believed one day you'd come back home, but I thought that was wishful thinking. When you left for London, I remember her saying that it's good to see how other people live, but she didn't want you to change. I laughed, because of course it would change you. But she was right. You're still the same Kerra at heart. I guess it's time I let that girl of mine make me look more presentable, then.'

'And I'll work on Uncle Alistair,' I reply, raising my eyebrows in a meaningful way that makes her chuckle.

Bertie bounds forward to greet us, swiftly followed by Felicity, who seems to have taken charge of him for the afternoon.

'Felicity, this is my auntie Marge. Felicity is Drew's...' I stop short, not quite sure how to finish off my sentence.

'Girlfriend,' Felicity adds, offering Auntie Marge her hand.

'Kerra, there's someone at the door for you,' Dad calls out, as he strides towards me and I make my apologies and hurry over to him.

'It's a delivery,' he informs me and then walks off in the opposite direction.

Delivery? On a Sunday?

Wending my way through the house, as I step outside, I take a quick look around. The street is packed with cars as usual, but there's no sign of anyone loitering with a parcel. Stepping through the gate I peer across at the lay-by and spot Ross's car. *Oh great, Dad, thanks a lot.*

'What do you want?' I throw the words at Ross as he steps out of the car, quickly shutting the door behind him.

He immediately puts up both hands, as if he's fending me off. 'Whoa... I'm not here to upset you, but I wasn't sure quite what to do.'

I look at him quizzically as he turns to open the rear door of the vehicle.

Miaow, miaow, miaoooooow.

It's Ripley. 'What on earth is she doing in your car?'

He shrugs his shoulders. 'She turned up at Treylya. I popped in with a few boxes and as I was about to leave, there she was. It's a bit of a trek for her and I didn't want to just drop her off and drive away, in case she made her way back there again. I won't be moving in for a couple of days yet.'

He's avoiding eye contact with me.

'Has she been up there before?'

Ross shrugs his shoulders apologetically.

'I have no idea. As the crow flies it's not that far I suppose, and I'm sure there are plenty of mice to hunt among the trees. Maybe she'd find her way home anyway, but I was worried.'

He scuffs the floor with the toe of his trainer and I try to ignore my hammering heartbeat.

'Well, thank you for bringing her back.'

I lift her out of the car, but she immediately jumps out of my arms and shoots straight across the road and in through the gate. She's clearly a little spooked. Was it the car ride, I wonder, or did she stray too far afield and it scared her? The front door opens and Nettie hurries over.

'Hi Ross, so glad you can join us. Kerra, Mrs Moyle says it's cake time and we're hoping you'll make a little speech for Sy and Tegan. Everyone's waiting.'

Ross doesn't quite know what to do and I ignore the awkward glance passing between Nettie and him, and hurry back inside. Plastering a smile on my face, I walk into the kitchen area where Mrs Moyle is beaming as she pops the last icing rose onto the cake and stands back.

'That's not a bad job if I say so myself,' she mutters.

'You did a great job, Mrs Moyle. Now let's round up the happy couple.'

Very gingerly I lift the plate and carry it outside. 'Sy, Tegan—come on everyone, we have cake!' I shout out at the top of my voice.

A few people are already gathered around the table on the lower patio area, where Dad is handing out glasses of champagne.

Sy and Tegan step forward and I can see they are touched.

'The cake is courtesy of Mrs Moyle,' I inform them, and Tegan blows her a kiss. 'Does everyone have a glass? Good.'

All eyes are on me to say something meaningful and yet

my legs feel like jelly beneath me, as I have no idea whether Ross followed me inside. I keep my eyes on the happy couple and tears begin to sting my eyes as they look at me, expectantly.

'It's time for a confession, folks. Luring Sy to Cornwall for a little break wasn't easy. This was a man who didn't own a pair of wellie boots and had never walked a dog before—let alone through muddy puddles.' There's a ripple of low-level laughter. 'But my right-hand man, who was always there for me in London, came because I asked him to.' I stop for a moment to turn and look at Tegan, grinning. 'Wearing my business hat, I knew that Sy would make himself useful.'

Tegan bursts out laughing, shaking her head at me.

'And he did. Maybe a little more useful than I'd intended, but I couldn't be happier. You see, what I didn't understand was that finding one's soul mate doesn't start with a list of requirements you can simply tick off. I'm used to putting business plans together and it's all about the facts and figures. But the Sy I used to know is not the man I see before me now. Being with Tegan has turned both their lives upside down and the result is that I've never seen either of them as happy as they are now. So, it is with great pleasure that I ask you all to raise a toast to Sy and Tegan on their engagement.'

There is a loud chorus of whoops and congratulations, as the couple come closer for a group hug.

'I never in my wildest dreams thought anything could keep Sy away from the bright lights of London,' I whisper conspiratorially. 'But he did it for you, Tegan. And you deserve this happiness. I love you guys.'

*

Ross has kept his distance, but one by one people take their leave and eventually it's down to Dad, Nettie, Ross, me and Ripley. Annoyingly, Ripley has been following Ross around the entire time and even refused my attempts to lure her away with a bowl of tinned tuna. Darn it, she's my cat and if she isn't, then she belongs to Drew. Her lack of solidarity has been irking me now for a couple of hours.

'Right,' Dad says, looking directly at Nettie, then glancing at Ross. 'Time we headed back to walk the dogs before settling them down for the night. Come on, Bertie, I think you've had enough excitement for one day. It was a grand party you put on, Kerra, and you've certainly livened things up around here, lovely.'

His words are particularly touching, because Dad doesn't often share what he's thinking.

'Well, thank you both for your help today; it was a joint effort, wasn't it?'

'It's been a long day for you and I expect you just want to relax for an hour, or two, now on your own.' This time he looks directly at Ross, who looks distinctly uncomfortable.

'Yes, it's time I made tracks. I'm glad Ripley has settled back down. Great to be able to catch up with you, Nettie and Eddie. I'll see myself out.'

'Lovely to catch up with you, too, Ross,' Nettie calls out, as he walks away. It's clear she has no idea what's going on. Or that while Dad has a lot of respect for Ross, it would be a different story if he thought there was anything going on between us. Dad isn't comfortable around people who have, as he puts it, airs and graces—as the Treloars do.

Dad secures Bertie's lead and Nettie goes in search of his water bowl.

'Don't worry too much about Ripley. I've seen her up in the woods from time to time. They often wander, but seldom does a cat get lost. Especially when they're so well looked after.'

'Thanks, Dad.'

As I see them out and push the door shut, I turn around and sag back against it. I've been living off nervous energy all day and I feel physically sick. Then I realise I haven't really eaten anything. Ripley has disappeared again and I run upstairs, looking for her.

Ding-dong.

'Ripley, are you up here? Come on, stop being a pain. I'm too tired for this and Dad's forgotten something.'

I rush back downstairs, thinking I must grab some food and swing open the door with a knowing smile. The smile quickly fades when I see Ross standing in front of me, with Ripley in his arms.

'I'm sorry. She snuck out and when I opened the car door she shot inside.'

As Ross tries to hold her out to me, a tirade of miaowing indicates she's not happy.

'You'd better bring her inside,' I instruct him, walking off. 'I need to eat or I'm going to faint.'

'Shall I settle her down on the bed upstairs and then make my escape?'

'Suit yourself.' Ross is doing this on purpose and I'm not in the mood to play games.

I slam about in the kitchen angrily and when he reappears, several minutes later, I ignore him. He stands there watching me, shifting from foot to foot. The fidgeting is annoying, to say the least. Why doesn't he just go?

'Honestly, Kerra, she must have darted out in the few seconds it took me to walk out the door and shut it behind me. I'm sorry. Actually, I'm sorry for a lot of things.'

So you should be. I throw together a cheese and cucumber sandwich, heavy on the cucumber, because it's one of my comfort foods. I add a pinch of pink Himalayan salt.

'You add salt to a sandwich?' Ross blurts out.

'Don't knock it if you haven't tried it. It's good salt, not the bad sort most people use.'

Why am I even talking to him?

'You said you had to get back. Don't let me stop you. Ripley was obviously unsettled with everyone here. Dad said he's seen her in the woods before, so I'm sure she'll be fine now,' I concede.

Ross ignores my dismissal and comes closer.

'You might not believe this, but I was too upset to eat earlier on and that sandwich looks interesting.'

His voice is velvety smooth, and I glance up, then put my head straight back down again to focus on what I'm doing.

'Fine. One sandwich and then you are out of here.'

Why am I doing this to myself? It's never going to work between us. Our families stand for different things—we stand for different things. Lust isn't love, I remind myself.

'Here. Eat and go.'

He takes the plate I slide along the worktop in his direction.

'Thank you. Do you mean take it with me, or can I sit and eat it?'

I give him one of my withering stares, then tilt my head in the direction of the table. Following him over, I walk around the table to sit facing him.

'Say what you obviously want to say, then leave me in peace.'

'The truth is that I don't know what to say, Kerra. What did I do that was so wrong?'

Having taken a massive bite of my sandwich, I make him wait for my reply. He's anxious and his body language shows how on edge he is, the fingers of his right hand tapping on the table as the seconds pass.

'You've talked for hours about your business and family worries. I've listened and you've asked for my opinion and now I feel like all I've been is a sounding board.'

He shakes his head vigorously.

'Do you seriously think I'd have shared that with anyone else, other than you?'

'Oh, that's supposed to make me feel better, is it? So you respect my opinion, but when it comes to moving out of The Forge you didn't think to mention it to me, even in passing? After saying I was always welcome, would I have turned up one day to find someone else living there?'

He groans.

'That's a ridiculous thing to say, Kerra, and you know it. I decided months ago that after the last booking in August I was going to put Treylya on the market. There are no happy memories for me there. Not a single one. But moving back in was a spur of the moment thing because of you.'

I'm determined not to let him rattle me, so I start eating again. I can see it's annoying him. I point at his plate and indicate that he'd better hurry up.

'I freely admit that at first I was as cautious as you about us being together. Then I thought, why do I care what people think? I only care, if you care—and you do, be honest. We're both scared we can't pull off what Sy and Tegan have done. So, we sneak around until we're cast-iron sure, because we're scared of failing, or looking foolish.'

'Or getting hurt. And you've hurt me, Ross. I sat there listening to you talking about your future plans and I had no idea what you were going to say.'

'Funny you should say that, as the moment I saw you it totally threw me. New hairstyle and make-up? It wasn't for my benefit, as you didn't know I was coming.'

I ignore his comment, dismissing it as a diversionary tactic.

'Is Bailey coming back into your life and you don't have the courage to tell me?'

Ross freezes, his face ashen. 'What?'

'It happens. I'm not stupid.' Hmm. Not exactly my most eloquent of moments, but he's getting the message.

'Bailey represents everything I got wrong in life,' Ross explains, his face wearing a pained expression. 'I thought I made that abundantly clear and you understood that I don't do things simply to please my family anymore. I'm selling Treylya to cut all ties with that part of my past. I'm moving in for a while because I want to be closer to you. I'm not having you driving back in the early hours of the morning on your own, or lying there next to me worrying about Ripley, like you were the last night we were together at The Forge.'

My hands drop into my lap, as I sink back against the chair.

'You'd stay up there all alone, just to make it easier for us to see each other?'

'Of course, I would. I don't want to be half an hour away if something goes wrong here and you need me.'

'But what happens when it's sold?'

Ross shrugs his shoulders.

'That's rather up to you. But, Kerra, I have no idea what your plans are, either, beyond your business venture with Sissy—which isn't going to keep you fully occupied. The office in the garden means you're probably looking to work from home long-term, but how would I know?'

Touché. With food in my stomach and my head thinking straight for the first time in several days, I feel like a fool.

'I'm sorry,' I say, reaching out across the table for his hand. 'I thought you were trying to let me know it was time to move on and couldn't bring yourself to say it outright.'

'Some sort of payback, because you rejected me all those years ago?' He laughs, but there's a sense of relief in his tone and his eyes have come alive as he grasps my hand.

'It wasn't rejection, it was fear that you'd see I was infatuated with you.'

We both start laughing at that.

'Kerra Shaw infatuated. Nope. Sorry, that doesn't ring true. You were curious what all the fuss was about, that's all. But I wouldn't have kept your interest, because I was still figuring out who I was and look how long it took me to suss that out. You, on the other hand, have always known who you are and that's why the moment I saw you again after you returned, I knew I was in deep trouble.'

Oh, my goodness—I said the exact same thing to Sy, and then to Tegan, about Ross!

'Trouble?' I press my luck, but I know it's too soon for Ross to put his feelings into the sort of words I long to hear.

'Well, you are trouble. And your cat is trouble, too.'

'What's next for us, then?'

Ross pushes back on his chair and in a couple of strides he's lifting me up out of my seat, cradling me in his arms.

'We take it one day at a time, and in future we talk openly and honestly about everything that effects either of us. I'm not one for big announcements, or making wild promises, but I get this feeling that we'll know when it's time to go public. However, there is one promise I can make, Kerra, that will never change. I'd rather die, than hurt you. In my wildest dreams back in the day, I wondered what it would be like to walk down the street holding your hand in mind. To have you look at me and feel safe under my protection. I know— it's a guy thing, and you're more than capable of looking after yourself. But the thing is I need to be needed. And there have been a couple of times since we've been together that—'

'—made you feel just that,' I half-whisper, pulling back to stare deep into his eyes. The look is raw and carries with it a sense of vulnerability. It's humbling and my heart feels like it's going to burst with joy and happiness. 'The truth is that it's something I could get used to, Ross. And I never thought I'd ever hear myself say that, to anyone.'

'Job done, then,' he muses. 'I knew I'd grow on you eventually. And I love the new hairstyle, but it threw me for a moment. It's a reminder of your other life and made me wonder if you miss it.'

Shaking my head to dismiss his fears, I close my eyes as he kisses me, hungrily and with a mounting urgency. Then, in the background there's a loud and protracted miaow. Reluctantly disentangling myself from Ross's arms, I peer around his shoulder.

'Okay, Ripley. I'll let you out the door. But you're going to have to get used to using that cat flap a little more often, lady. But at least if I'm not here, you know your way to Treylya.'

She sits there looking at me for the briefest of moments, twitching her whiskers as if she's smiling. Then she does a curious little tilt of her head that I can't recall seeing her do, ever before. Her eyes stray in the direction of Ross and then she saunters, very leisurely, across to him, rubbing up against his leg.

Ripley knew something was missing today and it was Ross. So, she brought him back to me. Not once, but twice.

The next step is to convince Dad that Ross is the one, but we'll figure that out. One thing Sy and Tegan's commitment to each other has served to remind me of, is that fear can turn you into an *if only* person and that's not who I am.

When I returned to Cornwall, I thought it was because I was honouring the promise I made to Mum, to be there for Dad. Did she know that I wasn't happy and that my life felt incomplete? I think she probably sussed that out during those long days we spent together, making the most of what time she had left.

There is one place she knew I'd be safe and that was with Dad keeping a watchful eye. It's only now, with hindsight, that I realise it might have been obvious to her that every man I met, I compared to my first love. And found them lacking.

Ross Treloar, you've been in my dreams for a very long time and now those dreams are finally coming true. And that's why my heart never left Penvennan Cove—this is where I was always meant to be.

Acknowledgements

This three-book series is very dear to my heart, as Cornwall has always been an enchanting destination for me since I was small. And I believe that everyone should have a Ross in their lives—I know I'm lucky enough to have mine.

I'd like to give a virtual hug to my editorial director, the awesome Hannah Smith. You are a true inspiration. The day we sat around my dining room table plotting a future for Kerra and Ross was just the greatest fun. The fact that we spent a lot of time talking about cats and dogs made me smile. The real stars of the story really are our four-legged friends.

Ripley, too, gets a special mention as she is a cat with attitude and a well-loved family member.

Grateful thanks also go to my agent, Sara Keane, for her sterling advice and motivation. And to the wonderful Vicky Joss—who is a dream of a marketing manager—her hard work is much appreciated!

A special mention goes to the lovely Dushi Horti. Not a comma, or a single dangling modifier escapes this lady's eagle eye and, oh, how I wish I'd paid more attention to those grammar lessons instead of scribbling lines of poetry. But

Dushi is there to make sure the things I miss are corrected and I know I can relax knowing that she will make sure the story is polished to perfection.

And to the wider Aria team – a truly awesome group of people I can't thank enough for their amazing support and encouragement.

There are so many friends who are there for me and who understand that my passion to write is all-consuming. They forgive me for long silences and then when I get a breather, we catch up as if I haven't been absent while I've been head-down writing.

As usual, no book is ever launched without there being an even longer list of people to thank for publicising it. The amazing kindness of my lovely author friends, readers and reviewers is truly humbling. You continue to delight, amaze, and astound me with your generosity and support.

Without your kindness in spreading the word about my latest release and your wonderful reviews to entice people to click and download, I wouldn't be able to indulge myself in my guilty pleasure … writing.

Feeling blessed and sending much love to you all for your treasured support and friendship.

Linn x

About the Author

LINN B. HALTON is a #1 bestselling author of contemporary romantic fiction. In 2013 she won the UK Festival of Romance: Innovation in Romantic Fiction Award. Originally from Bristol, she now lives in the Welsh Valleys with her husband and Bengal cat, Ziggy.

For Linn, life is all about family, friends and writing. She is a self-confessed hopeless romantic and an eternal optimist. When Linn is not writing, she spends time in the garden weeding or practising Tai Chi. And she is often found with a paintbrush in her hand indulging her passion for upcycling furniture.

Her novels have been translated into Italian, Czech and Croatian. She also writes as Lucy Coleman.

Linn is represented by Sara Keane from the Keane Kataria Literary Agency.

Visit Linn's website at: https://linnbhalton.com/

And follow her on Twitter: @LinnBHalton

Hello from Aria

We hope you enjoyed this book! If you did let us know, we'd love to hear from you.

We are Aria, a dynamic digital-first fiction imprint from award-winning independent publishers Head of Zeus. At heart, we're committed to publishing fantastic commercial fiction – from romance and sagas to crime, thrillers and historical fiction. Visit us online and discover a community of like-minded fiction fans!

We're also on the look out for tomorrow's superstar authors. So, if you're a budding writer looking for a publisher, we'd love to hear from you. You can submit your book online at ariafiction.com/ we-want-read-your-book

You can find us at:
Email: aria@headofzeus.com
Website: www.ariafiction.com
Submissions: www.ariafiction.com/
we-want-read-your-book

f @ariafiction
𝕏 @Aria_Fiction
◉ @ariafiction